Dreamers of the Day

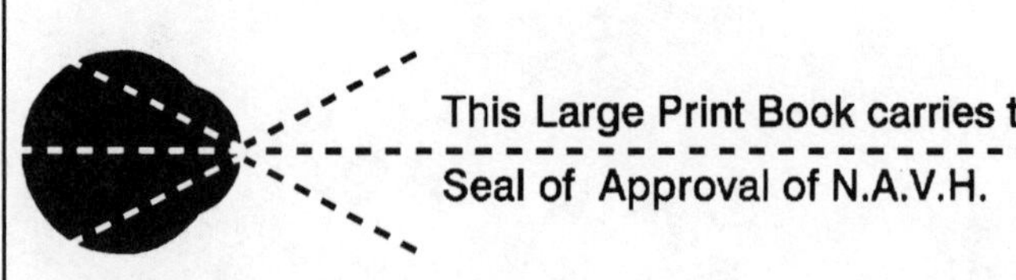
This Large Print Book carries the
Seal of Approval of N.A.V.H.

DREAMERS OF THE DAY

MARY DORIA RUSSELL

THORNDIKE PRESS
A part of Gale, Cengage Learning

GALE
CENGAGE Learning™

Detroit • New York • San Francisco • New Haven, Conn • Waterville, Maine • London

Photograph on page 301: Gertrude Bell Photographic Archive, Newcastle University.
Thorndike Press, a part of Gale, Cengage Learning.

This is a work of fiction. Though some incidents, dialogue, and characters are based on the historical record, the work as a whole is the product of the author's imagination.

Thorndike Press® Large Print Basic.
The text of this Large Print edition is unabridged.
Other aspects of the book may vary from the original edition.
Set in 16 pt. Plantin.
Printed on permanent paper.

LIBRARY OF CONGRESS CATALOGING-IN-PUBLICATION DATA

Russell, Mary Doria, 1950–
Dreamers of the day / by Mary Doria Russell.
p. cm. — (Thorndike Press large print basic)
ISBN-13: 978-1-4104-0709-2 (hardcover : alk. paper)
ISBN-10: 1-4104-0709-8 (hardcover : alk. paper)
1. Women teachers — Fiction. 2. Lawrence, T. E. (Thomas Edward), 1888–1935 — Fiction. 3. Churchill, Winston, Sir, 1874–1965 — Fiction. 4. Bell, Gertrude, 1868–1926 — Fiction. 5. Large type books. 6. Middle East — History — 1914–1923 — Fiction. I. Title.
PS3568.U76678D74 2008b
813'.54—dc22 2008009634

Published in 2008 by arrangement with Random House, Inc.

Printed in the United States of America
1 2 3 4 5 6 7 12 11 10 09 08

For
DAD, DON, and DAN

It's remarkable how much a woman can accomplish when the men in her life are strong and good.

■ ■ ■ ■

Part One: Middle West

■ ■ ■ ■

I suppose I ought to warn you at the outset that my present circumstances are puzzling, even to me. Nevertheless, I am sure of this much: my little story has become your history. You won't really understand your times until you understand mine.

You must try to feel the hope and amazement of those years. Anything seemed possible — the end of ignorance, the end of disease, the end of poverty. Physics and chemistry, medicine and engineering were breaking through old boundaries. In the cities, skyscrapers shredded clouds. Trucks and automobiles were crowding out horse-drawn cabs and drays in the boulevards below. The pavement was clean: no stinking piles of dung, no buzz of flies.

In 1913, America had a professor-president in the White House — a man of intelligence and principle, elected to clean up the corruption that had flourished in the muck of politics for so long. Public health and public schools were beating back the darkness in slums and settlements. The poor were lifted up and the proud brought down as Progressives reined in the power of Big Money.

In the homes of the middle class, our lives ticked along like clocks, well regulated and precise. We had electric lights, electric toasters, electric fans. On Sundays, there were newspaper advertisements for vacuum cleaners, wringer-washers, and automobiles. Our bathrooms were clean, modern, and indoors. We believed that good nutrition and good moral hygiene would make us healthy, wealthy, and wise. We had every reason to think that tomorrow would be better than today. And the day after that? Better yet!

The Great War and the Great Influenza fell on our placid world almost without warning.

Imagine: around the world, millions and millions and millions vital and alive one day, slack-jawed dead the next. Imagine people dying in such numbers that they had to be buried in mass graves dug with steam shovels — dying not of some ancient plague or in some faraway land, but dying here and now, right in front of you. Imagine knowing that nothing could ensure your survival.

Imagine that you know this not in theory, not from reading about it in books, but from how it feels to lift your own foot high and step wide over a corpse.

What would you do?

I'll tell you what a lot of us did. We boozed and screwed like there was no tomorrow. We shed encumbrances and avoided entanglements. We were tough cookies, slim customers, swell guys, real dolls. We made our own fun and our own gin, drinking lakes of the stuff, drinking until we could Charleston on the graves. *Life is for the living! Pooh, pooh, skiddoo! Drink up — the night is young!*

"I don't want children," said one celebrated writer after an abortion. "We'd have nothing in common. Children don't drink."

Does such callousness shock you? I suppose it does, but you see, by that time the plain stale fact of mortality had become so commonplace, so tedious . . . Well, mourning simply went out of style.

And just between you and me? Even if you find yourself among illustrious souls, you can get awfully tired of the dead.

Let me count my own. Lillian and Douglas, and their two young sons. Uncle John. And Mumma, of course. Six. No, wait! Seven. My brother, Ernest, was the first.

■ ■ ■ ■

I last saw Ernest in September of 1918. Slim in khaki, a mustachioed captain in the Army Corps of Engineers, my brother waved from the window of a train packed three boys to every double seat. They were headed for Newport News, where the battalion would ship out for Europe.

By the time Ernest left for the coast, five million European soldiers had already disappeared into "the sausage machine." That's what their commanders called the Great War. To understand why, you must call to mind some modern war. Think of the casualties endured in a year's time, or five years, or ten. Now imagine sixty thousand men killed in a single day of combat: meat fed to the guns. Imagine four years like that.

America stared, aghast and uncomprehending, while the Old World gorged on its young and smashed its civilization to pieces for reasons no one was able to explain. From the start, there was some war sentiment in America, but it was largely confined to those who knew there was money to be made selling weapons, uniforms, steel, and ships, should America join the fight.

Reelected, barely, on a peace platform,

our professor-president remained steadfast even when he was called a coward for refusing to involve us in the madness of foreigners. Then, eight weeks after Woodrow Wilson's second inaugural, a document was "captured" and made public. In it, the German foreign minister urged the Mexican government to join Germany in a war against the United States and, in so doing, to reclaim the lost lands of New Mexico, Arizona, and Texas.

Call me cynical. I always thought that document was a fraud. And if it were genuine, why send our boys to France if the threat was on our southern border?

Of course, I was just a schoolteacher — a woman without a vote of my own, or even a husband to persuade. The men all said that document changed everything. Certainly Mr. Wilson believed it did. When he turned the ship of state toward Europe, the nation cheered and felt gratified to have exciting newspaper stories to talk about at breakfast. Those of us who saw no need for war found the enthusiasm of our fellow citizens bewildering. I read all the papers, frantic to understand why this was happening to my country and the world. To me, Mr. Wilson's conversion was so shocking, it seemed Saint Paul had renounced Christ to become Saul once more. But there you are: the reason for going to war might be a shameless hoax, but the war itself was real and, by God, America was in it!

In fact, Mr. Wilson informed the nation, the Almighty Himself no longer wanted America to stand aloof from the slaughter in the Old World. "America," the president declared, "was born to exemplify devotion to the elements of righteousness which are derived from the revelations of Holy Scripture."

By turning the other cheek? I wondered. Silly woman . . .

No, exemplifying righteousness required America to fight a war to end all wars, a war so brutal and ruthless that war would never be waged again. Mr. Wilson assured us that this crusade was God's will and God's work.

If Abraham Lincoln had erred in allowing the press to criticize the government during our Civil War, Woodrow Wilson vowed, "I won't repeat his mistakes." The president didn't repeal the First Amendment; he had, after all, recently sworn to uphold the Constitution. The press could print what it liked, of course, but the post office didn't have to deliver it. The Wilson administration ordered the confiscation of anything unpatriotic, which is to say anything critical of his administration. Total war demanded totalitarian power, Mr. Wilson told a compliant Congress. "There are citizens of the United States," the president thundered, "who have poured the poison of disloyalty into the very arteries of our national life. Such creatures of passion, disloyalty and anarchy must be crushed."

Anyone who protested, or even voiced reluctance, was called a traitor. Mr. Eugene Debs was sentenced to decades in prison. His crime? He said that a war abroad did not excuse tyranny at home.

Mexico was all but forgotten in the excitement.

That's why, by the summer of 1918, a million American men had been mobilized to fight — from career officers like my brother, Ernest, to draftees straight off the farm. Ernest's train left Cleveland carrying nearly 250 soldiers, including a boy from Wooster who seemed to have a dreadful cold. When the troops arrived on the Virginia coast two days later, more than 120 of the soldiers already had the flu. Sixty others were ill within a day or two.

In Ernest's last letter home, he confessed that he was afraid he'd miss the war. He was so eager to embark! I doubt he mentioned his headache to anyone else. The next letter we received was from a friend of his. Ernest had been buried at sea before the boat was halfway to France. Later we learned that most of his battalion had sickened. Many died while standing on a French dock, awaiting orders in a chilly autumn rain.

In October, the military finally canceled leave and liberty, but it was too late to make a difference. Railways had distributed the influenza with the same swift efficiency that carried coal, wheat, and livestock to and from every corner of the continent. Within weeks, the flu was everywhere.

People spread the disease before they knew they had it, got sicker, brought it home, and died. Fiancées, parents, brothers, and sisters: kissed good-bye at train stations. Ambulance drivers, stretcher bearers, doctors, nurses: working until they died on their feet. Trolley conductors, shopkeepers. Teachers.

Waves of influenza broke across the nation and all the while, the war ground on in Europe. Cleveland sent forty-one thousand boys "over there." One of my students came to see me before he left — a boy named for the great Italian patriot Garibaldi. Gary, we called him at school. He was a good student.

Arithmetic was his best subject, as I recall. Off he went with the Fifth Regiment of the Ohio National Guard, to revenge bleeding Belgium and rescue poor brave France, to make the world safe for democracy and kill Huns for Mr. Wilson.

Gary visited me again after he got home, in 1919. "You were wrong, Miss Shanklin. The Grim Reaper isn't a metaphor," he told me. "The Reaper's real. I saw him. We went over the top and machine guns mowed us down, like a scythe through weeds. Row after row of us. You can't imagine, miss."

No, not that, but I had seen men struck down in the streets of Cleveland. They'd leave for the office in the morning feeling fine. During the day, they'd complain of being hot and achy. By evening, waiting on the corner for a streetcar, they'd fall to the pavement, already dead or near to it. Gary soon became one of them. Poor boy. He had just married his sweetheart and found a job as a bank teller. He left work feeling woozy and never made it home for supper.

Even then, before the worst of it, I wanted to escape from the sadness. I was older than the lost generation of the Roaring Twenties. I began the decade too shy to dance, too homely to imagine myself of interest even to a maimed veteran, too timid to break the

Prohibition laws and risk blindness drinking bathtub gin. But in the end? I was not so very different. I, too, yearned for new sights, new sounds, new people — and, yes: a new me. I wanted to believe again in peace, and progress, and prosperity.

Prosperity, at least, I would have and this one certainty: of all my natal family, I would be the last to die. My brief obituary would be written by a bored young newspaperman in 1957: "Agnes Shanklin, heiress, dead at 76, after a long illness."

That's what they called cancer then. "A long illness." And don't be fooled by that fancy word "heiress." No single estate was all that much, but taken together and added to $1,000 of soldier's insurance from Ernest, they totaled just enough to afford me a careful independence.

Frugality I had learned at my mother's knee. "Use it up, wear it out, make it do." That was Mumma's motto, especially after the bankruptcy and Papa's death.

In the beginning, I believe, my parents anticipated something close to the ideal marriage of the nineteenth century. They met and married late, both nearly thirty and too mature for silly romantic illusions about love. When they pledged their troth in the sight of God, they did so in the hope that theirs would be a union of souls. They understood that this would demand an equal sacrifice of personal interests. Papa would lose his place in the home; Mumma, her place in the world. He would strive for material sustenance and guard the family from the corruption of the marketplace. In return for cooking and needlework, the bearing and raising of children, she would receive shelter, food, and a clothing allowance.

Such marriages always ran the risk of becoming cold but practical business partnerships. In the case of my parents, mutual admiration rested upon an economic arrangement that seemed to suit them both. Mumma was a fine seamstress, Papa a mechanical engineer. You might not think they'd have had much in common, apart from their children, but together they reasoned out a design for a sewing machine foot that would make cording easy and automatic. In the tenth year of their marriage, walking home from church one Sunday, they hatched a plan. They would take all their savings and start a factory right in Cedar Glen, just east of Cleveland. The business could provide good, honest work for the sons of slaves who'd come north on the Underground Railway. Those men would demonstrate that Negroes were capable of skilled labor, and the business would benefit by undercutting the competition on wages.

Papa's probity and Mumma's piety were well known in Cedar Glen. Their good character convinced several members of their congregation that they could do well by doing good, and they agreed to invest in the venture. Papa took the idea to a banker, who steered him toward a partner said to be a person of energy and vision.

To our family's misfortune, Papa was an honest man in a time when business was increasingly often conducted between strangers who recognized no good or god excepting only Profit. In Washington and Columbus, politicians wearing masks of unctuous respectability legislated mightily to outlaw private sin and enforce private virtue, all the while accepting money to overlook the public crimes of industrialists and financiers who made incalculable fortunes by exploiting workers and swindling investors. In that climate, Papa's trustworthiness was the very hallmark of a "patsy." He built the factory; his partner and the banker disappeared with the money.

For Papa, it was a matter of honor that he

keep his employees working and make his creditors whole. That determination left hardly any time or money for his family. Mumma soon found it difficult to hide our circumstances, but Papa steadfastly refused help from her brother, a bachelor attorney with money to spare.

"Foolish pride," Mumma called that. "How am I to run a proper household with what you bring home?"

"Others are worse off," Papa said, time and again. "We shall manage without charity."

"Easy for you to say," Mumma would mutter, and the household would go very quiet, unspoken accusations loud in our minds.

Then one day a sympathetic neighbor lady remarked, "Your poor husband, working so hard! It's just not fair that he should have to pay back money others stole."

Something snapped inside Mumma. I could almost see it recoil in her. "I'd rather see Howard in his coffin," she said, "than fall to the level of the men who bilked him."

From that day on, Mumma made every penny count and did so with a zeal that awed us. She gave up our subscription to the family pew at church, and we found cheaper seats in the back. "God will hear our praise and prayers," Mumma told us, "no matter where we sit." If there was no money for tickets to attend an uplifting lecture, she went to the library for a book and read it aloud in the evening. If there was not much for supper, she would pop corn for us; it was a whole grain and filling. She raised chickens and collies, sold eggs and puppies for extra income. She gardened and canned the produce. She sewed uniforms for students at the Cleveland Training School for Nurses, and used the blue-and-white-striped scraps for the patchwork quilts that kept her children warm at night. She was so thin, so weary, on her feet from dawn to dusk. It seemed to me that she was all alone and yet so brave! What if something happened to her? Something awful?

I wanted to keep Mumma safe. Young and useless as I was, I tried to help but succeeded only in wearing out her threadbare patience. "Oh, Agnes," she'd sigh. "It's easier for me to do it myself than to take the time to teach you."

Looking back, I am sad to realize that I never thought about keeping Papa safe; it never occurred to me to worry about that benign but absent figure. When at last he had worked himself into an early grave, the business was out of debt. Mumma took over, bereaved but eager to put her own ideas into play. "Your father was not a fool," she told us children on the way home from the funeral, "but he had no head for business." And Mumma certainly did.

Her first move was to renegotiate arrangements with suppliers. "Thank you for your consideration," she'd tell them in her small, sweet voice. "There are those who'd be happy to take advantage of a poor widow with three children to support." Once she'd struck a bargain, her brother, John, wrote ironclad contracts to enforce the deal. "No more handshakes," Mumma told us grimly. "Those weasels will cheat you every chance they get."

I gladly accepted my duties as the "little mother," as the phrase of those times had it. I was proud to be trusted at last with household duties for which Mumma had no time. I cleaned and cooked and mended as best I could, gratified that I was less a burden to her than before and that I could sometimes make our dear mother's life easier. If she was too tired to notice my efforts or rated them poorly done, it was only because she worked so hard for us at the factory and she had high standards for everyone.

I was the eldest child, born a year before

Ernest and three years before our sister, Lillian. Of Lillie Mumma would often say, "We saved the best for last." And who could disagree? Strawberry blond and spritely, Lillian was like fireworks: bright and quick and colorful. She was a precocious chatterbox at two, following me around the house like a puppy and talking all the while. Once, when she was not quite three, we stood hand in hand, watching Ernest burn trash out back. I remember this so clearly! Lillie pointed at the sparks that rose skyward from stirred embers and piped, "Look, Agnes! Baby stars."

I adored her, but our brother was not so charmed. Lillian was fearless at four and took Ernest on in sibling squabbles, quoting from the Bible as she boldly scolded him for striking her because he simply could not think fast enough to hold his own in argument. At five, she wrote a letter to God, asking Him to take good care of Papa; her penmanship was already better than Ernest's. She skipped first grade, sailed through second, and won the spelling bee that year, competing against her elders. When she skipped a grade again, Ernest sulked, humiliated by a younger sister who was his equal or better in all things academic, but I was grateful for her precocity.

She would read aloud from my textbooks while I washed dishes or hung out laundry. Without Lillie's help, I never could have stayed in school.

By fourteen, I could see my life laid out before me. While Mumma ran the business, I would keep house for her and Ernest and Lillie. Later, I would become the sort of maiden aunt who lived in a spare bedroom and helped in the raising of nieces and nephews.

Marriage seemed out of the question — even then, when I was so young. You see, Ernest and Lillie were handsome persons with Mumma's red-gold hair and Papa's bright blue eyes. I shared their coloring and — in favorable light, from certain angles — a similar cast of feature, but for me, you must imagine a young Eleanor Roosevelt: bucktoothed, weak-chinned, strong-minded, with a father's bony angularity in place of a mother's delicate prettiness.

But Eleanor married, you might protest. *Why, her husband became president!*

Add, then, my freckles, considered a dreadful defect in those days. Next, be discreetly disconcerted by my crossed eyes blinking behind round spectacles.

Ah, you think now. *Ah, I have the picture. Poor Agnes . . .*

■ ■ ■ ■

In 1899, our little household changed forever. Ernest shocked us all by running away to join the army, taking with him Papa's mechanical talent and a firm desire for the male companionship our high-pitched feminine household did not afford him. I knew Ernest was unhappy at the factory, but he was barely seventeen and I'd never imagined he would simply up and leave home. Poor Mumma was beside herself when she discovered his note.

A few weeks later, she summoned me to her office to make her own announcement. After careful consultation with her brother, she told me, she had sold our Papa's patents and the factory itself to White Sewing Machines, a Cleveland concern with a reputation for plain dealing and decent labor policies. This decision realized sufficient profit to provide an income. There would be enough, Mumma informed me, to send both of her daughters to Oberlin College, one of the first coeducational academic institutions in America. Lillian's fine mind had already taken in all that our small school had to offer; she would be a good deal younger than most of our classmates, but we would matriculate at Oberlin together so that I could look after her. At Oberlin, Mumma expected, Lillian would find an educated young man worthy of her.

"And you, Agnes, will need a profession." Mumma looked toward my left eye, ignoring the right, which turned in when I was feeling tired or upset. "I have decided that you shall earn your teaching certificate. Well? Speak up. I should have thought you'd be grateful. Your nose is always in a book."

Well, yes. I loved to read, histories especially, but I had never imagined having enough money to go to college. I had begun, instead, to dream of going to the city, of making myself useful to society.

"Mumma, don't you remember? I — I told you I was thinking I might like to do settlement work."

She hardly moved. "Are you telling me that you do not wish to attend Oberlin with your sister?"

"Well, you see, Mumma, Miss Jane Addams thinks that those who serve the poor do better by going directly to work with the people who need us. She thinks we should avoid the snare of endless preparation —"

Mumma folded her thin hands in her lap and looked out the window, blinking rapidly. "Agnes, I am all alone," she whispered. "I thought when Ernest left me that I could count on you to behave." She shrugged helplessly. "It appears that you have become more self-willed than ever. And to think that I sold the business for you!"

To this moment, I can remember the wave of shame that washed over me. "Mumma, I didn't know you planned to sell the business! Settlement work wouldn't require any tuition money, so I just thought —"

"You thought. *You* thought! Without asking anyone's opinion, let alone approval. Oh, Agnes," Mumma said with a gentle melancholy that froze my heart, "you are as bad as your brother. I expected more from you. What will become of Lillian if you won't go to Oberlin with her? Is your happiness worth your sister's misery?"

If she had shouted, it might have been different, but Mumma was so small, so fragile. I always felt that if I used my strength, I might break her. Now I, who had only ever wanted to please, had hurt her so cruelly! Settlement work suddenly seemed like a pastime for silly rich girls who had nothing at all in common with me. I swore that teaching would suit me perfectly, that it was a marvelous opportunity, that I was wicked not to be grateful right away. Nothing I said made any difference. Before I knew it, I was weeping at her knees, begging for forgiveness.

Mumma's face remained the same: gallantly, if imperfectly, concealing her suffering as she recalled every sin, every promise broken by a tiresome, dishonest child. "Go to bed," she said finally, and sadly, still refusing to look at me. "And in the morning, try to be more cheerful. You owe me that much, at least."

And in the end, I was glad that Mumma's wisdom prevailed. Studying at Oberlin College was a great opportunity, and teaching was a profession that suited me well. Indeed, everything went according to her plans for Lillian and me — with a single small detour when I enrolled in Professor Douglas Cutler's course "History and the Old Testament." No one was more surprised than I when Professor Cutler found something in me to admire. And no one was less surprised than I when he found even more in darling Lillie to desire.

Douglas was in his thirties, a doctor of divinity, and a match for Lillie's intellect and Christian conviction. The moment I introduced them, it was love at first sight. They made such a handsome couple, full of plans and aspirations. Shortly after their engagement, Douglas informed us that he'd been offered a position at the American Mission School at Jebail, just north of Beirut in Syria, which in those days stretched all the way to the Mediterranean seacoast. Lillian's excitement over the news could hardly be contained, but Mumma wept and pleaded with Douglas to turn the offer down. She could hardly bear to think of her favorite child so far away, she told him. She had been so happy to believe that she would have a son-in-law to count on, what with her own dear Howard dead and her wicked son, Ernest, gone. It was awful to hear her distress, but Douglas had already signed the agreement, and a contract is a contract, as Mumma understood.

As for me, well, gracious! It had long been my dream to visit Egypt and the Holy Land, and now my very own sister would be living there, as the wife of a scholar and missionary! What could be better? I would miss Lillie desperately, of course, but she promised to write home every single week and tell me all about her travels and her life.

The wedding was to be in June, a few days after graduation. Lillie insisted that I serve as maid of honor. Eventually I gave in, though I was careful to remove my glasses and keep my eyes downcast for the wedding portrait, presenting neither my profile nor my eyes to spoil the photographs.

Lillie and Douglas spent their honeymoon walking in the footsteps of Jesus, and afterward, they took up residence in Jebail. That September, I left Cedar Glen as well, moving a few miles away to Cleveland, where I had accepted an appointment with the public school system. As you can imagine, Mumma was distraught at being left all alone, so I had a telephone installed for her and made sure the billing went to me. "You can call as often as you like," I told her.

"And let those operators listen in?" she sniffed. "No lady would do such a thing!"

She was getting on in years by then and reluctant to introduce an outlandish modernity to her home. Even so, I believe she was somewhat consoled to know that if she had a need pressing enough to summon a daughter, I was close by and lived right on the trolley line.

The district had assigned me to Murray Hill School in the Cleveland neighborhood known to all as Little Italy. The children in my classroom were mostly immigrants. Some of their fathers were quite rough, and nearly all the parents were illiterate. Few believed that education was worthwhile beyond the fourth grade.

"Pushcart Tony," Mumma called that

kind, though most of them were day laborers, not fruit and vegetable vendors. "Foreigners are taking this country over," she'd say.

"They didn't sail on the *Mayflower,*" I'd answer, "but they came here as soon as they could."

"Well, I don't know about *that,*" Mumma always said.

This remark was never capitulation, you must understand; nor was it ever an admission of ignorance. *You're wrong,* she meant, *but I don't care to argue about it.*

"And don't think I haven't noticed — that school is right next to a settlement," she let me know. Alta House wasn't really a settlement, of course. It was more of a community center with a playground and a gymnasium with a swimming pool. It was named for John D. Rockefeller's daughter Miss Alta Rockefeller, and it really was quite respectable, though Mumma never entirely believed that.

Each year, I am proud to say, there were two or three children who truly blossomed in my classroom. Often these were the most resistant in September: cocky little boys who wanted to look tough and were afraid to fail, or awkward little girls who hardly dared believe that they'd be good at anything.

With no children of my own to love, I had to be careful about letting my emotions run away with me. If my affection and attention were noticed, the boys and girls I liked best would be called "teacher's pet" and there'd be trouble for them on the playground. I quickly learned to be evenhanded in the classroom.

And I worked hard to expand all my students' horizons beyond Mayfield Road and Little Italy. We took field trips to the art museum, for example, and whenever a building was going up downtown, I'd try to get the architect to visit us. All the children were excited to see the postcards and letters I received from Lillie, and I organized Old World geography lessons around her mail. Each week, the student whose marks had most improved from one examination to the next would be rewarded with a postcard or a carefully loosened stamp from one of Lillie's envelopes.

When the war in Europe began, geography took on a different importance. The Ottoman Empire seemed likely to collapse at any moment, throwing the Middle East into turmoil. Lillie and Douglas came home, of course — they had their two boys to think of. Douglas, stoutly middle-aged by then, was awarded a full professorship at our alma mater, Oberlin.

When the war ended in November 1918, our family seemed to have reached a safe harbor, apart from the loss of poor Ernest to flu in the autumn of 1918. At thirty-eight, I believed that all the big questions of my life had been answered. I would never marry. I would earn my living as a teacher. When the time came, I would move back to Cedar Glen and care for Mumma in her old age.

And yet, I will confess to you, from time to time I envied my youthful self — that girl who could still dream and want more, who could still imagine someone who had never materialized, except during those brief weeks before Douglas fell in love with Lillie. However briefly, Douglas had seen my true self, and he had not laughed or sneered or sighed. He was only being kind, I suppose. But kindness is so important, wouldn't you agree?

It was early March in 1919 and I was correcting a pile of arithmetic papers when my landlady, Mrs. Motta, called me downstairs to receive a telephone call that changed my life. I expected to hear Mumma's voice, but it was Lillie on the line, and she was so excited! "Agnes, do you remember Neddy

Lawrence?"

I racked my brains but no one came to mind, so she reminded me of her letters from Jebail. She'd written of an archaeology student, a British undergraduate who planned to tramp around the Middle East alone, photographing crusader castles for his thesis. He and Lillie had become great friends as he studied practical Arabic with her colleague at the mission school — a young Christian lady whose name was Fareedah el-Akle.

"Neddy's grammar wasn't strong, but his memory was excellent and he absorbed Arabic vocabulary very quickly," Lillie recalled. After her return to the United States in 1914, she and Neddy had exchanged letters, the most remarkable of which was his request that she purchase for him a Colt .45 automatic pistol, which he meant to carry into combat. "Handguns are difficult to obtain in England," he wrote in explanation.

"We lost track of him after that," Lillie told me, "but he not only survived the war, he's become a hero! We called him Ned, but his name is really Thomas Edward Lawrence. *Lawrence,* Agnes," Lillie repeated, exasperated. "Doesn't that ring any bells?"

Frankly, it didn't, not then. In those days Colonel Lawrence was just on the cusp of the international celebrity that would soon be his. And in any case, I was distracted by how expensive this telephone call would be; Lillie never seemed to worry about things like that.

"There's a sort of Chautauqua lecture about him at the Palace on Thursday evening," she said. "We'll swing by to pick you up —"

"Lillie, no! Friday is a school day. I can't —"

"Oh, Agnes, you must come. It'll be *wonderful!*"

Lillie had a way of saying *wonderful.* Her tone carried the thrill of the word, its element of marvel and surprise.

"It will be like visiting the Holy Land," she said, "and you can tell the children about it in class. Anyway, we've already bought your ticket, so don't argue, darling. Just be ready at six forty-five."

And she was right, of course. It was a splendid evening. Truly unforgettable, for so many reasons.

She and Douglas drove in from Oberlin and left their boys with Mumma before picking me up at Mrs. Motta's. Lillie was like a schoolgirl — so excited and full of chatter — and she gave a little shriek when we saw the theater marquee.

LOWELL THOMAS PRESENTS
With Allenby in Palestine
and with Lawrence in Arabia!

Douglas left us girls in front of the theater and rattled off to park their ancient electric car. He kept talking about replacing it, but an Oberlin professor's salary was not quite up to one of the newer gasoline models. A light drizzle was falling, and we hurried inside to wait for Douglas in the lobby. By the time he arrived to escort us to our seats, the theater was almost full.

You might have thought we'd all had enough of war, and that was true in some ways. No one wanted to think about the horrors of the trenches, or those poor Romanov girls, or the ugly revolution in Ireland, but this was different. This was the rousing story of General Allenby, the modern Crusader, and his conquest of the Holy Land, and a glorious tale about the young man Mr. Lowell Thomas called "the uncrowned king of Arabia."

The presentation had received rave reviews in London. Drawn by the biblical setting and the tour publicity, Americans had flocked to the lecture in city after city. Now it was Cleveland's turn, and goodness gracious! Didn't we see a show!

Pots of incense were set alight; a captivating musky fragrance pervaded the hall. As the house lights dimmed, there was a swell of organ music, which resolved into a haunting Levantine melody. Mr. Thomas stepped onto the stage and into the spotlight. With a magician's flourish, our host proclaimed an irresistible invitation: "Come with me to lands of history, mystery, and romance!"

The curtains swept back to reveal the Nile awash in artificial moonlight that faintly illuminated distant painted pyramids. For the next two and a half-hours, Mr. Thomas took us to places in Arabia that no Christian among us had previously seen, and he did so with the world's first aerial motion photography. Gasping, we viewed the pyramids — from above! We felt vertigo when "our aeroplane" banked and flew along the very roads upon which had marched the armies of Godfrey de Bouillon and Richard Coeur de Lion, eight centuries before. Hands at our lips, we felt we witnessed with our own eyes a thrilling charge by the massed cavalry of the Australian Light Horse and Imperial Camel Corps.

Lillie loosed a tiny excited squeal at the

first image of the slim young Englishman she'd known in Jebail. She held my hand while Mr. Thomas related his own first glimpse of "Shareef Aurens," the boy my sister knew as Neddy.

"My attention," Mr. Thomas recalled sonorously, "was drawn to a group of Arabs walking in the direction of the Damascus Gate. My curiosity was excited by a single Bedouin who stood in sharp relief from his companions. He was wearing an *agal, kuffieh,* and *aba* such as are worn in the Middle East only by native rulers. In his belt was fastened the short, curved, golden dagger of a prince of Mecca."

It was not this person's marvelous costume that interested Mr. Thomas. "The striking fact was that this mysterious prince looked no more like a son of Ishmael than an Abyssinian looks like one of Stefansson's Esquimaux. Why, this chap was as blond as a Scandinavian in whom flows cool Viking blood! My first thought," Mr. Thomas assured us, "was that this might be one of the youngest apostles, come to life. His expression was serene, almost saintly in its selflessness and repose."

"He was a lovely young man," Lillie allowed, sounding amused.

"But saintly?" Douglas asked rhetorically,

and shook his head.

They were both firmly shushed by the gentleman who sat behind us. Mr. Thomas, unaware, continued his encomium. A brilliant young archaeologist before the war, Lawrence was "a born strategist who outthought and outwitted the Turkish and German commanders in practically every engagement." At the head of his troops, in the thick of every battle, Lawrence rapidly rose from junior lieutenant to full colonel. "But he dislikes titles," Mr. Thomas told us, "and prefers to be known as plain Lawrence to general and private alike." In fact, this modern Galahad was rather shy, Mr. Thomas confided. "Indeed, the Terror of the Turks can blush like a schoolgirl." Those terrified Turks had put a princely price on his head, but so beloved was the twenty-eight-year-old commander, no one had betrayed him. Thus, we were told, the blue-eyed scholar became, in less than a year, the most powerful man in Arabia, leading the greatest army raised in that land in five centuries.

Indeed, Mr. Thomas seemed to have forgotten General Allenby entirely, and gave young Neddy Lawrence personal credit for the downfall of the entire Ottoman Empire. "Mesopotamia, Syria, Arabia, and the Holy

Land — all freed after centuries of Turkish oppression! Why, I would not be surprised," Mr. Thomas concluded, "if centuries from now, Lawrence of Arabia stood out as a legendary figure along with Achilles, Siegfried, and El Cid."

Well, my goodness! You can just picture us emerging from the theater, dazzled by what we had seen and heard, astonished to find ourselves back in plain old Cleveland. Unwilling to let the evening end, little groups congregated on the street: strangers drawn together by shared experience. The earlier drizzle had turned to a cold, spitting rain, just this side of sleet, but we were so caught up in the moment! Illness was the last thing on our minds.

Go to any symphony hall, any cinema, and you'll hear a few who cough through the event, just as we did that night. You don't think a thing about it, and neither did we. During the 1918 influenza, some cities had passed laws requiring everyone who went out in public to wear surgical masks over the lower face. Most people refused, or forgot and left the masks at home. In any case, the epidemic seemed over and done with. It would have felt absurd to take any such precautions in Cleveland that night.

Lillie and I were nearest a man who

sneezed and wheezed through the lecture, but it was Douglas who sickened first. Maybe he had shaken the hand of an acquaintance when he was entering the theater after parking the car. Or maybe one of his students was coming down with the flu and had exposed him earlier that day. Who knows?

Unsuspecting, Lillie and Douglas drove back to Mumma's to pick up the boys after dropping me off at Mrs. Motta's boardinghouse, on Mayfield Avenue. I myself went to school as usual on Friday, eager to share with my students what I had learned the prior evening. Instead, I shared something I did not know I had.

That afternoon, I developed an awful headache but put it down to being up so late the night before. God forgive me, I spread the flu to my students. Several died, including one of my favorites. Elisabeth Maggio. I'll never forget that poor child's name, but I remember very little of the days that followed.

Near the end of the Great War, just before he was killed, the poet Wilfred Owen provided us with a simple searing description of the damage war had done to his spirit while his men were destroyed in wholesale lots: "My senses are charred. I don't take the cigarette out of my mouth when I write 'Deceased' over their letters." Later, when the fighting ended, Mr. Aldington and Mr. Graves described trench warfare with such bitter exactitude, it seemed to me a mercy that Ernest had died before he reached France, if die he must. Like the doomed Persians of Aeschylus, "he was happiest who soonest gasped away the breath of life."

The pointless savagery of the Great War forged a generation of writers, so I've always found it strange that no one here at home chronicled the Great Influenza or its effects on us, although Miss Katherine Porter did write the brief and touching story of her soldier-love, who died of the influenza that he caught while nursing her. Without literature as a guide, I expect you think of the flu as a homey, familiar kind of illness, not a horrifying scourge like the black plague or smallpox. You may believe you know what the flu epidemic was like for us.

Pray, now, that you never learn how wrong you are.

The onset of the disease was abrupt, very much like that of meningitis, which is what the doctors thought it was, in the beginning. The initial symptoms were a severe headache and a high fever, followed by those of an awful cold: a terrible sore throat, an endlessly dripping nose, violent coughing. And then —

Well, I cannot make poetry of our great trial, as Mr. Owen did of combat, but permit me to act the schoolteacher and explain to you the workings of the lungs. In health, they are the lightest of all our organs. Their surfaces are a lacy gauze of fine blood vessels. Across this diaphanous borderland between the body and the world, the scientists tell us, life must be renewed each moment of the day and night by the exchange of gaseous waste for fresh, clean oxygen.

Early in the epidemic, frantic to find the cause of this vicious illness, pathologists cut open chests and discovered that those delicate soap-bubble lungs were as heavy and solid as a liver — saturated with bloody fluid, the air passages leading to the throat completely blocked. Those who died turned blue-black for want of air. In the morgues, bodies the color of slate were said to be stacked in piles "like cordwood." In a single year, fifty million people died that way — millions more than died in combat on all sides, on all fronts, in four and a half-years of the Great War, itself an orgy of killing.

My own experience was one of delirium and long nightmares of drowning. Over and over, I would slide down a thick hemp rope toward water. Hour after hour, I tried to climb that rope, desperate to keep my head above the surface. My leaden arms would fail me. I'd slip beneath the water, and then I'd awaken myself: coughing, coughing, coughing.

I, who never wished to be a bother to Mumma, called and called to her in my dreams, but she never came. Around me, fellow sufferers groaned and wept. I heard muffled voices — masked doctors, nurses, hospital attendants, I realized later. Those poor heroes and heroines must have been overwhelmed and exhausted, trying to care for hundreds of patients who were hemorrhaging from the nose and throat. It was an inferno worthy of Dante, for them, and for us.

Whenever it became clear that patients might survive, they were removed from the hospital to make way for others. *"Poveretta,"* Mrs. Motta cried as I was carried up to my room in her boardinghouse. "Poor little t'ing! I make a bath. You want I wash your hair?"

It was such a comfort, feeling her soapy hands gently rinse away the waxy sweat and stink of illness. That good woman nursed me with motherly tenderness, as though I were her own, but when I asked why my own mother did not come, or why I had not been taken home to Cedar Glen, Mrs. Motta never answered my questions. "You rest now," she'd say firmly, and then she'd leave me alone to sleep.

Only when my recovery seemed assured did she hand me the stack of telegrams that had been delivered while I lay ill. Douglas. Lillie. Their boys. Uncle John. Mumma. All of them were gone.

"I'm sorry, signorina," Mrs. Motta said, wringing her hands as I read the messages, one after the other. "I'm real sorry."

When I laid the flimsy yellow sheets aside, Mrs. Motta handed me a business card. I recognized the name. Mr. James Reichardt was a junior partner in Uncle John's law firm.

"He come round here twice, for to see you," Mrs. Motta told me. "He say dere's a 'heritance, signorina. And he wanna know, what you wan' him-a do wit' dat dog?"

Over the years, Mumma had raised and sold generations of puppies: first collies, then cocker spaniels, and finally dachshunds — all long, benchlike dogs, decreasing in size as her stamina declined.

"The dachshund is a perfectly engineered

dog," Ernest once observed. "It is precisely long enough for a single standard stroke of the back, but you aren't paying for any superfluous leg."

Perhaps it was the dachshund's economy of material that appealed to Mumma, but her timing with the breed was unfortunate. She had tried to popularize the long-haired variety, believing its temperament was better, but people preferred the familiar short-haired red. Later, when the war started, no one would buy anything remotely German. By 1918, Mumma was practically giving the pups away. She decided to sell the breeding stock and get out of the business entirely.

As luck would have it, I was present for the final whelping. The last to emerge was a black-and-tan female with a badly kinked tail and an unattractive blue dapple splattered across her back and face. These were defects that doomed a puppy to a quick end. Mumma kept a bucket of water in the kennel for just that purpose. You may think her harsh, but it is a conscientious breeder's duty to be critical. Mumma had tried crossing dapples in the past, and the results had sometimes been disastrous. This little female might be healthy enough, but her own offspring could be born eyeless, or earless, or brainless. Mumma had never worked out a way to predict when or why that would happen.

"No sense exhausting the bitch's resources on a pup that shouldn't be bred," she said briskly.

"Wait!" I said, and stayed my mother's hand when she reached for the dapple. "I'll take her."

Mumma stared.

I dropped my gaze, ashamed of my wayward eye, but I couldn't stop myself from arguing. "You always say I don't get enough exercise. Walking a dog will be good for me."

Mumma couldn't dispute the principle, but picked up the puppy anyway. "Well, you don't want *this* one. You want the sable."

All my life, Mumma had told me what I didn't want. "Oh, you don't want *those* earrings," she'd say. "They'll draw attention to your eyes." Oh, you don't want *that* dress. It will make you look like a stick. Oh, you don't want *eggs* for breakfast. You want oatmeal. It's better for you in cold weather. Well, I didn't want oatmeal. I never wanted oatmeal. I hated the stuff, but I choked it down, all winter long, because Mumma put it in front of me and told me that was what I wanted.

Suddenly, and I cannot tell you why, a determination came over me like I don't know what! I did not want that puppy's perfectly lovely red sister or her handsome sable brother. No, I wanted the defective little black-and-tan. I wanted her ferociously, indignantly, unbendingly — blue dapple, kinked tail, and all.

Mumma was just as determined to save me from my own bad judgment. "Agnes, you're not making any sense" became "This is a mistake. That pup is inferior" and finally a tearful "I am only trying to guide you, Agnes. There's no reason for you to speak to me in that tone."

Nevertheless, and for the first time in my life, I dared insist and I got my way. I named the pup Rosie. Before the day was over, I was so in love, it was difficult to leave her, even to go to sleep.

The plan was for Mumma to raise Rosie until she was housebroken. (House-training, I must tell you, is a formality that can elude young dachshunds for some time; this is particularly true in climates that affront their sensibilities with outrageous meteorological insults. Rain, for example, or a startling gust of wind.) I always visited Mumma on weekends, of course, but knowing Rosie was waiting for me would make the routine a treat. When the school year was over, I would return as usual to spend the summer in Cedar Glen, helping Mumma with the garden and the canning. In autumn, I would take Rosie back to Cleveland with me. Either my landlady would agree to this, I decided, or I would just have to find a new place to live.

Mumma had the satisfaction of being right about Rosie in some ways. My little pet was indeed a poor specimen of her breed. She matured to sixteen pounds — on the awkward border between the miniature and the standard for the breed. Her coat grew in long but thinnish. She was timid as well as unprepossessing, and spent her puppyhood hiding behind boxes in the kennel, darting out to steal food or toys from the stronger members of her litter.

"She's sneaky," Mumma would report whenever I telephoned to check on her and Rosie. "She plots and she schemes."

"She's clever," I'd reply, "and resourceful."

"Well, I don't know about *that.*"

Those were the last words Mumma said to me, in life, a few days before the influenza swept my family away.

Weeks later, when Mrs. Motta handed me all those awful telegrams, I hardly reacted at all. I was so . . . depleted, I suppose, that I simply did not have the energy to weep.

In fact, I did not cry at all until I was strong enough to meet the lawyer at my mother's house. You see, Mr. Reichardt brought Rosie with him that morning. She remembered me. And she came to me when I called.

Well, three times out of five, anyway. Dachshunds have their own agenda and can be stubborn about seeing their plans through to completion. What Rosie lacked in consistency, she made up for in enthusiasm. Most of the time when I called her name, she sprinted back, her long ears cocked and flying like a little girl's pigtails. Each encounter was a glorious reunion, even if we'd been parted for only a minute or two. I had never felt so beloved.

She went with me everywhere, and there was so much work to do! Mr. Reichardt took on as much as he could of this necessary tidying of lives cut short, but he had many such estates to settle, so a great deal fell to me. The probate courts were jammed. Rosie and I spent hours waiting in queues that often turned out to be the wrong ones. More than once, someone in the line fainted, sending panic through the room. Since we'd been caught out by the second wave of influenza, illness was never far from our minds.

Douglas and Lillie and the boys had lived on the campus in a house provided for them by Oberlin. The dean told me that I could take all the time I needed to vacate the premises, but then he checked my progress every day, and frowned significantly when a bare week had passed. Not wanting to be a bother, I had their belongings boxed for transport and delivered to Mumma's house in Cedar Glen. I turned next to Uncle John's estate, hoping it would be relatively simple. He was a bachelor lawyer who had left his affairs in good order. Even so, there were many accounts to process and outstanding fees to collect, and his apartment to clear out, on top of the legal mechanics of settling any estate.

I was beginning to realize that a surprising amount of money would come to me eventually, but in the meantime, ready cash was in short supply. I hoped to raise funds by selling Uncle John's furniture, but with so many estate liquidations, secondhand dealers had more stock than they could handle and paid just pennies on the dollar. And there was no market for anything Victorian anymore. Brash confidence might rule the business day and boozy flamboyance might dance through the night, but when people left the speakeasies? They wanted to go home to cozy houses filled with brand-new suites of "colonial" oak or the awful stuff that people of taste called "Flapper Phyfe." As the weeks dragged on, the final expenses of three households piled up. The costs of caskets and burial plots had been added to all the usual bills: electricity, coal, telephone; grocery accounts, department store purchases. My salary from Murray Hill School had ceased the day I fell ill, and I fretted constantly about how long I could put off creditors while the estates were in probate.

Then, while I was going through the contents of my brother-in-law's files, a small miracle was revealed: Douglas had carried a life insurance policy. Though it was meant for Lillie and the boys, I was listed as contingent beneficiary, so the money would come to me: un-looked for, unwished for, but welcome all the same.

My financial worries were allayed, but there was still the physical labor of sorting through the entirety of other people's things. Minute by minute, I made thousands of little decisions: what to keep, what to sell, what to give away, what to have hauled to the dump. Until you've done it, you have no idea how draining that can be.

Mumma's death seemed only half real to me, surrounded as I was by her possessions. Even before I shipped Lillie's things home, Mumma's house — mine now, I slowly realized — was jammed with a half century's accumulation, and there was no inch of it that did not speak to me of her.

Her desk, a massive rolltop in a makeshift office, was formidably well organized, but the sheer volume of paper was daunting. There were yellowed newspaper clippings about dog shows, records of bloodlines, AKC registrations. Feed supplies and veterinarian bills. Records from the sewing machine business: accounts receivable and accounts payable, employee pay stubs several decades old. Mail of all kinds, each item read and returned to its carefully slit envelope, dated, and filed, "just in case." Everything had to be opened, read, and dealt with.

Mumma had lived through lean times: nothing potentially useful was ever discarded. Old clothes, old shoes, old handbags. Empty bottles of all descriptions, washed and stored in a closet. Bits of string — short lengths tied end to end, wound like yarn into balls. There were oak-slat baskets in every corner, filled with quilt pieces and rag rugs in progress; cigar boxes held skeins of ribbons, hoarded buttons, and wooden spools of thread. She kept the empty spools, as well. Just in case.

As her only heir, I would benefit from Mumma's parsimony, and from the carefully conserved proceeds from the sale of the sewing machine business, but I simply could not think in those terms, not yet. Overwhelmed, I often wandered from room to room, helpless in the face of it all, alone but surrounded by the dead, for every flat surface was peopled with framed studio portraits. Ernest and Lillian as children. Lillian and Douglas at their wedding. A series of the two boys, almost growing up. A stranger might have thought Mumma had only two children, but pictures of me were nearly always disappointing, you see. Why pay a photographer for something that wouldn't bear looking at? I understood this, even as a child, though I won't deny a lingering sense of invisibility.

I found other evidence of my existence, however: my grammar school report cards, tied with blue yarn, were tucked away in a desk drawer. These, Mumma had evidently decided, were suitable keepsakes of her eldest child's youth. And then there were the ghosts of birthdays past that she had stashed away. Dusty candy boxes filled with fossilized chocolates. Books of poetry, their spines uncracked. Heaps of unused embroidered handkerchiefs. I sometimes broke down in tears when I came across a Christmas present that I had carefully selected for her, and that she had left untouched for years at the back of a cupboard or on the top shelf of a bookcase. It's the thought that counts, of course, but it was disheartening to find evidence of how consistently I had failed to please her.

I suppose you find my laments self-absorbed and unseemly. *Your mother left you a wealthy woman. You should be grateful, Agnes. Many a war widow was worse off.* True enough, though in my own defense, I will point out that I was not at my best, having been so recently so ill.

That said, I will be honest with you. I'd have traded every penny of my inheritance for the memory of one word of love, or a single fond caress.

Like many modern mothers of her time, Mumma was much influenced by Dr. Emmett Holt and Professor John B. Watson. Young people raised in the aftermath of the Civil War were effete and flabby, these experts declared. They had been spoiled by sentimental, unscientific mothers who weakened the nation's youth with loose schedules and sloppy displays of affection. In his manual *The Care and Feeding of Children,* Dr. Holt warned mothers that babies were not sweet little angels but small animals with fearsome appetites whose spirits needed breaking, just like those of wild horses. To rear a responsible adult, regularity in all things had to be imposed, for a well-adjusted adult was defined as one with iron habits and rigid self-control.

Above all, mothers must avoid displays of tenderness. "Mother love is a dangerous instrument that may inflict a never-healing wound," Professor Watson warned. Merely to touch a child unnecessarily would place at risk that child's future success and happiness. Maternal solicitude was not merely unsavory and unwise but a corrupting dereliction of duty.

In your time, adults strive to be "good parents," but in my day, it was the business of children to be good and the solemn duty of parents to punish them when they were bad. In the spirit of scientific modernity, and with a calm sense of moral certainty, therefore, Mumma trained her children and her dogs with similar cool competence.

The childhood discipline that Ernest ran from — and that Lillie laughingly evaded — I truly desired to be governed by. I might have been annoying and, too often, I asked questions before I did as I was told, but I was as obedient as I knew how to be, even when I was small. How, then, had I so signally failed to elicit Mumma's approval and pride? Why, I wondered, had my questions rankled when Lillie's charmed? Was it merely that Lillian was a pretty child and graceful, while I was homely and awkward?

Like Rosie, I was a poor specimen of my breed. My wandering eye may have seemed to Mumma a constant silent accusation that she'd given birth to flawed stock. And as a toddler, I wailed so loudly when she splinted my arms to keep me from sucking my thumb that she gave in; my spoiled teeth were no doubt a rebuke to her weakness every time I smiled, but I don't quite believe that was the whole explanation.

You see, Mumma was easily able to answer Lillie's questions about the Bible and God and what Jesus wanted from us, about what was good and what was sin. My questions were most often not "What?" but "Why?" Why did people think one thing and not another? Why could things not be different from the way they were? Why would God blame little babies for what Eve did? If Jesus was God, and God was going to forgive Original Sin after the Crucifixion, and the whole Trinity knew that was going to happen, why did Jesus still have to die on the cross? It didn't make sense to me.

Once, I remember, we were walking home from services on Sunday, and I was terribly upset about the sermon. "I don't think God's being fair," I said. "Asking a person if he wants to spend all eternity in heaven or hell is like asking a little boy like Ernest what he wants to be when he grows up. We can't understand infinity. Why would God punish a little finite person forever? And what could a finite person do to deserve an eternal reward?"

Alone, in what I still thought of as Mumma's house, I could hear echoes of her exasperation with such questions. "Oh, Agnes," she'd sigh. "The things that pop into your head and out of your mouth . . ."

And that would be the end of that.

The estate work seemed endless but, through it all, Rosie was nearby and her company made the tasks more bearable. Dachshunds like to burrow, and Rosie would scoop out a cave in a basket of quilt scraps or crawl under an errant sweater. She could be content for hours, fast asleep, but if I sat back in my chair or laid my head in my hands as melancholy or exhaustion overtook me, she'd hop right out, and I'd feel small, soft paws go pitty-pat on my knee.

Pay attention, Rosie tapped in dachshund Morse. *You aren't alone. I'm here.*

I'd pull her up into my arms. She was the size and weight of a four-month-old baby, and it was comforting to hold her against my chest until I'd recovered my composure. "What do you think, Rosie?" I'd ask her then. "Shall we go for a walk?"

At the sound of the word "walk," she'd hurl herself off my lap with a steeplechaser's leap, then pirouette at the doorway, delicate pointed nose tossed repeatedly in the direction of the road. As I put on my hat and gloves, she'd spin again to register her approval. *Good girl, Agnes! Yes, yes, yes! Most certainly! Time for a walk!*

Outdoors, she was joy embodied, trundling cheerily at my side, or veering off to track an elusive chipmunk, or falling behind to investigate some loathsome reminder of another animal's passage. If you'd seen us, you might have rolled your eyes and thought, *How pathetic. An old maid and her spoiled little dog.* But Rosie was less a pampered pet than a prizefighter's trainer, insisting that I do my roadwork twice a day, always pressing to go a bit farther.

Though she never allowed me to sink for long into discouragement or loneliness, Rosie seemed to understand when I simply had to rest. Recovery from the Great Influenza was slow. The fever broke, the aching ended, breathing became easier, but for months afterward, one had hardly any mental energy and tired very easily. For a long time, I napped every afternoon with Rosie curled beside me, warm and sweet.

There is a difference, I discovered in those shuttered hours, between mourning and grief. Mourning is soft and sad. I mourned my brother, Ernest, and Lillie's husband, Douglas, and my two young nephews, especially. I thought of what those fine boys could no longer enjoy and of what they would never experience. To die so young — just as they had begun to fulfill their promise . . . My sadness was for them, but not much for me.

Grief, by contrast, is sharp and selfish. The loss feels like deprivation, as though something rightfully one's own has been unjustly stolen away. Oh, how I grieved for Lillian! I missed desperately the elements of surprise and gaiety she so often brought to my unremarkable days.

Pull yourself together, I could almost hear Mumma say. *Make a list. Get things done.*

Good advice, of course. Each morning, I wrote down my tasks for the day. Each evening, I crossed some off and added others, chipping away at the mountain of responsibilities, bit by bit. It was all I could do to take care of my own small affairs at my own slow pace. As I struggled through my duties, I thought sometimes of President Wilson, who had just returned from Europe after the Versailles Peace Conference and was dealing in those same days with great affairs of state.

I was not among those who applauded the president's decision to take us into the Great War, but I always try to be fair-minded. He and our soldiers deserved credit for hastening the conflict's end, in the opinion of many Europeans, who had once believed their nations would be forever locked in stalemate, with the war killing mothers' sons as steadily as they could be born, raised, drafted, and sent to the front. America broke that impasse and released them from despair, and the Europeans were truly grateful.

Mr. Wilson's trip to England and France was, therefore, a triumph. He was showered with flowers, our newspapers reported, and cheered by throngs of admirers as his motorcade crept through the streets of

London. He and Mrs. Wilson were house-guests at Buckingham Palace. At dinner that first night, King George noted that Woodrow Wilson was the first president of the United States to visit England, and he toasted Mr. Wilson as the leader of a "mighty commonwealth tied to us by the closest of ties."

Ah, I thought, reading that. Our little revolution is officially forgiven.

The American party soon set sail for France. Mr. Wilson looked fit in photos taken as he debarked in Brest, where thousands celebrated his arrival. He received a gold medal from the city of Paris and met with diplomats to discuss the coming peace conference in Versailles. He spent a week at the American army headquarters in Chaumont but declined a visit to the cratered moonscape of the battlefields. "I don't want to get mad," he explained in an interview. "I think there should be one man at the peace table who hasn't lost his temper."

It was a noble ambition, to retain some composure on that ruined continent. Nevertheless, for all the grief it cost our country, others at Versailles pointed out that only 150,000 of the ten million war dead were Americans. Mr. Wilson might be inclined toward magnanimity; not so, the other victors. Their aim was to punish those who'd set the meat grinder in motion: to destroy forever the ability of Germany, Austria, and Turkey to wage war.

If Mr. Wilson had been one of my students, I'd have advised him to do as my students did when trying to grasp something difficult: read aloud. Hear the weight of these numbers in your own voice, sir. Ten million soldiers dead. Twenty-one million wounded. Seven and a half million men missing in action: blown to shreds, grim fertilizer for the poppies that would grow in Flanders Field and a hundred other battlegrounds.

Nor was the cost reckoned in lives alone. The total for four fiscal years of combat was estimated by Mr. E.R.A. Seligman at $232 trillion. And that, remember, was before inflation took hold in the twenties.

The youth and wealth of empires had been poured out onto bloody mud, but Mr. Wilson went to Versailles intending to ask still more of them. His Fourteen Points called not just for free seas, free trade, and arms reduction, and not only for the voluntary withdrawal of all armies from all conquered territories. Why, he demanded the end of all colonial claims! He intended to fight for the right of the whole world's conquered and colonized peoples to determine their own autonomous development. His peace plan was simply this: America writ large.

He wished for all nationalities a nation like our own: of the people, by the people, for the people. His greatest allies at Versailles were the defeated Triple Alliance and the many small nations of the Balkans and the Middle East that had begun to emerge as the Ottoman Empire crumbled and collapsed. All of them laid their hopes for a better future on the altar of Mr. Wilson's peace.

Now think again of those awful numbers, and you will, perhaps, understand the hatred, the rage, the thirst for vengeance among the rulers of England, Belgium, France, and Italy. From those empires, Mr. Wilson's plan required the sacrifice not only of men and money but of importance. Who among them would willingly cede that?

Try to imagine what a miracle of peacemaking, what relentless powers of persuasion, what Herculean intensity of physical and intellectual effort such a peace would have required! And learn this, if you wish to understand the twentieth century: Woodrow Wilson was hospitalized with influenza just as the Versailles conference began.

While the president lay hallucinating and delirious, representatives of the victorious empires redrew maps as they pleased and took what they wanted. Too ill to carry the day, Mr. Wilson never really regained his strength of body or mind. He left France, scorned, and sailed back to Washington, a sick and disappointed man.

While I sorted through boxes of my nephews' toys and my sister's letters and her husband's books; while I cleaned my mother's closets; while I sobbed sometimes and napped regularly; while I walked with Rosie a bit farther every day and slowly reconciled myself to a changed world, Woodrow Wilson struggled to convince his bereaved and preoccupied nation that we must make the whole world over in America's image. To do so would require a League of Nations that could adjudicate the creation of new nations of, for, and by their people. And for that League of Nations to prevail, America would have to pledge troops and treasure to an international armed force sufficient to guarantee the independence and territorial integrity of every member state. The fate of the world was in our hands.

Mr. Wilson and his eloquent pleas were ignored by heedless boys, too young to have fought, who wore raccoon coats and kept lists of bootleggers in their pockets. He was ignored by carefree girls who bobbed their hair and rolled their stockings down, and knew just how alluringly their white thighs flashed at dance clubs where cool black musicians blew hot jazz and made their cymbals shimmer. He was ignored by busy, striving citizens who had troubles of their own and who were sick of the Old World's expensive, incomprehensible, murderous politics. He was ignored as well by contemptuous senators and congressmen, whose eyes were on their next election campaign and who cared nothing for airy-fairy ideas like the League of Nations.

Exhausted, derided, Mr. Wilson suffered a crippling stroke before he could sway public opinion. Europe was already doomed to a conflagration that would make the Great War seem almost quaint, with its horse-drawn caissons, its Christmas truce, and the chivalric notion that soldiers should fight one another instead of carpet-bombing civilians or gassing noncombatants by the trainload.

Read aloud the names of the nations and the colonies whose dreams were fired by Mr. Wilson's promise of freedom, then burned to cinders by his fever. Germany, Austria, Hungary. Serbia, Croatia, Bosnia.

Kosovo, Albania. China, Korea, Tibet, Vietnam. Palestine, Syria, Mesopotamia. The Lebanon and the Philippines, the Congo and the Sudan. Algeria, Egypt. Ethiopia, Eritrea. Somalia, Mozambique, Angola . . .

Or simply look at a globe, and weep.

Despite it all, there was still a chance for peace, even then, in some few places. If no single person could make things right after the Great War, young Neddy Lawrence still hoped to make them less wrong in one corner of the world. The rest of my story is a small part of his, and a large part of yours, I'm afraid.

When did the idea of going to Egypt begin to take hold? Sometime around Christmas in 1920, I think. Certainly by February of '21, I had booked passage and was packing for the trip. By then I'd served nearly two years' hard labor as the executrix of three estates and had largely completed my duties. A second solitary Thanksgiving had come and gone, and I'm afraid I was feeling quite sorry for myself.

To stave off "the blues," I set myself a task I'd put off until then as unimportant: the bundling up of hundreds of magazines for the paper-and-rags man who collected them for paper mills.

Long after she sold the sewing machine business, Mumma had continued her subscriptions to *McCall's* and *Vogue* and *Vanity Fair* and, of course, she had saved every issue, "just in case." For a whole day, I stacked them and tied them up with string, but I often paused to gaze at the Palmolive advertisements on the back covers. There, the soap's green tint was lent a foreign glamor by a slender olive-skinned girl who sat beneath palm trees and beckoned the customer toward starlit pyramids.

Another Ohio winter lowered the skies; for days at a time, noon was as dark as dusk. During the holidays, I passed many a long empty evening reading Douglas's mission diaries about Egypt, Palestine, and Syria, or paging through Lillie's scrapbooks of their travels. The idea of sun and desert heat began to make a compelling case as Rosie and I took our short, cold walks. Rosie loved the snow and would tunnel through it after chipmunks, digging with relentless determination until the ice balls between her toes made movement impossible and she had to be carried inside. I tried to emulate her energetic pleasure in the season but felt increasingly adrift as silent nights became dismal days.

You may be wondering why I didn't go back to my job in the Cleveland school district. Well, at the end of the war, women had achieved the suffrage, but the Nineteenth Amendment didn't carry with it the right to make a living. There were so many demobilized soldiers needing work that we ladies were often summarily dismissed from employment. With plenty of money and no family of my own to support, I could not bring myself to protest when I was replaced by a returning veteran. Even so, I missed my students and my colleagues.

Rosie was not my sole companion in those days, although she was the only one of flesh and blood. In the years after the Great War and the Great Influenza, many of us were visited by apparitions, and I saw — or, rather, heard — my share of spirits. There was no one alive to find fault with my dress or hairstyle or habits, but Mumma seemed to look over my shoulder whenever I stood before a mirror to brush my hair or put on a battered hat. Of course, in those days, I didn't believe in superstitious nonsense like ghosts and ghouls or hauntings, but I could hear Mumma's voice so clearly! *What will people think? Land sake, Agnes! I never let a daughter of mine leave the house looking as slovenly as you do now.*

In all times and in all places, a teacher's salary has required fiscal discipline. When I was working, my tastes had inclined toward books, not clothing. I could have afforded more now, but for me the acquisition of a new dress had always been less an amusing indulgence than a depressing chore. When I began teaching, women's clothing was made to measure, tightly fitted around unbending corsets that wordlessly proclaimed: *This is decidedly not a loose woman.* The styles of that era celebrated an ampleness I did not possess, though Mumma did her best for me. "Oh, Agnes," she'd sigh, gathering ankle-length skirts into high fabric waistbands to hint at shapely hips I did not have. "What am I going to do with you?" she'd mutter as she created abundantly pleated bodices to enhance what nature had begrudged. It was unrewarding work for her, and I hated every moment.

Then the war came on, and suddenly it was patriotic to conserve fabric more nobly used to clothe our boys in uniform. Skirts crept toward the knees. Pleats disappeared. Hats became smaller, with none of the elaborate wire structure that earlier millinery had required and armament factories now requisitioned. Mumma was scandalized by the new styles and would have none of them. I simply waited the war out, wearing what I had, but Lillie enjoyed the changes. She had a real knack for fashion. A professor's wife couldn't be extravagant, but my sister could toss an old piano shawl around her shoulders and look chic. When I tried that, I looked like a pile of rough-dried laundry pulled straight off the clothesline, and . . .

Well, to be honest? I just gave up.

By 1920, even without Mumma's otherworldly disapproval of my shabbiness, I knew I needed clothes. The trouble was, I dreaded becoming the object of a dressmaker's pitiless assessment but I had also forbidden myself the alternative. The new fashions sold in department stores had thrown skilled American seamstresses out of work, you see. They'd been displaced by immigrant girls doing piecework for a pittance in terrible sweatshops. I refused to patronize a garment industry that exploited its desperately poor workers so heartlessly.

And if that wasn't enough to keep me out of stores, there was this as well: I was determined to resist that shameless sister of war propaganda — the advertising industry.

President Wilson had been reelected on the slogan "He kept us out of war," but it wasn't long before he'd organized the Committee on Public Information. Its brief was to provide citizens with facts that would persuade them that entering the war was a good idea after all. To the administration's dismay, its facts did not convince; rather than reconsider his own conclusions, Mr. Wilson decided that what our country really needed was a new slogan. Thus, the C.P.I. launched its memorable motto: "Make the world safe for democracy!"

Soon Americans were surrounded by posters with childish, frightening images like giant spiders wearing German helmets and crouching over Cleveland. Street boys were paid to hand out flyers with maps that had UNITED STATES crossed out and NEW PRUSSIA scrawled across the nation. Newspapers printed bogus pro-war letters to their editors, planting them next to articles that vilified anti-war dissenters in the crudest terms possible. In theaters, paid "spokesmen" gave four-minute patriotic speeches during intermission. Even at school, we teachers sat through pro-war slide shows with the children, who were sent home to shame their parents into supporting what the facts had not.

"The war taught us the power of propaganda," one of the C.P.I. men said after the armistice. "Now, by God, when we have something to sell the American people, we know how to sell it."

A few moments, it seemed, after the end of the war, "the nation" became "the marketplace" and the exalted word "citizen" was promptly replaced with the loathsome, bovine "consumer." Women had achieved the vote just as civic discourse shifted from political rights to the "freedom" to buy ready-made dresses and lipstick and jewelry, or the "liberty" to drink and smoke and dance. With the world rendered safe for democracy, our civic duty was redefined: buy the cake and biscuit mixes, the canned meats and soups that had once fed the troops.

If the ad men had learned from the war that a good slogan could sway the masses, they learned from Dr. Sigmund Freud that people are governed less by reason than by unconscious sexual desires. "Critical eyes are sizing you up," the advertisements warned, but Aqua Velva aftershave would make a man's face "fresh, fit and *firm!*" All women were naturally homely and ordinary, but Elizabeth Arden and Coco Chanel could make us beautiful — for a price. Inattention to external appearance was no longer high-mindedness, a *Vogue* editorial warned; rather, it destroyed "those potential personalities that psychologists tell us are lurking behind our ordinary selves."

It was insulting and demeaning, but if you hear something often enough and long enough? Your resistance gets ground down. Absurdities start to make sense. Yes, you start to think. How true . . .

Not even I could be oblivious forever to frayed cuffs, run-down shoes, and a threadbare antebellum overcoat. One dark day in late December, with nothing to look forward to as 1921 approached, I came upon a newspaper ad for Halle's Department Store. "When a woman begins to regard her appearance as a fixed, unalterable quality, that same moment some vital, shining part of her is extinguished forever."

Agnes, I told myself, some work for immigrants is better than none at all. And if you try to repair this waistband again, you risk public catastrophe. *But you don't want to go to Halle's,* I could hear Mumma's "ghost" add. *It's much too expensive! Sears and Roebuck's is entirely good enough for you.*

I dithered another hour before telephoning the mechanic who valiantly kept Douglas's obsolete electric running. I would be driving into Cleveland in the morning, I told Brian, and would he be kind enough to put a charge into the batteries tonight, please?

I drove as little as possible in those days, not because I was afraid, you understand, but because each outing required me to withstand another lecture on the technical and economic superiority of gasoline engines. Holding the telephone's earpiece away from my head, I pretended to listen as Brian swore that he couldn't keep that old rattletrap wired together much longer. It wasn't safe for me to drive it into town. It might break down, and then where would I be? On the side of the road, freezing in this weather. Now listen here, I was instructed, just come on down to the garage and take a look. He had a used flivver that would do fine for my use. Just take a look, that's all he asked, but he asked relentlessly, and I hated being nagged. Only Rosie's exultation made the ordeal worthwhile. I can't imagine anything in the wolf lineage to account for a dog's delight in automotive travel, but Rosie loved to ride in cars.

The next day, the electric delivered me without incident to a parking spot on Euclid Avenue. *Oh, for heaven's sake,* I could imagine Mumma saying. *You don't belong here. Go to Sears!* And I admit that I hesitated at the sight of Halle's liveried doorman, but once I made my mind up, I could be more determined than you might think. Clutching Rosie under one arm as though she were a furry football, I squared my shoulders as Papa used to and swept right through that door, as though my little dog and I had a perfect right to be in a place where a blouse costing less than nineteen dollars was hardly worth cutting up as a dust rag.

My spectacles fogged immediately. It's Mumma, I thought, then told myself firmly, Nonsense, Agnes. It's condensation.

I set Rosie down, took a handkerchief from my bag, and carefully polished the mist from my lenses. When I replaced them on my nose, my icy courage thawed and puddled under the heated gaze of three spruce shopgirls, each of whom seemed to have spent her entire salary at Halle's.

Despite the advertised reduction in prices, few other shoppers had ventured out that bitterly cold morning. With no one else to wait on, all three girls advanced on me like an army vanguard, each wearing a combat uniform that was some clever variation on the theme of cultured pearls and a dark French frock with a white collar and cuffs.

"I only want to spend eighty-five dollars," I told them, backing away. "I — I need clothes. And a pair of sturdy shoes. And an overcoat."

There's just the thing, Mumma said when my eyes fell on a sensible brown tweed. *It will wear like iron.*

The least beautiful but most confident of the three girls came straight up to me. "A dachshund!" this young blonde cried. "Oh,

I love dachshunds! Half a dog high, dog and a half long — that's what my boyfriend, Les, always says. Les is such a card! What's her name?"

"Rosie," I said, a little startled.

"Well, nice to meetcha, Rosie. My name's Mildred." With that, she snatched Rosie up with such aplomb, the dog hardly wiggled as she was lifted. "Take off your coat," Mildred urged me, popping her gum. "Let's see what we've got to work with, Miss — ?"

"Um, Shanklin."

Goodness, she's rude, Mumma remarked, but I soon found Mildred's breezy cheer a welcome change from the dreary posthumous conversations I'd grown used to, all those months alone. That's simply the way young people speak now, I told Mumma, even to their elders.

I unbuttoned my old coat and handed it over, feeling strangely liberated when Mildred tossed it aside with the disdain that it deserved, but my heart, buoyed momentarily, sank to its accustomed level while she considered the challenge before her. Familiar with the sensation of being appraised by someone clear-eyed, pretty, and remorseless, I awaited judgment like a condemned criminal. *Agnes Shanklin, I find you flat-chested, hipless, hopeless —*

Mildred sighed. “You are so lucky! Miss Shanklin, you’ve got the perfect figger for a dropped waist. Perfect!”

Dumbfounded. There’s no other word for it. I was dumbfounded by the notion of possessing any sort of perfection, let alone one that was physical. When I stammered my disbelief, Mildred seemed genuinely astonished and told me in no uncertain terms that every fashionable woman between the ages of fifteen and forty-five yearned — positively yearned — for the very “figger” I’d been cursed with.

“But all that hair!” Mildred rolled her eyes. Fingers busy behind Rosie’s ears, she dropped into a sort of baby talk. “Mommy’s hair has to go. Isn’t that right, Rosie? Awful, awful, awful.”

Shifting Rosie to the crook of her left arm, Mildred lifted an in-store telephone’s earpiece with her right hand. “Antoine’s!” she ordered into the speaker, eyes on mine, as though there were nothing wrong with what looked back at her. “They’ll say they don’t have time,” Mildred predicted. “Don’t worry. I’ve got Antoine twisted right around this,” she said, displaying a little finger tipped in blood-red enamel.

And it appeared that was the case. Before I could change my mind, Mildred had secured an immediate appointment for me. Still carrying Rosie, she escorted me up several escalators to the store's hairdressing salon, where I was relieved of more of my clothing and swathed in a yellow rayon wrapper.

There was a brisk discussion with the slender and artistic Antoine. A bob, they decided. Just the thing.

"Oh, gracious," I said. "I don't think —"

Mildred pulled a silver flask from her pocket and handed it to me as though that were just another service she provided to her customers. "Canadian courage," she whispered, urging me to take a sip. "I know an 'importer,' " she said with a wink, and then offered to take Rosie out for a walk.

Recognizing the word, Rosie wiggled and whined rapturously. The two of them disappeared together. Antoine picked up his scissors.

Two hours later, the salon receptionist summoned Mildred in time to see me whirled in my chair to behold Antoine's handiwork. Everyone in the shop applauded when I gasped. What had always been long and frizzy and disobedient was now short and shining and perfectly waved.

"Miss Shanklin," Mildred declared, "you are the bee's knees."

"Well! I don't know about that," I murmured. But truly? From that moment on, I was Galatea to Mildred's Pygmalion.

The weather had gotten worse while I was being shorn; with the store now nearly empty, its bored staff was entirely available to bring a dazzled and unresisting customer into the twentieth century. As we sailed down the escalator, Mildred called out assignments to her stylish young colleagues, detailing the elements of my wardrobe each should supply from the Better Coats Department, from Sports Wear, and Dresses, and Ladies' Shoes. All of Halle's took on a party atmosphere and I allowed myself to be borne along on the enthusiasm. It reminded me of rainy afternoons in childhood when Lillie would cry, "Come on, Agnes! Let's play dress-up!" Only, this time, *I* would be the fairy princess.

Mildred led me to an elaborately mirrored private dressing room, lifted Rosie's paw, and wagged it in the direction of a curtained screen. "Off you go, Mommy," she said in a baby voice, as though Rosie herself were speaking. "You're going to park that girdle for good!"

The new underthings laid out for me were dauntingly simple and unconstructed, but with my hair decisively cut, there was no turning back. While I changed, Mildred perched on a stool, chattering about her rapid rise at Halle's from stock girl to sales and telling me all about her boyfriend, Les Hope, who was thinking of changing his name to the jazzier Bob. "He's a terrific dancer," Mildred said, and I didn't have the heart to point out that "terrific" means very frightening, not good. "He gives lessons, but that's just temporary, y'know. He's going to be a star — just you wait and see! Here, now, try this on."

She stuck a hand through the curtains; in it was a limp length of ivory charmeuse. "No, really, Mildred," I started to protest. "I have no use for —"

"Just try it!"

The fabric slid over me like a waterfall, and I let Mildred adjust its drape before I looked in the three-way mirror. Then — my fingers went to my lips. What had been woefully inadequate in the era of the Gibson girl was now a slim, elongated, shimmering elegance. And the color made my complexion look fresh as cream.

Mildred clapped her hands like the delighted child she was. "I just knew you'd be a knockout in that dress! Do you have pearls? Oh, my gosh, you'd be positively stunning in pearls!"

Agnes, don't be foolish. You don't want that dress, said Mumma. *It's completely impractical. What you want is a good woolen skirt and a nice cotton blouse that can take bleach and stand up to hard use. Where on earth would someone like you wear a silk charmeuse — ?*

"I'll take it," I heard myself say.

Piece by piece over the next two hours, a wardrobe was assembled. Like a butterfly in reverse, I drew on one cocoon after another. With every change of outfit, a new and different Agnes appeared in the mirror, and Mumma hated them all.

Tailored frocks with boyish collars and turned-back cuffs, belted low. *(You look like a stick in those things.)* Simple straight skirts in good Scottish wool, to be worn under the most beautiful costume tunics in crepe de Chine and printed silks. *(They'll be ruined the first time you wash them.)* Round-necked voile blouses with hand-drawn embroidery work. *(You'll snag the openings, Agnes, you know how careless you are.)* Shoes next, three pairs. *(Two are enough, surely. One for church and one for everyday. Why would anyone need three pairs of shoes?)* A long loose overcoat in jade green wool, with a deep shawl collar — stunningly expensive, but the loveliest thing I'd ever worn.

I brought you up to think of others, Mumma said with a defeated sigh. *The moment I'm gone, you sink into selfish profligacy.*

I will give an equal amount to charity, I promised silently.

"I'll take it," I said aloud.

With the dressing room filled and me beginning to wonder where on earth I'd hang all these clothes once I got them home, the jubilant Mildred crooked a varnished finger and led me out to a cosmetics counter. While my purchases were being bagged and boxed, my lips were to be rouged and my eyes smudged with kohl.

"Oh, Mildred, really, I couldn't!" Balking at long last, I gestured toward my forehead and confided my reluctance. "It will draw attention to —"

"What?" she asked.

"My eye," I whispered.

"What about it?"

"Well, it — it crosses."

"Which one?"

"The right. It crosses. When I'm tired."

She shrugged. "So? Take naps." She stared hard and finally admitted, "I suppose it does turn in, but it's not that bad. Makes you look . . . like you're really paying attention. Anyway, you've got lovely lips. We'll play them up."

Mildred and the Elizabeth Arden lady consulted on colors and application, and when they were finished, Mildred produced a bell-shaped cloche hat made from the same green wool as my beautiful new coat. She settled it onto my head and tugged it down until it dipped rakishly over my right eye. "In case you get tired," she said, winking. "What do you think?"

I walked to the nearest full-length mirror and saw someone chic and modern, youthful if not young. In a daze, I stood there reassessing everything I had ever thought about myself. "Mildred," I whispered finally, "you are a miracle worker."

"Don't you dare cry!" she warned. "You'll ruin your makeup."

We embraced then as though we were old friends, and I waved to half a dozen other girls beaming happily at the magic they had accomplished. I didn't even ask how much the bill had totaled. It doesn't matter, I told myself. I am not a penny-pinching schoolteacher anymore. I am a lady of means.

Not if you keep up this kind of spending, Mumma warned.

Paying no attention, I sailed out of the store followed by three boys laden with the boxes and bags they would carry to my car. The doorman, who barely noticed when I entered Halle's five hours earlier, looked at me now with frank and cheeky admiration as I departed.

I tipped the boys a dime apiece when the car was loaded, and gave a nickel to the valet who held my car door open. Rosie hopped in, and for a time I sat still, gazing at the green-gloved hands resting on the steering wheel. I felt as transformed as the society I lived in.

The spell was not broken, but only slightly cracked when a trickle of melted snow slipped down a newly bared neck that had never before gone out in such weather without a sensible crocheted scarf. Even inside the car and out of the winter wind, my silk-stockinged legs felt exposed and cold beneath the knee-length skirt.

You'll catch pneumonia, Mumma said.

Maybe so, I could hear Mildred say, *but she'll die happy.*

What about Egypt? you ask. *What has any of this to do with Egypt?*

Well, I'm getting to that, but you have to know all about Mildred to understand why I went to the séance. You see, Mildred and Mumma began to argue on my way home, and they never seemed to stop. Every time my mother rebuked me for that spending spree or anything else, for that matter, Mildred's voice would come to my defense.

What would she be like if you'd let her make the most of herself instead of the least? Mildred demanded, bold as brass. *You always acted like her life was over before it got started.*

But a silk charmeuse dress! A waste of money if ever there was one. It'll sit in the closet forever.

Not necessarily . . . Why, it's perfect for a cruise! It's the very sort of dress ladies wear when they eat at the captain's table on a cruise.

And what would you know about such things?

More than you would! I have lots of customers who go on cruises. Anyway, Agnes should get out more, see more things, said Mildred. *Say! A change of scenery would be just the thing! She might meet someone on a cruise.*

Meet someone? Why, the very idea!

And why shouldn't she?

She's nearly forty!

She doesn't look it, not when she's all dolled up.

It went on like that for a week. Nothing seemed to quiet the dispute I heard inside me. And it was in that state of mental instability that I found the courage to do something else completely out of character. I visited a medium.

I know, I know. You're absolutely right. The séances popular in the twenties were shameful, silly affairs, designed to fool the gullible and take advantage of grieving families. I grant you that, but then again, here I am, telling you this story! So you just never know, now, do you? And remember, please, all the other invisible forces that had so recently become a part of our lives in those days. Madame Curie's radiation, and Signore Marconi's radio, and Dr. Freud's unconscious. Even before I died, it seemed possible that there might be some scientific basis for communication with the unseen soul. There might be a sort of telephone of the spirit, or maybe radio waves, which were there to be heard if only one were tuned to the right frequency. Why not try to assuage our hunger for one more moment with the shockingly, suddenly absent? Why not yield to the desire to contact the dead, to ask one last question, to receive one last message?

And I did so long to hear my sister Lillian's voice again! Maybe she could settle the differences between Mumma and Mildred.

All of which is why I am not embarrassed to tell you now that my decision to go to

Egypt was set in motion by the eerie male voice I heard in the darkened room of a glassily bejeweled woman who called herself Madame Sophie. "Years from now you will be more disappointed by the things you didn't do than by the ones you did," the disembodied gentleman predicted. "Throw off the bowlines! Sail away from the safe harbor, madam! A sea voyage is what you need!"

"That is the spirit of Mr. Mark Twain," Madame Sophie whispered, leaning over the fringed paisley shawl that covered a small round table. "He was a skeptic in life, but he visits me frequently."

Well, I don't know about that, I thought, but I listened anyway because, like Mildred's, this voice too insisted that I travel, that I see the world from a different perspective. And a coincidence like that seemed the sort of thing to which one had to pay attention.

"Mr. Twain," I said, feeling more than a little foolish, "while I am a great admirer of your work . . . Well, sir, since the influenza, I — I dream of drowning, and sailing would be —"

"— just the thing!" he exclaimed. "Like getting back up onto a horse after you've been thrown."

Then it happened. Clear as a bell, I heard Lillie's dear remembered voice. *The best time for Cairo is March,* she said. *And then go on to Jerusalem, as I did . . .*

You can wear the silk charmeuse, Mildred added.

"What about Rosie?" I asked, my hand running down her back as she snuggled in my lap. "I have a small dog —"

"That will be no problem at all!" the putative Mr. Twain assured me warmly. "Take her with you, dear lady. All the best ocean liners are delighted to accommodate the pets of valued guests such as yourself."

Of course, it didn't take a great deal in the way of deductive reasoning to work out that Madame Sophie was the *inamorata* of a gentleman who ran the Thomas Cook Travel Agency, located one door down the corridor from her second-floor salon, but I simply didn't care. Within the hour, I had booked passage on a steamship to Egypt. And then? I drove directly from Cook's to Halle's to consult Mildred about a wardrobe for warm weather, and bought a beautiful set of matched luggage to contain it.

As you can imagine, Mumma argued nonstop, the whole day long. *It's nerves,* she said as I steered the electric off Carnegie and angled up the hill toward Cedar Glen.

You've no regular work, nothing to take you outside yourself. You have a great deal to be grateful for, right here at home, young lady.

I've been good all my life, I told myself and Mumma. I've been oh, so good for oh, so long! Just once, I'd like to trade good for happy.

I suppose now you'll tell me you can buy happiness.

Not happiness, but maybe a little fun.

But Egypt, of all places! You'll get a disease. You'll be kidnapped by white slavers!

Lillie and Douglas did just fine there. Maybe I'll be a missionary. Why, I could teach at the mission school in Jebail.

Well! Mumma didn't know about *that.*

Neither did I, truth be told. I had never fully shared Lillian's joyous, confident faith, although I did believe in God. Indeed, as the weeks passed and my departure date neared, I knew I ought to ask for divine guidance, but my courage failed me. What if God answered? What if He agreed with Mumma?

The thought of renouncing this trip made me go cold and dark inside, but when I looked at my new luggage and contemplated packing it with all the lovely flattering things Mildred had helped me pick out, oh my! I felt like Moses' staff — like a dead stick miraculously bursting with new possibilities.

I felt . . . happy.

And afraid. And guilty, but excited as well.

Yes. More than anything: excited.

On the Monday before I sailed, I withdrew a great deal of money from my bank account. I had prepared answers to the questions I expected, but the teller had no clue that I was doing something wildly self-indulgent, nor would he have cared had he known. My next stop was the post office, where I gave instructions to hold deliveries, and felt compelled to explain, "I'm going away for a few months. To Egypt, actually."

"Oh, how nice," the postmaster said. "Next!"

Then it was on to the law office of Mr. Reichardt to make arrangements for my absence. I expected a lecture on thrift and the husbandry of my funds. "Do you a world of good," he said instead. "Send me a postcard, Miss Shanklin."

In fact, no one seemed shocked or even very interested in my plans. That, in itself, was strangely thrilling. Nobody came to see me and Rosie off either, and that was rather sad.

We boarded the eastbound train on a blustery, wet evening in early March. The bad weather chased us, arriving in New York City just as we did. The storm intensified as we transferred from train to steamship in a taxicab, its windows fogged and smeared by sheets of freezing rain.

Things got even worse as we sailed, and the crossing was atrocious. Furious winds drove the rain with such force that it splashed down gangways and ran into corridors, bringing on panicky thoughts of the *Titanic.* Together, Rosie and I learned what "sick as a dog" really meant. I never ate at the captain's table. Indeed, we hardly ever left our cabin, and when we did, I was definitely not wearing the silk charmeuse. When I had the influenza, I struggled to live, but seasickness made me yearn for a pistol.

That's what you get for listening to shopgirls and fortune-tellers, Mumma said, satisfied to see me pay a price for my willfulness.

Finally, as we neared the coast of Europe, the tempest blew itself out. My stomach, and Rosie's, settled. One fine morning, we left our cramped cabin and walked out onto the promenade deck, feeling rather well. There we discovered that some confidence trick of climate and current had delivered us into a full and bracing spring.

That night we steamed past Gibraltar: a

towering black shape studded with tiny, twinkling lights. The next morning we slid by Spain, where the peaks of the Sierra Nevada loomed over the jagged summits of the Alpujarras. A day more, and the lavender rocks of Sardinia appeared. Forty-eight hours in Naples, to take on coal in the shadow of Vesuvius, and it was onward toward a dawn that revealed golden Mediterranean isles, shadowed in amethyst, set in a sea of sapphire and diamond.

Gray winter weather, selfless good works, the opinions of others — all these faded like the dim memories of a fever dream.

I listened hard but heard only my own thoughts, or perhaps those of my ancestors when they made the Atlantic crossing westward. *No one at home knows where I am or what I am doing. No one here knows who or what I am, or have been, or shall be.*

At last, the splendor of my audacity began to warm me. I lifted Rosie into my arms and turned my face east, toward a dazzling sunrise.

I can do anything I please, I thought, and no one at home need ever know what I've been up to.

"We're free," I whispered to my little friend.

Free. Free. *Free . . .*

■ ■ ■ ■

Part Two: Middle East

■ ■ ■ ■

Accept from me, please, a bit of timeless travel advice. Should you inquire about a potential difficulty during a journey, beware the agent who assures you, "Sir," — or Madam — "that will be no problem at all."

What he means is, "Sir," — or Madam — "I personally shall not be troubled in the slightest by what you anticipate. When you encounter it, I shall be safe at home, and snug in my own bed."

To be fair, I had only asked "Mr. Twain" if there would be a problem traveling with my dog. I had not thought to inquire about being admitted to my hotel room in Cairo with Rosie at my side.

The Semiramis, I was given to understand, was one of the finest hotels in the world. Certainly it was one of the most expensive, but by the time I made the reservation, I was long past pinching pennies. I put down a substantial deposit and, having parted with that kind of money, it never occurred to me to ask, "Will Rosie (who you very well know will be traveling with me) also be permitted to stay at the Semiramis?"

After the cool, blue beauty of the Mediterranean, the port of Alexandria greeted our steamer with milky heat and a buzzing horror of flies. Above us, vultures wheeled or seemed to stall, stationary in the sky. Peddlers on the squalid dock hawked sugarcane and dates and lemonade in an aggravating singsong serenade. Beyond them, woeful donkeys complained while being grossly overloaded by sweating stevedores.

An alarming crowd of nearly naked men had gathered, hoping for work, I supposed, but with a sullen temper that certainly would have discouraged me from speaking to any. One stood out, however, handsome in a white turban, his bare brown legs beneath a long blue gown held close by a vivid red belt. Raising a hand to shield his eyes against the glare, he seemed to search the deck. Just as I saw "Cook's Porter" emblazoned across his chest, he spotted me and called out, "You travel Cook, madams? All right! I am here!"

Courteous and efficient, this gentleman saw to it that my bags and my person were safely and efficiently transferred to the train station, and that I had exchanged ten dollars American for the equivalent in local currency. Rosie was always a good traveler and seemed to know that she should take care of business before we boarded the southbound train. That accomplished, the two of us were ushered into a first-class compartment. It was well appointed if a bit garish, and stifling hot, but provided blessed relief from the flies that covered one like soot outside.

The man from Cook's stood at the door, looking expectant. I opened my pocketbook and held out a handful of Egyptian coins. "Um . . . how much is appropriate?"

He delicately selected two piastres, making sure that he did not touch my palm as he did so. "Thank you, madams. My pleasure, madams. Speak well of me to Cook's, yes?" And with that, he was gone.

"Well, Rosie," I whispered, "here we are in Egypt! Imagine that!"

I was trying to be thrilled but so far, Egypt had failed to charm, although the porter was quite nice. Maybe it was just too warm to generate any excitement. Rosie was panting and couldn't be bothered to work up so much as a growl when two gentlemen slid open the compartment door and took their seats across from us. After murmuring courtesies, they flicked on the lights and two small electric fans I had not noticed mounted above the luggage rack.

"Egypt would be materially improved if relocated to a better climate," the first one remarked in a lovely accent.

"Yes," his companion agreed amiably. "We seem to have situated all our colonies in the world's worst geography."

I smiled and was about to ask if they were British, but they each rattled open their newspapers, making it clear that no conversation was invited.

The train lurched and pulled away slowly, seemingly reluctant to leave the station. That reluctance lingered for no reason I could discover. Rarely topping thirty miles an hour, we creaked slowly through the tan Egyptian landscape, the surface of which was cracked like pound cake baked at too high a temperature. Outside, beyond the dusty window, the high-pitched train whistle barely drew the attention of brown-bodied peasants who stood as unmoving as scarecrows in the scorched fields we traveled through.

"Gracious! Look at that!" I cried, pointing at a building that seemed to float above its foundation, twenty degrees above the horizon in the shimmering air.

The gentlemen barely glanced out the window. "A mir-a-age," one informed me, drawing the word out, as though speaking to some pitiable dunce.

"First visit?" the other asked, brows raised.

"Yes," I admitted, and felt as though I'd committed some unpardonable gaffe. They shot small knowing smiles at each other and went back to their reading. Embarrassed that I was not equally blasé, I moved Rosie's hot little body off my lap, fussing over her a bit to change the subject in my own mind, if not my companions'.

Mirages became routine. Like Rosie, I dozed as the time passed, molasses slow. Eventually we entered the Delta, where the temperature moderated and the landscape changed dramatically. Natives working in the startlingly green countryside looked more energetic and alive. The train picked up speed as well. I thought, At last — we're getting somewhere! But a few minutes later, we slowed again and stopped.

Up ahead, the track curved and I could see a pair of automobiles waiting. An English army officer's spectacles flashed in the light. A few minutes later, a native conductor in a red uniform with a gold sash slid open the door of our compartment. "Gentlemen, your motors are waiting," he announced, and they disappeared down the corridor with him.

I felt stupid, not sure if we had arrived somewhere or not. I might have asked, of course, but I'd already exposed my ignorance once and was unwilling to invite additional scorn. Before I could decide what to do next, the train lurched forward. I sat back, anxious and confused.

Once again the train picked up speed. Cairo came into sight: an immense agglomeration of low, clay-colored cubes and rectangles. Sidetracks appeared, ran parallel, converged. Suddenly, the roadbed was lined by a mob of furious-looking men in white dresses who screamed and chanted something that sounded to me like *"Ah-bah sure-shill! Ah-bah sure-shill!"* Rocks began to hit the windows. I shrank back into the compartment, clutching at Rosie, who flung herself toward the window, barking and snarling. Then, just as suddenly, the train outran the mob, and a few minutes later we pulled into the darkness of the Cairo station.

The compartment lights went out. The fans stopped. I sat still, dazed in the eerie silence. The conductor reappeared briefly and indicated that I should leave.

I gathered my things and joined the rest

of the passengers in the aisle, keeping Rosie tucked up in my arms so she wouldn't be stepped on. We emerged into a chaos of jostling, shouting, and rushing.

Rosie and I hurried through the crowd toward the baggage car and waited for my belongings to be unloaded. I sat on my steamer trunk, doing my best to appear both fearless and serenely expectant that someone wearing Cook's livery would arrive. Time passed. Rosie relieved herself nearby. I pretended not to notice. No one from Cook's appeared, and the platform was all but deserted. Tired and close to tears, I could just hear Mumma say, *Well, you got yourself into this, Agnes. Are you just going to sit there like some greenhorn immigrant, fresh off the boat?*

I drew myself up and waved to a passing workman two tracks away. We engaged in a brief, shouted conversation, during which he made reassuring Egyptian noises in response to my distressed American ones. With gestures and smiles, he indicated that I should stay where I was, and then he hustled away.

Eventually the workman returned, grinning happily. He was accompanied by a railway porter who spoke some English and was at pains to point out that the chanting had ended and that the mob outside had dispersed. “No worries, madams,” he soothed, while he and the workman heaved my baggage onto a luggage dolly. “No worries atall!”

The two of them leaned forward to push the cart outside, where lines of wagons and taxis waited. Believing I was now to find my own way to the hotel, I reached into my handbag for some coins. The workman accepted one with much gratitude and left. The porter, on the other hand, displayed an expression of such offended sensibilities, you’d have thought I’d asked if I might eat his favorite child.

Stammering an apology, I closed my pocketbook. The porter looked relieved. With an attitude of intense dignity, he whistled down a donkey-cart driver. This “dragoman” was to be engaged to convey me and my luggage the final few miles to the Semiramis Hotel at a price that the porter would determine.

Establishing the fee involved much vituperative negotiation. The dragoman glared at Rosie. She returned the favor. I might have been alerted to the impending difficulties by their mutual hostility, but that was when the porter said severely, “Six piastres, madams! Not more for him!” The porter himself then stood still, which seemed to indicate that his services to me were complete. Tentatively I reached into my pocketbook, and this time my offering was accepted with a charming, toothy smile.

I was assisted into the cart. The dragoman slapped the reins. His donkey lurched forward in its traces.

And then: Cairo. Goodness gracious! How to describe that city? The smell! The racket! Even without a mob chanting incomprehensible slogans, the normal everyday noise of the place was an almost physical assault. There were no traffic lights and no policemen to direct the cars through intersections. Lane lines, where they existed, were ignored. The streets were jammed with pedestrians and vehicles of all descriptions. All this seemed to shock and exasperate the dragoman, who flicked his whip at everyone who came within range and screamed for them to give way.

Shrouded women pressed themselves against alley walls as we passed. They balanced a variety of burdens on their heads, and most carried small children in their arms. These ladies nearly all wore veils or held over their noses a portion of the long black garments that trailed them through the trash-strewn byways. Lillie had written that such concealment was a sign of modesty, but now that I was in Cairo, I wondered if the practice had originated as a defense against the city's odor, which was a perfectly nauseating blend of sewage and citrus, burning tobacco and roasting meat, unwashed bodies and jasmine.

In contrast to the mute and shrouded hordes of Cairo's women, the city's men yelled constantly. Regardless of topic, every exchange seemed to be composed entirely of bitter recrimination. Men bargained loudly in tiny shops and stalls, where every item offered in trade provoked rancor, disgust, and a mutual loathing in buyer and seller. Others played games — checkers or chess or cards — at the outdoor tables of street cafés, and each was vocally convinced that his opponent was the worst kind of cheating lowlife. At one point, I braced myself to witness bloodshed as two chess players shrieked and gesticulated in the most menacing way. Then, to my astonishment, they stood up, mounted the same little donkey, and rode away together.

Each time our cart rounded some corner, my presence drew rapt attention. Groups of arguing men paused and stared over the rims of tiny china cups, or sucked on long tubes attached to smoke-filled glass jars containing water that bubbled with each breath. I felt like a film star with my cloche hat and dark glasses, dressed perfectly for the late-afternoon warmth in a linen dress that stopped at my knees. I fancied that the Egyptian women envied me. Poor things, I thought, sweltering in their robes and veils!

My dragoman pulled onto a lovely boulevard, and the noise receded as his donkey tugged us along its palm-fringed pavement. "The Nile, madams," the dragoman called out, pointing with his whip. "The Semiramis," he said a few minutes later.

Sitting on the cart, I caught a glimpse of the hotel's interior, which made a general impression of polished brass and marble across which teams of energetic bellmen carried hatboxes, toiletry cases, and wardrobe trunks. The Semiramis promised to be every bit as grand as I had anticipated, but the Nile itself? Well, I must admit that the Nile was a disappointment. Given my present situation, the irony is considerable, now that I think of it.

I suppose I expected too much of a river that has been called "liquid history." Mr. Joseph Conrad wrote that the Nile was an immense uncoiled snake with its head in the sea, its body at rest, curving afar over a vast country, and its tail lost to sight. Mr.

Conrad was, of course, a literary genius, whereas I was merely a schoolteacher. Imagine a hundred-foot rope, I would have told my students. Tie a knot in it ten feet from the end. That knot is Cairo. Now, to represent the Nile's delta, separate the strands that make up the ten-foot end to form a triangle. The Nile's length is marvelous, but when seen crossways from the boulevard, its width was unimpressive. And its depth? Well, in March, when I was there? Its depth was just plain silly.

Why, the Cuyahoga River is more to look at! I was thinking when a fresh round of shouting broke out nearby.

I have read that most travelers quickly come to feel a sort of detached immunity in truly foreign places, and I certainly experienced that myself. In the time it took to go from train station to hotel, I had come to the conclusion that Cairo's unrelenting uproar was a phenomenon that could not possibly involve me. Then Rosie began to snarl, and I slowly realized our own arrival was the cause of the latest dispute. The combatants were a native doorman and my dragoman. Their field of battle was the stairway into the hotel. Fingers jabbed in my direction. Glares were aimed down substantial noses toward my luggage, my dog, and myself.

"I have a reservation," I said in the voice I used to bring classrooms of unruly immigrant children to order. "I made all the arrangements through Thomas Cook's in Cleveland, Ohio."

Struck dumb, both men paused to stare at me.

"That's in America," I explained in the sudden silence.

For a moment they were joined in astonishment, as though they had just seen some revolting insect stand on two of its six legs and speak. An instant later, the dispute resumed; if anything, the attempt of a woman to take part in her own affairs provoked both men to further fury. The doorman, eyes and blood vessels bulging, blocked the dragoman's effort to carry my bags into the hotel. The dragoman matched him in every particular, trying to gain entry by dint of volume and main force. Rosie's high-pitched yapping adding to the bedlam.

Even in Cairo, this was sufficient to draw attention. Thin brown children appeared as if from nowhere, their delight in the entertainment multiplied by the element of comedy contributed by a dachshund's miniature ferocity. Several Egyptian policemen converged on the scene and joined in the shouting. Inside the hotel, a large group of European gentlemen halted halfway down a curving staircase that descended into the lobby. There were dozens of them, some in khaki uniforms, others in well-cut suits. All of them were looking at me. In their midst, like a queen surrounded by courtiers, stood a majestically tall woman in her fifties. More commanding than any of the soldiers around her, she took in the scene and frowned.

At that point, I still believed that if I could just step inside and tell the desk clerk about my reservation, everything could be resolved in a civilized tone of voice. Explaining this to the accumulated variety of Egyptian gentlemen, I tried to move toward the lobby, but Rosie was engaged in a series of feints at the end of her leash. Though she had clearly identified the doorman as the source of our trouble, she took several distracted opportunities to snap at the excited children who danced away from her. I bent over to pick her up. Shrieks of childish laughter, and a shout of shared horror from the men informed me that the movement had exposed my legs upward of their midpoint. Mortified, I straightened, with Rosie squirming in my arms.

The whole thing was starting to look like

an audition for a comic vaudeville revue when the queenly woman broke away from the Europeans on the staircase and strode across the lobby toward me, with a very slight and very cool smile. She had a strong oval face surrounded by a mass of graying red hair folded into a pompadour beneath a densely flowered picture hat. Despite the weather and the decade, she was swathed in layers of Edwardian striped silk overlaid with lashings of Belgian lace. From the silver fox boa slung over her shoulder to the black high-topped shoes with their fine pearl buttons, the ensemble was tasteful and expensive.

It was also, I knew from Mildred's tutelage, hopelessly passé.

I felt very chic in comparison and secretly superior, until she swept past me on her way toward the doorman. Direct, verdigris eyes met mine. *I'll deal with you later, young lady,* she seemed to tell me with a glance. And though she said not a word, I felt like a third grader caught in the cloakroom showing her pantaloons to the boys.

"Mrs. Cutler?" I heard someone call from within the hotel. "Lillie! Is that you?"

A blond man, about thirty years old, wove through the main party of Europeans on the staircase and came toward me smiling broadly, blue eyes wide with astonishment. He was wearing a cheap brown suit, not flowing white robes, but I recognized him immediately from the many photographs in Mr. Lowell Thomas's presentation. Colonel Lawrence in person was compact and more strongly built than I had imagined, and moved with the taut, athletic grace of a tightrope walker. As he approached, I was surprised to find that he barely exceeded my own quite modest height. Five foot four, perhaps? A bit more, if he would stand up straighter.

His pace slowed and his smile faded when I took off my dark glasses and he realized he was mistaken about my identity. *Yes, that flat-voweled Ohio accent is familiar,* his embarrassed little laugh seemed to say, *but you are definitely not the lovely Lillian Cutler.*

Hoping Rosie would mind her manners, I set her on the ground — bending carefully at the knees this time. "You must be Colonel Lawrence," I said. "I'm Agnes Shanklin, Lillian Cutler's sister."

"How extraordinary," he murmured after a brief handshake that seemed as reluctant as his words were warm. "It's a pleasure to meet you at last, Miss Shanklin. Lillie and Douglas told me so much about you." And then, once more, he giggled.

You doubt me, perhaps. *No, Agnes. Lawrence was a scholar and a soldier. Surely such a man would not giggle like a girl!* But that giggle turned out to be as much a part of him as his small stature and great strength of will. Often, it invited you to follow his quirky logic. Sometimes, it was a warning. More rarely, it was a spontaneous outburst of genuine amusement. On the occasion of our first meeting, it simply conveyed relief that he had not, after all, shouted across a busy hotel lobby at an utter stranger.

He glanced beyond me toward the tall woman, who had by now dismissed the policemen and was taking the doorman and the dragoman aside. Perhaps because she herself spoke softly, their dispute became a conversation. Colonel Lawrence seemed to accept this lady's intervention as a given. "If you wish to insult a Muslim, call him a dog," he told me in a low, quick voice. "The gist of the doorman's case is that your pet is unwelcome."

"But — No!" I cried. "The Cook's agent in Cleveland said —"

"Gerty will sort it out. How is Lillie? Is she here with you?" Colonel Lawrence asked eagerly. "No," he said when he saw my look. "How?"

"Influenza."

"My father as well," he told me then, in the brief way we all had in those days. We'd acknowledge a private drop or two of grief in that ocean of general mourning and change the subject without providing the full roll of our dreadful losses.

"So. What brings you to Cairo?" he asked, blue eyes narrowed, his glance sidelong. "Are you a missionary, as your sister was?"

"Heavens, no!" I said with a bit more vehemence than I intended. "I've never been sufficiently confident in my faith to offer myself to others as exemplary."

"My mother has recently decided to bring Christianity to the Chinese," Colonel Lawrence informed me, then dropped his voice to confide, "She could, I'm afraid, testify that being exemplary is not a requirement for missionary work."

My land! What a thing to say about his own mother, Mumma cried, and indeed, Colonel Lawrence snickered like a naughty boy aware of his transgression.

Perhaps, I thought, I am not the only one whose mother whispers unwelcome commentary. To my own surprise, I said, "I take it you learned cynicism at home, Colonel Lawrence?"

Another giggle, this one with a darker note that confirmed my guess. "Why Cairo then," he asked, "if not to spread the faith?"

Well, I could hardly say, *Mark Twain advised me to travel.* I searched, and found a different truth. "The war, you know. The influenza. I think — Well, one needs to make new memories, don't you agree?"

For a little time, he seemed quite far away. So many veterans had that look. "Yes," he said finally, blinking himself back into the present. "Yes. Well put."

We fell into an instant friendship, our conversation built on the scaffolding of our shared regard for Lillie. "I shall never forget how welcoming and kind she was," Lawrence told me. "I was a penniless undergraduate, but she treated me like a prince."

He was just suggesting that we meet for tea the next afternoon when the towering woman he called Gerty took her place at his side. Deliberately, I think, she put an arm over his shoulder, in a gesture that was both maternal and proprietary. In that pose, she asked, "And who have we here, dear boy?"

Colonel Lawrence moved away from her touch, becoming formal and adult. "Miss Gertrude Bell, may I introduce Miss Agnes Shanklin? I knew her sister, Lillian, before the war. Miss Shanklin: Miss Bell, who knows everyone and everything Middle

East. What have negotiations accomplished, Gert?"

"Take her to the Continental," Miss Bell told him. "They'll never let her in here."

Her lips hardly moved when she spoke. I thought of Mumma taking down a hem, telling me to turn with her mouth full of pins. Unnerved, I lifted Rosie into my arms and stammered into her fur. "But — I made a reservation. I — I put down a deposit. The Cook's agent in Cleveland said —"

"Hold your head up," Miss Bell commanded. "Look people straight in the eye and state your position without hesitation. It's the only way to get anything done."

I felt both admonished and encouraged, like a failing student who's been told how to earn a better mark on the next assignment. It took all my self-possession not to say, "Yes, miss. Thank you, miss."

She took a small, flat silver case from her handbag and extracted a cigarette with stained yellow fingers, tapping one end on sterling to settle its tobacco. "The dear boy and I stayed at the Continental before the war. We were colleagues at the Arab Bureau," she said. "The rooms are quite adequate. I'll ring ahead for you and make the arrangements."

"Will they allow Rosie in?" I asked.

"If I tell them to."

She seemed barely to register my thanks as she placed her cigarette between lips permanently puckered by the habit and leaned expectantly toward Colonel Lawrence.

He spread his empty hands and suggested, "Ask Winston."

She rolled her eyes toward heaven. "The dear boy has no vices, Miss Shanklin. Very tiresome for those of us who do."

"I have many vices," Lawrence said. "It's a vesta I lack." A match, he meant. That's what British people called matches back then.

Miss Bell sighed, and turned, and raised her hand to catch the attention of a balding, thickish person who stood gesticulating with a cigar amid a knot of gentlemen in the lobby. "Winston Darling!" she called. "Light me, will you, please?"

With that, she sailed off and docked at Mr. Darling's side. He produced a lighter, and again she leaned forward — almost coquettishly steadying the flame with a hand upon his wrist. Pulling in the smoke with evident pleasure, she released a long plume into the air and took the round arm he offered. Mr. Darling was evidently undismayed to appear so short and soft in comparison to Miss Bell's own commanding physique.

"Don't worry, dear boy," Miss Bell called over her shoulder as she and Mr. Darling swanned away in a cloud of tobacco smoke. "We'll save a seat at the table for you. Lawrence has been drafted to escort a lady in distress to the Continental," she told the others in ringing public tones, and then laughed gaily before adding, "He'll rejoin us *shortly.*"

Colonel Lawrence's face went very still. I winced. "Next," I whispered with sympathetic annoyance, "she'll say something to me about seeing straight."

Lawrence giggled, but rather grimly this time. "I don't know why I let that kind of thing get up my nose, but —"

"Maybe she's self-conscious about being so tall," I suggested.

Lawrence gestured toward the door, where the dragoman still waited, and changed the subject. "Winston is His Majesty's secretary of state for air and the colonies," Lawrence began. "He was navy during the —"

"Oh, and Miss Shanklin?" Halfway across the lobby, Miss Bell had turned around to address me once more in her loud, carrying voice. "Do find something more suitable to wear while you are in the Middle East," she advised. "That clothing is far too revealing. The doorman took you for a whore."

After helping Rosie and me back up into the cart, Colonel Lawrence climbed aboard himself and gave the dragoman directions, using Arabic and gestures. "It's not far," he told me. "Ten minutes, across the river." For the whole of that time, the colonel filled the silence with travelogue and chat. The boulevard we rode upon divided Cairo in two, he told me. The western half was *frangi,* or French — the word was used locally for anything foreign. The whole district used to be inundated yearly by the Nile's flood, but after European engineers dammed the river, it was possible to build on the high ground. Foreigners were allowed to settle, and *frangi* Cairo came to look like a southern European city, filled with banks, hotels, consulates, and Art Nouveau residences. There was even a Sporting Club with a race course. To the east was *beledi* Cairo, the real city, in his opinion, where ordinary Egyptians lived and worked amid mosques, coffee shops, tiny stores, little factories, markets, and schools.

The Continental Hotel was *frangi,* set in the Gazirah neighborhood, a quiet enclave popular with Europeans. "*Gazirah* means island," the colonel said, as the dragoman turned off a broad boulevard onto a handsome bridge that crossed one of the Nile's strands.

The Europeans I'd seen at the Semiramis were a group of British officials. "Winston and his Forty Thieves," Lawrence called the delegation. They had been assembled for a few days in Cairo to finish some business left undone at Versailles. Much of it had been decided years ago, in London and Paris, but details remained to be worked out.

I nodded and murmured as he spoke, touched by his kind awareness of my speechless embarrassment. Only when we arrived at the Continental did I feel capable of asking the question that made my cheeks burn. "Colonel Lawrence, at the Semiramis . . . Was it my dog who was objectionable, or was it myself?"

He sat still a moment, staring at his shoes, which were as scuffed as a schoolboy's. "To a Muslim, all dogs are objectionable," he informed me, "but those with short legs are especially to be despised." He glanced at me to see if I was "buying it." I must have looked skeptical, for he added, "I have no idea why, but that *is* the case."

"And Miss Bell's suggestion that I — ?

That the doorman thought — ?"

"Oh, don't mind Gert," he advised with a patience that reminded me that he'd also found it necessary to overlook her tactlessness. "She really is quite extraordinary. There's a saying here: If you think you understand Middle Eastern politics, they haven't been explained to you properly. Gerty knows every nuance. No one in the West can match her. Still, she can be a bit —"

I didn't catch his last word, but I confess: I supplied my own.

With that, he left the cart and disappeared inside the Continental, returning presently with the news that Miss Bell had been as good as her word. At her telephoned request, my room was ready; the deposit paid to the Semiramis would be forwarded to the Continental by the local Cook's branch office.

When I tried to thank Colonel Lawrence, he giggled again — this time, I gathered, to indicate the absurdity of gratitude for a small service willingly undertaken. A bellman appeared to transfer my luggage from cart to lobby. Lawrence apologized for leaving me on my own. He had to return to the Semiramis "before Gert sorts out Mesopotamia on her own," whatever that meant.

There was the dragoman to pay. He wanted ten piastres, given the extra trouble he'd been put to, but we settled on eight. When I turned to say good-bye to Colonel Lawrence, he was already halfway down the block, apparently intending to walk back to his hotel. Farewells, I was to learn, were a nicety the colonel frequently found dispensable.

Rosie was indeed made welcome, even though she chose to relieve herself just outside the entry. ("Better out than in, madam," said the very dark gentleman who whisked away the evidence.) A few minutes at the desk, and two bellmen were assigned to ferry my things up three flights of stairs and down a quiet, carpeted corridor at the end of which was an ornately carved door. This was opened to reveal a high-ceilinged and airy room. "Will this do, madam?" I was asked.

"Oh, yes!" I breathed. "Oh, it's perfect. Thank you."

With Rosie in my arms, I stepped outside through tall French doors that opened onto a little private balcony overlooking a formal green garden. The first brilliant stars had begun to appear in an ultramarine sky. Palm trees slanted on the horizon, black against a tangerine sunset.

"Look, Rosie!" I whispered. "We're in a Palmolive ad!"

While I stood rapt and idle as a princess, my things were unpacked and hung up or folded neatly into drawers. Feeling quite worldly and experienced, I waited to tip the gentlemen until their tasks were completed to their own satisfaction.

Alone at last, I peeked into the bathroom and was delighted by gorgeous cobalt tiles, a deep copper tub, and thick white towels stacked high on a shelf. I served Rosie a drink from a china whatnot dish and ran a bath for myself. She wriggled under the bathmat and fell asleep while I soaked in pleasantly tepid water.

Refreshed, I made a call downstairs to inquire about room service. I was informed that Miss Bell had already ordered a supper to be delivered to my room at eight-thirty, but that it was ready to be sent up right away. Minutes later, it arrived on a rolling cart, complete with a plate of meat scraps and a bone for Rosie. There was even a stack of newspapers to lay out for the dog afterward. It was a very nice gesture, and I thought better of Miss Bell for it.

Thus a day that had begun in heat and noise 140 miles north, in Alexandria, ended as I slipped between crisply ironed sheets in a quiet Cairo hotel. Rosie nosed beneath the light cotton coverlet and corkscrewed round and round, all the while producing the wheezes and mutterings peculiar to dachshunds attempting to get comfortable for the night. At long last she settled and sighed and slept. I expected to do the same momentarily. I was as tired as I had ever been in my life: the journey, the heat, the novelty, the anxiety, the bliss of arrival! But sleep would not come.

Instead, the scene at the Semiramis played over and over in my head. Humiliation is not the same as embarrassment, I realized. If you know yourself to be clumsy and never pretend otherwise, you might well be embarrassed when you trip over your own feet upon entering a room, but you won't be ashamed. You can laugh at yourself and shrug the embarrassment off.

Humiliation, by contrast, does not merely require open recognition of an acknowledged foible. Humiliation is public exposure of some secret vanity. You might gaze into a mirror holding your head just so, and your eyes sparkle at your own best self. Then perhaps you leave a bathroom at college, for example, thinking that you really look rather nice this morning, all things considered, only to overhear someone remark, "Good

Lord, if I looked that bad, I'd never go out in daylight." You discover that not even your own modest opinion of yourself is shared. You are not merely homely but also deluded, and vain, and ridiculous. That is humiliation.

And someone had lied to me, but who? Colonel Lawrence or Miss Bell? Was it a short-legged dog or a bare-limbed woman who had aroused such animosity? Was the lie a kind one, told to spare my feelings, or a harsh one, meant to cut a potential rival who had dared to be friendly with Miss Bell's own dear boy?

Or had each of them told me a part of the truth? Certainly there was something about Lawrence's tone that might have implied, *Yes, I was lying about why the doorman blocked your way, but I found a perfectly good explanation that saved your pride, and that's merely good manners, don't you agree?* And perhaps Miss Bell had provided accurate information about local custom, even though she chose to do so in a way that seemed calculated to inflict as much mortification as possible.

You should have known better than to dress so immodestly, Mumma said. *None of this would have happened if you'd just stayed home, where you belong.*

It doesn't matter, Mildred told me. *You'll probably never see those people again. Just wear that nice silk cardigan when you go out. Or the navy linen jacket — that goes with everything.*

Exhaustion eventually claimed me, but during that first night, my sleep was disturbed, perhaps by some unfamiliar sound outside. I rolled over in bed and saw — silhouetted by moonlight — a man standing calmly in my room.

Frightened out of my wits, I screamed and sat up, clutching at the covers, and struggled to turn on the bedside light.

By the time I found the switch, the intruder had disappeared into the darkness. With my heart beating violently, I expected help to arrive at any moment. But the minutes passed. No one came, and this upset me more than the initial fright. I had screamed for help! And no one came!

"Why doesn't anyone ever come?" I wailed aloud.

Rosie awoke at the sound of my voice, and only then did I realize that she'd been fast asleep. How on earth could she have slept through the shriek that still echoed in my own ears?

Still terrified, I lay back, torn between the utterly convincing nature of my experience and indisputable facts: neither hotel staff nor other guests had arrived to investigate my loud distress, and Rosie had missed the entire drama, if drama it had been.

My pulse slowed. Reason reclaimed me. I eased out of bed, pulled on my robe, went outside to the balcony. Serene starlight revealed nothing of note in the blue-shadowed world beyond. I quietly closed the French doors against a chill that had crept across the desert and traveled along the Nile. Rosie watched me curiously from beneath a fold of sheeting.

This is an ancient place, I thought, getting back into bed. There are souls here who cannot find their way.

It was utterly unlike me to think that way, but I swear that's what came to mind. From my present vantage, that dream makes perfect sense, but at the time? I shook off the unease and settled onto the pillow.

"A late supper's nightmare — that's all," I told Rosie. "A bit of Mr. Scrooge's undigested cheese. It was a dream. Just a silly dream . . ."

"Lie down with dogs, rise up with fleas," Mumma used to say. She was referring to moral corruption that came of falling in with bad companions, although she also thought that people who let their dogs sleep indoors were asking for trouble.

Ah, but those who lie down with dachshunds rise up with smiles, even if their own night's sleep has been disturbed. Dachshunds are structural comedians; their very existence is a cause for amusement. In the full light of morning, I awoke to the spectacle of Rosie lying flat on her back: pointed nose in the air, stubby forelegs folded demurely across her chest, hindquarters sprawled in lewd abandon.

"Trollop! Just look at you," I murmured, stroking her belly. "No wonder Arabs think short dogs are odious."

Waking, she rolled over. Yawned, her long tongue unfurling like a paper noisemaker.

Stretched, a two-part motion: first fore, then aft. A cylindrical shake from one end to the other, and she leapt into my arms, all exuberance and kisses, as though we had been cruelly parted for days, not sleeping in the very same bed all night long.

Someone just outside my door must have heard my laughter, for there was a tiny knock and a piping voice. "Walk you dog, madams?"

I pulled on my dressing gown, lifted Rosie, and opened the door to a small boy wearing a barely respectable white cotton shift and sandals. This little capitalist held up a worn leather leash, probably scavenged from some European's trash. "Yes, madams? Walk you dog?"

Rosie customarily barked at strangers, but perhaps she did not yet consider the hotel room entirely her own. And this child had, after all, uttered a magical word. She looked at him and then up at me, trembling with anticipation. *He said 'walk,' Agnes.*

"How much?" I asked.

We quickly brokered a price and I attached his leash to her collar. Before I even learned the boy's name, he and Rosie raced down the corridor toward the stairs.

I don't know what I was thinking. I suppose I simply presumed that the concierge had sent the boy. When he and Rosie failed to reappear by the time I'd washed up and gotten dressed, dreadful possibilities began to occur to me. Was this how poor Egyptians obtained meat — by walking foreigners' dogs? What if the boy held her hostage and demanded a ransom? What if the doorman of the Semiramis had sent the boy here to execute the offensive animal? That was absurd, but still . . .

Idiot! I thought. Why didn't you call the desk clerk before sending her off with some little stranger?

Five more sickening minutes, and I left the room, hoping at every step to hear a child's pounding footfalls and Rosie's scrambling scamper up the staircase. With no sign of them three flights down, I was close to frantic as I approached the concierge. "Sir, I'm afraid I've made a terrible mistake," I began, embarrassed at the quaver in my voice.

Just then I heard a deep male voice cry, *"Ein Wursthund!"* right outside the hotel door. There was a stream of delighted German followed by a question in Arabic that was answered by the boy, who entered the lobby and lifted his chin toward me.

The German gentleman appeared with Rosie draped happily over one strong forearm. He was a rather handsome person, quite tall, and broad in the chest. My age. Perhaps a bit younger. When he saw me, his smile widened beneath a luxuriant mustache, and he leaned over to place Rosie on the floor.

Crying "Woo-hoo!" she sprinted across the lobby and pirouetted at my feet as if to say, *Look, Agnes, look! I found us a new friend!*

I picked her up, careful to bend at the knees, and straightened just in time to see the gentleman hand the little boy a coin and dismiss him with a word or two in Arabic. "You are English, miss?" the gentleman inquired cheerily with a slight but pleasant accent.

"American," I said.

"You must forgive my forwardness, Miss — ?"

"Shanklin."

"You see, Miss Shanklin, I had a dachshund when I was small, just the same as your — ?"

"Rosie."

"Such memories your Rosie brings me! My Tessa was just the same," he said again, astonished by this coincidence. "Black and brown with markings just the same." He held out his hands with a pleading look, begging for the opportunity to hold Rosie once more. Disarmed, I passed her to him, and the hussy allowed herself to be transferred without a struggle.

"She is a vamp," the gentleman said with mock disapproval, as though reading my mind. "My Tessa was the same. But I forget my manners as well." Rosie looked put out when he offered me the hand that had been stroking her long back. "Permit me to introduce myself, Miss Shanklin. I am Karl Weilbacher. Please," he urged, extending an arm toward a sunny room just off the lobby. "You must allow me to buy you and Rosie some breakfast."

This meal was included in the price of my accommodation, or it had been at the Semiramis. Uncertain if the same arrangement obtained at the Continental as well, I turned toward the desk clerk to inquire.

Herr Weilbacher must have misread my hesitation. "Please, Miss Shanklin, I assure you that my intentions are entirely honorable."

The notion that a man's intentions toward me were anything else seemed improbable but intriguing. I tried to think if I was properly attired for a meal in public, and yes — even preoccupied by Rosie's fate, I'd taken time to select the longest frock

Mildred had allowed me to purchase and had pulled the navy jacket on over it. I wore neither gloves nor hat, but I could feel the marcelled wave that Antoine had created swagging low and becomingly over my wayward eye. And I was in Cairo! I was far from home, you see, and free from all my own ideas of myself. It seemed just possible that —

"Not another thought," Herr Weilbacher declared. "Please, do me this favor," he pleaded, looking sweetly sad as he added, "It has been so long since my Tessa has been gone from me."

When I agreed, his face lit up. Chatting cheerily, he led me to a dining room ringed with ferns and orchids where gleaming silver and cut glass on white linen caught the glorious morning light. The waiters all seemed to know Herr Weilbacher, and if they were unenthusiastic about Rosie's presence in their domain, his good humor — and perhaps a history of genially distributed tips — overcame their dismay.

"Now, what would you enjoy for breakfast?" he asked, rubbing his hands together with anticipatory relish.

"Anything, as long as it's not oatmeal," I said and listened, dazed, as he ordered for us while keeping up a steady stream of amiable small talk. Soon a team of waiters delivered large trays bearing tea and coffee, and boiled eggs, and rolls with butter and marmalade, and sausages, and oranges and melon.

I thought it was all delicious, but Herr Weilbacher's face twisted as he chewed and swallowed a forkful of meat. "This is not so good as our sausages at home," he told me in a low voice and then explained, "Like serious Jews, Muslims eat no pork and so: there is rarely any sausage worth eating in Egypt, not even in hotels that cater to Europeans. This sausage is fit only for dogs." His face lit up again. "But we are in luck: here is a dog!" he cried and slipped a tidbit to Rosie.

"Oh, don't feed her from the table," I objected.

"It is only a tiny piece," he said, winking. "When I was a boy, my brothers and I fed Tessa, just so."

"But didn't she learn to be a beggar?"

"Of course, but she was very adorable," he said with a shrug and a look that asked, *Why should we resist?*

His face was remarkable, capable of all sorts of vivid, interesting things as he spoke. Straight and serious one moment, crooked and amused the next, his expression changed as quickly as his topics, which were as varied and light as clouds racing across a spring sky. He was so interested in me and Cleveland and how I'd come to be in Cairo — why, before ten minutes had passed, he made me feel as though having breakfast with a German gentleman in an Egyptian hotel was the most natural thing in the world for a lady from Ohio.

"And where is your home, Herr Weilbacher?" I asked.

"Please," he said, buttering another crusty roll. "Call me Karl. I am from Stuttgart, in Württemberg." When I grew thoughtful, his mobile face quieted. "You are thinking: he was the enemy."

"Not at all!"

He smiled at my lie, and I looked down at my plate. "We Germans are not all the same," I heard him say in his resonant, musical voice. "Germany has a north and a south as your country does, Miss Shanklin. We southerners are quite a different breed from Prussians, who love war and wish to rule." He leaned over the table. "The kaiser came to Stuttgart when I was a child. My friends and I threw stones at his parade," he confessed merrily. "In the beer hall, men gave us boys pretzels when we sang silly songs or recited a rude poem about the kaiser."

"I know just the sort of boy you must have been. I was a schoolteacher," I said, and began to speak about my students back in Little Italy. I meant to tell him about how hard they studied and how quickly they learned English, but Herr Weilbacher seemed so curious, so sympathetic . . .

And the truth is, I can never seem to stick to a subject, as you've probably noticed, and I really do apologize for that, but everything always seems so connected to me! Anyway, before long I found myself recounting my struggles with resentful, bitter parents, frightened by their children's success. Americanization was a Faustian bargain for such immigrants, I told Herr Weilbacher. Yes, their children could go to public schools with no bribes, no fees, and no questions asked, but American tuition was paid in estrangement. Daughters told mothers that they dressed funny, they cooked funny, they talked funny. Sons stayed out late and went to dance halls, and quarreled with their fathers over who would keep the money earned from after-school jobs.

Fed up, the parents would decide enough was enough. A father would appear at my classroom door. Hat in hand but defiant, he would declare, "My kid don't wanna go to school no more." Listening to those men, you'd have thought their sons and daughters wished for nothing more earnestly than to work for a pittance in a steel mill or a laundry.

"And the children stood there, dying inside," I told Herr Weilbacher. "I could see it! The boys would hang their heads. The girls would weep. I could do nothing, and it just broke my heart — because honestly? What the father meant was, I'm losing my power. I am diminished every day as this child grows more knowledgeable —"

I realized suddenly that Herr Weilbacher, so charming and chatty before, had fallen utterly silent.

You simply cannot see it when you bore others, Agnes, Mumma whispered. *He doesn't care that you were a schoolteacher. My land! He's only being polite to sit with you at all, and here you are with your crossed eyes, braying about immigrant children. You'd drive gentle Jesus to drink, Agnes. Honestly, you would.*

I stared at my lap, hands clawed around my napkin. "I — My apologies, Herr Weilbacher," I stammered, trying to drop my voice an octave and to soften its harsh midwestern timbre. "One does get carried away."

Still he said nothing. He is disgusted, I thought. Disgusted by me, by my opinions, and my loudness and my accent. He is struck speechless by disgust.

He bent and lifted Rosie, one hand cupped under her muscular behind, the other supporting her chest. She could be wary with strangers, but there was something calm and assured about his hands. He shifted Rosie to the horizontal and stroked her back all the way to her feather-duster tail. His fingers stopped moving when he felt the misshapen bones.

"She was born that way," I said, ashamed of her and of myself. "Her tail is a defect. I know that." I glanced up then and saw that his face had become . . . Well, I don't know how to describe it except that he seemed impressed and entertained, at once.

"You are compassionate," he said softly, as though he knew that I had saved her life by taking her for my own on the day she was born. "I was not much of a student," he confided then, "but perhaps I would have been if I'd had such a teacher as you, Miss Shanklin." He set Rosie on the floor decisively. "I had an appointment this morning, but it was canceled. Cairenes are so unreliable. Everything with them is *inshallah* —"

"If it be God's will," I said, remembering the word from Lillian's stories.

"Yes, but also 'perhaps,' or 'someday.' Or 'not bloody likely,' as the English say. Today, I think, this is good luck. It would be my pleasure to show you something of the city, if you and Rosie would do me the honor?"

Agnes, no! Mumma cried. *He's a complete stranger, and a foreigner.*

Here in Cairo, Agnes is a foreigner, too, said Mildred. And that was true, of course.

"What a lovely offer," I said brightly. "Just let me get my hat."

We left the lobby with Rosie trotting ahead on her leash while Herr Weilbacher pointed out the sights. "Gardens like these are among the many European amenities in this neighborhood. This part of Cairo reminds me of Paris. Have you been to Paris? No? *Ach!* You must see Paris someday! Notre-Dame is on an island in the Seine just as Gazirah sits between two parts of the Nile. That is the Cairo Opera House, just there. It was built to celebrate the completion of the Suez Canal. Do you enjoy opera, Miss Shanklin?" When I allowed as how I'd never had the opportunity to hear one, he cried, "Then we must make an opportunity. I'll try to get tickets for a performance. Perhaps *Aïda*! What could be better than *Aïda* in Cairo?"

Halfway across the Gazirah Bridge, noise began to lap at us like waves against a shore. Arriving on the *beledi* side of the city, we were suddenly in the midst of it all: camels, carts, crowds, and an astonishing number of trucks and motorcars. Many were Fords, in considerably reduced condition. Stripped to their essentials, they made the kind of deafening racket that might have been produced by a thresher attempting to harvest a stone wall. Behind each ramshackle vehicle, a crowd of boys followed, "hoping for a breakdown or an entertaining collision," as Herr Weilbacher put it. "Amazing how few parts a Ford needs," he shouted when a particularly skeletal flatbed truck clattered past. "If something falls off, a Ford rolls right on — although it complains rather loudly."

"No wonder people here yell all the time," I remarked at the top of my voice. "Everyone in Cairo must be hard of hearing!" And I was thrilled when Herr Weilbacher produced a booming laugh, amused at my remark.

Engulfed by Cairo's kaleidoscope of odors, Rosie dashed to the end of her leash in every direction, as eager to sample Cairo's scents as I was to see its sights. Before long, however, her jaunty rolling trot slowed, and Herr Weilbacher scooped her up. "The world is very large for a sausage dog," he observed. "It's a short life but a hairy one, *ja,* Rosie?"

With humor and insight, he began to interpret the street life for me, giving meaning to yesterday's exotic chaos. The ladies' long black garments, he explained, were allowed to trail in the dust purposely, to erase the tracks of their bare feet — in which an evil spirit might read hieroglyphs that could bring their families bad luck.

"Look at that," Herr Weilbacher murmured, speaking close to my ear. I followed his glance and was amazed by the sight of a woman balancing on her head a large chicken coop — complete with chickens! A man walked a step or two in front of her, carrying nothing more than a cigarette between his lips. "Probably her husband, or perhaps a brother," Herr Weilbacher said. "Egypt is a man's world. Women bear all the burdens of Cairene life. Clay jars, children, baskets of goods . . . You are lucky, Miss Shanklin, to be independent and free. What an extraordinary woman you are to come so far — all on your own!"

We turned down a side street. For a short time, the noise around us diminished to the crunch of discarded pistachio shells beneath our feet and the *ka-lop, ka-lop* of delicate donkey hooves, followed by the rumble of wooden wheels on cobbles when a little cart passed by, laden with oranges. Soon, however, we entered an enclosed passageway where shouts and cries echoed against ancient stone walls.

"I think we will not go farther inside. Just look from here," Herr Weilbacher advised. "It is too dirty for your pretty shoes." That was just the sort of thing Mumma might have warned against, but on Herr Weilbacher's lips, the instruction seemed to convey concern for my welfare and carried no implication that my own judgment was inadequate to the situation.

The covered bazaar was called a *souk,* he told me, and it teemed with jostling shoppers haggling over sacks of spices and beans, and piles of melons and cucumbers. Each item was the occasion for the sort of shouting matches I'd observed the day before, and when I inquired, Herr Weilbacher explained, "The negotiation is designed to make every transaction take as long as possible. It is a form of sport and justifies the time men spend on it. When they are tired from their bargaining, they must sit and smoke, or play dominoes for a while — to recover their strength, naturally."

Rosie wiggled in his arms, and he paused to set her on the pavement just as a gang of small boys gathered around us calling, *"Baksheesh! Baksheesh!"* Herr Weilbacher shook his head and waved the children off, but one of them noticed Rosie, who was backing up, circling. When she curled like a comma to deposit her own malodorous contribution to the bazaar's collection of garbage, donkey droppings, and camel urine, the little boy alerted his friends. In an instant, the whole group doubled up with glee. Herr Weilbacher tossed a coin into the *souk.* The boys ran off to retrieve it and were quickly lost amid the hawkers' wares.

"Baksheesh," I said. I remembered the word from Lillie's letters but couldn't recall the meaning. "Is that a sort of fruit?"

"Yes, in a manner of speaking. Foreigners are the tree and all Egypt harvests us." When I smiled uncertainly, he explained, "From the Persian *bakhshidan,* to give. It means a tip or a small gift."

"And how have you come to be in the Middle East, Herr Weilbacher?" I asked as we strolled onward.

He stopped walking and waited with a

hurt expression for me to look back. "Please, must I beg?" he asked, sounding comically aggrieved. "Call me Karl."

"Karl." The word was soft in my mouth. "And you must call me Agnes, of course."

"That's better." He had a smile like sunrise. "Before the war, I supervised the construction of a railway my government built for the Turks."

"You are a civil engineer, then? My brother was an army engineer," I said, delighted by the coincidence.

"An engineer?" He laughed, but kindly. "I'm afraid I have no head for such things. No, Agnes, I was — let us say — an observer. I reported on progress to my superiors. There was a considerable investment of money. Many important people were interested in the project."

Toward noon we circled back toward an impressive square, which was, Karl told me, the very heart of Cairo. There, all the colors of humanity were in evidence. "Sudanese," Karl whispered, indicating a family so dark as to be nearly purple. As we strolled, he nodded toward Greeks and Italians, Jews and Armenians, Syrians and Lebanese and Cypriots: all sallow and hirsute in varying degrees. "But look there!" Karl said quietly. A slim, square-shouldered youth passed by, slender brown limbs moving with fluid grace beneath his homespun cotton robe. "That is the true Egyptian, Agnes, just as he is depicted on the walls of ancient tombs."

Together we gazed at the young man's beauty until Karl was distracted from it by a pair of white-skinned men. "Turko-Circassians," Karl said. "They ruled Egypt until recently but were displaced by the French and then the British. Which reminds me! Was that not the famous Colonel Lawrence I saw with you yesterday? How do you know him, Agnes?"

I spoke of my sister's connection and then of Mr. Thomas's presentation. Karl smiled knowingly. "The world's most famous spy, our Lawrence — barring only Mata Hari, I should say. They both enjoyed dressing up as Orientals."

"I'm sorry, Herr — Karl. No, I don't believe you have the right man. Colonel Lawrence is a British army officer."

"Among other things." Karl smiled. "I have followed his career for many years, Agnes. We met near Baghdad before the war, when he was an 'archaeologist' at Carchemish."

"You say 'archaeologist' as though it were some sort of joke."

"Not a joke, but part of the truth, only. Lawrence was competent in his field and Carchemish was an important Hittite site, but there are many such sites. Why choose one and not another?" he asked playfully. "Because Carchemish was very near a bridge we were building for that new German railway, of course! Lawrence spent a good deal of time taking photographs and making notes that would be of use during the war we both knew was coming. I came to know him rather well . . ." Suddenly, a cloud seemed to pass over him. Karl shook his head sadly. "He was built like a young bull in those days — not tall, but great strength in the shoulders and chest." The colonel had not struck me as robust, and I must have looked doubtful because Karl remarked, "It was a hard war for him, I fear."

He brightened up as we approached the famed Egyptian Museum, an immense building of peony-pink stone. "They held an international competition for its design. Worthy of the splendors it contains but, like Egyptian history, it contains too much. I will remain outside with Rosie while you spend just forty-five minutes in the museum — no more or you will be overwhelmed, dear teacher! You can come back again and again, and you will look at the same objects with different eyes. Learn inside, learn outside, then learn more on your return!"

The museum was laid out clockwise, with the oldest objects to the left of the entrance. Circling, one encountered five thousand years of rulers: Pre-Dynastic, Old Kingdom, New Kingdom, Ptolemaic, Roman, Ottoman.

Despite Karl's wise advice, I tried to take it all in. The striding vitality of Ka-Aper, whose gleaming eyes seemed alert and lively; the seated Khufre, whose throne is enveloped by the protective wings of Horus; the lifelike statue of Princess Nofret, whose "real" hair can be seen poking out from beneath her royal wig. The sad, severe face of Ramses II, once mighty but now a beak-nosed, lipless mummy exposed to the vulgar curiosity of tourists.

My eyes swept over death masks, coffins, armchairs. Statues of falcons preparing for flight and of crocodiles lying in wait. Alabaster perfume bottles that would not have looked out of place on a modern woman's dresser. Gold jewelry that Tiffany's might have sold that very day in New York City. I paid as much attention as I could to the exhibits so that I would have something interesting to tell Karl when I returned to him, but I will be honest with you: I was as giddy as a schoolgirl with a crush.

Looking back now, it seems plain that I had passed into a sort of delayed adolescence on my first visit to Halle's Department Store. After decades of defining myself by what I would not do, what I did not want, what I could not be . . . Well, my young friend Mildred had allowed me to see myself in an entirely new way — as a grown woman really, making my own choices, hearing myself think.

And what I thought that first afternoon in the Egyptian Museum was, Forty minutes . . . thirty minutes . . . ten minutes, and then I will see him again.

I made myself stay inside a while longer to keep my eagerness to rejoin him from being too obvious. When at last I allowed myself to go back outside, Karl was sitting on a stone bench in a cool green square a few steps from the entrance and waved to catch my attention.

"An hour!" he called, releasing Rosie and grinning as she dashed toward me and danced at my feet, wagging herself almost in half. "I warned you, didn't I? Quite overwhelming!"

He had assembled a picnic for us: tomatoes, creamy goat cheese, disks of soft flat bread dotted with blackened, bubbled dough. "These tomatoes are delicious," he told me when I joined him on the bench. "I am thinking of importing them to Europe. A man could make his fortune that way. And so, Agnes, what was the best thing you saw?"

I chewed, and thought, and swallowed. "Akhenaten," I said, and then described the winsome oddity of that strange pharaoh with his soft little potbelly and long lantern jaw. There he sat, basking in the sun with his beautiful wife, Nefertiti. I was especially intrigued by their peculiarly adult children, sitting on the royal laps or playing at their parents' feet. The children looked like Mr. and Mrs. Tom Thumb.

"A touching image," Karl agreed. "And here we are, you and I, under the very same sun, with our little deformed daughter!" It took my breath away, that casual joke. "All those gods," he went on, "each demanding attention! Amun, Osiris, Isis, Horus. Anubis, Ra. Maat, Geb, Bes! Monotheism must have been a welcome simplification," he remarked, and I shocked myself by laughing at what I suspected was blasphemy. "Of course, polytheism has its advantages," Karl pointed out. "If you fall suddenly in love with an unsuitable person, you may say, I am struck by Cupid's arrow and helpless to resist! Or if something awful happens, you needn't ask, What have I done to deserve this misfortune? Or, How could a just God permit such a thing? You merely say, Alas! Poor me! The gods are playing in the sky, and I have stumbled into their path."

With that, he licked the last of the tomato juice and cheese from his fingers and stood, telling me regretfully that he had an appointment that afternoon. "And you, I think, must now have a rest — *siesta,* the Spaniards call it. A nap in the heat of the afternoon. You must keep up your strength, Agnes, for more adventures later."

After the warmth and noise of *beledi* Cairo, my *frangi* hotel room was a cool and quiet oasis. I took off my street clothes, put on my robe, and lay back on the soft bed with Rosie at my side. Hands clasped behind my head, I watched the bed's white cotton netting lift and sway in the slight breeze that drifted through the balcony doors. I felt enveloped, and . . . cared for.

It occurred to me then that no one had ever really taken care of me. Papa was always working and, you'll recall, Mumma was never a great one for fussing over children. I learned early not to need much. After Papa died, it fell to me to look after everyone else. So, you see, to have someone like Karl anticipate my need to learn, to eat, to rest, to enjoy — that was profoundly moving.

Old as I was, I was innocent, but innocent as I was, I knew the difference, even then, between love and an infatuation. Infatuation is a mirror in which one gazes at one's own longing for love and acceptance. Mirrors are fragile. Love endures.

What I felt in those first hours with Karl was a sense of excitement at discovering a person who seemed to find me witty and perhaps even a little attractive. His joy in sharing his knowledge of the city made my own enthusiasms seem well proportioned and justified. He had a great deal to teach but did so without talking down to me. That meant a lot. Until I met Karl, I was a daughter before parents, or a student before teachers, or a teacher before students. Even with my brother and sister, my responsibilities took me somewhat out of their spheres. I would not have said so at the time, but I suppose I had been lonely all my life. Karl was a companion, you see. Someone who treated me as an equal, worthy of his thoughtfulness and care.

He even mentioned Cupid, Mildred whispered.

And, of course, when a couple walks side by side, they look out at the world together, not at each other. The voice becomes more important than the face, you see. The soul and the intellect can be more beautiful without the dross of physicality.

Well, not entirely without.

Built like a bull. Great strength in the shoulders and chest. Karl's description of Lawrence seemed more a self-portrait . . .

"Ah, vain delusion!" wrote the poet. "The fancy that flits before my mind is not the truth."

There's no fool like an old fool, Mumma sneered.

Pay no attention! Mildred advised. *She's just jealous.*

"What do you think, Rosie?" I asked as she chewed meditatively on her toes. Receiving no clear reply, I answered for her. "You think he's a nice man who feeds you sausage, don't you!"

And for the moment, that was good enough for me.

I was awakened in the full heat of late afternoon by the sound of knuckles rapping on wood. Convinced now that the room was hers to defend, Rosie hurtled off the bed, barking maniacally until I could make myself decent, pick her up, and open the door.

It was Karl. Merry eyes averted, he murmured apologies for interrupting my nap and explained that he'd overheard the desk clerk's instructions to deliver a message immediately and wait for an answer.

Blinking and benumbed by interrupted sleep, I traded Rosie for the loosely folded note Karl offered on a silver salver as though he were the hotel bellhop. "I took the liberty," he admitted and waited, smiling broadly, for my reaction.

The handwriting was small, upright, and worth no better than a C for penmanship. *"Miss Shanklin: Dinner party this evening. The Semiramis, 8 pm. Short notice, but may I send a taxi for you? TEL"*

Colonel Lawrence had by that time completely slipped my mind, but he had not forgotten about me. I looked at Karl, astonished, then abashed. "Oh, no, I — I couldn't possibly."

"Agnes, why not?" Karl cried quietly, coming inside and pulling the door closed behind him. It seemed so natural — not forward or frightening. It was the simple act of one who wished a private word with a friend. Perhaps you, too, have met a stranger with whom each hour is so open and so enjoyable that you feel you have always known each other?

Anyway, Karl sat down on the slipper chair in the corner of my room and lifted Rosie onto his lap. "Agnes," he said, face serious and hilarious at once, "the Uncrowned King of Arabia invites you to dinner and you will refuse him? Tell me why, please. This, I wish to understand."

Bit by bit, Karl pulled the story from me. I was trying to make a comedy of my excruciating experience at the entrance of the Semiramis when Karl raised a hand to stop me. "Winston Darling?" He looked confused and then delighted. "As in the Barrie play of *Peter Pan*? Like Wendy's father, yes? Mr. Darling? Agnes, you are adorable!" he declared, then continued with specious formality: "My dear Miss Shanklin, if I am not mistaken, the gentleman's surname is Churchill, not Darling. You really must tell me what you think of him when you meet him. I am not inclined in his favor, but I will trust your judgment."

For my part, I trusted Karl's own goodwill toward me, and my growing confidence in this friendship was confirmed when I got to the part about Gertrude Bell and her obnoxious remark about my clothing.

"Ah, Miss Bell," Karl said with a roll of his eyes. "Immensely knowledgeable but not beloved, I may say to you. She must make everyone aware immediately that she is a person of importance — telling you who she knows and where she has traveled and what she has done. She believes herself the equal of any man on earth, saving her father. No doubt she is more capable than most. She can often bring men round to her way of thinking, but it must annoy her to work always through her inferiors. As for other women, well . . . You are distressing reminders that she herself is female. And now that all women are claiming the freedom she took for herself many years ago, she is not so special, do you see?"

Karl looked into the middle distance, considering the circumstances of our encounter. "Miss Bell used to travel like a queen — her caravans had a cook, muleteers, servants. Twenty camels. A bathtub for her tent! Wedgwood china and silver cutlery for her meals. In those days she was quite stylish — Paris shops would send crates of clothing to her tents in the sand." His merry eyes met mine. "Perhaps," he said with a wicked grin, "when she saw you, she was dismayed to realize that she has fallen rather behind times?"

Oh, Miss Shanklin, he really is a living doll, said Mildred, and I admit I found Karl's suggestion deeply satisfying.

"That said," he continued more soberly, "the entire female population of the Middle East is a millennium behind the times. Dress rules for Muslim women are quite strict. They don't apply to infidels, but it wouldn't go amiss if you were to cover up a bit while in public. A matter of courtesy, if you like. However, at a dinner for Europeans? You may be as fashionable as you like! Miss Bell may not even be attending, but if she is?" His hands spread and his brows rose in a theatrical display of guilelessness. "After such a catty remark, it would be fair play to show her up a bit, don't you think?"

The ivory silk charmeuse, Mildred whispered. I turned to the wardrobe and pulled the dress out. "With pearls?" I asked.

A long, slow smile bloomed on Karl's face. "Perfect. It's settled. You will go to dinner with Lawrence and I'll take care of Rosie, and you will tell me all about it when you get back!"

It was a quarter of nine before my cab arrived at the Semiramis that evening. Colonel Lawrence was waiting for me at the hotel's taxi stand, propped against a low stone wall with arms folded over his chest. He had on the same badly fitted brown suit he'd worn the day before. Oh, my, I thought, am I completely overdressed or is that the only suit he has?

He leaned in to pay the driver and held my door open as I climbed out. We could clearly hear the chant of *"Ah-bah sure-shill! Ah-bah sure-shill!"* a few blocks away.

"I'm sorry to keep you waiting," I said. "The police have roped off the road down at the corner. There's some kind of demonstration."

"Egyptian nationalists," Lawrence said. "Allenby keeps smashing their uprisings, but everyone blames Winston for the bloodshed." He took up the chant and translated it. "*À bas* Churchill: Down with Churchill."

"*À bas?* But that's French, isn't it?"

"Ever since Napoleon was here, it's been traditional to riot in French. Where is your little dog?"

When I said I'd made arrangements for her at the Continental, Lawrence seemed disappointed. He'd been prepared to do battle on Rosie's behalf, he told me, and produced a bad-boy giggle.

"Brace yourself," he advised then, cryptically.

He stood aside as I approached the exalted precinct of the Semiramis lobby, grinning when I stopped dead, immobilized by a quarryful of marble, mines of gold leaf, forests of precious woods. The Continental had seemed extravagantly appointed to me, but this! This was —

"Enough to turn you Bolshevik?" Colonel Lawrence supplied, reading my expression.

"Ghastly," I agreed.

He touched my elbow briefly to get me moving again. "The dining room's worse," he warned and a good thing, too, or I'd have been stupefied by the display.

Just beyond tall double doors we could see a dozen round tables. Set for eight, each was crowded with extravagantly gilded porcelain surrounded by a myriad of crystal stemware and enough silver to supply the U.S. Mint with a decade's worth of dimes. Filled to capacity by close to a hundred guests, the room was vivid with flowers and patterned silk and beaded bags. Black tuxedo jackets and red dress uniforms contrasted dramatically with white linen tablecloths. Champagne fizzed and sparkled within candlelit cut glass. Cigarettes in ebony or tortoiseshell holders dipped and waved. Now and then, shrills of feminine laughter rang out above the manly buzz of conversation.

The entry to that Aladdin's Cave was guarded by a gentleman who stood well over six feet tall and had the physique and demeanor of a prizefighter who has yet to lose a bout. Some of my students' fathers were more frightening, but none of them was more imposing. He and Lawrence exchanged a few words before I was introduced to the colossus. Naturally, I offered my name and waited to hear this gentleman's in return. He seemed surprised and gratified that anyone would bother and said, "Detective Sergeant Thompson, miss."

I don't know what came over me. Certainly I had taken an instant dislike to the ostentation of the Semiramis and its guests, whereas Thompson seemed one of my own kind — outranked and out of place amid that dazzling assembly. Perhaps — with Karl's encouragement — I was simply feeling confidently well dressed, and that let me imagine what Mildred might say, although with better diction. "Nice to meet you, Sergeant," I said brightly. "Have they got you here to keep the riffraff out of the party or to guard the silver?"

He stifled a laugh. "Bit of both, miss." And then he turned his attention to the next pair of glittering party guests, arriving even later than Lawrence and I had.

"Thompson is Scotland Yard. Churchill's bodyguard," Lawrence informed me quietly as we entered the dining room. "You're not supposed to notice him."

"He's rather difficult to overlook," I pointed out, smiling over my shoulder at the policeman.

The colonel gave a little giggle, for Thompson had indeed made him look half-grown by comparison. In my heels, even I was taller than Lawrence but, as we moved through the throngs of ramrod-straight soldiers and their willowy ladies, I realized that Lawrence was deliberately making himself look worse. Slouching and shoving his hands into the pockets of his cheap brown suit like a snippy schoolboy was a sort of reverse snobbery, I think: a brazen if silent disparagement of the occasion and the company.

"Gerty!" he cried suddenly, spotting Miss Bell. "You two've met," he said with a significant stare, which seemed to remind that lady that she'd been put on notice to play nicely with the new girl.

Miss Bell, tall and sharp-jointed, was covered from neck to ankle in gauzy lace and mushroom-colored silk. My sleek, defiant dress received a cool appraisal, but I held my head up and met her gaze, just as she'd instructed. She nodded, acknowledging this, and I took the opportunity to thank her for sending the lovely dinner to my room the night before. She appeared puzzled. Both of us turned toward Lawrence.

He coughed and found somewhere else to look.

"Dear boy! How very diplomatic," Miss Bell remarked dryly. "And yet, you do find a way to get credit in the end, don't you."

Before Lawrence could respond, she introduced me to the gentleman on her right: "Lieutenant Colonel Arnold Wilson, until recently His Majesty's high commissioner in Mesopotamia," Miss Bell informed me. "We worked together in Baghdad."

In his late thirties, this person matched Miss Bell's own considerable height and had an equally commanding gaze, but seemed annoyed by the way she had characterized him. There was something muttered about "Persia, these days," and oil, and then their interrupted conversation resumed without us.

I whispered to Colonel Lawrence as we moved on, "Those two don't like each other much, do they."

"It's been a long day, and they've spent it

arguing. Gert believes that no people will enjoy being governed very long by another. She's for indirect rule in our Middle Eastern protectorates. Wilson is of the firm opinion that — apart from a few troublemakers — His Majesty's colonial subjects desire nothing better than to be granted material and moral progress under the tutelage of Great Britain."

I snorted, by way of comment. It was a bad habit, the unattractiveness of which Mumma often noted, but Lawrence smiled with enigmatic satisfaction. "I thought an American might be amused."

"Americans," I recalled, "were notorious colonial troublemakers."

"As the Arabs promise to be," Lawrence said quietly. "A considerable portion of Mesopotamia rose against Wilson's administration last summer." Lifting himself on tiptoe to see over and around the shoulders of the crowd, he scanned the room while remarking, "Cost His Majesty's Government eighteen million pounds to put the rebellion down. The Exchequer has been hemorrhaging money onto the sand ever since. Ah. There's Winston, who's angling for chancellor and earnestly desires there be something left in the Exchequer to preside over when he gets the job."

Lawrence introduced me to His Majesty's secretary of state for air and for the colonies, and I received a pleasant welcome from the man I'd originally thought was "Winston Darling." Thickset and square, with a stooping head and hooded eyes, Mr. Churchill was not yet the bulldog he would come to resemble, but all the signs were there, even in 1921. He, in turn, introduced me to his wife, Clementine, a vivacious woman in her mid-thirties, visibly in love with the husband who was perhaps a decade her senior.

Other introductions followed, the names and titles coming at me so quickly I caught only a few of them. There was an elderly couple named Cox who were some sort of nobility, I gathered. Was I to call them Lord and Lady in direct address or some other variation on that imperial theme? The honorifics stuck in my democratic throat. "How nice to meet you both," I said warmly and let it go at that.

Just then a uniformed gentleman pulled Lawrence aside. I was immediately taken up by a stylish young woman whose name I'd already forgotten. She was holding what may not have been her very first cocktail of the evening and made a point of exclaiming over my dress.

"How lovely! And so becoming!" I was

told in a voice meant to be overheard by Miss Bell. "Wherever did you get it? Cleveland? Oh, but it positively screams Paris!"

I returned her compliment, for she was wearing a brilliant green-and-gold gown cut sleeveless and low. Breathlessly up-to-the-moment. She moved to stand at my side so that we could both observe Miss Bell, layered in elaborate Edwardian drapery and holding forth among the gentlemen.

"I heard what the dreaded Gertrude said to you," the young woman whispered. "You're not the first, believe me. She made the very same remark to me when my husband and I arrived in Baghdad last year. Horrible old thing . . ."

Having found this ally, I was hoping to be seated at the children's table with her, but Colonel Lawrence reappeared at my side and steered me toward a damask-covered expanse with the Churchills and the Coxes, Miss Bell and Colonel Wilson.

"Cleveland," Wilson noted, having heard the drunken girl's cry. "Standard Oil, of course. And do you know Mr. Rockefeller?"

"Colonel Wilson served in Mesopotamia until recently," Lady Cox informed me with a condescending pat. "He is with the Anglo-Persian Oil Company now."

My reply was delayed by the arrival of an

army of Egyptian waiters. Wearing spotless white gloves and starched linen jackets, they distributed the first of what would become a farcical number of courses. I hoped everyone would forget that I'd been asked a question, but the table remained attentive, so I answered, "Mr. Rockefeller and I do not ordinarily move in the same circles, Colonel Wilson, although I did work near a settlement house named for his daughter. I was a teacher until recently. I'm here on holiday."

"How nice for you," Mrs. Churchill said after an awkward pause that conveyed what everyone was thinking: *Why on earth has Lawrence invited a nonentity like her to the table? Is this some sort of prank?*

"Miss Shanklin's sister was my hostess in Jebail when I was starting my thesis on crusader military architecture," Lawrence told them.

I'd spent enough time with schoolboys to find his tone suspiciously innocent, but everyone else seemed happy with his explanation. Parallel conversations quickly developed. With a teacher at the table, Mrs. Churchill took the opportunity to talk about her children, the latest of whom was a daughter named Marigold, of all things. No, the children were not traveling with their parents, my query was answered. The Churchills had been separated a great deal during the war. This trip to Cairo was a chance for the couple to enjoy some time together, a sort of second honeymoon.

Over and around Mrs. Churchill's praise for the nanny who was taking care of her younger children while she traveled, snatches of the conversation across the table reached me. Colonel Wilson, Mr. Churchill, and Miss Bell were all engrossed in the topic of oil and the administration of the lands it lay beneath. Lord Cox merely harrumphed occasionally, as though dismissive of everything he heard. He reminded me of the mummies at the Egyptian Museum: fleshless, lipless, rigid. On my right, Colonel Lawrence grinned, taking it all in and occasionally tossing out an incisive remark, rarely more than a few words long. Happily left out of that discussion, I leaned toward Lawrence to ask, "Were you by chance a middle child, Colonel Lawrence?"

"Temporarily," he whispered. "I was the second of five brothers, and you're right: one had to be quick to slip a word in."

"What you must understand, Wilson, is that the British people are sick of war," Mr. Churchill rumbled in a slightly slurred baritone. "We simply cannot sustain an expenditure of thirty millions a year to control the place."

"You know as well as anyone, Winston: the Royal Navy needs oil," Colonel Wilson replied. "There's every indication that Mesopotamia has fields as productive as Persia —"

"The cost is all out of proportion to whatever we can expect to reap from that wilderness. If we pull the troops back, Trenchard assures me that we can keep order with airpower."

"Nonsense," Wilson snapped. "We need more troops on the ground, not fewer."

"And with Marigold ill with influenza, the whole experience was positively nightmarish!" Mrs. Churchill was saying.

I tried to look interested and sympathetic, but I was distracted by a rising tension between Miss Bell and Colonel Wilson. They sat side by side, staring straight ahead, but now addressed their remarks to each other. Mrs. Churchill and Lady Cox began to discuss the scandalous state of "checkers." When I looked lost, Lawrence told me in a low voice that they were speaking not of the board game but of the prime minister's official residence. "Chequers was built in the reign of Henry II for his clerk of the Exchequer. Hence the name," he said. The home was last remodeled in 1580. I gathered it was in need of repair.

"Arnold," Miss Bell was telling Colonel Wilson, "when we have made Mesopotamia a model state, there won't be an Arab in Syria or Palestine who won't want to be part of it, but they will never accept direct rule. You saw that last year."

"Gertrude," he countered, "you cannot simply draw a line around Mosul, Baghdad, and Basra and declare everything inside it a nation! It won't matter whom you use as the figurehead."

"Well, of course," Miss Bell said airily, "we'll have to take Kurdish sentiments into account."

"I rather like our Gertrude's idea," Mr. Churchill declared. "Saves the expense of administration in triplicate."

"It will cost more in the long run," Colonel Wilson insisted. "What do you propose to do about the Shi'a in Karbala and Najaf? The level of religious bigotry in those regions is staggering! The Persian clergy spends half its time fostering hatred —"

"And what age of child do you teach, Miss Shanklin?" Mrs. Churchill asked, trying to draw me back into the ladies' conversation.

"Fifth grade," I said. "That would be ten-year-olds, for the most part."

"Tikrit!" Colonel Wilson cried. "Don't talk to me about Tikrit — that city is home to the most brutal, boorish, savage —"

"Ten? Why, that's just my Randolph's age," Mrs. Churchill said, raising her voice slightly as Colonel Wilson's grew louder.

"You must miss him very much," I offered, hoping to send her off on a maternal soliloquy so I could hear what Miss Bell would say in reply.

"I simply do not understand that child," Mrs. Churchill confessed. "His sister Diana is high-spirited, but Randolph!" She lifted her eyes heavenward, and I saw the look of exasperated incomprehension that my own mother so often wore in my childhood.

Half-listening to Mrs. Churchill's complaints about her son, I thought it obvious that the boy was doing everything he could think of to get his peripatetic parents to stay home for a change and pay some attention to him. With no children of my own, I had no right to voice an opinion, so I confined myself to mute courtesy during her despairing account of the governesses her son had driven away with a dismaying series of insurrections.

"Yes, like the one last summer," said her husband. I thought he was referring to his young son's rebellion, but Mr. Churchill went on, "And not just in Mesopotamia. We'll be lucky to hold off the Bolsheviks in Persia — there's no shifting them from Russia now. There's trouble in Ireland, and India. And Egypt! And Palestine! And why our esteemed prime minister has decided to back the Greeks against the Turks in Cyprus simply passeth understanding."

To my astonishment, the cadaverous Lord Cox turned unblinking eyes toward me and growled, "We have your President Wilson to thank for these rebellions. All that talk about the end of colonial rule —"

"The Great Promiser," Mr. Churchill sighed. "Freedom and democracy for all!"

"Arab nationalism is a fraud. Their loyalty is to their tribe," Lord Cox declared, glaring at me. "They have no concept of *democracy,*" he said, making the word sound as though it were a synonym for "turd." "They believe freedom is an object that can be delivered, like a parcel that arrives in the post."

"They must surely know what freedom isn't," I said. "It isn't having British troops all over their land. It isn't taxation without representation."

At the sound of that ringing phrase, Miss Bell informed me tartly that the taxes we Americans had protested were incurred when the Plymouth colonists started a war with the Wampanoag and wiped out the buffer tribes that had shielded them from the Iroquois Confederacy. "You needed troops and we taxed you to pay for them," she told me, and then addressed the table: "Our American cousins . . . often ignorant, but never without opinions."

"Well, perhaps if you'd asked our opinion about the troops and the taxes, you might have avoided a war," I replied. Lawrence giggled happily, and thus encouraged, I went on, even though the others began to look uncomfortable. "It appears to me that Britain proposes to follow American footsteps in the Philippines," I said, "and I don't recommend it. We helped the Filipinos overthrow the Spanish, but did we allow them then to choose their own form of government? No! We annexed the islands. We installed a colonial administrator, and for the next fourteen years, we had one hundred and twenty thousand American troops there! Four thousand of our boys were killed — fighting the very same guerrillas we encouraged to rebel against the Spanish. Who knows how many natives died? Is that what you want in the Middle East?"

"Goodness, you are quite well informed,

Miss Shanklin," said Mrs. Churchill, her voice sweet. "And what do you think of your new president? Mr. Harding is from Ohio, I understand. That's near Cleveland, isn't it?"

"I passed through Cleveland on the way to Niagara Falls from Chicago," said Miss Bell. "Dreadful. Did you vote for Harding?" she asked me, her brows arched. "Many women did, of course. Handsome man, if vacuous. So much for suffrage."

" 'O! Why did God, Creator wise, that peopled highest Heaven with Spirits masculine, create at last this novelty on Earth, this fair defect of Nature?' " Mr. Churchill declaimed, his fork stirring the air. "Be careful, Miss Shanklin. Our Gertrude has as low an opinion of her sex as the immortal Milton. She lent her considerable energies to the Anti-Suffrage League when she was at home before the war."

I was, I must tell you, stunned speechless. Karl had warned me that Miss Bell was hardly a believer in female solidarity, but to oppose votes for women actively? Well, the shock must have shown on my face.

"The role of women in society is fundamentally different from that of men," Miss Bell said firmly. "They have no business meddling in the affairs of state —"

"Never stopped you, Gert," Colonel Lawrence remarked, to general amusement.

"But then, I am hardly representative, am I, dear boy? The intelligence and experience of a few do not argue for giving the vote to masses of illiterate and exhausted women surrounded by screaming toddlers and infants wailing for milk."

"Perhaps if they had the vote," I said, "they could choose representatives who'd protect their interests. What they need is education —"

"Spoken like a teacher," Lawrence said.

"I, for one, welcome the opportunity to vote," Mrs. Churchill said, taking my side.

"But surely you're not old enough, my dear," said her husband.

"Women must be over thirty to vote in England," the elderly Lady Cox informed me with another pat.

"That alone will keep most of them from the ballot box until they're fifty," Miss Bell added.

"I am quite old enough to vote, thank you," said Mrs. Churchill primly, "and not too vain to admit it."

"Clementine, don't tell me you were a suffragette!" Lady Cox cried.

"Heavens, no! I supported votes for women, but not like that awful Mrs. Pankhurst and the harridans who followed her," said Mrs. Churchill bitterly. "One of those women tried to push Winston in front of a train, Miss Shanklin. They threatened to kidnap our children! We had to hire armed guards."

"Well, I suppose they felt forced to such extremes," I said recklessly. "In America, women asked courteously for the vote for sixty years. We collected hundreds of thousands of signatures and rolled up miles of petitions. We met with politicians again and again. They reneged on every promise — and when we howled at their lies, they told us we were too emotional to vote!" I said, infuriated by the memory. "Well! When six decades of nice manners fail to produce a result, you have to become a nuisance or you'll never get justice."

"I doubt the Arabs will wait sixty years before becoming a nuisance," said Colonel Lawrence softly. "I'm curious, Miss Shanklin. The Marquis de Lafayette. Generals Kosciuszko and Pulaski . . . they all came from Europe to aid the American colonists' fight for independence from the British Empire. What do you suppose would have happened if they'd proposed afterward to divide North America between France and Poland?"

The notion was startling. I thought a moment, imagining the betrayal we'd have felt if such heroes had turned on us after the Revolution. "We certainly wouldn't have named cities and parks after them," I said. "After all, if British rule was obnoxious to us —"

"With a shared language, shared laws, centuries of shared history," Lawrence murmured.

"— we wouldn't have accepted rule by a different colonial power. We'd have fought Poland and France just as the Filipinos fought us. Five years, fifteen . . . we'd never give up! Never, never, never."

Across the room, someone finished telling a joke and laughter erupted, but a withering quiet had settled around our table. Miss Bell sat still, her hands in her lap, shrewd eyes on Lawrence, who grinned gnomishly back. The Cox corpse tossed a linen napkin onto the table in disgust, and Colonel Wilson's face was stiff.

Well, Agnes, Mumma said, *I think you've had quite enough to say for one evening.*

Evidently Mrs. Churchill agreed. For the rest of the meal, she gracefully steered the talk toward topics unlikely to elicit American commentary. Decisively exiled from polite conversation, I finished my meal in silence, trying not to blush. I meant what I'd said, of course, and I'd only been answering

Lawrence's question. Even so, dessert came as a relief. Grateful for a sign that the evening was nearly over, I spooned at something custardy, only vaguely aware of the others until Colonel Wilson leaned over the table and addressed Colonel Lawrence with such venom that we all took notice, one by one, around the room.

"You were in Basra for two weeks! And on the basis of that vast experience, you presumed to lecture those who've given years to the region!" Wilson said, punctuating his accusations with a blunt index finger that thumped the table again and again. "You did immense harm to Great Britain at Versailles. Our difficulties with the French in Syria I lay at your doorstep."

Astonished, I shifted in my seat to look at Lawrence, and so did everyone else in the room. He was smiling slightly, the corners of his wide mouth turned up in a curious, predatory curve, while he watched Wilson with lazy, heavy-lidded eyes. The snickering schoolboy, the Oxford scholar, the teasing gadfly — all these had disappeared; in their flashing, prismatic place was a strong, slim figure of intensely male beauty.

It was like seeing an opal turn to diamond.

Massive and austere, Colonel Wilson continued to pile denunciation upon indictment with a measured cadence that revealed how often he had rehearsed this litany in his mind. Miss Bell, who had no love for Wilson, grew increasingly agitated and seemed to blame Lawrence for provoking the assault. Certainly his lack of response was driving Colonel Wilson to barely contained fury. Finally, Wilson seemed to remember that they were equals in military rank and changed his tack. "If you commanded an army of Arabs and I had so much as a division of Gurkhas —"

Lawrence spoke at last. "You would be my prisoner," he said simply, "within three days."

This was evidently the last straw for Miss Bell. "Lawrence!" she hissed through unmoving lips. *"You little imp!"*

Lawrence blanched, then flushed, the sudden pink startling against his yellow hair. You cannot imagine how ruthlessly insulting the remark was, especially in that company. It was the sort of thing a kindergarten teacher might say to a naughty child, and the patronizing scorn with which it was delivered silenced even Colonel Wilson.

An instant later, Lawrence had mastered his reaction. Fixing Miss Bell with a steady blue gaze beneath raised eyebrows and above a small skewed smile, he sat still, letting the silent awkwardness gain weight and solidity.

"It's getting late," he observed at last, "and if this is the best we can do for political discourse . . ." He shrugged as if to say, *There's no point waiting around for brandy and cigars.*

With that, he stood. Inclined his head to our dinner companions. Bowed slightly to the other guests in a general sort of way. Then he put his hands in his pockets, and sauntered out of the room.

I was there at Colonel Lawrence's invitation and, in any case, I had no wish to remain at that table. Without apology or farewell, I picked up my handbag and followed him out of the dining room, through the lobby, and into the midnight moonlight beyond.

By the time I caught up to him, he'd come to rest across the street and stood with one hand against the thick cylindrical trunk of a palm tree, talking to himself and looking almost nauseated by anger. "The sheer arrogance of the lies!" he was snarling, evidently halfway into a topic. "The relentless concealment! The British public were tricked into this adventure in Mesopotamia by a steady withholding of information," he told me when I arrived at his side. "They have no idea how bloody and inefficient the occupation has been, or how many have been killed. The whole business is a disgrace to our imperial record. And those people" — he jabbed a finger in the direction of the hotel — "those people are determined to make it all worse!"

Too agitated to keep still, he set off along the boulevard. I hurried to keep up as he went on vilifying the bureaucrats and diplomats he had to work with here and back in London. Like Wilson's, this diatribe seemed to have been accumulating for some time, and I felt honored to be of use to him, if only as a sounding board. For a while I simply listened, but I knew something about self-consciousness and injured pride, and waited to address that which I suspected had truly wounded him. *Little imp . . .*

When Lawrence's anger began to circle toward the personal, I saw my opening. "Wilson and Cox are the worst kind of India Office bureaucrats," he muttered as he strode along. "And Gertrude — sitting there with Cox, agreeing with his nonsense. That's her flaw — she always gravitates to the man in power!"

Arms crossed, I stood my ground, as though I myself were furious. "And all three of them are entirely too tall!" I declared, matching his emotion but trying to make him see the funny side of the situation. "It's very disagreeable, and really quite unnecessary."

Lawrence turned to stare at me. For an uncomfortable moment, I wondered if he understood that he was being joshed and worried that I'd misread him. Then he slumped, and laughed a little, and nodded. Some of the tension went out of him, and we walked on, though not quite as quickly.

"It's the condescension I can't abide," he continued, calmer now but still needing to talk it out. "The self-satisfied presumption of supremacy! 'Silly wogs,' " he said, mimicking Colonel Wilson's clotted tones. " 'How improvident not to be born into the British aristocracy and how perverse to stay that way! We'll soon sort them out. White man's burden, don't you know!' Who, exactly, is carrying that burden? Arnold Wilson never lifted anything heavier than a polo mallet in India. I just wanted him to say it all aloud, to reveal it for what it is —"

"So you did provoke him." I had stopped again, and he looked back. "And you *knew* I was going to say all that about the Philippines as well."

Caught out, he let a guilty giggle escape. "I certainly hoped so," he admitted, and we walked on.

"You let me make a complete fool of myself," I accused, "and in front of all those lords and ladies."

"The toffs at that table needed to hear what you told them. I've said the same, but . . ." He grew serious once more. "Perhaps it will carry more weight coming from a citizen of a *former* colony —" He looked down and came to a halt so suddenly that my own momentum carried me a few steps beyond him. "Your poor feet!" he cried. "I'm sorry! Would you like a taxi? I should have thought!"

My buckle shoes were going to punish me, but it was too late to change that now. "It's not far," I said. "After a meal like that, the exercise will do us good."

As we approached the Nile, the air was rippled by fluttering bats swooping through invisible clouds of insects. What at first seemed silence was actually filled with the rhythmic trilling of crickets and cicadas — surprising, there in the middle of the city. A large, pale bird swept past us on powerful wings, passing so near that I clearly saw its heart-shaped face and bright brown eyes. "A barn owl," I said, amazed. "We have them in Ohio, too."

Standing on the Gazirah Bridge, we

paused to watch the majestic bird gliding out along the riverbank, head cocked, searching for rodents.

"How," I asked, "could you be sure that I would say what you wanted the 'toffs' to hear? What if I'd been what Miss Bell assumed I was? Some superannuated flapper, too featherbrained to vote."

"I knew your sister," Lawrence reminded me, resting his forearms on the stone balustrade. "She knew your politics. You were intelligent and argumentative, she said. You'd follow an idea and get lost in the journey. And when you forgot yourself and spoke your mind, it was . . . *wonderful,*" he whispered with Lillie's own dear emphasis. "She admired that in you."

I turned away, pretending to study the black water moving sluggishly beneath the bridge. With quiet kindness Lawrence asked, "Would you like to visit Jebail, Miss Shanklin? To see where Lillie and Douglas lived? I could arrange it. After the conference."

I cleared my throat and blinked into the darkness. "Yes. I would like that very much. That would be lovely. If it's no trouble."

We started again toward Gazirah. "So!" I said briskly. "Miss Bell wants to rule the Arabs, but sneakily. Colonel Wilson wants to rule right out in the open. Mr. Churchill wants to save money and rule on the cheap. What do you want, Colonel Lawrence?"

He took a deep breath and let it out, glancing at the moon riding low over the deep blue geometry of Cairo's cityscape. "A state for the Kurds," he said, "and one for the Armenians. Separate kingdoms for Basra and Baghdad. A national home for the Jews in Palestine. And biff the French out of Syria!" Embarrassed, he sniggered in recognition of the absurdity: big ambitions, little me.

"And what do the Arabs want for themselves?" I asked, since no one else seemed to have.

"Independence," Lawrence said. "A single caliphate: a single state encompassing all the tribes and all the territory that was unified under the Ottoman Empire."

"Well, then!"

"Miss Shanklin, there are at present nine men claiming to be caliph. None of them can unify Shi'a and Sunni Muslims, let alone hold the lands ruled by the Sultan."

"I — I'm sorry. Sunny Moslems?"

He corrected my pronunciation and explained that after Muhammad died, the question arose as to who would lead the Muslim community. The Shi'a believed that Muhammad had named as his successor his cousin Ali — who was also the husband of the Prophet's daughter Fatima. The Sunni denied that any such appointment had been made. They believed the Prophet desired that Muslims be guided by a caliph: a leader who arises from within the community and who lives according to the precepts and example of the Prophet.

There was more about tribes and emirs and sherifs, but it was late and my feet hurt. This has nothing to do with me, I decided, feeling very American and far removed from the fine points of impenetrable foreign customs. Before long, Lawrence saw that I was lost and waved it all off.

"Doesn't matter," he said. "France will never agree to Arab rule in the Middle East. They want Syria and the Lebanon for themselves, and they're bargaining hard to annex the Mosul oil fields. The India Office will fight me as well. So one must focus on the possible," he said decisively. "Tomorrow I hope to convince His Majesty's Government — in the person of Winston Churchill — that our Middle Eastern protectorates should not be our last brown colony. They should be the British Empire's first brown dominion."

We turned a corner. Karl was out in front of the Continental, lounging against a huge potted plant, smoking an evening pipe. Rosie noticed me at the same moment and gave a strangled little whine of joy. Karl let slip her leash. She sprinted down the quiet street. For the next two minutes, I was wholly occupied by her exuberant, wiggling greeting.

When at last I could return my attention to the two gentlemen, my broad smile faltered. From this distance, Karl seemed relaxed and amused; Lawrence was motionless as a snake. Their eyes were locked. Lawrence seemed absorbed in some sort of mental calculation.

Rosie struggled to be let down, and I bent to put her on the pavement. "No harm done," I heard Lawrence say breezily. When I straightened and looked around, he was no longer at my side. Mouth open, I watched him disappear into the darkness.

"An Arab dominion," Karl said. "Like Canada. Or Australia . . . Self-governing for internal affairs, but without a separate foreign policy. It's an interesting solution. The Arabs might be less offended than by the notion of being 'protected' by the British, but Lawrence is correct: the India Office will oppose him."

We had already chatted for nearly half an

hour by then, sitting in the club chairs of the Continental's quiet lobby. To be honest, I wanted to go to bed, but Karl had been waiting all evening to hear about the dinner party and I couldn't disappoint him.

"Why would the India Office care?" I asked.

"Great Britain rules India, and India has the largest Islamic population on earth. An Arab dominion in the Middle East would give dangerous ideas to millions of Indian Muslims."

You're probably thinking, *Agnes, India is mostly Hindu, not Muslim!* But, remember, this was back in 1921, before India became independent and before Pakistan became a separate country.

India was the primary source of British prosperity, Karl continued. "It is governed by bureaucrats who live like royalty with palaces and servants," he said. "Who among them would give up wealth and privilege for such airy ideals as liberty and equality for brown people?" He puffed on his pipe for a time before shaking his head. "No. It cannot happen. And in any case, Lawrence is right about the French, as well. They'd never agree."

"What have the French got to do with anything?" I asked — a little irritably, I'm afraid. Lawrence's abrupt departure had thrown me off balance. Rosie was shedding all over my dress. My feet were killing me.

There was nobody else around, so I kicked off my shoes. To my astonishment, Karl lifted my feet to his lap and began to knead the soles. Like so much of what Karl did, the gesture seemed equal parts caring and casual, merely a small physical favor done for a friend. I shouldn't have allowed it, but it felt so good! Frankly, I'm amazed I remember anything he said after that, but the gist of it was that France had lost an entire generation of young men to the war. Their politicians had begun to debate polygamy as a way to repopulate the nation! Having paid such a price, the French believed themselves entitled to the greatest spoils.

"They want real colonies, not self-governing members of some international gentleman's club," Karl said. "If the British give self-rule to their protectorates, it will stir up trouble in French possessions. Just a few months ago, the French had to crush a revolt in Syria that was led by Lawrence's friend Feisal. They won't want to risk that again."

His voice trailed off and Karl sat silently, the glow of his pipe going dark while his mind was far away. His hands had stopped moving, too, just as I had sunk into the sensation of his fingers on my feet and had almost begun to imagine . . . well, more.

A few minutes passed. Feeling invisible and let down, I lifted my feet out of his lap and slid to the edge of the chair.

Karl noticed the movement and shook off his thoughts. "Agnes, forgive me," he said, his face showing genuine concern. He reached toward my hair and lifted it slightly away from my temple. My eye must have been wandering, because he said, "You are exhausted. I can see this. And perhaps bored. Yes! Don't deny it! Let me walk you to your room."

The concierge nodded as we passed and wished us a good night. It felt cozy and intimate: to be sleepy and on the way up to bed, to laugh quietly together at Rosie's comic leaping progress up the stairs.

Her short little legs reminded me of Lawrence's sensitivity about his height, and I asked Karl about that. "Yes," he told me, "Ned's brothers were quite tall, but he broke his leg as a boy and never grew after that. Here's irony: if he'd been drafted instead of volunteering for intelligence work, the Uncrowned King of Arabia would have been relegated to a 'bantam brigade' filled with malnourished little men from the countryside! For anyone to be underestimated seems a personal affront to him, I think. He is drawn to the underdog."

While I fit the key into my door, Karl asked, "Agnes, what are your plans for tomorrow?"

"Goodness! I've lost track of the days. Was today Saturday?" I asked, and he nodded. "Well, I have a tour of the city booked with Cook's on Sunday and —"

"Cancel it," he urged. "You must rest, I think. Take a day or two to recover from your travels. Sleep late. I'll make sure the boy comes round to walk Rosie for you."

I unlocked my door. Rosie trotted ahead and waited to be lifted, tossing her nose toward the pillows expectantly. Made shy by the hour, and the quiet, and the bed so near, I busied myself with her, embarrassed by my own thoughts.

"I have business in Alexandria," Karl told me, "but on Tuesday? Please, allow me to take you to the Old City. It is one of my favorite places in Cairo. I would like to share it with you."

"That would be lovely," I said for the second time that evening, "if it's no trouble."

Karl's face changed again, softening but

serious. Eyes on my own, he took my hand and brushed it with his lips. "Truly, Agnes, I believe this: to be enjoyed, life must be shared."

Even now, I can remember how I felt that night as I watched him turn and stride down the corridor. Can you see why I loved him so quickly? I hope you can. He was such a nice man.

As Karl promised, the little boy came for Rosie first thing in the morning. I stumbled back to bed. Half an hour later I roused myself briefly to welcome her return and paid the child what was obviously too much, given his reaction. Utter disbelief was rapidly replaced by a studied nonchalance that said, *Oh, yes, madams! This is most assuredly the common fee for walking foreign dogs and includes, naturally, a surcharge for being seen in public with a loathsome short-legged one.*

Dachshunds have a remarkable capacity for resting even under the most leisurely of regimes, but thirty minutes on foot was a twenty-mile hike for Rosie. Reunited, we went back to bed and slept again until it was nearly noon. Feeling refreshed at last, I dressed in no great hurry and ordered a light lunch from room service.

"Goodness gracious," I said to Rosie. "Two days ago, we were still on the boat! We've ridden the whirlwind to Oz, haven't we! But this will be a lazy day," I promised us both.

When we'd finished with our meal, I carried a lemonade out to the balcony and made use of the wicker chair and table there. Rosie settled in my lap. Contented and becalmed, I stroked her long back and watched the sky begin to whiten. The day was going to be hot, though it was still early spring and vast flocks of birds were traveling northward. Squadrons of pelicans, storks, and cranes soared high above a layer of violently flapping warblers and swallows. Nearby some sort of shrike gripped the hotel's telephone wires. Boldly patterned if dully colored, it opened its wings and swept downward, noiselessly capturing what might have been a grasshopper or perhaps a small lizard. Horrified and fascinated, I watched the bird impale its tiny victim on the thorn of a climbing rose that scrambled up the hotel wall, a few yards from where I sat.

Retreating to the printed page, I spent a quiet hour browsing through my guidebooks, reading with special attention about the Old City. I was wondering just how one pronounced the name of the Church of El-

Moallaqa when an immensely long black car rolled up to the entrance of the Continental.

The sun was at full strength. Yesterday's warmth was now real heat and made me think of July in Cleveland. Even so, I felt a shiver of dread when I saw Mr. Churchill's enormous bodyguard climb out. Of course, there were plenty of other guests in this hotel and no reason in the world to imagine that I was the subject of Detective Sergeant Thompson's errand, but a minute later the telephone in my room rang, just as I'd feared.

"Miss Shanklin?" a weary voice asked. "Thompson here. I'm in the lobby of your hotel, miss. Mr. Churchill requests the pleasure of your company this afternoon. We're going to see the pyramids."

Well, who wouldn't want to see the pyramids? But I had imagined I might go with Karl. "Sergeant Thompson, that's a very kind invitation, but I was counting on a quiet day today and —"

"Miss? I was assigned to this duty six weeks ago," Thompson told me in a tone that suggested his spirit had been broken. "I've learned this much about my boss already: it's no good arguing with him. Please, miss. I'd take it as a personal favor."

I let out a long breath. Rosie did love car rides. "I couldn't leave my little dog in the room. May I bring her along?"

"Miss Shanklin, you can bring the contents of Noah's ark, if that's what it takes," Thompson said, sounding infinitely relieved. "Honestly, miss, thank you. Once he's made up his mind . . . you have no idea."

Well, I didn't then, but I would soon obtain one.

Sergeant Thompson was waiting for me at the far end of the lobby. With the stiff and stoic look of a man who was duty-bound to follow foolish orders, he escorted me outside. "I was supposed to have the afternoon off as well," he told me while Rosie made use of a flower bed, "but he took it into his head to paint the pyramids. It's a disease with him, painting. I'm fed to the teeth with it. You couldn't pay me to walk into a museum now. I'm not a bloody porter, but he's got me carrying his damned boxes of paints — pardon my French, miss — and his easel, and his umbrella, and his chair."

Rosie was already panting. I shrugged off the linen jacket I'd tossed over my dress. The car was going to be hot, and I'd be among Europeans.

"We've been attacked by mobs twice since we docked in Alexandria," Thompson continued. "I'm supposed to be guarding his life, not carrying his bloody boxes." He leaned past me then, to open the door, but not before muttering, "If something happens, miss, I'm required to protect him. Get yourself back to the car and stay away from the windows."

Have you ever found yourself agreeing to something because you're simply too polite to object? If I'd had a moment to think things through, I might well have said, "On second thought, perhaps I'll take a rain check," but it was all such a surprise that I just ducked into the car and hoped for the best.

Inside, it was hot enough to bake bread and large enough to house an immigrant family. Sweating and jovial, Mr. Churchill sat in the center of the broad leather bench — away from the windows, I noted — and indicated that I was expected to perch on a folding jump seat opposite. "Miss Shanklin! And her dread dachshund, terror of the Semiramis!" he rumbled cheerfully as Thompson took his place up front. "Thank you for your companionship. Clementine and I operate on entirely different schedules. She's up before dawn and does a full day before I so much as stir. Then — just as I'm finishing the day's meetings and ready for some recreation — she's off to take a nap. It's a wonder we see each other at all! Still, we've had four children, so we're not doing badly, are we?"

Our driver, a young man in the blue uniform of a Royal Air Force corporal, coughed his surprise. I myself hardly knew what to say, but it didn't seem to matter.

"My mother is an American," Mr. Churchill went on, without taking a breath. "It was a treat to hear your accent last night! Such interesting inflection, and the vowel shifts are fascinating! I thought, Wouldn't it be grand to invite our American friend along this afternoon and hear some more of it?"

"Where in America is your mother from?" I asked.

"She was born in Brooklyn. Her father was a titan of Wall Street! Made fortunes and lost them just as quickly. Family moved to Paris when Jennie was four. She grew up in France."

That would seem to make his mother French rather than American, I had intended to remark, but Mr. Churchill evidently didn't need to hear very *much* of the American accent I had been invited to supply. Instead, he himself spoke at length of his mother. Jennie, as her son always called her, was one-quarter Iroquois, which made her fascinating, in his opinion. She was an enduringly glamorous, if rather capricious woman for whom the conventional was simply too boring to bear. As evidence, her son described her as an accomplished pianist whose recitals showcased a tattooed snake coiling around her left wrist.

She had married several times. Widowed by her sons' unlamented father, she was quickly divorced from a second husband twenty years her junior and nearly the same age as Winston himself. Despite that less than agreeable episode, she had recently married another young gentleman. This third husband no longer lived with her. Jennie's social life remained energetic in his absence.

All of this was conveyed to me in considerable detail and with much affectionate tolerance while the car crawled through the Cairo traffic. By the time we reached the outskirts of the city, I had stopped trying to follow the twisted skein of names and relationships and began to be glad that Mr. Churchill's conversation did not require a great deal from his companions.

I'm going to melt, I thought and blotted up a trickle of perspiration with my hankie. "How much farther is it to the pyramids,

Mr. Churchill?"

"Oh, but we're not going to the pyramids." My surprise must have been obvious, for Mr. Churchill immediately shouted, "Thompson! Did you tell Miss Shanklin we were going to the pyramids?"

Sergeant Thompson did not turn around. "I believe I said we'd *see* the pyramids, sir."

"Hah! Well! There you have it. Forgive the confusion, Miss Shanklin. An understandable misunderstanding, eh? I shall be very happy to include you in our excursion to Sakhara next Sunday. This afternoon, however, we'll remain at a distance so that I may obtain some useful perspective. Did Thompson complain about my paints? Hah! I expect he did. 'I'm not a bloody porter!' Yes? Do I have him?"

I smiled. Rosie panted.

"Do you paint, Miss Shanklin?"

"Why, yes," I said. "I've studied watercolors since college and —"

"Watercolors! Watercolors! I have no word of disparagement for watercolors, but with oils you can approach your problem from any direction!" Mr. Churchill cried. "You need not build downward from white paper to your darkest darks. Attack where you please! Start with the middle tones, then hurl in the extremes when the mood strikes.

Lay color upon color! Experiment! And if the attempt fails? One sweep of the palette knife will lift the blood and tears of a morning from the canvas, and you're ready to make a fresh start!"

Blood and tears? you ask. Yes, indeed. You can imagine my own surprise decades later when that casual remark would become his ringing wartime declaration, "I have nothing to offer but blood, toil, tears, and sweat." In 1921 he was merely remarking on the advantages of oils over watercolors, but all his life Churchill recognized a good turn of phrase when he created it and was not above reusing one when the occasion presented itself.

"Oils are delicious to squeeze out," he confided cozily. "Splash into the turpentine! Wallop into the blue! You really must try oils before you die, Shanklin. You will see the whole world differently! There are so many colors on a hillside, each one different in shadow and in sunlight. I had never noticed them before I turned forty and began to paint. I saw color merely in a general way, as one might look at a crowd, for example, and say, 'What a lot of people!' "

Beyond our windows were men, women, and children, donkeys, dogs, and poultry.

All small, all dusty, and all the color of khaki in the afternoon glare.

"I must say I like bright colors," he said, following my gaze. "I cannot pretend to feel impartial about colors. I rejoice with the brilliant ones and feel sorry for the poor browns. In heaven, I expect, vermilion and orange will be the dullest colors needed. When I get to heaven, I mean to fill a considerable portion of my first million years with painting. Armed with a paint box, one can never be bored!"

He went on like that, all exclamations and opinions, for the entire drive. When he shouted, "Perfect! Here! Stop here!" the order was lost in the general stream of enthusiasm, so I twisted on my jump seat to tap the driver's shoulder and convey the order to pull over.

Amid squealing brakes, outraged shouts, and honking horns, we cut across traffic to circle back toward the place Mr. Churchill had selected. The car jolted to a halt at the side of the road. Thompson immediately left the car to survey the site from a policeman's point of view. The driver came around to open our door. Rosie jumped out and darted to the end of her leash. I unfolded myself to follow.

Relentlessly eloquent, Churchill emerged

last, heaving himself toward the door, expounding all the while on Egypt's fierce and brilliant light. Still talking about the "triplex theme of Nile, desert, and sun," he strode off, carefree, with Thompson stalking along behind him, alert for trouble.

That left me alone with the driver, who touched his cap. "Davis, ma'am," he introduced himself. Then, eyes on Churchill, he sighed and said something that sounded like — and I am being approximate here — "Lord luv a duck, but 'e ain't arfa talker."

I took a few steps away from the heat of the car's scorching metal and lifted a hand to shade my eyes. You can easily imagine the vista for yourself. It is familiar from ten thousand illustrations: massive triangles on the horizon, the defaced and enigmatic Sphinx squatting in the foreground. The sun was lowering and the shadows were dramatic. I could see why Mr. Churchill had chosen this time of day for his expedition, but I envied his wife her nap.

What surprised me was the nearness of modern life to these ancient monuments. Motorcars and trucks clattered and roared ten feet behind me, blaring their horns at the camels and donkeys and pedestrians with which they shared the thoroughfare. Clusters of Europeans snapped photos of each other with their arms extended, pretending to hold the distant pyramids in the palms of their hands. Filthy barefoot boys begged or sold postcards or figs or soft drinks.

Tongue lolling, Rosie plumped abruptly down on her haunches. Taking pity on her, I opened my purse and motioned to a tiny child who staggered beneath a vestlike contraption that held a jug of tea and a few small crockery cups.

"Don't buy anything, miss," I heard Sergeant Thompson call. "We have lemonade and clean glasses."

His tone of voice made his meaning clear, for the child shot him a look of purest hatred, then aimed liquid eyes full of pleading at me.

Thompson trotted back to the car, glancing repeatedly over his shoulder at Churchill, who stood immobile, apparently absorbed in artistic rapture. The sergeant gave Davis orders to "haul out those damned boxes — pardon my French, miss." This Davis did, muttering in the same Gallic dialect. "I'll find something for the dog. Just give me a moment, miss," Thompson pleaded, gathering the rest of the equipment. With that, he and Davis scuffed profanely through sand and scrubby weeds toward Mr. Churchill, who awaited delivery without moving a muscle.

Rosie looked close to prostration. After tapping my lips for silence, I motioned to the tea boy and held up a coin. In an instant, I was surrounded by a half-pint mob of children waving their pitiable wares and crying, *"Baksheesh! Baksheesh!"*

Dropping the easel and a box of paints, Thompson sprinted back to run the children off. "Buggy little beggars," he snarled. "I told you, miss! Don't buy from them! If you give them anything at all, they're all over you."

"Well, I'm sorry, but Rosie's thirsty! Look at her! And I hardly think lemonade is something dogs should —"

"There's milk for the tea," Thompson said, rummaging through a picnic basket in the trunk of the car. With a tense courtesy that said, *Please, don't make my job any harder than it is,* he handed over a thermos. I opened it and poured a drink into the cap for Rosie, refusing to feel guilty.

Ten yards away, Davis was setting up a large umbrella. With his easel erected, Mr. Churchill had begun to work, and this was inevitably a matter of professional concern to his bodyguard, for any public painter will naturally attract a crowd. There is something magical about the process of turning blank canvas and blobs of color into something recognizable and pleasing. Presently, a group of blue-jacketed British airmen came along, off duty and nonchalant. When they stopped to watch, Sergeant Thompson relaxed slightly and returned to my side. "That lot can handle trouble if it's offered. Mind if I smoke, miss?"

"No, but I mind if I'm lied to," I said. "*See* the pyramids, indeed."

"There they are," Thompson replied, all innocence. He lit a cigarette, pulled in, and coughed. "I used to smoke a pipe, but —" He jerked his chin in the direction of his charge and mimicked Churchill's stuffy sonorities. " 'Put that beastly thing out! If you must smoke, smoke a cigarette, and make it a Turkish one.' Pretty rich, coming from him, with those endless foul cigars."

Sitting with his back to the gawking airmen, Mr. Churchill dabbed at the canvas with a paintbrush in one hand and a stogie in the other. Smoke curled upward and began to pool beneath the green sunshade that rendered his own color bilious.

"Looks like an upholstered toad," Thompson observed with deadpan venom, "slowly incinerating itself."

The assembled airmen were no more

respectful, delivering artistic appraisals in stage whispers that we could hear from where we stood. It wasn't until one of them suggested that the gentleman might be better employed painting the outside of a blimp hangar that Mr. Churchill turned to look at him.

"Gawd! It's Winston," the young man cried.

Appalled by the discovery that they'd been "razzing" such an important personage, the airmen backed away. Churchill grinned and motioned them nearer, happily criticizing his own work, detailing what he thought was still missing, and set about trying to put it in.

For all the artistic paraphernalia Mr. Churchill had for himself, there was nowhere for us to sit, apart from the car, which would have roasted Rosie alive. Years of teaching had made me tolerant of standing, but for heat and flies, summer in Ohio couldn't compete with a spring day in Egypt.

"How long do these painting sessions last?" I asked Thompson. He just rolled his eyes.

Churchill shouted another stream of peremptory orders, this time for Thompson and Davis to unpack the picnic hamper and share its delicacies out among the airmen. While the boys ate sandwiches and slurped tea, the great man painted and chatted about his plans to put additional air force installations in Egypt. If the Sudan and Mesopotamia could be policed from the air by flyboys like themselves, it would represent a great savings to the empire. "Trenchard agrees," Churchill told them. "What do *you* think?"

The airmen were voluble on that topic and a variety of others. Mr. Churchill seemed particularly interested in their canteen and barracks. When a sergeant mentioned that the married quarters assigned to noncommissioned officers were abominable, Churchill promised to look into the problem personally.

"They don't realize it, but they're giving him a report on their morale and readiness for combat," Thompson remarked, waving flies away from his face. "You're watching His Majesty's secretary of state for air at his best. Do anything for those boys, he would, but with his own staff?" Thompson shook his head. "Thoughtless, selfish, rude. That's his class: casual tyranny. Treating the help like menials."

"Including professionals who deserve better," I surmised, scratching as discreetly as I could at an insect bite on my ankle.

"We've had a few short, sharp discussions," Thompson admitted. "End of the day, I'll be walking out the door to go home to my supper — he'll announce we're off to inspect some military base on the coast, or we're going back to his London office. I've got kiddies, same as him, and a wife who expects to see her husband from time to time, same as his! I doubt he remembers that. Keeps insane hours and assumes I've nothing better to do than stand behind him and watch. But he's mad for his airmen. Do anything for them, and they can tell. Good balance for their real commander. Trenchard. Block of ice, that one. 'Boom' Trenchard, they call him. 'Bomb it!' That's his solution to everything. I've never known a man less able to reach people or be reached. Good match for the Sphinx, I'd say. Sorry, miss. I don't usually blather."

"I imagine you build up a conversational head of steam, listening to him all day." I pressed the hankie against my neck and thought of murder. "Why don't you ask for a transfer?"

"I tried, miss. This assignment was supposed to last two weeks. Marched into my chief's office at the end of it and said, 'Sir, I'd like very much to be relieved of this protection duty.' Chief just laughed. 'Well, it's yours whether you want it or not,' said he. 'Winston's asked for you to be with him permanently.' It's this or quit the Yard."

"And you have a family to feed."

"I help my brothers and sisters out, as well. I'm one of thirteen."

"Gracious! Is your family Catholic, Sergeant Thompson?"

"Methodist." He shrugged as if to say, *No excuses.*

"Your mother must have had . . . great stamina."

"I worked it out once. She was preggers for one hundred and seventeen months." The sheer scale of the feat lingered while he tossed the cigarette butt into the sand and lit another. "I've seen my Kate go through it four times." He blew smoke high into the air and vowed, "No more for us!"

His own story was a familiar one. Like many of my students, he'd had no difficulty learning whatever he was taught, but he'd worked from the age of nine, helping to provide a bare living for his family. Mornings, he told me, he'd run three miles from home to a draper's, where he took down two dozen big wooden shutters and carried them to a storage cellar. He'd clean the windows, polish the brass, and then run to school. He'd return at lunchtime to deliver parcels for an hour, and return again late in the evening to haul the shutters out and replace them for the night.

"Heavy work, even for a big, strong boy," I said. "How did you keep your eyes open in class?"

"I didn't, often enough. And I was caned for it. Justice in this matter was not served, from my point of view. You cane your students, miss?"

If I had, I wouldn't have admitted it to a giant with a long memory. "No," I said honestly, "but my classroom was notoriously undisciplined. Cost me more than one reprimand from the principal."

"Good job you didn't," Thompson said. "Caning eats at a boy." He dug out another thermos and two small glasses. "Have some lemonade to drink, miss. This heat."

I hesitated initially to drink all that he urged on me that afternoon, but the bone-dry air pulled moisture from me so quickly that I never felt the need to relieve myself. My skin, on the other hand, gradually took on the color of sunset, despite my best efforts to stay in Thompson's considerable shadow. "So how did you get into police work?" I asked, to pass the time and because I really was interested.

"Suffragettes," he said.

By 1913, British suffragettes had moved on from merely disrupting political meetings with acts of public disorder to staging full-scale riots and burning down churches. The shift in tactics horrified women like Clementine Churchill, who was a suffragist. I imagine everyone's forgotten the difference between suffragists and suffragettes after all these years, but believe me, it was significant. Anyone who favored votes for women was a suffragist, whether male or female. Suffragettes were women only, radicals determined to wrest their rights from the patriarchy by any means necessary, including the occasional plot to push a government official or two under the odd locomotive.

In response to their campaign of violence, Scotland Yard was ordered to expand the Special Branch. Thompson was working in a factory that made shirts and collars at the time. "Wasn't enough money to marry Kate on, though. Neighbor of hers said, 'Big strong lad like you! You could join the police force.' Took the written exam. Week later, I'm a detective, loitering in Kingsway, tailing suffragettes to their meetings. Arrested Emmeline Pankhurst once. Never knew a woman to speak so!"

"French?" I guessed.

He chuckled grimly. "But they weren't all like her," he said. "One lass — pretty little thing — she knew I was tailing her. When it started to rain, she waited for me, and we shared her umbrella the rest of the way."

For the next hour, Thompson told story after story of the undercover work he'd done. Wartime London was a hotbed of anarchists, Irish rebels, and German spies, all of whom "had a go" at Mr. Churchill, who seemed to invite both hatred and attack.

"I never thought I'd be working for him," Thompson said. He poured each of us another glass of lemonade, and when I had accepted mine, he asked out of the blue, "How long have you known Karl Weilbacher, miss?"

"We just met," I said, surprised. "He had a dachshund just like Rosie when he was young. When I checked into the Continental, he —"

"Weilbacher's not interested in you," Thompson said bluntly. I must have looked stunned and confused. Thompson cleared his throat. "He's the kind who is more likely to be interested in Colonel Lawrence, miss."

To cover my surprise, I poured some more milk for Rosie, hoping it hadn't gone bad in the heat. *I knew it all along,* I could hear Mumma say. *That German's just using you to get near important people.*

That's not fair! Mildred cried. *Colonel Lawrence is a celebrity. Everyone's interested in him.*

"Everyone's interested in Colonel Lawrence," I said, straightening. "He's a celebrity!"

"Did Weilbacher tell you about Carchemish, miss?"

"Yes, as a matter of fact, he did," I said. "Karl is German," I admitted freely. "I understand that he was your enemy. Well, the war is over." And America never should have been involved with it anyway, I thought. Karl isn't my enemy!

"Funny, though, wouldn't you say, miss? A German agent who knew Lawrence before the war suddenly shows up now?" Thompson's gaze was level. I looked toward the Sphinx, feigning indifference, but Thompson went on: "It may be a question of blackmail, miss. Breach of security."

"Well! I'm sure I wouldn't know anything about that!"

Thompson waited.

"Being suspicious is your job," I pointed out. *And it's none of his business,* Mildred whispered. "And in any case," I said huffily, "my friendships are none of your business, Sergeant."

"Just be careful," Thompson said with such mildness that I was disarmed. "My job, miss. I don't like to see people hurt."

"Well, put your mind at rest. Herr Weilbacher has been a perfect gentleman."

"I'm sure, miss."

"Is that why I was invited to come along today? So you could quiz me about my social life?"

Thompson's eyes were on his boss, who was shouting again. "No, miss," said the sergeant with a sigh. "You were invited because that man cannot stand to be without an audience for more than ten minutes, and he knows I've stopped listening. You'll excuse me? Duty bellows."

Off he went, leaving me alone with my thoughts and my discomfort. Without Thompson's conversation, there was nothing to distract me from the accumulating facts: the sun felt like an open flame against my face; my feet ached; the biting insects of the Nile Valley were many and various. Rosie began to scratch as well. Worried about fleas, and scorpions, I toppled decisively into a foul mood.

"Rosie," I said, "what on earth are we doing out here?"

Glaring across the scrubby sand, I rehearsed what I would say: Mr. Churchill, I am neither a paid member of your staff nor an adoring wife hanging on your every word. I am not a colonial subject, and I am not a British airman on duty, and I am not charmed by you, your slutty mother, or your theories on painting. I prefer watercolors, which require subtle skill, and I have had just about enough of standing out here in the broiling sun while you talk yourself blue, thanks all the same!

"Mr. Churchill!" I called loudly. "I — I'm afraid I may miss a dinner engagement. Will we be leaving soon?"

There was no response and I grew angrier by the moment at him, at the bugs, and at my own cravenly courteous white lie. Just as I was imagining the satisfaction of gaining his attention by dumping half a thermos of heat-curdled milk on his head, His Majesty's secretary for the colonies and air stood to announce that the light no longer served his artistic purposes.

The airmen moved off, laughing and keyed up by their brush with fame. Paint boxes, easel, umbrella, canvas chair, and picnic hamper were folded, furled, packed, lugged, and stowed. Davis paused in his duties long enough to ask, "You right, then, miss? You look a bit off, like."

"I'm not used to the sun," I told him. "It was the dead of winter when I left Cleveland."

One by one, we climbed into the furnace heat of the long black car. Quiet for a change, Mr. Churchill pulled a carved wooden secretary box to his lap, opened it, uncapped a fountain pen, and began to make notes, careful not to perspire into his ink. Thompson slammed his door shut. Davis put the car in gear and we lurched out onto the highway.

Dizzy and slightly nauseated, I rolled down the nearest window and held Rosie up so that her ears could fly in whatever breeze our progress might generate. Sergeant Thompson looked over his shoulder and thought to tell me to raise the glass. He reconsidered when he saw my face and the threat that was easily read on it: *If my dog dies of heatstroke, you will not be defending your boss from* Arab *assassins, buster!*

Mr. Churchill observed this silent exchange and chuckled, but he was wise enough to refrain from comment. For twenty minutes there was no sound but the whine of the tires, the noise of the evening traffic, and the scratching of a pen nib on rag paper.

By the time we reentered the city, the sun had set and it was noticeably cooler. Rosie's misery lessened and my arms were tired. I decided she'd do fine on the floor and leaned over to set her down. That was the only reason the first rock missed my head.

Churchill lurched to his left, quickly rolling up the window. More rocks thumped and banged against the car. An instant later, the mob was on us physically, beating on the tonneau with sticks, shouting the now familiar chant: *"À bas Shershill! À bas Shershill!"*

"Stay down!" Thompson yelled over his shoulder.

I heard a whine of fear; I honestly cannot tell you if it was Rosie or I who produced it. Cowering on the floor, I curled myself around her as much for comfort as to protect her from the stones and shards of glass that came crashing down around us.

"Get out on your side!" I heard Thompson command, but I was too terrified to move and, in any case, he meant Davis. The light brightened briefly as both front doors flew open, then slammed shut. Roaring, Thompson plunged into the mob, punching any face that came within reach. Davis had a big iron wrench in his hands and brought it down repeatedly. Howls joined the screams and chanting.

Churchill, pink and cheerful, had capped his pen and remained upright in the center of the backseat, watching the mayhem like a spectator at a prizefight. "Seems Lawrence was right," he observed. "They respect hand-to-hand combat, he said, but don't pull a pistol on them."

A rock bounced off the seat, onto the floor. I strangled a scream. Churchill gazed down at me benignly.

"Dachshunds have extraordinarily expressive eyes," he remarked. "It's the whites around the iris, I think. Most dogs have no sclera, but dachshunds are possessed of an almost human eye. This is the great appeal of the breed — Thompson! Behind you!"

I looked up. Just beyond the window, I saw a wooden club lifted overhead. Warned, Thompson ducked, and I lost sight of him after his shoulder drove his fist into the belly of the man who'd meant to brain him.

"So, Miss Shanklin!" Churchill exclaimed. "Whom did you vote for?" He might have been speaking Chinese for all the sense this question made to me. "In the presidential election," he prompted. "Were you taken in by the attractive Mr. Harding, as our Miss Bell suspected?"

A brick shattered the windshield. "Debs!"

I screamed. "I voted for Eugene Debs!"

"Debs! Really, Shanklin, you surprise me. I took you for a sensible woman. You should have voted for Cox! He was a better man than Harding in every way, and he stood a chance of winning. You wasted your ballot on Debs."

"I did no such thing!"

"Yes, you did. It was a foolish choice. A foolish *woman's* choice!"

"I am a woman, sir, but not a fool! My choice was just as valid as the next man's!" I cried, flinching at the dent a truncheon made in the side of the car. "Eugene Debs spoke truth to power!"

"He's no better than this rabble. He is a radical and a troublemaker who deserved prison."

"He had every right to speak out against the war and the lies that got us into it. He is a martyr for the Constitution!"

"Hah! He is a Communist and a subversive."

"He is no such thing! He was for racial equality and workers' rights. He believed that all men are created equal — even if some of them are women! He believed everyone should have a voice and a vote, even Negroes!"

"Even Arabs like these?"

"Especially Arabs like these! It's no wonder they're angry! If powerful people won't even ask what you want — it's as if you don't matter a bit. And that's not fair, because we all matter the same amount!" I insisted, cringing away from the shrieking, gesticulating men I was defending. "President Wilson was right about that! All nations matter the same amount, even if they aren't rich and powerful like Great Britain!"

"Piffle."

"Don't you 'piffle' me!" I said, infuriated. "You ask British airmen what they think, but you don't ask Egyptians. That's why they hate you. It's — it's like — like oatmeal!" I cried, my voice breaking on the word when a stone thudded onto the back window and came to rest in a spider's web of crazing. "Oatmeal is a perfectly fine breakfast, but some people just don't like it. It's only good manners to ask! 'Would you like some oatmeal?' What's so hard about that? Maybe they'll say, 'Yes, please.' Maybe they'll say, 'No, thank you. I'd really rather have eggs.' Or maybe they just want coffee! Well, then — that's their choice! These men are throwing rocks because you think everybody wants to be like you and — and eat oatmeal because — because that's what you want —"

Churchill was grinning. I looked around and slowly became aware of shrilling police whistles, clomping boots, and a sudden relative quiet. Just like that, the riot was over, and I realized that I had been making an utterly incoherent argument about political rights and breakfast food at the very top of my lungs for some time now.

Assured that Churchill was unharmed, Thompson and Davis conferred with the Egyptian police. Mr. Churchill helped me back up onto the jump seat and leaned over to remove a shard of glass from my shoulder, as though he had noticed a bit of lint there. "How is your dog?" he asked.

Rosie was practically catatonic: trembling and panting, eyes half out of her skull. And those were not the only signs of her distress.

"Oh, my goodness. Oh, I — I'm sorry," I stammered. "She never — She's always — Oh, Rosie, you've disgraced yourself! I'm so sorry, Mr. Churchill."

"Please! Call me Winston." He pulled a monogrammed handkerchief from his pocket and wrapped up the offending material with a flourish. "Quite a common reaction to combat," he confided, and tossed the linen packet into the street.

Up front, Davis and Thompson cheerfully compared contusions, swapping extravagant stories of earlier brawls they'd enjoyed. As we continued our drive, Winston sat back, thoughtful and removed. I murmured soothingly to Rosie, who buried her head in my lap and shook.

When we arrived at the Semiramis, the car's battered condition quickly drew a British crowd. Performer that he was, Churchill regaled the assembly with his version of what had happened, making it all seem like a grand day out. Drawn by the excitement, Lawrence appeared at the hotel door. In three quick steps, he was at my side. "Are you hurt?" he asked, his voice low and controlled. "Do you need a doctor?"

"A doctor! Hah! She needs a soapbox! The woman could run for Parliament!" Churchill cried. "Thompson was punching faces and young Davis here was breaking heads with a wrench. And there sat Shanklin: a pillar of moral strength, lecturing me on constitutional law and Arab suffrage!"

"That's not how it was," I told Lawrence shakily.

"Battles are always better in the telling," he said with a wry smile that did not change his eyes. "Do you want to come inside, or would you like to go straight on to your hotel?"

"Back to the hotel, thanks —"

"Nonsense!" Churchill shouted. "She's been eaten alive by savage Egyptian mosquitoes. No argument, Shanklin! Quinine water is your only hope. Someone get this woman a gin-tonic!"

"It's not a bad idea," said Lawrence. "You're very pale."

"You should thank her, Lawrence," Churchill cried. "I've decided your friend Feisal can have a kingdom after all. Gertrude! Wilson! Our Miss Shanklin has given me the solution to the election problem in Mesopotamia. Take everything but oatmeal off the menu! They'll choose what we want them to have."

For the next few hours, Winston kept my drink topped up during the general merriment he made of our adventure. I was briefly aware that he was eliminating the emptying glass that might have warned me of overindulgence; very soon, it didn't seem to matter. I rather liked the taste of the gin and tonic, and began to feel quite gay. The terror of the riot was swept aside by conviviality, and everyone was being so nice to me! For the first time in my life I began to understand why people enjoy drinking. Barriers are dissolved. Conversation is easy and unexamined. Nothing you say seems stupid, and everything seems amusing. No wonder gin parties were all the rage back home!

I had a vague impression that Lawrence was keeping an eye on me. While I do not remember getting into the taxi with him, I do recall his tolerant chivalry when I warned him that I was probably going to be sick. The colonel snapped an order to the driver, who pulled to the side of the road halfway over the Gazirah Bridge. Lawrence got out, opened my door, told Rosie to "Stay!" and steadied me on the way to the railing, where I abruptly contributed to the general fetidness of the Nile.

"Oh, good Lord," I gasped, hilarious and horrified as I took the handkerchief Lawrence offered. "I just puked in front of the Uncrowned King of Arabia."

"My dear Miss Shanklin," Lawrence said with a gallantry I have never forgotten, "I was an undergraduate at Oxford. Believe me: I've seen worse."

Vomiting was only one of several elements I left out of the tale I told Karl at breakfast on Tuesday morning.

It was just as well that he was away from Cairo until late Monday night, for I had spent the whole of that day nursing a sunburn and a gin headache that seemed hardly less incapacitating than the malaria that tonic water was meant to prevent. Perhaps to distract myself from my own misbehavior, I spent many of those wretched hours in contemplation of Thompson's suspicions about Karl Weilbacher. At the very least, I had to admit that Karl might be using me as a conduit for information about the conference Lawrence was attending.

And so, between bites of breakfast eggs and toast, I did my best to make amusing anecdotes of Sunday's adventures, telling Karl all about Winston painting the pyramids, and the riot, and the hilarious drinking that followed, but slyly withholding the slightest mention of Colonel Lawrence. This was, I'm ashamed to admit, a test like the ones that Mumma often set me when I was young.

Such tests were by their very nature covert. When I passed, there was no reward; when I failed, silence was my only clue. Mumma was never a particularly chatty person, so a heavier quiet might go unrecognized in the beginning. As the days went on, however, it would become clear even to me that I had failed her in some way. Belatedly, I would rack my memory. Was it something I'd said or neglected to say? Was there some forgotten chore or promise? Or something more, something worse? How long had I been oblivious to her dismay? Feeling myself the most wicked of daughters, I would creep into her office late at night and ask, "Mumma, please, what have I done?"

She would look at me with those sad eyes and that brave, unmoving face. "I shouldn't have to tell you, Agnes. If you loved me, you would know."

With no clue as to the nature of my offense, I could only redouble my efforts to please and hope to be restored to Mumma's good graces. Eventually she would signal the sufficiency of my penance with a gift of heirloom jewelry, perhaps, or a china figurine. "This belonged to your grandmother," she'd say. That closed the matter in her books, but for me? Always, always, the sword of silence hung over my head. It wasn't until after Mumma died that I began to wonder why she hadn't simply told me what she wanted. Why did I have to guess and grovel and work my heart out for some trifling object like a porcelain lady with a parasol? It made no sense to me.

Well! My years at Murray Hill School had taught me that a child can't correct something if he doesn't know it's wrong. That's like expecting him to learn to spell when his teacher won't mark his papers and keeps the dictionary hidden! And the Great Influenza had taught me how suddenly life could end, how quickly people could disappear from your life, how important it was to say what you mean and mean what you say. If ever I came to care for someone, I vowed, I would never waste our time together with guessing games. I would speak my mind aloud and clearly.

And yet there I was, setting Karl a secret test every bit as subtle and underhanded as Mumma's: *If you love me, you won't ask about Lawrence.*

At each turn of my story, I braced myself for Karl's comments, dreading the moment when he would bring up the colonel's name. And was Lawrence there that night? Karl might ask casually. What did he do then? To whom did he speak? And what did that person say?

Told of Churchill's tedious monologue on painting, Karl shook his head. "I said I was not inclined in his favor. Now I am against him. He sounds a self-satisfied bore."

And of the riot: "He put you at such risk! *Ach,* Agnes! That is unpardonable."

Then: "Now I think my opinion must change a bit. How clever he was to distract you from the danger!"

And: "No, I understand perfectly what you meant about the oatmeal. When Germany or Belgium or France seize colonies, the intent is to gain wealth and power. The British believe they are doing a selfless service when they impose their empire on others. They are always surprised when their generosity is unappreciated, but to be frankly conquered is less demeaning, I think."

Then: "Yes, yes, the British set great store by gin and tonic, but I am not so certain. Were you feverish yesterday? Are you entirely well this morning? I must say, your sunburn is quite charming, but if you feel ill, you must tell me at once. I know excellent doctors here in Cairo."

And finally: "After such an experience, perhaps Rosie will never again set foot in an automobile. I hired a taxicab for the day. What do you think, Rosie? Are you brave enough to go for another drive?"

At the sound of her name, Rosie pricked up her ears, and when the word "go" was uttered, she snapped to attention with a whine of anticipation.

So there! I told Sergeant Thompson in my imagination, for Karl had passed the test he didn't know he was taking: he had not once mentioned Colonel Lawrence.

And I? I was as serene and naive as a child pulling petals off a daisy. *He loves me, he loves me not . . . He loves me!*

The morning was cloudless, as all mornings in Cairo seemed to be. The weekend heat had moderated delightfully. Rosie and Karl and I were all in high spirits as our hired car conveyed us along an excellent highway that paralleled the eastern bank of the Nile.

Egypt dominated the known world once, Karl remarked, but in the millennia since, it had always been on the receiving end of empire. The land along the Nile had been overrun by foreigners with a regularity not unlike the river's yearly flood. "Nubians, Assyrians, Persians," Karl listed as we motored along. "Greeks and Romans. Arabs and Ottoman Turks. The French. The English. In the Old City, you can stand in one place and see evidence of five great imperial epochs."

Our driver pulled over a few yards from a stepped entrance to a walled enclave where tourists milled near a narrow gate. We made our way through groups of English ladies wearing sun veils and carrying linen parasols, and German hikers in full white shirts sporting short trousers that showed their knees. There was even an American woman wearing knickerbockers and flat shoes who was describing her house in Santa Barbara with a carrying voice that made me cringe. As usual, we foreigners were mobbed by entrepreneurial Egyptians shouting their offers.

"Buy wood of wonder-working tree!"

"I show you where Pharaoh daughter, she find Moses!"

"I show where Holy Virgin, she hide with Christ child!"

"Two thousand years temple for saints!"

The other tourists engaged a guide or

stuck close to a Cook's tour group and entered the city through the gate, but with a few words of Arabic, Karl let the Egyptians know we were not in need of their services. At worst, these "guides" would rob us, he told me quietly. At best, they would lead us to a smelly crypt or dirty cellar that might well be two thousand years old but of no particular significance.

Their stories were all nonsense as well, Karl said, and he treated the natal narratives of Moses and the Christ child with the same blithe disdain I felt for wonder-working trees. " 'I found a baby in the river!' 'A god visited me in the night!' " he said in a high voice, mocking such explanations for untimely births. "And then we have the opposite: when a wife drops an inconvenient child down a neighbor's well. 'Gypsies stole my darling!' 'Jews used his blood for matzoh!' " He shook his head. "What a lot of trouble such women cause!"

I shushed him, concerned that he might offend others. "Are you an *atheist,* then?" I whispered, and I admit that I felt a small thrill simply saying a word I had never dared to apply to anyone, let alone a friend.

Karl threw back his head and laughed, blithely unconcerned. "I am an *avis* even more *rara,*" he told me merrily. "I am a realist. And you know what they say, don't you? Birds of a feather . . . ?" He looked into my eyes until I blinked and looked away. He laughed again, though not at all in an unkind way. Rather, his devil-may-care amusement made me feel that he had seen the person I kept hidden even from myself, and that he approved of her and would be happy to see more of her if she dared reveal herself.

With Rosie bounding ahead at the end of her leash, he led me toward a hill just outside the walls, and if I was a bit winded when we achieved this minor pinnacle, the view itself wholly took my breath away. To the west, across the apex of the Nile Delta, a buff-colored floodplain stretched toward the Gizeh pyramids and beyond. Due north, we could make out the green European enclave on Gazirah. To the island's east lay Cairo: spiked by minarets, bejeweled by tiled domes, dotted with dovecotes, immense and golden in the morning sunlight.

"Memphis is the earliest of the five cities you can see from here," Karl said, pointing toward the pyramids. "It was founded perhaps four thousand years ago. The remains of the city itself are not much. Mostly they are covered by palm groves, but you can see there an enormous statue of Ramses II and the necropolis at Sakhara."

"Sakhara! That's — Winston invited me to go there next Sunday! Although given what happened the last time he invited me somewhere . . ."

"Ah, well, I think you must go, Agnes," Karl said reasonably. "I believe you shall be safe there among many tourists. Ordinary Egyptians are very eager that business not be interrupted by the unpleasantness of politics."

Near us, forming the western corners of the Old City walls, were two towers. Cylindrical and huge, they were constructed of bricks that were flatter and longer than any I had seen before. "They are Roman," Karl said, "part of a fortress established about two thousand years ago. The fort itself lies above an even older city founded by the lawgiver Nebuchadnezzar. Down there?" he said, indicating the tourist entrance in the Roman wall. "That was once a water gate. The Nile used to run right along here, but its course has shifted since the time of the Romans. Their fort was built by Trajan about the era of Jesus."

He turned westward and looked across the river toward an island. "That building on the point houses a Nilometer. Before the dams went in, the Nile would swamp this whole valley most years. When it retreated, the soil it left behind was very rich. Since ancient times, a Nilometer has measured the flood. If the river rose high, there was a festival of thanksgiving to the gods. If it was low, the priests would pray very hard because the crops might fail and there would be famine."

"The seven lean years," I said, remembering Joseph's interpretation of Pharaoh's dream. "That was when the Hebrews first came to Egypt."

"Yes, and four hundred years later, Moses said, 'Let my people go!' But there is an ancient Egyptian version of the Exodus as well," Karl told me. "In their version, the Hebrews were not merely numerous but also tempted good Egyptians to apostasy. The Yahweh cult was an affront to the gods who ruled the Nile. And so? The floods failed. Catastrophe! In the Egyptian story, Pharaoh told our leaders, 'Take your people and leave!' He tried many times to kick us out, but we Jews refused to go because Egypt is so lovely. Finally it was necessary to drive us away with chariots."

I laughed, amazed by the notion, and said, "I suppose there are two sides to every story."

"Or three, or four," he said.

And then it hit me. *Us. We Jews.*

"You yourself are . . . ?"

"Jewish. By heritage, yes," he said, his lively features now quite still. "Are you shocked, Agnes?"

I had gotten used to the idea that Karl was a German, but now there was this, and it *was* a surprise. When I said nothing, he tried to make a joke of it. "See?" he offered, removing his hat and bending over to show me the top of his head. "No horns."

You must understand — as Karl himself did — that in those days Christians believed it rude even to say the bare, bald word "Jew." In public we might say that someone was "of the Hebrew race," but never that someone was "a Jew." In private, I am ashamed to tell you, the word was an insult among Americans of my time. When Mumma got a supplier to drop his price, there would be a glint in her eye as she whispered to us at dinner, "I jewed him down by half." Or if someone got the better of her, she would admit, with grudging admiration, "He's as clever as a Jew." Even when there were good Christians on both sides of a transaction, to be a Jew was to be a sharp bargainer, avaricious and untrustworthy. And to socialize with Jews was simply unthinkable among people like . . .

Well, like me.

I'd never even met a Jewish person back in Ohio, as far as I was aware. To work in Little Italy among papist children was scandal enough, given that I was not there to evangelize among them. Yes, Cleveland had a growing community of Jewish immigrants from Poland and Russia, but they lived in the Glenville neighborhood, where no one nice would ever think of going.

Standing there, watching my mute struggle with convention, Karl's expression was one of suspended judgment, waiting for evidence of my true character. He busied himself with his pipe, packing it with tobacco, but something about the way he held his shoulders, the slight stiffness of his posture, made me aware that he was braced for the snub, prepared to be scorned. This man — so urbane and confident, so friendly and generous — this dear man could be wounded to the quick by what I said next.

Feeling another slender thread to my old life snap, I found my voice. "It makes no difference to me," I said with what I hoped would sound like insouciance.

He lit the pipe, puffing rhythmically, eyes on mine, and the silence felt like a rebuke. *Come now,* his expression seemed to say, *let us have nothing less than truth between us.*

"It did," I admitted then, my seriousness matching his own. "It used to, but . . . that was before I met you."

Another moment passed. He drew in smoke, held it for a moment, and finally released a long, somewhat uneven breath, waving his hand at the plume. "Like a dragon, yes? I think that is why I took the habit up, when I was young," he said. "I loved stories of knights and dragons, but I was always sympathetic to the poor misunderstood dragons."

"They had a side, too," I said, and Karl's approval was plain.

It was such a simple idea, really, but many things seemed to click into place for me. It was not scandalous or sinful or dangerous to understand a different point of view. I had been raised to believe that to do so was to risk error at least and damnation at worst. Knowing Karl taught me that it was simply good manners, and a more interesting way to live.

Karl, too, had recovered his aplomb. "Frankly," he confided as we retreated down the hill, "I think the world will be a better place when science has swept all religion into the dustbin of history. What is religion but a shared belief in things that cannot be known? When we substitute concurrence for fact, fantasy quickly replaces knowledge. Why? Because knowledge is much more trouble to acquire!"

And yet, he seemed fascinated by all religions that day as we strolled from church to synagogue to mosque. Our first destination within the ancient city walls was the nearly unpronounceable El-Moallaqa, whose name I had noticed in my guidebook just before Winston arrived to ruin my day. Karl directed me toward a shuffling group of tourists, and as we trudged up a long stone staircase toward a set of twin bell towers, he asked, "You see how this church uses the Roman tower for some of its wall? This is the earliest place of public Christian worship. Legend says that Saints Peter and Paul both preached here."

"You don't believe it?"

"I believe there is a festival each year on their feast day. Lots of visitors bringing lots of contributions." He pointed to a sign in many languages and several alphabets, displayed above a rack of postcards sold in support of a children's home. I expected him to tell me that there was no such place, but Karl dropped a coin into the box and urged me to take a souvenir. "The orphanage is real," he assured me, "and so are the needs of the children."

At the top of the stairs, Karl tapped the tobacco from his pipe, letting the ashes fall over the balustrade. With a wink and a finger on his lips, he picked Rosie up and kept her tucked close to his chest, hoping to sneak her in, and in the event, nobody seemed to care.

We passed through tall doors standing between chiseled pillars topped by lavishly tiled arches. Inside, three barrel vaults rested on graceful arches completely covered by gorgeous geometric mosaics and supported by columns with beautifully carved capitals. "Eleventh century," Karl said. "A good time for masons. The icons date to the late seventeen hundreds —"

"But . . . I thought you said this was the first Christian church?"

"I'm sorry. I was perhaps not clear. This is the first *public place* of Christian worship. The church itself has been demolished and rebuilt many times. There are always fires here in Cairo, and earthquakes."

"And conquerors," I said, pleased when he smiled.

"Most of the wall decorations are modern Coptic, but look at that pillar. You see, third on the right? That is probably ninth century."

"Karl, I've heard the word 'Coptic' before.

but I don't really know what it means."

"The Christians of Egypt are called Copts. The word is a corruption of the Greek for Egypt: *Ai-gup-tios.* The Arabs turned *gup* to *qop,* and the medieval Latinists made that *Coptus.* Typical of Egypt: layer upon layer," he said with a smile. "The Copts claim to be the true descendants of the ancient Egyptians, and they may be correct. Look there! Can you see how the Egyptian *ankh* has become a Christian cross? Paintings of the Virgin suckling Jesus are very like those of Isis nursing the baby Horus. Most Egyptians converted to Islam thirteen hundred years ago. Coptic Christians are very few today. They have not much influence."

Here and there, the blaring voices of tour guides competed for attention with Karl's quiet instruction. "Now that the war is over, it seems the entire population of Britain has booked a tour with Cook's," he remarked. Then he leaned closer to speak quietly into my ear. "This church retains some aspects of an ancient synagogue. You see the wooden dividers?" he asked. "They are to separate the men from the women, yet the overall design is that of a basilica. The main altar is behind those screens." He gestured toward exquisite panels of cypress and sycamore. "They are very old. The most elegant in

Egypt, I think."

We passed out of the murmuring darkness into the narrow street beyond, and Karl took me to visit two more churches. Of them, I recall only the passage from sun glare to near blindness in the shadowed stony chill inside, and the disorientation I felt until my eyes adjusted enough to discern exotic artwork in sputtering candlelight.

Far more interesting were the lively neighborhoods into which these churches were wedged. Tourists busily shopped for rugs, brasses, and ivories in little stores. Local people haggled over onions, leeks, and cabbages piled high on rickety carts. Most vivid of all were the gaggles of children who pointed and laughed at Rosie or offered to sell us freshly carved scarabs and spurious antiquities, which Karl warned me not to buy. My students at Murray Hill had seemed poor, but they were kings compared to those stunted, barefoot urchins. Many were disfigured by scabby eyes or withered legs or scarred hands crabbed by burns. Parents sometimes deliberately maimed a son to make him more appealing to tourists, Karl told me. A visibly defective child might be sold or rented out to Fagin-like professionals who sent groups of little beggars out to collect alms, which they turned over to their masters. And yet those children all smiled gloriously, teeth gleaming white in their small dark faces. They seemed to me angels, or imbeciles, or both, by turns.

Around noon, we stopped at an outdoor café tucked into a blind alley off a side street. It was patronized by Egyptians and old Cairo hands, Karl told me, and therefore of no interest to tourists or beggars. He placed our order in Arabic; it was received with enthusiasm by a thin young man, who salaamed and disappeared inside his tiny place of business.

A few doors down, a barber was sitting cross-legged on the cobblestones. In lieu of a shop with a striped pole, he had spread a scrap of cloth upon the pavement and laid out a set of archaic-looking tools next to a copper bowl filled with water. Customers appeared out of nowhere. Young and old, one by one, each shook the barber's hand and then squatted down facing him to await their turn.

Our coffees were delivered on a beautiful brass tray, in tiny glass cups set into filigreed metal holders. Sipping at the syrupy, sweet drink, I watched the barber at work, fascinated by this example of private life lived in the open air. Mustaches were trimmed to tidy points. The sides of curly mops were clipped close until heads resembled white-walled cottages beneath thatched roofs. When the barber finished, Karl told me, each customer would pay whatever he considered the job to be worth: one piastre or two — the equivalent of a penny or nickel at home.

"Karl, there was a beggar boy who caught my eye — he had a large square patch of hair shaved out, right on the top of his head. Did you notice him?" I asked while we waited for our meals. "Does that style mean something?"

"I suppose it is just for fancy," Karl said, "or maybe for a wedding."

When our plates of lamb and rice appeared, Karl spoke to the young waiter for a few minutes. Motioning at the top of his head, he evidently described the boy with the odd haircut. The waiter unleashed a broad and happy grin and spoke at length. To my surprise, Karl invited the waiter to sit with us.

His name was Ashour, the young man told me in remarkably good English, and the little boy's unusual haircut was indeed in honor of a recent wedding, which was Ashour's own. Ashour was twenty-three and admitted that was very late to marry. "For five years, I try to make wedding," he said earnestly, "but I have bad luck. Each year somebody die, and I cannot."

"If someone dies, there are no weddings for a *year?*" I asked.

"Yes, madams. Each year I try, and then at the new year, a baby die or an old gentlemans, and it cannot be."

Last month, the great day had at last arrived. Ashour's wedding was a grand affair. "There was big tent and everybody he come. From my village. From Cairo. From American Express Company! I wait tables, and I know many peoples, madams. Everybody he come and eat and drink. Tea, coffee, cocoa. Champagne and wine, and many other things. Meat and apricots and chicken, more than you ever saw." Eyes shut, he swayed in memory of the magnificence. "And music! For three days, with eight womans to dance. Eight! Me, I not drink, ever," he assured us piously, "but on third night, I am so tired, I am falling like drunk. So much food and music, so much dancing womans!" And he reeled in his chair, miming the effects of the endless meal, the exhausting beat of the music, the relentless dancing.

Ashour was quite a catch, I gathered. His job at the café had afforded him a house with three rooms, and he was able to provide his bride with a wedding dress from a store. Everyone was impressed when she sat down among the veiled women of two families. His bride's hair was dressed with gold bangles, and she brought with her a dowry of gold necklaces and gold chains for her waist. She was, Ashour assured us, "very pure."

Karl asked something in Arabic, and there was a brief, prideful answer and a short discussion before Ashour spoke again in English. "At first she cry," he admitted to me, as though I, too, had followed their exchange. "Every day she cry. But soon she will make me a son, and she all the time very happy. And she keeps my house clean. Very clean!"

Once again, he and Karl fell into Arabic. The conversation ended in Karl's polite demurral, handshakes, and a large tip left on the table.

"What was all that about?" I asked, walking away.

"He invited us to his village to be his guests, but I said no."

I tried to hide my disappointment. "It might have been interesting."

"I think it would be too sad. Ashour's wife is only twelve years old."

"Twelve!" I stopped dead and stared.

"But very pure," Karl said, echoing Ashour's guileless pride. "And she keeps his house very clean! That's why he wanted us to visit: so we could see what a good housekeeper he has."

"Good gracious! No wonder she cries every day!"

"Islamic theology is sublime, Agnes. For Jews, I think, it is more familiar than Christianity — a true monotheism, unlike the Trinity. But at the level of the family?" He shook his head, and we walked on. "Most religions seem to concentrate on making sure that men do not raise someone else's sons. And if little girls are married off at twelve —"

"There is less opportunity for the gods to visit in the night."

"And fewer inconvenient babies."

We walked on in silence, alone with our thoughts, until Karl stopped at the austere facade of a building he identified as the Ben Ezra synagogue. "After the Romans destroyed Jerusalem, many Jews fled to Alexandria. A few came here, where there has been a synagogue since the time of Jeremiah. There is a tomb inside. Legends say it is Jeremiah's, but I think not. He lived in Taphanes."

"Are we allowed to go in?"

"There's not much to see." Karl seemed oddly distracted, as though his mind were elsewhere even while he explained, "The most interesting thing about Ben Ezra was its *geniza* — a treasury of ancient writings. Egyptian Jews believe that any paper bearing the name of God must be preserved. When the building was being repaired in the last century, many documents were found. They are a detailed account of medieval life in Cairo, but in Hebrew, naturally. I learned some Hebrew when I was a boy, but I have forgotten it all." His shrug was not embarrassed or regretful but, rather, seemed a reflection of a deepening gloom. "In any case, the documents were removed to Cambridge University."

We walked on toward Amr Ibn al-Aas, the "ur-mosque," Karl called it. Like the suspended church and the Ben Ezra synagogue, it had been destroyed and rebuilt repeatedly, he told me, but the site had been dedicated to the worship of Allah since the year 641.

Rosie, of course, would not be allowed inside. So as not to give even a hint of disrespect, Karl stayed with her across the narrow street from the entrance. "That fountain is for ablutions," he said, indicating a small stone object that dribbled water into what appeared to be a wading pool. "You must remove your shoes at the entrance. Walk through the water to wash your feet. Give the old man a piastre when you are finished. Then you may go in."

It was a large, airy, open place, as unadorned and empty as the churches had been sumptuous. Like them, it was peopled almost entirely by tourists. In the center, however, stood three white-robed worshippers: two young men and an elderly one, who did not seem to notice that they were objects of foreign curiosity. Serene in their devotion, they dropped to their knees and bent forward until their foreheads touched the ground between hands held palms to the floor. Then they settled back on their heels, stood, and repeated the ritual.

"Muhammad was driven from Mecca for introducing that posture of prayer," Karl told me when I returned. "He was forty when he was seized by God and commanded to recite the Koran and to preach *islam:* submission to Allah. To bow, forehead to the ground? That was outrageous and disgusting to the merchant princes of Mecca. Eventually, Muhammad defeated them in battle, and today a devout Muslim can be identified by the callus his forehead bears."

As the day went on, Karl remained informative but distant from me, as though a pane of glass had come between us. I was increasingly distressed by the sense that I myself was the cause of his detachment. It was a familiar sensation: this feeling that I had unknowingly disappointed someone or failed to rise to an occasion when better behavior was expected of me. Anyone's silence or despondency seemed to carry me back to childhood, as if I were still trying to imagine what I'd done to sadden Mumma and frantic to make it up to her.

That morning, Karl had risked rejection by revealing his religious persuasion to an American provincial who might well have cut him dead for it. I thought of his expression — poised between defiant pride and the expectation of insult — and my heart melted. He had taken a chance on learning something dismaying about me, while earlier, I had secretly tested him. It wasn't fair, and I felt terrible about it now.

By the time Karl and I decided to return to our hired car, my mind was made up: I owed him a chance to be honest with me about his reason for cultivating my friendship. Besides, what did I care if Sergeant Thompson was right and Karl was a German spy? The war was over. I wasn't a British subject. Why shouldn't I help Karl learn about the conference?

As we strolled back to the hired car, I said tentatively, "I've been meaning to ask you something. Colonel Lawrence was kind enough to explain the difference between Shi'a and Sunni Muslims." I summed up what I could recall and asked if I had fully understood what Lawrence had told me.

"There's an ethnic difference as well," Karl said. "Persians are nearly all Shi'a, just as southern Europeans are mostly Catholics. There is a human element in Shi'a Islam that is also similar to Catholicism. There are Shi'a saints and shrines. The Prophet's cousin Ali is venerated, as the Virgin is venerated among Catholics. Shi'a clergy — the imams — are connected to Ali lineally, as a pope is said to have a lineal connection to Peter. Traditions and the judgments of the imams are given great weight, as Catholics give weight to papal interpretations and tradition. But Arabs are nearly all Sunni," Karl said, "as northern Europeans are usually Protestant. The Sunni despise Shi'a traditions as superstition and heresy. Such differences sometimes turn bloody."

"So that's why Colonel Lawrence said no modern caliph can unite Muslims?" I asked.

"It would be like English Protestants deciding to embrace Catholicism again when Bloody Mary took the throne of England."

"Or vice versa, when Elizabeth succeeded her," Karl agreed. "Worship Jesus the wrong way and you risk the rack or the stake."

"Drawing and quartering. Heads and hands chopped off." I shuddered. "Savage, when you think of it."

"And quite recent, in the sweep of history. Not England's most admirable era, although they obtained Shakespeare into the bargain. People forget that much of the Renaissance took place during constant religious warfare."

As for the political element, he largely agreed with Lord Cox and Colonel Wilson. "Islam is a bond that unites western and central Asia, but there is no sense of nationalism associated with it, except when outsiders force the issue."

I was a little taken aback by that, probably because I had disliked the "toffs" so much. "So Colonel Wilson's right and that's why Muslims can never rule themselves?" I asked. "Because they are a feudal people, and they require British rule to lead them out of the dark ages?"

"Fifty years ago, Germany was a collection of feudal duchies, and Italy not much better. By the logic of Colonel Wilson we must conclude, therefore, that Christians cannot rule themselves! Besides," he added dismissively, "who are the British to tutor the people of the Middle East? Civilization here was thousands of years old while the British were wearing bearskins and painting themselves blue."

"You sound like Lawrence, now." It was another opening for him, you see: an opportunity to steer the conversation back to things a German spy might want to know.

Karl merely shrugged. "Foreigners nearly always wish to simplify the Middle East, Agnes. They cannot tolerate to feel ignorant long enough to understand it."

"And how did you come to be so patient?" I asked, beginning to relax.

"My mother was a Persian Jew, from Teheran. My father was with the German embassy there for a few years — that's how they met. They raised their children in Stuttgart, but my mother took us to Persia every summer to visit her family. My grandfather once befriended a British scholar," he recalled. "This gentleman studied Persian folktales, which are engaging but naive, as was the gentleman himself. My grandmother said that Persian poetry would have provided him a more accurate picture of the East. It is elegant and sophisticated." His tone shifted from reverie to judgment. "Here is the trouble for a colonialist in the Middle East: he shall always be the natural victim of *ketman.*"

"Ketman?"

"The art of fakery," Karl said dryly, "whereby underlings preserve their dignity by fooling authority. In Persia, the practice is combined with a Shi'a concept: *takkiya* — religious permission to lie when dealing with infidels."

It was then that I asked about Lawrence's friend Feisal and recounted Winston's odd remark "We'll take everything but oatmeal off the menu! They'll choose what we want them to have."

For the first time since we met, Karl seemed truly surprised. "He can't be serious! Churchill said this, yes? Not Lawrence, surely! This is a terrible idea, Agnes!"

"But why? Is there something wrong with Feisal?"

"No, not at all! Feisal is, without question, a strikingly attractive leader," Karl said with much feeling. "He inspires great love, great devotion. He is intelligent, refined. Handsome, soulful. A beautiful man!"

My heart sank deeper with every adjective. This is embarrassing to admit, but I have tried to be completely honest with you. It was not only Karl's professional interest in Lawrence that worried me. No, there was something else that Sergeant Thompson's phrasing might have implied and that I was loath to believe. "He's the kind who is more likely to be interested in Colonel Lawrence," Thompson had said, and I'd begun to wonder if he was warning me off Karl for reasons that had nothing to do with politics.

Mumma was certain she understood what the detective was getting at. *I knew he was that kind all along,* she claimed. *Look at him! He wears a bracelet watch.*

They're called "wristwatches," Mildred pointed out. *All the soldiers wore them in the war. You can't pull a pocket watch out in the middle of a battle.*

And all that catty jabber about Miss Bell's dresses? "Wear the silk charmeuse and show her up!" Mumma mimicked. *A real man would never say such a thing. And a real man wouldn't care about you, Agnes. He's defective himself or he wouldn't give you the time of day from that sissy bracelet watch of his.*

I hated to think it, but even I had wondered. Karl was not unaware of male beauty, and he displayed a certain vivacity and expressiveness that I found both pleasing and unusual. I had never met anyone like him, you see, and I simply didn't know if he was different because he was foreign, or Jewish, or homosexual, or simply . . . Karl.

"Churchill is serious about this?" he pressed. "If the British fix an election that will make only Feisal available — *Mein Gott,* a Sunni Arab to rule Shi'a! I cannot believe Lawrence will agree to this. His love for Feisal is genuine, I think. When the French drove Feisal out of Damascus last year — no doubt, Lawrence felt very much that terrible humiliation. Naturally he wishes to redress such a wrong and to strike back at the French for it, but Feisal has never set foot in Mesopotamia! No, no, no! This is the wrong king for Mesopotamia. And the wrong kingdom for Feisal. Surely Lawrence will see that."

Karl fell into a brooding silence that persisted even after we reached our hired car. The driver woke up and rushed from side to side, opening the doors. Karl helped me and Rosie inside. There was some chat with the driver — Yes, we had a lovely time, and so on — but the trip back to the Continental was marked by the thickening of a despond that I'd made worse with my clumsy effort to engage Karl's interest in Lawrence.

When we arrived at the hotel entrance, the driver leapt out again and stood at attention by my door. Karl remained in the car, his face tense and still. I, too, stared blankly, unable to rouse myself enough to get out. Rosie was sitting upright in my lap, her little haunches balanced on my thighs, stubby forepaws resting against my chest. She often sensed my mood, and now she watched my face with such intensity and concern! Aware that I was distressing her, I laid my cheek against her own and stroked her long back over and over. "It's all right, little girl. Everything's fine," I murmured. "I'm all right."

"You have such beautiful hands," Karl said softly.

I looked at him, astonished. He smiled through his melancholy. "I'm sorry, Agnes. I have infected you with my bad mood. Ever since we spoke with Ashour, I have been unable to be cheerful. I can only think of his little bride, crying every day." Karl looked away, toward the north. "Twelve years old. I have a daughter just that age," he said. "So young, so young . . ."

If you had been there with us, you might have whispered in my ear, *Agnes, he has a daughter. He's married.*

I would have answered, He's here alone.

Perhaps he's a widower. Perhaps he's divorced. Perhaps he never married the mother of that girl.

In truth? I had not a single moment of concern for some unknown German woman who might be dead or discarded, after all.

I did not ask, "Oh, and does your family live here in Egypt? In Alexandria, perhaps?" I did not say, "And is your daughter an only child?" I did not once think, He is a husband with a family.

I thought, You see, Mumma? He is not that kind! It wasn't my fault that he was sad. And he said that I have beautiful hands.

For the next few days, Karl and I met frequently, sometimes for breakfast, sometimes for dinner. Whenever he had a few open hours, we strolled through parks and visited museums. We ate *falafel* in flat bread and *mahshi* — vegetables of all kinds stuffed with spiced rice and tomatoes and onions. We drank cup after cup of sweet, thick coffee and talked and talked while Cairo's kaleidoscopic populace passed before us. What I remember from that week is not so much what we did or saw but the warmth of Karl's presence and the sound of his pleasingly accented voice, rising and falling.

His world was so much wider than my

own, so mostly I just listened, smiling, when he tossed off international observations like "The English are the only people on earth who pay vast sums to private schools designed to cripple their children emotionally. In Germany, we do that at home. Not as efficient, but far less expensive."

Or, "In the past twenty years, Egypt has been ruled by a *khedive,* a sultan, a king, and a constitutional monarch whose parliament has just been spanked and dismissed. Throughout all these, the British have maintained order, but they will receive no thanks for it. And if the radicals succeed in gaining Egypt for the Egyptians? It will be chaos. The Egyptians couldn't organize a beer festival for themselves."

Or, "Agnes, the war had nothing to do with the archduke! It was planned for years. The Prussians told the kaiser, 'Germany will be at the peak of military power between 1913 and 1915, but France will catch up by 1916.' When a footrace is to begin, a shot is fired, yes? But the gunshot is not the reason for the race. The assassination of Archduke Ferdinand was not a reason for the war. It was merely the gunshot that began it."

Not everything was serious, for dear little Rosie was always with us, waddling along with a sailor's rolling swagger. In stores or cafés that catered to Europeans, she was welcome; elsewhere Karl would bluff his way in with her or wait outside while I explored on my own.

With so much walking, you might have thought that dog would be as slim as six o'clock, but Karl persisted in feeding her from the table, and she got tubbier by the day! She'd stretch up and go pitty-pat on his knee. He'd lean down to put his ear close to her delicate muzzle. "Can you hear, Agnes?" Karl would ask me, his eyes sparkling. "She is saying, *Baksheesh! Baksheesh!*" And then he'd slip her another bit of *pita* or a shred of lamb. Once I returned from a museum visit to find Rosie fast asleep in Karl's arms, flat on her back with her short legs twitching. "She is dreaming of ancient times," Karl whispered with soft solemnity, "when sausage dogs were tall." Then he added thoughtfully, "Foolish, isn't it? Such love we squander on these little dogs . . ." By the end of the week, it was hard to tell whom the hussy loved better, Karl or me!

Whether by accident or design, neither of us mentioned our families. I had no interest in learning what I did not wish to know, and Karl did not speak of his daughter again. Then, one afternoon, we were sitting in an outdoor café when a rare pair of pariah dogs slunk by. Rosie tried to pick a fight with them, barking from the high ground of my knees. When the strays had been driven off by the waiters, I said, "She has no idea how small she is! My theory is that dogs believe they are the size of whomever they bark at, which is why small dogs are so fierce and big dogs are often gentle."

"That could be true," Karl replied. "When I was a boy, we had also a big sheepdog. He disliked my Tessa very much but was frightened of her. He would gobble her food but he was a very sloppy eater, and she was able to survive on his jowl droppings. It was a terrible flaw in his plan to starve her."

We sipped our coffees, contented in the sunshine, and Karl turned thoughtful. "Dr. Freud observed that dogs love their friends and bite their enemies. In this, he said, they are quite unlike people, who always mix love and hate in their relationships. Tell me, Agnes, what were you like as a child?"

I tried, but my story turned into Mumma's: her widowhood, her courage, her labor and generosity. Karl listened with great attention, smiling when I confessed the pride I felt in being the "little mother" who cared for Ernest and Lillian. "Tell me about them," he urged.

"And what of your father?" he asked next.

"Have you noticed?" he asked a few minutes later. "No matter what I ask, the answer is always 'Mumma.' "

I laughed and put my face in my hands. "I know, I know! Mumma always told me, 'Agnes! Do *try* to keep to the point!' But one thing always leads me to another, I'm afraid." And off I went again, in my rattle-trap way.

Karl's face, ordinarily open, became quite unreadable until I got to the part where Mumma sold the factory so that we girls could go to college. To my surprise, he laughed, his eyes widening in disbelief. "Agnes, your mother did not sell the factory for you and your sister! She sold it because your brother refused to work for her."

"Oh, no, it wasn't that —"

"But, yes! Don't you see? Your brother knew he would be under her rule forever, so? He ran from her to the army. When her plans were opposed, she threw the factory away in anger."

"Karl, no! It wasn't like that at all —"

"And your sister left, just as your brother did! Do you think it is only chance that she moved so far from home?"

"But that was missionary work! Her husband was —"

"A man who could take her far from Mumma, and for an irreproachable reason," Karl said, rendering me speechless. "Your father did just the same. He worked hard because it was his duty, but it was also an honorable way to escape his wife. He could not bring himself to abandon his family. So? He chose to work himself to death."

"Well! That was hardly a choice," I said huffily. "Papa had debts, Karl. He had to make good —"

"It is remarkable what people choose to do, and then insist they had no choice. You had plans to leave as well, but your Mumma cried. Some tears and *paf!* You gave up your dreams."

I had no answer for him. I was stunned, astonished that he would turn on me like that.

"Your mother believed she was harmed when your brother left," Karl said, "but no! That was disappointment." He sat back in his chair and waved his pipe in the direction of an imaginary vista. "If your home has a beautiful view of a forest on someone else's land, you may enjoy the view, but you have no right to it. It does not belong to you. If one day the owner decides to cut down all his trees for lumber, you may be disappointed, but you are not harmed. It is his, not yours, to dispose of as he wishes. Your mother acted as though your lives were hers. When your plans differed from hers, she lost a view of the future that she imagined but had no right to." He leaned over the table, his eyes as merrily compassionate as his words were harsh. "Agnes, your mother was a tyrant."

"Karl!" I gasped. "You don't — How can — You're not being fair!"

He laid his pipe in the ashtray and reached across the table to take my hands in his. "Think!" he commanded with a curious kindly insistence. "Was there ever a time when your mother did not get exactly what she wanted?"

How often had I imagined that he would take my hands? But not like that, not after saying such awful things about Mumma — about my whole family!

"The only way to end her tyranny was to leave," Karl said, "but she cried, and you gave up. Your life is your own, Agnes. You are handsome and accomplished and brave. You must leave your mother behind or you will never become the woman you were meant to be."

I pulled away, and when we parted a little while later, I felt lost in a fog of anger. Back in my hotel room, I wept and paced, furious and alone except for Rosie. Karl had no right to say all that. He didn't know Mumma or Papa, or Ernest or Lillie. He didn't know me! He had no right to call poor Mumma a tyrant. She never asked for anything for herself. She was good and generous and hardworking. He could ask anyone in Cedar Glen. They'd all tell him that!

But I'll bet he's right, Mildred whispered. *Sooner or later, she always got what she wanted, didn't she? And she had kind of a mean streak.*

Mumma herself was strangely silent.

Any grade school teacher knows the demonstration. Lay a bar magnet on the table. Sprinkle iron filings evenly across the surface of ordinary white typing paper. Hold the paper taut between your fingers. Carefully move the paper above the magnet, then give it a slight shake to overcome friction's resistance.

When you set the particles in motion, the children gasp and clap. As if alive, the iron filings rearrange themselves, fanning out above the positive and negative poles at opposite ends of the magnet, curving inward to form concentric ovals around its shaft.

"Why did you decide to come to Cairo?" Karl had asked me on our first day together as we strolled, side by side, with Rosie in the vanguard. "It is an unusual choice for someone who has not been abroad before. Most Americans go to Paris or London. Or Rome."

I told him how Lillian had urged me to visit her in the Middle East, back before the war. She had even quoted Muhammad: " 'Do not tell me how educated you are,' the Prophet said. 'Tell me how far you have traveled.' "

The explanation seemed to satisfy Karl, but it was not the truth, not if I was honest with myself.

Why do we travel, really? If we are of a thoughtful nature, we may wish to improve our minds, to examine the manners and customs of others and compare them to our own. For these reasons, we study guidebooks and make lists of the churches, palaces, galleries, and museums we'll visit. We take photographs and write our impressions in diaries. We might even justify the expense of the trip by planning to share our knowledge with others upon our return.

But is it really an education that we yearn to acquire when we travel? Or — be honest, now — do we more sincerely desire souvenirs? What tourist returns with lighter bags than those he packed at home? We want something to display, a memento, a "conversation piece" that will silently inform a guest: *I have traveled. I have awakened under a fierce foreign sun.* We look for a painting, a sculpture, a vase that will whisper: *I have shopped in* souks *and bargained in bazaars, and I have this to show for it.*

In all practicality, of course, one could buy such objects at home. After all, there are importers, antique shops, and art galleries — even in Ohio. Why, then, do we undertake the expense and risk of travel? Why leave the comforts of home for flies and disease, heat and dust, crowds and the risk of theft? Because souvenirs remind even the traveler of his journey: *I was not always who and what I seem, sitting in this Ohio parlor. Here is a talisman of a magical time when nothing — not even I — was ordinary.*

If we are timid or rebellious or both, then travel — by itself and by ourselves — forces us to leave our old lives behind. Travel can overcome habitual resistance and set the soul in motion along magnetic lines of attraction. On foreign soil, desires — denied, policed, constrained at home — can be unbound. What hides beneath the skin-thin surface of the domesticated self is sensual, sexual, adult.

Why then, truly, had I come to Egypt? To flee everything that was conventional and predictable and respectable. I wanted to lock up my mother's house in Cedar Glen and walk away from my own dull mediocrity. I wanted to escape anyone and everything that had ever told me *No.*

As the hours passed, so did my anger with Karl. I understood at last what I'd experienced while planning this journey: the excitement and fear, the happiness and guilt. Surely those were the very emotions one might have felt when planning a tryst with a secret lover.

You are handsome and accomplished and brave, he'd said, taking my hands in his.

In those hours, far from home, beyond the scrutiny of those who knew me in Ohio, the very meaning of sin began to change. To leave the apple unpicked — that was sin. To choose loneliness if love — even illicit love — were offered, that seemed worse than sin.

That would make of my life a tragedy.

The next morning there was a knock at my door. Expecting Rosie's little boy, I ran my hands through my hair, pulled on my wrapper, picked Rosie up, and opened the door.

The room service man bid me, "Good morning, madam," and wheeled in a cart heavily laden with silver platters, pitchers, and bowls. Behind him in the hallway, Karl was holding flowers and newspapers. On his face was a sheepish look that asked, *Agnes, am I forgiven?*

Rosie danced and spun and barked at our feet. Karl tipped the waiter. Grinning crookedly at me, he traded me the flowers for Rosie's leash. "Walk you dog, madams? I gave the boy a day off. We'll be back in half an hour."

I brushed my teeth and bathed and combed my hair. A bit of makeup. A fresh dressing gown. Ready, and slightly breathless, I stepped out onto the balcony to watch the sun climb, listening to the hiss and clatter of palm fronds that rattled in the morning breeze.

I will do this, I thought. I am forty years old, and it is long past time. My life is my own.

At last, I saw Karl on his way back toward the hotel, with Rosie trotting merrily ahead of him. I stretched and waved. The motion caught his attention. He paused, shading his eyes with his hand. When he saw me, he went motionless.

It's difficult and rather pointless to deceive

yourself when you are dead, and I can admit it now: Karl was startled to see me waiting for him, still dressed only in a robe, but I chose to read his expression as mere surprise. There was a long pause before he shortened up on Rosie's leash and stepped to the edge of the sidewalk, glancing each way for traffic. Something he saw made him raise his face to the sky, eyes closed. Then he looked at me and shook his head, smiling ruefully. He and Rosie darted across the street and were lost to my sight as they passed beneath the hotel marquee.

Moments later, I saw what Karl had: Churchill's long black automobile with miniature Union Jacks affixed to its front fenders. The car rolled to a stop at the Continental. The young driver Davis got out. I heard Karl's heavy steps hurrying down the hallway. He and Rosie burst into the room just as the telephone rang.

"I completely forgot!" Karl whispered hoarsely. "It's Sunday! You must go —"

"Yes, of course," I was saying into the mouthpiece. "I'll be down in a few minutes." Stricken, I replaced the handset in its cradle.

"I'll take care of Rosie," Karl said.

"I should have made some excuse!" I cried, exasperated with myself. Perhaps if I had been in the habit of lying, it would have been different, but my mind just didn't work that way. I lifted my hands in despair. "Karl, what on earth does one wear for a camel ride to the pyramids?"

Galvanized, he threw open the double doors of the room's tall sandalwood wardrobe and considered the possibilities.

Without thinking, I blurted, "And I had been hoping you would undress me!"

Both of us froze, equally shocked.

Eyes wide, I clapped my hands over my mouth, but the absurdity of it all suddenly blossomed. I began to laugh. An instant later, so did Karl. For a few precious moments, we were helpless in each other's arms, wailing until we were weak.

"They're waiting," I gasped and waved a hand toward the wardrobe. "Pick something! I have no idea!"

Karl flipped through the clothing, pausing when he got to the sport suit Mildred had recommended in case I was invited to play golf or something. Wool flannel, in a smart navy blue, the jacket was fingertip length with braided trim around the cuffs. It looked vaguely equestrian, which seemed appropriate given that camels might be considered vaguely equine. "But it comes with a skirt," I said.

"Don't worry," Karl said. "Tourist saddles

allow ladies to sit with modesty."

I snatched a cream-colored blouse off a hanger and dashed into the bathroom to change. I emerged still buckling a wide belt over the blouse. Karl held out the jacket. I spun into it and grabbed a tan cloth hat with a turned-back brim. Kid gloves in hand, I presented myself for inspection.

"It needs one thing more," Karl said. He selected a striped scarf and, coming close, knotted it cleverly around my neck. He stepped back, looked me up and down, and pronounced the ensemble "very smart."

"Now go," he said. "You can tell me all about it when you get back."

Then he kissed me and sent me on my way.

It would have been more thrilling, of course, had Karl kissed me on the mouth, but no matter. I flew down the staircase aware of the lingering sensations: his hands on my shoulders, his lips against my forehead. Now that my mind was made up, delay and anticipation could only make romance more delicious. I was off on an adventure, and Karl would be waiting for me when I got back.

"Morning, miss," said young Davis, holding the door for me. When he declared,

"Don't you look nice!" I accepted the compliment without argument.

The Churchills and Detective Sergeant Thompson had gone ahead earlier with the Coxes, Davis said, and so I had the grand car to myself. The weather had turned fresh and cool overnight. At home I'd have called it Canadian air, and it made my wool worsted suit seem as perfect as the morning. When we arrived at the staging ground, it became apparent that there was no British consensus about what to wear for this event. Miss Bell was off smoking by herself, dressed for the Arctic in high-topped button shoes and an ankle-length woolen coat with a huge fur collar that hid her neck. Her dark felt hat was squashed-looking and small, quite unlike the wide straw sun hat Lady Cox was wearing.

"There is something infuriating about a man's wardrobe," Lady Cox remarked, fussing with the woolen cloak she'd pulled over a long day dress. "The only question he ever has to ask is, 'Dinner jacket or tailcoat?' "

The men, however, were as variously attired as the ladies. Several were in uniform, but headgear ranged from topee to field cap. Colonel Lawrence, Sergeant Thompson, and Lord Cox wore ordinary suits and neckties, their trilbies' small brims turned up all round. Only the burly Winston Churchill had a topcoat on, and its added bulk made him look more than ever like Mr. Toad of Toad Hall.

"I considered a bedsheet and a pillowcase," he rumbled, "but Lawrence told me it was not the done thing."

"You just didn't want to compete with me," his wife teased, Clementine herself being swathed top to bottom in a head scarf and white canvas driving duster as voluminous as Arab robes. "I should have consulted with you, Miss Shanklin. A golfing suit is such a good idea! I brought knickerbockers but —" She glanced toward Miss Bell and leaned over to whisper, "I was afraid to wear them."

The atmosphere was festive and may have been fueled by something other than tea. Already giddy, I shook my head and smiled a demurral at the dour and thin-faced native who presented a brass tray offering me one of the little cups.

A few yards away stood several large male pack camels. Laden with equipment boxes, wicker lunch baskets, and rolled carpets, the animals produced a constant bizarre gargling noise unlike anything I'd ever heard before. The smaller riding camels crouched nearby with ropes wrapped around their folded knees to prevent them getting to their feet. Dozing with long-lashed eyes half-closed, they seemed serenely indifferent to the bustle around them. Their only movement was to lower their heads now and then to rub their chins against the ground.

Seeing me, Sergeant Thompson trudged through the sand, looking profoundly doubtful about this mode of transportation. "Tried to talk him into driving to Sakhara," Thompson said, glowering at Winston, who'd gone off to speak with Lawrence. "He's like a child. 'Oh, goody! Camels!' They're picturesque from a distance, but when you get up close? Filthy, vile, stinking brutes."

"Attar of camel is unlikely to gain commercial acceptance," I agreed, but really? I was as thrilled as Winston by the prospect of riding one.

Each of us was led to a mount and informed of the animal's name. Mine was Dahabeah, an austere and self-contained individual whose six-foot-long neck was slung with colorful woven lavalieres that jingled with tiny silver bells. Two camel boys gripped her tasseled halter on either side and looked at me expectantly.

Dahabeah herself snaked her head out of reach when I tried to make friends by scratching behind her ears. One side of her split upper lip curled in distaste. *What do you take me for?* she seemed to ask. *Some sort of horse?* And then she spat.

A week — a day, an hour — earlier, I would have shrunk from her, convinced of my own inadequacy. Instead, I laughed, transformed by a kiss and a man who had pronounced me handsome, accomplished, and brave.

"Hold here, madams," the nearer boy instructed. "Yes, and sit, so! Very fine, madams! Very comfortable, yes?"

"Comfortable" was not the word that came to mind, but I smiled anyway and looked around to see how the others were doing. The ladies and most of the men sat sidesaddle. Winston, by contrast, had arranged himself astride, his thick legs gripping at a substantial hump while his feet, in street shoes and spats, dangled. This did not promise to be an effective tactic; Colonel Lawrence was resisting an anticipatory grin. He himself appeared to be sitting at home in an easy chair: legs crossed at the ankles, feet resting on his camel's left shoulder as though it were a hassock.

I settled myself the same way and tugged my skirt down to cover myself a bit better. "Hold tight, madams!" the bigger boy warned and slipped the tether from Dahabeah's knees.

Released, she lurched and rocked upright, back legs rising high before her forelegs straightened. All around me, women gave little shrieks that carried far in the still, cool air. Even a few of the men shouted their surprise. Miss Bell rolled her eyes at our amateur attempts to regain balance, but Lawrence laughed and traded amused commentary with a number of marvelously robed Arab dignitaries, who were evidently going to accompany us on horseback.

Lady Cox immediately demanded to be let down. "I am far too old and spoiled for this nonsense. I shall go by auto and meet you there."

Beside me, Sergeant Thompson looked as though he'd have joined her, had the humiliation of such a decision been less than mortal. He confined himself to muttering his own peculiar dialect of "French" while his camel jacked herself upright. The motion very nearly pitched Thompson onto the ground. It would have been quite a fall, Thompson himself being an exceedingly tall man perched at a great height on a camel much larger than my own.

"Nothing to grab but sky," he snarled, fear making him angry. "How the hell do you steer this thing?"

"Pull this, I think!" I held up a light cord that ran from the forward pommel to the camel's right nostril.

Thompson tugged on his, but the effect was not as hoped. Rather than circling clockwise, the animal swiveled her head around to look directly back at him with an expression so alarming, the policeman felt for his pistol by reflex.

In the midst of all this European incompetence, the Arab horsemen called out advice, which Lawrence translated, sometimes. "The camels know where they're going," he said. "Relax and give them their heads."

That was easier said than done, of course, but after a certain amount of circling and roaring, the lead animal finally plodded off toward the pyramids on padded feet the size of dinner plates. Our caravan soon strung out into a line, just as one sees in storybook illustrations. The pace was not torrid, which was just as well, for the gait of a camel is complex and disagreeable. Each advance of four linear feet entailed a set of jerks, twists, and contortions. Up and down, side to side — those are familiar to anyone who has ridden a horse. A camel adds forward and back to the dance.

All of us who were new to the experience

concentrated mightily on keeping our seats while trying to discover some predictable pattern to the herky-jerky rhythm. After a few minutes, I was confident enough to raise my eyes and joke to Sergeant Thompson, "I feel like a cooked noodle!"

Thompson made no reply, in English or in French, for his entire attention had shifted from his own plight to that of Mr. Churchill. I followed Thompson's horrified gaze some twenty yards ahead. There, with stately slowness, His Britannic Majesty's secretary for air and the colonies was, by degrees, tipping sideways off his mount. Topcoat billowing, round arms waving frantically, Winston clawed at the saddle with increasing desperation, searching for some purchase. At last he managed to get a grip, but not a reprieve. The saddle itself was only resting momentarily on the camel's flank, and with each of the camel's six-element strides it ticked . . . ever . . . downward.

When the inevitable moment of separation came, Winston looked resigned to it, almost. I wish I could say that we were kind when he thudded onto the ground, but alas! Even his adoring wife, Clementine, was convulsed, and every attempt to stifle our laughter made things worse.

"The animal must be an Egyptian nationalist," someone shouted.

"Offer her a caliphate!" someone else called out.

To Thompson's alarm, our Arab escorts wheeled their steeds around and raced toward Winston, who still lay glaring upward from the ground. "Christ!" Thompson cried. "They'll crush him, and on my watch!" But no — these were superbly skilled riders on beautifully trained Arabian horses. With a splendid spray of fine yellow sand, they pulled up just in time and leapt gallantly to the ground, shouting their distress.

"They plead with the great man," Lawrence translated, straight-faced, "that he will, by God, exchange mounts with one of them, and not hazard himself again by sailing on a ship of the desert!"

Growling, Winston rolled onto his hands and knees, stood himself up, brushed himself off, and looked around for his hat. "Tell them I started on a camel," he ordered Lawrence, "and I'll finish on a camel!" To the rest of us, he declared, "I'll have you know I ranked fourth in my class of cavalry candidates at Sandhurst."

"Yes, and I'm quite sure your animal was aware of that," Lawrence soothed as he slid lightly off his own mount and came to the side of Winston's. "When she realized she'd have the honor of carrying you" — Lawrence heaved the heavy saddle upward — "naturally, she puffed up with pride. Then she felt how badly you rode and decided there must have been some mistake." Lawrence bent at the knees, then rose to ram a shoulder into the camel's belly. The animal exhaled with an audible rush of stinking breath and he jerked the belly strap tight before continuing: "Since she was obviously being ridden by some very common person, she decided to unload you as speedily as possible. So she let out the air, the girth loosened, and off you came."

Slapping the animal's neck, Lawrence turned around. The schoolboy grin had been replaced by a workmanlike confidence. "It won't happen again."

The errant camel was once more brought to her knees, and Winston was helped to remount. At that point, the two great men exchanged a few private words, Churchill glowering and bullish, Lawrence quiet and reassuring. Whatever Lawrence told him, it seemed to make a difference. Churchill rode without incident afterward.

As for the rest of us? Well, even without an inglorious public plummet, we were soon humbled. You see, camel saddles have two high horns, front and rear. Their wooden frames beat rhythmically on bones, while their coarse woolen covers grind like pumice against any unprotected skin. My garters chafed and buttons prodded, and judging from the increasingly open squirming and shifting, all the other greenhorns were equally discomfited. Within twenty minutes conversation ceased as we passed from quiet dismay to open misery. In a fury of wretchedness, one or another of the men would kick and snarl at his beast, trying to rouse it to a trot, but these were tourist camels, disinclined to hurry. Their response was not an increase in speed but bared yellow teeth and a bitter, misanthropic commentary of their own.

I suspected that more than one of us envied Lady Cox's snap decision not to embark on this trek at all. How easy it is to begin a journey in ignorance and how quickly one can come to regret it, I thought. We had gone too far to turn back now, though the pyramids seemed no closer on the horizon. Indeed, our goal seemed to recede as time ground on, but there was nothing to do except stay the course.

To distract myself, I watched the two experienced riders in our party. Miss Bell was admirably stoic and skilled in the saddle, but Lawrence's boneless, unresisting grace was a marvel, and I found myself relaxing as I tried to mirror his supple motion. Dahabeah gradually drew even with his slowing mount. Without much thought, I called, "Colonel Lawrence! I'm surprised that you —"

At the sound of his name, he straightened, and I realized he'd been sleeping. He came to himself with startling quickness, but I could see that it was not merely boredom and the rocking rhythm of the camel that had lulled him. His cornflower eyes were red-rimmed and sunken in bruised-looking, bluish skin. His features seemed stretched taut across the bone. *Poveretto!* I thought reflexively, and it came to me that my landlady, Mrs. Motta, had taught me the proper way to respond to affliction: not with an admonition to buck up or count one's blessings but with simple kindness and compassion.

"You poor thing," I said aloud, and firmly. "Colonel Lawrence, you look exhausted."

"The longest fortnight I have ever lived," he admitted. "Forty points of view, forty opinions to bring into balance . . . And then it all has to be written up." He smiled briefly and looked away. "Winston's idea of working hard is to assign an impossible task to others and wait for the report." He leaned toward me slightly and confided, "War was easier."

For a time he rode silently, haggard and depressed, then shook the tiredness off, stretching like a cat before settling back into his saddle. "What was it you . . . ?"

"Oh! Yes! I'm so sorry I woke you. It was just something silly. I wondered why you didn't wear your Arab robes this morning."

"Clothing is a tool, Miss Shanklin. What one wears depends on whom one hopes to influence. When Winston brought me into the Colonial Office, everyone expected me to be colorful and difficult. 'What? Wilt thou bridle the wild ass of the desert?' " he quoted with self-deprecating amusement. "They were prepared to resist anything I said or did. So I have been plain and brown as a wren, and used their own surprise as a lever."

"And have you achieved what you hoped? Will your friend Feisal get his kingdom?" He hesitated, and I promised, "I won't say anything to Herr Weilbacher, if you'd rather I don't. I know Sergeant Thompson thinks Karl is a German spy."

"Thompson is an excellent policeman," said Lawrence, although his tone seemed to imply, *The man is out of his depth.* "Has Karl asked about me?"

"He mentioned that you knew each other before the war."

Lawrence grinned into the sun. "In a manner of speaking. Of course, he was doing his job and I was doing mine."

"Anyway, I'd like you to know that Karl is simply —" My breath caught before I finished: "A dear friend."

"Yes . . . He can be charming." Lawrence looked away, his eyes measuring the distance to the pyramids. "You have my leave to inform Herr Weilbacher that the British Crown plans to repair the injury done to the House of the Sherifs of Mecca." All this was said in the bland, measured tones of diplomacy. Then he smiled his beaming, cryptic smile and added, "The French won't like it."

"You could tell him yourself," I suggested. "Have dinner with us."

He giggled. "It might be entertaining to watch the veins stand out on Thompson's forehead, but no. Thanks, all the same." Lawrence yawned and rubbed at his face. "Another day, and this part of the job will be done. *Inshallah,* it will last. Are you still planning to come to Palestine with our party? We're scheduled to leave day after tomorrow."

"Oh! Jebail! That's right —" I'd become so enthralled by Karl, I'd forgotten all about Colonel Lawrence's invitation. But I could easily imagine what Karl would say. *To see the Holy Land in such company! Agnes, you must go! We have time. I will be here when you return.*

Lawrence and I discussed our itinerary. There would be three days in Jerusalem before going north to the American Mission School, where Lillian had taught. Then I asked, "And what are your plans when all this is over, Colonel?"

"Back to the groves of academe, I suppose. I'm trying to write a memoir. A lot of that going around," he said, as though authorship were the flu. "Have you heard the old joke about Job sitting on his dunghill?" he asked, his tired eyes flickering with amusement. "He tells his friends all his troubles and at the end, one of them says, 'Yes, but you know . . . there could be a book in it!' "

He had recently written an introduction for a new edition of Doughty's *Arabia Deserta* and hoped to make "a few quid" from the same publisher by providing book translations from French to English. We talked of novels next, and I was surprised to learn that he had read Dornford Yates's Berry tales, which were light and humorous courtroom stories. Those were, Lawrence told me, the only things that could make him laugh after the war. He was fond as well of W. W. Jacobs and George Birmingham but particularly taken with Richard Garnett's study *The Twilight of the Gods.* "Garnett's scholarship is so easy and exact, so deep, but so unobtrusive," he said with boyish enthusiasm. Lawrence had begun to consider reinterpreting *The Odyssey,* which he had carried in the original Greek throughout the desert campaign. He thought a soldier's perspective would add dimension to a translation like Butler's.

When he got back to England, he was eager to meet poets like Hardy and Sassoon and Blunden. They had some secret he hoped to learn — a technical mastery of words that he wanted to study, as an apprentice carver learns the use of mallet and chisel. Writers, painters, and composers fascinated him, and he believed their essential labor differed only in the medium they employed. He'd approached several artists about illustrations for the war book that he was writing. It was going to have photographs, woodblocks, paintings, even cartoons. In fact, he'd offered himself to the artists as a model and looked forward to long, quiet days watching them work and asking questions.

At a bare two miles an hour, the camels plodded down dunes where the sand gave way like fresh snow, then joltingly stumbled up the next ridge, sliding a foot backward for every eighteen inches of advance. In the presence of that busy, far-ranging mind, time passed quickly and I began to understand, to some small extent, how he had kept sane during endless empty hours in the desert. But when we crested yet another ridge with nothing to show for it, I thought, This is hell. And a little while later, Sergeant Thompson said as much aloud.

Hearing that, Lawrence excused himself, touched up his camel, and shouted something to our Arab escort. Suddenly our pack animals were beaten into a loping run and the sheiks on horseback dashed away as though on a bandit raid, leaving us to plod along behind them.

Several ridges later, we crested to find a cup-shaped depression in the land where boxes and baskets of supplies had been emptied and arranged for us to use as chairs. Two circular tents were erected, umbrella-fashion, each upon a center pole, their fabric pulled taut on ropes fastened to stakes driven into the sand. The closest was an unadorned black woolen affair in which a native cook worked over a large stove of admirable simplicity. It consisted of nothing more than an iron trough on legs, its bottom pierced by small holes like those of a sieve, for air. On its bed of burning charcoal, the cook had set out an array of battered pots and kettles. Their contents smelled divine.

Groaning, we rocked and flopped and lurched as our mounts folded up their long legs and jackknifed onto the ground. One by one, we slid off stiffly with chuckling cries of pain. Ladies and gentlemen separated into two simple washing areas behind plain canvas walls. When we emerged, tea was served by the camel boys, who'd turned themselves into waiters by putting on red tarbooshes and belting their long white gowns with matching red sashes.

The dining tent was brilliant against the colorless noonday desert, decorated with abstract appliqués cut from heavy canvas in dazzling colors: crimson and blue, chrome yellow and acid green, rose and turquoise and violet. Inside the tent, Oriental rugs covered the sand, and off to the right there was a serving table with wine, Scotch, and soda. Flanked by camp stools, long tables were laid with white damask, china, glassware, silver cutlery, and tall brass candlesticks. Soup was served, then grilled fish fresh from the Nile. We ate roasted chicken, and mutton with rice, a salad with squab. There was a pudding for dessert. At the very end, the boys passed small dishes of nuts, raisins, and candies, and platters heaped with segments of exquisite local oranges. Replete, we staggered outside and dropped in small groups to rest on the carpet-covered sand and yawn, and yawn, and yawn.

Contentedly on my own, I lay back and closed my eyes. The sun's radiant warmth was perfectly balanced by a springtime breeze that cooled my face and hands. Drowsing, I listened to the desert wind singing in my ears and to the mournful, minor chanting of the Arabs as they packed up the equipment . . .

A smoker's cough roused me. I opened my eyes and beheld Miss Bell, who seemed twelve feet tall from where I lay. She had a cigarette dangling between her lips and a china cup in each hand. "May I join you?" she asked.

"Not if you're going to tell me my skirt is too short," I replied.

"I didn't think you had that in you," she

said, sounding as though she approved. "Coffee?"

I sat up and accepted the drink, sipping carefully so as not to disturb the muddy sludge of grounds at the bottom. Miss Bell lowered herself beside me and leaned back on an elbow. For a time, we were silently companionable while I watched some sort of beetle scooping out a home. As the sand moved backward, the beetle's rear feet caught and threw it farther behind him. His frenzied determination reminded me of Rosie maniacally digging through snow. Now that I was looking, I noticed a whole colony of such beetles; we were surrounded by tiny geysers of sand.

Clementine's musical laughter floated out on the still air. Miss Bell, for whom desert beetles had long since lost their novelty, stared balefully over the rim of her coffee cup at the Churchills. "When Winston was away at the front," she told me, "Clementine ran soldiers' canteens that fed a thousand men at a sitting. Raised the money, bought the supplies, hired the staff, ran the whole operation. Now look at her!"

With both small neat hands, Clementine had clasped her dumpy husband's round arm and laid her forehead against his shoulder, fawning.

" 'And the two shall be as one,' " Miss Bell intoned. "The one, of course, is always the husband. Why have *you* never married?" she asked abruptly, but allowed no time for a reply. "I had my chances," she said, "but . . . the war, you know."

Her eyes shifted to Colonel Lawrence, who was sitting on the other side of the encampment with two of the men in uniform. "We were close once, or so I believed. We hardly speak now. Tell me, Miss Shanklin, is the dear boy satisfied with this fortnight's work? He should be," she said, not waiting for an answer. "I wouldn't have thought it, but he has a talent for negotiation. It is something female in him. He despises it, as an intelligent woman would, but uses it nevertheless. You see how he listens and listens?" she asked, lifting her chin toward the three men. "When all the others have talked themselves out, he will suggest just the right words, just the right formula . . . The art of diplomacy: everyone gets something, no one gets everything."

The French would get Syria and the Lebanon, she said, to govern and exploit as they wished. In return they had accepted nominal Arab rule in the British protectorates. The oil fields of Mosul would most likely go to the British; that was still to be worked out. Miss Bell herself had drawn the borders that would bring the Kurds, the Sunni, and the Shi'a together under a single administration in a new country to be called Iraq.

Why had she chosen to tell me all this? Was it to display her importance? To make it clear she had more than skirt lengths on her mind? I honestly didn't know. Maybe I was all she had: no one else in the party had invited her company. People who are respected but not liked often seek out newcomers, hoping for admiration if not affection. Maybe she was lonely.

Or perhaps she was just summing up the outcome of the conference for her own purposes, trying to decide who had won and who had lost. Hussein, the elderly sherif of Mecca, would not rule a vast post-Ottoman caliphate, but in return for his goodwill toward the British government he would receive a yearly cash *douceur.* His chief rival to the south was a man named Ibn Saud, and to promote tranquillity in the rest of Arabia, that person was to be given a subsidy equal to Hussein's, though Ibn Saud's would be doled out monthly.

"That will keep him on a shorter leash," Miss Bell remarked. Perhaps it was the mention of a leash that reminded her that I was listening. "You haven't understood a thing I've said, have you."

That's why she's telling me all this, I thought. Talking to me is like talking to a dog. To her, I might as well be Rosie. That's what all of them think, I suppose.

And yes, I had probably gotten lost in some of the details, but I understood more than she thought, and something began to shift inside me. While I had been willing to promise Lawrence not to say anything to Karl, I had no such feeling of loyalty or friendship for Miss Bell. She clearly believed that whatever she said to me would go in one side of my empty head and swiftly out the other.

There is a difference between looking and being inconsequential, I thought then; I am not the cipher you think I am. "And what of Lawrence's friend Feisal?" I asked. "Will he rule Iraq?"

Yes, Miss Bell informed me with satisfaction, she had beaten Colonel Wilson in that contest of wills. Feisal would be "elected" king, as soon as the British had removed his native rivals from the local scene.

Like Karl, Miss Bell admired Feisal, but she believed that he would be welcomed with rose petals in Baghdad. The new king would, of course, manifest his gratitude by acting in accord with advice tendered to him by Sir Percy Cox, for our cadaverous dinner companion would be named high commissioner of the new nation.

Across the sand, one of the officers with Lawrence suddenly stood. We could hear his voice, raised but indistinct. "The dear boy must have told him the bad news," Miss Bell observed. "Winston is going to pull nearly all our ground troops out of Iraq. Trenchard will police the region from the air. Watch. The general will now cry carnage and ruin," she predicted, and indeed both officers were visibly upset, though Lawrence remained calm and reasonable. "If Boom Trenchard says he can keep order with the R.A.F., he probably can, but . . ." Miss Bell shrugged. "Arnold Wilson thinks the plan is doomed. Without three hundred thousand British troops to keep order, he expects the Arabs to rise against any government with ties to us. Feisal will be tainted by association. Why bother with the dumb show? We should simply rule, as we do in India."

"And what do you think?" I asked.

She motioned for more coffee. One of the waiters hurried over to pour, starting at the cup and raising the long-spouted brass pot high to elongate the stream dramatically before cutting it off — just so — without spilling a drop. "The arrangement is not ideal," she admitted finally, "but things can't go on as they have." She lit another cigarette and shot smoke upward before adding bitterly, "It will cost less to fail from the air than to fail on the ground. And fewer soldiers will die for the mistakes of politicians. God!" she cried suddenly. "They are all so proud of the British art of muddling along — as though ignorance and bad planning were a virtue!"

The man she didn't marry, I thought. He must have been a soldier.

She stopped to pick a shred of tobacco from her lip. "There was a time when I had an infinite capacity for coffee, cigarettes, and cajolery," she said, more with wonder than with wistfulness. "I knew every Arab chieftain. Whom they loved, whom they hated. Every name, every relation, every nuance of alliance. I could flatter and push, suggest and demand. No more! Diplomacy and marriage — I'm past them both. I simply haven't the patience."

She must have been a beauty once. Now her pink scalp peeked out amid thinning strands of half-grayed hair. Even when her mouth was empty, her lips pursed as though frozen in the act of smoking. Oh, yes, she was past it now, poor thing, but I wasn't, and at that moment I knew that Gertrude Bell was everything I did not want to be in ten years: an elderly virgin who'd had her chances but didn't take them, whose yellowed eyes were full of defensive disdain and hidden envy for a married couple who doted on each other as the Churchills did.

"It must have been hard on you," I said. "All those years alone, so far from friends and family."

She barked a dismissive laugh. "Happy and contented people don't make history, Miss Shanklin. I've done that much, at least."

And yet, there was no place for Gertrude Bell in the British plans. She had drawn the boundaries of Iraq and willed it into existence, but she would not be high commissioner. Percy Cox would rule.

She set her cup down, and stood, and looked north, her expression pulled taut as a pale, thin glove. "I can work with Feisal," she said then, but not to me. "He'll need a friend. Someone to guide him. Good God, the poor man's never even been to Baghdad!"

She raised her voice and beckoned to the others. "All right, everyone," she called out ringingly. "Let's get on with it, shall we?"

■ ■ ■ ■

We gathered and remounted, an excruciating process now that we'd had time to stiffen up, but as we drew closer to our destination, the scent of clover blew in from the riverbank, freshening the air and our dispositions. At the distance of two miles, the pyramids seemed to hover in a tremulous haze of sand, grand and imposing above the palms. An hour more, and then —

Well, it doesn't matter how many photos and paintings you have seen. The pyramids will take your breath away. They are immense in a way that is incomprehensible unless you experience them up close and in all four of Professor Einstein's dimensions: length, breadth, height, and time.

What will it mean to you if I say that the Great Pyramid is an almost solid mass of stone that covers thirteen acres? That each block at the base was a third the size of a railroad boxcar? Not much, I imagine.

All right. Try this: the Great Pyramid appears from a distance to terminate in a point, does it not? In fact, the apex is a flat square platform nearly thirty feet on a side, so large that an ordinary home in Cedar

Glen would fit on it with room to spare. Such an imaginary penthouse would sit forty-eight stories above the desert — and at that, the Great Pyramid is only a suggestion of its original size. Three thousand years old when Jesus was a child, it has served Egyptians as a quarry for millennia. Most of its smooth limestone facing stones were carried off for reuse long ago. What you see today is only its rougher, smaller core. Yet even in that reduced state, it was the tallest man-made object on earth through all of human history until 1889, when the Eiffel Tower was erected.

Around that corrugated mountain of hewn rock, hundreds of tourists dominated the landscape while mobs of half-naked children cried *"Baksheesh! Baksheesh!"* and robed men in tarbooshes offered their services as guides. The Great Pyramid itself swarmed with climbing trios of steadily diminishing size. Nearly every foreigner was accompanied by two Egyptian stevedores who clambered up and over the shoulder of each huge block of stone, then reached down to grab the raised hands of their freight. Thus they hauled the tourist up by his arms, from one ledge to the next, chanting relentlessly in English singsong: "All right! Very good! Hard work! Pay soon!" Politely, they left off what seemed to me implied: *Or prepare to be hurled to your death, should you fail to meet our remunerative expectations, O wealthy representative of colonial power!*

Detective Sergeant Thompson was easy to pick out in the multitude, since he stood a good deal taller than your average man, English or Egyptian. Moving in his direction, I waved to him and called, "Are you going to make the climb?"

He opened his mouth, closed it, started again to say something, and thought better of it. "No," he said finally, and carefully, and quietly. "I feel like I've been beaten with clubs." He started to jerk his head toward Churchill in the distance, but winced and curtailed the gesture. "At least he's decided we won't go on to Sakhara after all. Just the bloody Sphinx, then back to the hotel."

Indeed, merely walking around to the other side of pyramid was more than enough exercise to satisfy the most athletic and ambitious among our party. The stepped pyramid at Sakhara was impressively visible to the south and I'm sure it was very interesting, but it was all I could do to hobble the last little distance to the Sphinx, where our camels would be waiting for us.

To make even that small additional effort seemed unlikely to be worth the trouble but, once again our pain was rewarded by the stunning difference between anticipation and reality. The Sphinx is larger, more somber, and more surprising than one can prepare for, no matter how familiar its image. Its body was said to be that of a lion at rest, though it looked to me like a monumental Labrador retriever. Each huge paw was fully fifty feet long, by my pacing measurement. The head would require a three-story house to contain its volume; the ears alone are just over four feet from top to bottom. Sadly and famously, its nose is mutilated, but the face remains quite beautiful. With the impassive dignity of a handsome Negro man, its stony eyes have seen empire after empire rise and fall, and disappear into the desert.

"Yoo-hoo!" In a parking lot nearby, Lady Cox was waving a hankie to get my attention. "Miss Shanklin, where is everyone?" she called in a shrill voice that cut like a train whistle through the sightseers' babble.

I picked my way across the sand. Lady Cox and I exchanged stories. Mine was filled with discomfort and wonderment, hers with boredom and annoyance. "I've been waiting hours," she complained.

"We're going to have a photograph," Clementine called out just then. "Everyone!

Get back on the camels for the picture!"

There was a fair amount of French commentary on that notion. We were all wretched. Hips, shoulders, back, knees — everything ached, and every point of contact with the saddle felt raw. Joints and muscles had begun to seize up like a Model T engine after its crankcase has jolted apart on a stretch of rutted road. I hated to think what I would find when I undressed. Blisters, boils, bruises . . .

Nevertheless, most of the British remounted at Clementine's request, and that photo is in the history books. There we all are: the people who invented the modern Middle East and those who came along, or fell in with them by chance. The Sphinx is nearby, the pyramids in the distance. You can see Clementine and Winston, Miss Bell,

Colonel Lawrence, and Sergeant Thompson high on camelback, along with several officers in uniform. I hung back, shy as always of being photographed. Clementine insisted, so I hurried over and stood next to Lady Cox. You can see the two of us, on foot, off to the left. We are standing next to an Arab whose name we did not ask.

Mercifully, Lady Cox offered me a ride back to Cairo in the consulate car; I accepted with gratitude. When young Davis asked, "Did you enjoy the day, miss?" I hardly knew what to say, for if the world offers a more lacerating, bone-shattering, muscle-wrenching mode of transportation than riding a camel, I never discovered it. And yet, memories of that day are among the most vivid of my time in Egypt. Indeed, they remained among the most vivid of my life, and I would not have traded them for an experience more comfortable or luxurious.

I returned to the Continental Hotel early that evening in a state of utter aching affliction. Karl was the very soul of understanding and lifted Rosie into my arms for her delirious greeting when he realized I was too stiff and sore to bend over and pick her up myself.

"*Ach!* Agnes! I well remember my own

first journey on a camel," he said, and insisted I take some aspirin immediately. He'd had my room tidied. The morning's flowers were artlessly arranged in a lovely faience vase. "A gift," he said. "Rosie and I found it in a shop this afternoon."

While Karl ordered something from room service, I retreated to the bathroom. Within minutes I was nude, as I had imagined I'd be early that morning, but soaking alone in a tub of warm, scented water that Karl had drawn for me himself. Half an hour later, Rosie announced the arrival of room service, and I climbed, whimpering, out of the water. A light supper was waiting for me when I hobbled out of the bathroom, tying the belt of my silk wrapper over my nightie.

The sun set. I ate an omelette. Karl prepared a pipe and listened while I told him everything I could recall of what Miss Bell had said. In one way, to share it all seemed homey and natural, and brought to mind the evenings when Mumma and Papa had discussed their plans to begin a business together. At the same time, it was exciting to feel a part of something clandestine and important.

It was premature to draw out the British ground troops, Karl thought. "Trenchard will need a year at least to build the air bases. The army should remain for now." He was also wary of the man the British had decided to work with on the Arabian Peninsula. Ibn Saud openly wished to conquer the Hejaz and Mesopotamia, Karl told me. His goal was to spread Wahabism, an ascetic form of Islam to which no one outside his tribe adhered.

"Can the British truly believe that ten thousand pounds a month will buy Ibn Saud's friendship? They'll simply end up financing the trouble he makes for them. What a pity that Sufi Muslims are outnumbered!" he remarked. "No one thinks of them, but the Middle East would be better if they ran it."

He was also quite gloomy about Miss Bell's map. "This Iraq of hers makes no sense — politically, tribally, religiously."

"Miss Bell seemed to think that Lawrence's friend Feisal could bring the region together," I said.

"Perhaps, for a time, but all men are mortal. What will happen when Feisal dies? A very real civil war, I fear, to end a very artificial state. No," Karl said decisively, "I see nothing to be gained by Miss Bell's new boundaries, and I am surprised Lawrence compromised on this. His plan was sensible. Keep the three Ottoman districts separate:

Kurds in the north, Sunni in the middle, Shi'a in the south. Unless . . ." Puffing on his pipe, Karl looked out the window toward the deepening aquamarine where a thumbnail moon was rising. "Perhaps the idea is to play the Kurds off against the Arabs and the Persians. Cox may believe he can use native rivalries to prevent them from organizing a resistance against British influence."

Karl sat for a time, lost in thought, and when he came to himself, he seemed slightly boggled. "And so! Just like that," he said, snapping his fingers. "The Treaty of Sèvres is abrogated: no homeland for the Kurds after all. And nothing for the Armenians. Two nations, brushed aside in the name of compromise." He lifted the teapot and topped off my cup before asking, "And what of Palestine?"

"No one mentioned it."

"Odd. I heard that Sir Herbert Samuel arrived for the negotiations yesterday. He's the high commissioner for the Palestine Protectorate."

I thought back, but nothing came to mind. "I don't recall hearing that name at all, but — Oh, I keep forgetting! Lawrence has invited me to come with the British party that's visiting Palestine!"

I expected Karl's usual response: *Agnes, you must go!* Instead, his face clouded over. "I'm not certain this is a good idea, Agnes. Churchill is unpopular here, but he is truly hated in Palestine."

"Do you think I should decline?" I chewed a bit of buttered toast, trying not to look delighted at the idea of staying here with Karl. "Lawrence wanted to show me where my sister used to teach, in Jebail, just north of Beirut. That's where he and Lillie met before the war, but perhaps you could take me there instead?"

He said nothing, and there it was again: a silence that felt like punishment. Even a few seconds distressed me, and the old habit of appeasement and ingratiation reasserted itself, as though a switch had been thrown.

"Karl," I said tentatively, "wouldn't it be useful to you? If I were to go with them, I mean? People just talk to me. I don't think they realize . . ."

". . . that you are a woman of intelligence?" he suggested.

"Well, I guess I just look so harmless, nobody imagines — And really, I just listen, but maybe I — I could — I could be useful."

"Mother's little helper." With a deep breath, he looked away, deliberating. At last he made up his mind. "Lawrence would not have invited you, I think, if he were not confident that you will come to no harm. All right," Karl agreed. "You must be careful, but yes! This is an extraordinary opportunity." There was a long moment while he held my gaze, and then he added, "For both of us, I think." And I felt a sort of bone-deep relief, as though Mumma had told me that she was pleased by a gift I'd given her.

While I finished my supper, we discussed the vagaries of traveling with Rosie. She certainly made everything more complicated, but I could not have imagined leaving her at home in Ohio. "And if you had, we never should have met," Karl said. "So I am glad that you brought your *wursthund* with you." In the end, we decided that Rosie would be perfectly happy to let Karl feed her sausage for a few days. He had business in Alexandria, but she could easily come with him on the train, whereas things were likely to be much less flexible on a British diplomatic excursion to one of the empire's embattled protectorates.

Karl would make arrangements for the concierge to help me pack for the trip to Palestine tomorrow; the bulk of my belongings would be stored while I was gone. "And when you come back to Cairo, what would you say to a voyage up the Nile?" Karl asked, his eyes sparkling. "It is the least I can do for such a helpful friend."

"That would be *wonderful,*" I said.

"It's settled, then! Would you like more tea? No? Have you had quite enough to eat? Yes? Then it is time for you to rest."

He turned down the bedcovers and gently took the robe from my shoulders, offering a steady arm as I climbed groaningly into the bed. Rosie, boosted up beside me, promptly nosed her way under the sheets, settling against my aching, blistered hip.

"I'll come round for her in the morning," Karl said softly, turning out the light. I heard the door latch click when he left, and nothing more after that.

I suppose you're wondering if I was disappointed to be retiring alone that evening. After all, just that morning, I had made up my mind to — well, you know.

To tell the truth, I was rather relieved. Yes, of course, "Birds do it, bees do it," as the song goes, but it was not so easy to throw off the fear that decades of spinsterhood had rested upon, and reinforced. Since Papa died, I had lived by the maxim "You can because you must." Duties, tasks. Self-control, self-denial.

To delay a little longer — to wait a week or so for the next step — that seemed the better part of valor. Under the circumstances, then, to be fussed over and tucked into bed was not merely sweet but entirely satisfying — for the time being, at least.

When I get back from Palestine, I'll be ready, I thought. And I slept very soundly that night.

Most dogs, when they meet your eyes, intend to intimidate you. For example, when a collie stares, he is giving an order: *Be quiet, you! Go stand in that group where you belong!* All the world's a flock of sheep, to a collie.

Not so with dachshunds. Dachshunds gaze. When a dachshund like Rosie looks softly into your eyes, her sweet expression seems to say that you are the most important person she has ever met in her whole life. Moreover, she considers it a high honor and distinct privilege to be your pet. She's only being nice. Within that absurd tubular body beats the heart of a princess. She gazes at you to demonstrate the very devotion she expects, but she is also issuing a warning: *If you leave me home alone, you'll be sorry.*

Abandon a dachshund and upon your return, you may well be confronted with a small token of her displeasure. This, for the dachshund, is an undignified but necessary form of training. Eventually, you will learn your lesson, which is to take her with you everywhere. When you have finally accepted this, you will be generously rewarded for your good behavior by a jaunty, joyful companion.

I was an exceedingly well-trained subject. Leaving Rosie with Karl was awful. "I can't stand it. Look at that face! Look at those eyes!"

"She'll be fine," Karl insisted, kissing my forehead. "She'll have many walks and an entire sausage every day."

"Don't overfeed her."

"Agnes, you're going to be late for the train."

"You be a good girl, Rosie. I promise, I'll come back."

"Agnes, if you don't make a fuss, she won't be upset. Into the taxi with you!"

Reluctantly, I did as I was told. Rosie, by contrast, set off happily with Karl on their first walk of the morning, her meaty little hindquarters sashaying gaily down the street. She never looked back, and as the taxi turned onto the bridge, it was I who had to reconcile myself to the separation.

The cab picked up speed and I watched the city slide by. Cairo was slow to awaken:

dawn not so much greeted as slept through. Despite the wailing calls to prayer from every minaret, the commercial boulevards remained nearly empty until noon. A donkey cart loaded with dates might clip-clop along a road. A baker's deliveryman might bicycle across a square, balancing a huge tray of fresh bread on his head while he pedaled. A sweet-potato seller might pass, pushing his rumbling wagon toward a market. Then quiet would descend again.

Thus, my taxi had hardly any competition in the streets that separated the Continental Hotel from the main Cairo train station. I smiled, thinking back to my adventures on the dragoman's cart, amazed to realize that just ten days had passed since Rosie and I arrived here. In that short time, I had hobnobbed with diplomats, explored the great Egyptian Museum, sipped coffee with a child-bride's husband, ridden a camel to the pyramids, and met the love of my life. One could hardly ask for more from a vacation, I thought giddily. And now, it was on to Palestine, and to the Lebanon beyond!

I paid the cabbie and followed the sound of British voices to the train. Passengers were assembling on the main platform, and the place was crawling with British soldiers. Suddenly, I found my path decisively barred, and though the soldiers were quieter about excluding me than the doorman at the Semiramis, they were equally determined, and I had nothing to prove I'd been invited. The longer we discussed the matter, the more likely I was to miss the train, and I'm afraid I raised my voice when pointing that out. To my relief, Detective Sergeant Thompson emerged from one of the first-class cars and saw the difficulty I was in. I expected him to come to my rescue, but he scowled and stalked toward me like an unusually menacing heron.

"What are you doing here?" he demanded.

I glanced over my shoulder. There was nobody behind me. "I — I'm going to Palestine."

He looked flabbergasted. "Is this Churchill's idea? I don't care if it is — I won't take a chance on exposing you to that kind of danger."

"But I was invited!"

I meant to repeat Karl's logic: that Lawrence wouldn't have asked me to come along if there were any serious danger. It seemed, however, that I was merely the latest in a series of infuriating events in Thompson's morning. Before I could say anything further, the sergeant gripped my elbow with one large hand and steered me off to the side of the platform.

"Do you see that man over there?" he asked, though it was more of a command. "That is Russell Pasha, the chief of police here in Cairo. The man next to him is Sir Herbert Samuel. He runs Palestine. Do they look relaxed, miss? Do they look like we're off on a holiday excursion?" I opened my mouth, but Thompson continued: "No! They don't, and why? Because we have reason to believe there will be a serious attempt on Churchill's life in Gaza. Despite what anyone else says, I am responsible for security on this trip, and if you think I am going to let a lady like you get on that train, you are —"

"My guest, and welcome," said a low, quick voice just behind us.

I turned and almost dropped my handbag in my surprise. It was Colonel Lawrence, but he was not wrenlike this morning. The trilby hat and the badly cut brown suit were gone, replaced by a rich brocade *burnoose* and heavy white robes. These were cinched at his waist with a tooled and gilded leather belt that held a breathtaking gold dagger in a silver-gilt sheath. The effect was dazzling and, as I took it all in, I expected a self-deprecating giggle from him, or some wry remark about playing dress-up. Instead my eyes met an unwavering blue gaze.

"Different people to impress?" I asked.

"Dressed to kill," he said, and he meant exactly that. Lawrence noted my tiny shiver. "Thompson's not overstating the situation, but he's done his work well," the colonel said then, inclining his head toward the big man. Thompson crossed massive arms over a broad chest and glowered at the compliment. "Russell Pasha has vetted the driving, signaling, and coupling crews," Lawrence continued. "We're sending a pilot train ahead, and there are police details deployed wherever the trains must slow enough to be boarded by unauthorized personnel."

"Unauthorized personnel," Thompson muttered. "Assassins, you mean." He looked at me pleadingly. "That riot near the pyramids was nothing to what we can expect in Palestine, miss. If you insist on coming, I can't be responsible."

"I shall be," said Lawrence. And with that he produced one of his glorious beaming smiles, which were so benign and reassuring it seemed silly to have any qualms at all. When he beckoned, I followed, and the attention of the poor harassed detective was immediately redirected toward some other crisis. Leading me through knots of British officials, Lawrence said, "Thompson's paid to worry, but I have matters in hand."

Was that remark bravado? Genuine confidence? A drive to display mastery amid all these diplomats and generals, after weeks of blandishment and coaxing? Though Lawrence gave no sign of it, I suspected that he felt a secret thrill of satisfaction as imposing men in Savile suits and tailored uniforms took note of his approach and, murmuring, gave way. They were on his ground now, dependent on his judgment of the situation. Their lives were in the hands of that small Englishman in outlandish Arab dress. He knew it. So did they.

Inside the train, we headed for a compartment at the trailing end of the third carriage. "If we detonate a mine," Lawrence said with cheery schoolboy relish, "it'll take out the engine and coal tender, but you'll be fine down here. Most likely."

He was grinning, and I took it as a joke, but it drew goggle-eyed stares from two men Lawrence called "Mutt and Jeff" once we'd squeezed past them. Indeed, they were as mismatched physically as those comic characters — or as Lawrence and Thompson were, for that matter. The tall one, with his long bony limbs and ginger hair, looked like a metal farm implement left to rust in a field. His companion was pink and round, and during the hours of our acquaintance, I don't believe he ever stopped eating for more than a few minutes. Their uniforms seemed to have been borrowed from someone's clothesline, but they were officers of the Palestinian Police, Lawrence told me, assigned by Sir Herbert Samuel to help guard Churchill. Even to me, the two of them, fully armed, did not seem a good match for an Arab beggar. No wonder Thompson was worried.

We arrived at the Churchills' compartment, and Lawrence slid the door open. Winston looked up from sheaves of paper. Clementine, in a chic gray cloche with a black grosgrain ribbon, laid her book down on her lap. Neither seemed surprised to see me in Lawrence's company. Winston happily inquired about Rosie. Clementine invited me in and introduced me to the uniformed gentleman sitting across from them.

"Lord Trenchard," I said, offering my hand to the chief of the Royal Air Force, who would soon be counted upon to bomb the new Iraq into existence. "I've been hearing your name all week."

This person acknowledged my existence with a look of puzzlement followed by a funereal smile that consisted of a slight tightening of his cheek muscles. Not a word escaped the man Thompson had called a "good match for the Sphinx," but he did move slightly away from the window, which I gathered was his way of offering me a seat.

Lawrence left. Clementine, fanning herself quietly, went back to her novel. Winston, merely by adjusting his spectacles, seemed to create a perfectly businesslike office of his surroundings. There was an additional ten minutes of frantic official preparation outside. Finally, with a jolt and a squeal of steam, the locomotive began to drag us through and away from Cairo.

The Israelites fleeing Pharaoh required forty years for that which our train accomplished in a matter of hours. This difference in travel time, I believe, is partly responsible for the distinct dismay so many travelers have felt upon crossing into the Holy Land from Egypt. If one had spent weary decades wandering through sterile *wadis* and scalding plains of baking sand and gravel, then the eastern shore of the Mediterranean Sea might have seemed an oasis of milk and honey by comparison. But to the modern traveler, especially one accustomed to the rain-swollen streams and the rolling, fertile farmland of Ohio? Palestine was a dreadful letdown.

"It is a hopeless, dreary, heartbroken land," wrote Mr. Mark Twain — the real one, not Madame Sophie's gentleman friend back in Cleveland. Its valleys were unsightly, with feeble vegetation. Outlines were harsh with no lavender shadow of clouds, no dreamy blue mist to soften the perspective. The lumpish naked hills, Twain reported, appeared to have committed some terrible sin for which they had been stoned to death.

Fifty-some years later, I saw nothing to amend that dismal assessment. Not even Winston could discern a scene worth painting, and we were there in spring, when the countryside was said to be at its best.

For thirty centuries, "Cut down all the trees!" was every general's order at the beginning of every siege. Most recently, the British armed forces had cleared half the region's groves to deny Turks and bandits any cover from which to attack. Before them, the Crusaders had destroyed the land to save it for Christendom. Before them, when Pompey came to take Palestine for Rome, he leveled the forests. Josephus tells us that Titus axed every remaining tree within ten miles of Jerusalem a few decades later. And if any survived the armies, there were the locusts to denude them and goats that climbed into the topmost branches to crop their leaves.

The barrenness of the land was partly why Karl believed the Jewish "Back to Israel" movement was a foreordained failure. "There is no soil or water there," he'd told me at breakfast that morning. "No coal, or iron. No oil or wood for fuel. Nothing to buy, nothing to sell. Agriculture is all but impossible, manufacturing impractical, business unfeasible. My people value education almost above God, but what can an educated man do in Palestine? Farm rocks and dodge bullets?"

The Repeatedly Promised Land is what Karl called Palestine, and he was not referring to the pledges of Yahweh. With the Balfour Declaration of 1917, the British Crown promised the formation of an Israelite national home in Palestine, on what authority one could only wonder. In Karl's opinion, "It was propaganda, merely. The British knew how many German Jews were fighting for our nation and they hoped to sap our loyalty." Only a year or so earlier, the secret Sykes-Picot agreement had guaranteed the French a goodly share in the region, even as Colonel Lawrence was promising the Arabs independence in return for their alliance with the British during the war against Turkey and Germany.

In an effort to untangle this knotted skein, the British considered establishing a New Zion in one of their African colonies. Uganda was a healthy, fertile, and beautiful land, and the Jewish leader Herzl was inclined to accept the offer. The idea was dropped for a variety of reasons. "You see, when the Great War began, only Germany manufactured acetone, which is needed to make TNT," Karl told me. "There was an immigrant Russian living in England when the war broke out — a chemist named Weizmann — and he developed a way to make acetone from horse chestnuts. His claim for the invention was disputed. The Crown eventually granted a patent to an Englishman, but in return for not pressing his suit Weizmann asked that his service to Great Britain be rewarded with a homeland for his people in Palestine."

Now the League of Nations had given Palestine to Great Britain as a protectorate to be dealt with as His Majesty's Government thought expedient. "Russian Zionists call it 'a land without people for a people without land,' " Karl said, "but nearly a million people live there, Agnes. A tenth are Jews, and half again as many Christians, but three-quarters are Arab, and they will never give that wasteland up. It may be awful but it is theirs, and they value it above their children. They proved to Turkey that they would kill or die for it, and now that Lawrence has encouraged Arab nationalism?" Karl shrugged. "They will feel the presence of British colonialists and Zionist settlers as needles in their living flesh. The irony is that Palestine is such a desolation, and yet so many have desired to possess it."

Looking out the window of the train, I couldn't imagine why.

Until you see Palestine, Karl told me, you cannot truly understand the many passages of Scripture, Old and New, in which the commonness, cheapness, and troublesomeness of stones are drawn upon for metaphor. To dash one's foot against a stone is a tiresome vexation; to cast seed on stony ground, an exercise in futility. To gather stones out of a vineyard is to engage in a never-ending task. To ask for bread and receive a stone is to be heartlessly disdained. "King Solomon made silver to be as stones in Jerusalem" gives an excellent notion of that king's storied wealth.

"The Arabs, too, have a legend that explains the stones of Palestine," Karl said. "When Allah made the world, he put all the stones that were to be used across the entire earth into two bags and gave them to an angel to distribute over the land. While the angel was flying above Palestine, one bag broke."

And nowhere were those stones more in evidence than in Gaza.

Near the seacoast, the town was one of the largest in Palestine, which wasn't saying a great deal. Fifteen water wells rendered the location habitable in what is otherwise a desert. Those wells have made it a prize along the route of every invader from Tutmoses III to Allenby. In its newest cemetery, three thousand British graves bore witness to its importance in the Great War.

Of course, no city is at its best near its railroad tracks, but Gaza truly was the most complete municipal horror I ever looked upon. From behind dusty glass we saw fly-ridden and filthy children standing along the right of way and between mud-brick hovels, all of which were in a state of utter dilapidation. I remember thinking that the biblical Samson might be counted fortunate to have been rendered eyeless during his time in Gaza. There was nothing beautiful, nothing gentle, nothing delightful in that terrible place. There was nothing thriving, nothing unstinted excepting only stones and fury. Those, Gaza had in howling abundance.

The children's pebbles bounced harmlessly off the windows, and it seemed that this attack might be nothing worse than schoolboy horseplay. In a matter of seconds, however, the boys were lost in a huge mass of grown men running alongside the train. A sudden tempest of rocks rained against the side of the car. Window after window splintered. The stench of manure, the odor of unwashed male bodies, and the stink of coal smoke poured in, sharing the air with the stones.

Next to me, Lord Trenchard conveyed icy disapproval by compressing his thin lips into a tighter line. Chewing on a spent cigar, Winston laid aside his pen. Clementine stopped reading. "Not again," she sighed, looking more annoyed than interested as she picked a piece of glass from her skirt and flicked it outside.

"I blame Shanklin," Winston rumbled cheerfully. "There's a riot every time she takes me somewhere."

Sergeant Thompson appeared, slid back the compartment door, and motioned us away from the windows. A moment later, he made way for Mutt and Jeff. These were the two Palestinian police officers Thompson was counting on to recognize Arab ringleaders, and he deferred to them now.

Mutt bashed out the remaining window glass with his elbow. Jeff leaned forward with something in his hand. I shrank away, expecting him to fire on the mob. To our astonishment, he held not a pistol but a camera! He was taking photographs — God knows why, unless it was to build a case against the assassin he expected to succeed in killing Churchill.

Snarling, with his own pistol drawn, Thompson reached past Mutt and hauled Jeff out of the compartment with his free hand, all the while threatening to throw both policemen to the (French) wolves and take a (French) photograph of their (French) bodies to send to their (French) widows.

Lawrence arrived a moment later. In the corridor just beyond our compartment, he and Thompson discussed the situation in low voices, the sergeant tense, the colonel unperturbed.

"You can't be serious!" Thompson cried suddenly. "I'm not letting him off the train in this hellhole!"

"It's all arranged," Lawrence said mildly.

"You're demented! Look at those people!"

We had slowed to a stop in a sort of public

square with the station platform on one side and a large mosque opposite. Lawrence braced himself against the doorjamb and leaned across us to peer through what was left of the carriage window, as if gauging Thompson's assessment of the mob against his own.

The train was surrounded now, and the plaza was crammed to the edges with furious chanting men, all of whom seemed intent on murdering the odious "Shershill," given the least opportunity.

"I think we'll be all right," Lawrence said peaceably. "We're going to that big hall next to the mosque. Winston will speak. I will translate. The ladies can listen at the back, but —"

"You aren't thinking of taking the women through that," Thompson objected, astonished.

"They'll be quite safe with me," Lawrence said, and gave the sergeant no opportunity to argue. "Thompson, you will come with us as far as the door, but stay outside. Stand before it until we come out again. Stand without moving, understood?"

Thompson was bug-eyed with disbelief, but outranked. "Where do you want Mutt and Jeff?" he asked, jerking his chin toward the pair standing in the aisle. Both seemed quite shaken, and honestly? I'm not sure who frightened them more: the mob or Sergeant Thompson.

"They're Sir Herbert's worry," Lawrence said dismissively.

"You don't feel the need of them?" Thompson persisted. "They're a couple of extra guns."

"They're a couple of extra jokers" was the muttered response. "We'll lose them in the crowd, on the way." When Thompson looked aghast, Lawrence added cheerily, "Don't worry about those two — they'll survive."

"It's not those two I'm worried about," Thompson called, but Lawrence was already striding down the aisle toward the door at the far end of the car.

I must preface what I tell you next, for in the years that followed the Cairo Conference a considerable controversy developed about T. E. Lawrence and his part in the desert revolt. The war book he mentioned to me on our way to the pyramids was eventually published and received polar reviews. *Seven Pillars of Wisdom* was hailed as a literary masterpiece and denounced as a pack of lies. Lawrence himself was lionized and vilified, his exploits in the desert often confirmed and frequently denied.

I shall not pretend that I am unbiased.

After spending time in his company, I grew quite fond of him. In the years afterward, we sometimes corresponded and I followed his career from afar. I did not like to hear stories that were meant to undermine his reputation, but I do try to be fair-minded, and I read many of the biographies.

Chief among Lawrence's detractors was Mr. Richard Aldington, who published a peculiarly venomous book twenty years after Lawrence died and two years before I did. The book was first released in France under the title *Lawrence l'Imposteur,* which gives you the flavor of its contents; its title in English was not so bluntly libelous, but *Lawrence: A Biographical Enquiry* was no less hostile.

I myself enjoyed Mr. Aldington's novel about the Great War. *The Death of a Hero* is ironic, sarcastic, ferocious, and funny — very modern, actually, and quite entertaining. *Seven Pillars,* by contrast, is a brilliant but difficult book; when its author wished to conceal himself, its prose could be as monstrous and opaque as *Moby-Dick's.*

Nonetheless, neither *Death of a Hero* nor its author ever achieved the status bestowed upon Lawrence and his work, and Lowell Thomas's public lectures were just salt in Mr. Aldington's literary wound. They glorified war and mortal combat in ways no bitter veteran of the Western Front could tolerate, and on behalf of his dead comrades — gassed, machine-gunned, blown to mincemeat in the trenches — Mr. Aldington must have resented the attention paid to Lawrence's more photogenic but relatively minor desert campaign. Just as galling: in the years after the Great War, Lawrence fled from his fame — a fact that must have greatly annoyed poor Mr. Aldington, who would have enjoyed it more. Worse yet: after his death in 1935, Lawrence was treated as a secular saint. The world heaped on him the honor that it continued to withhold from a rival Lawrence never knew he had. Perhaps that was when Mr. Aldington resolved to cast as much doubt as he could on every exploit and accomplishment and talent attributed to the man who bested him, even from the grave.

Then again, I suppose it's possible that everything Aldington wrote about Lawrence was true. I certainly cannot judge the accuracy of the wartime memories upon which Lawrence built his seven-pillared worthy house, but I can tell you this much: I can tell what we saw that day in Gaza.

We moved toward the trailing end of the railroad carriage, and as we approached the vestibule, the noise swelled: two thousand men shouting, chanting, screaming. Never had I witnessed emotion as violent as that which greeted the arrival of Winston Churchill and Sir Herbert Samuel in Gaza. Those two persons were the very embodiment of colonialism and Zionism: His Britannic Majesty's secretary for the colonies and the British high commissioner for Palestine, who was himself a Jew. As Karl had anticipated, their mere presence in Gaza was "like a needle in the living flesh" of the men who made up that roaring sea of waving fists.

Without a word, Lawrence stepped from the shadow of the carriage into the sunlight that poured down between the cars. Having made himself visible, he lifted one hand slowly. A loose white sleeve fell back from a thin-boned, sinewy wrist. Like the pope of Rome, he raised the first and second fingers above the other two, as though in blessing.

And there was . . . silence.

In an instant, faces distorted by hate and fury were transformed: by startlement, by joy, by adulation. A moment later the crowd erupted, transported by the simple sight of him. Imagine winning the World Series at a home game. Imagine the grand finale of a Fourth of July fireworks display, or an ovation at the end of Beethoven's Ninth.

Thousands chanted his name. *"Aurens! Aurens! Aurens!"* Some wept.

Smelling of cigar, Winston gazed over my shoulder. "I'd heard," he said, awestruck, "but if I hadn't seen it myself . . ."

"And if the war had continued another year?" Sir Herbert suggested quietly, just behind me.

"He might have ruled the East," Winston agreed. "By 1919, that little man could have marched to Constantinople with all Arabia at his back."

Outside, Lawrence stepped down onto the platform. The crowd fell silent again and moved back, to make a space for him. Somewhere in the distance, we heard a goat bleat. A child at the edge of the crowd piped a request and was lifted onto his father's shoulders. When Lawrence turned, the crunch of coarse sand beneath his sandals was audible. He held out one hand toward us, his face serene and eyes seraphic. "Come along," he said, twitching his fingers in invitation. Casual as could be.

We looked to Thompson, who shook his head but shrugged helplessly, then nodded. One by one, we descended the three steps and followed Lawrence in the eerie quiet as the crowd made way for us. Many reached out to touch him, murmuring *"Aurens!"* as he passed.

Across the square, the door of the ramshackle public hall swung open to reveal a gathering of tribal chieftains and municipal officials, sweating and perfumed. A great cheer went up when Lawrence was glimpsed through the battered entrance of this jerry-made building, but he stepped aside, deferentially waving Winston and Sir Herbert ahead with a low sweep of his hooded arm. Clementine and I followed; with a slight movement of his eyes, nothing more, Lawrence reminded us to remain at the back of the room. Thompson took up his post just outside, looking as though he just *dared* the crowd to start something. And there he stayed, formidable and unmoving, as Lawrence had instructed.

I don't really remember much of what Winston said in that meeting hall. My eyes were on Lawrence, who contrived to make himself a wren again, even in his resplendent robes. Standing to one side and a bit behind, eyes downcast, he repeated Churchill's speech first in Arabic and then in fluent French — the real stuff, not Thompson's kind — when someone in the audience requested it.

This done, he conveyed the concerns and comments of the gathered dignitaries. No matter what they asked or said, Winston produced nicely phrased political pleasantries, and though the meeting took the better part of two hours, he uttered nothing of substance. What, after all, could he say that was both honest and unlikely to spark renewed passion?

In the back of that stifling room, yearning for fresher air and somewhere to sit, I suddenly realized that, though Winston held their national aspirations in his own pudgy hands, this might have been the first time he'd met with any Arabs. As far as I knew, not a single individual who actually lived in the region had attended the Cairo Conference, even as an observer. Last week, in private, Winston and his Forty Thieves had sealed the fate of everyone here and of generations to come. Public meetings like these were just for show.

In Versailles and in Cairo, I think it's fair to say, Lawrence did his best to represent the people of the Middle East, but he was just one man, with conflicting loyalties at that. His self-imposed mission was to balance internal imperial interests with international politics, and both of those with the expectations of millions who themselves had competing interests. Arabs, Lebanese, and Djebel Druses. Syrians, Kurds, and Armenians. Native-born Jews and European settlers. Turks, Persians, and Mesopotamians. Egyptians, Palestinians, and a thousand Bedouin tribes. All of these, and more, wanted something that usually involved taking land from someone else.

It was an impossible task. Within a few years, Lawrence would know that he had failed, but he didn't then — not that day in Gaza.

After standing for hours in the sun, the crowd outside had grown restive. The noise we were beginning to notice increased when the door was opened just long enough for Thompson to lean inside. He made a sign to Lawrence with a finger drawn across his throat and jerked a thumb toward the train. Lawrence lifted his chin. The next ten minutes were devoted to flowery farewells, during which time competing chants developed in the town square. Free at last to leave, we gathered our things and converged on the doorway, but Thompson held us inside, closing the door behind him. The mood outside had turned ugly again, he reported. Fights had broken out. Some Palestinian policemen had arrived on the scene, but their presence seemed to have made things worse.

"I can't read these mobs," he admitted,

over the muffled chanting outside. "Sometimes it seems they're just enjoying the excitement, but this looks serious."

"How long will they keep us here?" Clementine wanted to know. She was clearly concerned for her husband's safety, and with good reason.

"I think they only want to look at Winston," said Lawrence.

"The longer we wait, the more I shall deteriorate," said Winston. He looked pasty and drained, now that he was offstage, so to speak.

"What are they chanting?" I asked.

" 'Cheers for Great Britain,' " Lawrence said, lying so smoothly it was evidently meant as a joke. " 'Cheers for the minister.' "

I heard Sir Herbert's grim chuckle. " 'Cut their throats,' " he translated. " 'Down with the Jews.' "

Lawrence excused himself and stepped in front of the rest of us. For a moment, he stood before the entrance, physically still, as though gathering himself. Then he pushed open the double doors with a powerful two-handed shove.

He probably expected this to attract the attention of the mob, but no one saw him. The lack of notice would have been comical under other circumstances, but what had been a noisy demonstration was fast becoming a genuine riot.

Just beyond the door, two Palestinian policemen were swinging lead-loaded staves at whoever came within striking distance. Across the square, reinforcements had arrived on horseback and their officer shouted his intention to force a passage for us. At his order, the mounted police drew sabers and spurred their horses straight into the crowd. They might as well have tried to ride down a brick wall. Strong brown hands seized the horses' bridles and pulled the riders out of their saddles. One of the two chants was beginning to dominate. *Cut their throats! Cut their throats! Cut their throats!*

Thompson stepped outside and stood behind Lawrence. They exchanged a few words. Just as I was wishing that Karl had insisted I stay in Cairo, Thompson fired his pistol into the air.

Clementine cried out. I clutched at my heart, startled witless.

Fearsome, long-nosed, and keen-eyed, the Gazans turned our way. A moment later, the shouted rhythmic chant again became *"Aurens! Aurens! Aurens!"* Men rushed toward him, alight with excitement. Smiling easily, Lawrence accepted their joyful greetings and salaamed in return.

They didn't want to see Churchill, I thought. They were waiting for you.

The same thought must have been in his mind, for Lawrence became the courtier once more. Turning toward the door, he stood aside, ushering forth Mr. Churchill with a courtesy and humility that clearly told the crowd, *I wish you to treat this man with respect and as my own guest.* Holding up his hand, he received silence and spoke a few soft words. The chanting resumed, but this time the name *"Shershill!"* was taken up without its customary *"À bas!"*

Winston stood in the doorway, beaming like a chubby choirboy. I thought the cheers would never stop, but when he judged the time was right, Lawrence made another small sign. The crowd parted for us, and the dignity of our little procession was unmarred all the way back to the official carriage.

Backed by Lawrence and Thompson, Churchill climbed up to the vestibule platform to receive the town's farewells. The train whistle tooted. The locomotive began to pull. A company of Arab horsemen raced the train and stayed beside it for nearly a mile before we drew away.

From Gaza on, our progress to Jerusalem

was repeatedly interrupted by crowds that choked the railroad tracks. Sometimes civic delegations wished to present a petition to "Shershill." Sometimes mounted Bedouin simply wanted to lay their eyes on the great men who rode the train. Everywhere Lawrence was greeted with the enthusiasm we had witnessed in Gaza, and in the days that followed, he was welcomed "home" by tribal leaders, high and low, and by absolute rulers of remote lands with names like Zakho and Jeziret ibn Omar. Grand or humble, when they arrived, their affection and respect for Lawrence were plain to see.

So I am inclined to accept their reckoning of the man. They knew "Aurens." Mr. Aldington and later historians did not.

With the window glass gone, we had the creosote-scented breeze in our faces, dust and cinders flying into our eyes. The gentlemen urged Clementine and me to sit with our backs to the engine, but I declined. I wanted to see what we were headed toward and didn't mind the soot.

Naturally I missed Rosie and wondered how she and Karl were doing. It was unquestionably wise to have left her in Cairo, but she would have loved the trip to Jerusalem — apart from the riot, of course. I could easily imagine her stretching up from my lap to face the wind — ears flying, nose to the world as we steamed through dun-colored desert valleys dotted by long black Bedouin tents, crisscrossed with military roads, and knobby with the tumbled fragments of ancient masonry. Everywhere I looked I saw broken columns and walls, or the curving hint of a small amphitheater, or ruined mud-brick huts, or the crumbling tower of a castle. And in between each shard of civilization: sheep, and scrub, and stones, stones, stones.

It was well into the evening when we crossed the plain that has been the high road of conquest for five thousand years, whether "Egypt struck from the south or some cauldron boiled over in the north," as Jeremiah put it. And there at last was the Mount of Olives, glorified by the lingering brilliance of a golden sunset, its own purple shadows veiling hills that rose and retreated, height upon blue height.

Only a few years before, Kaiser Wilhelm had confidently expected to win his own rung on Palestine's long ladder of absentee emperors. In anticipation of that day, he had caused his eastern imperial palace to be built on Olivet. The war, however, hadn't gone his way after all, and now the kaiser's royal residence was called simply Government House, where the British civil administration of Palestine was lodged in Teutonic splendor.

Young Britons, smartly uniformed, snapped to attention as we passed beneath the imperial eagle of Germany carved into the main gateway to the palace grounds. Inside was a courtyard, open to the platinum moonlight but surrounded by roof gardens that would give it shade in the next day's sun.

We were ushered past the door of one vast, ornate room, and our attention was directed to a sign, in German and on gold, proclaiming it "The Kaiser's Bedroom." Across the hallway, and only slightly smaller, was "The Kaiserin's Bedroom." Those accommodations were reserved for such honored guests as Winston and Clementine, but I was shown to a lovely room, small and beautifully appointed. There I rejoiced to find a telegram placed on the night table in anticipation of my arrival.

ROSIE MISSES YOU STOP BEARING UP BRAVELY STOP LOTS OF WALKS AND SAUSAGE STOP K STOP

Smiling, I washed the grit of travel away, and smiling still, I gratefully received supper on a silver tray, delivered to my room by a nice young man. After dinner I got into bed and read the telegram over and over, smiling all the while.

I awoke full of energy, ready to see the city in daylight. I would be on my own while we were in Jerusalem. Lawrence and the other gentlemen were busy with matters of state, of course, and Clementine gracefully made it understood that she had no interest in accompanying me on my explorations. Mumma might have taken this as a snub but truth be told, it was fine with me. After nearly two weeks of continuous company, no matter how beloved or remarkable, it would be nice to have a few days when I answered only to my personal desires for rest or meals or walks.

"Don't bother hiring a guide," Lawrence advised at breakfast. "Since the war ended, Jerusalem has filled up with American and English tourists," he added, which was just what Karl had said about Cairo. "You'll overhear as much as you can bear."

And I had, in fact, brought along my own guide: my sister Lillian's spirit. Before I left my room, I'd reread several of her honeymoon letters, telling of her walk along the zigzag path of the Via Dolorosa to the Holy Sepulchre. Here, in Jerusalem, my sister's faith had been strengthened and confirmed as she and Douglas — newlywed and much in love — retraced the Savior's path. I meant to follow in Lillie's footsteps as she had followed those of Jesus. In so doing, I hoped to find a ford through the river of carping questions that lay between my sin of pride and my sister's shadowless belief.

I've told you so much, so I shall confess to you as well that when I was still teaching and lived in Little Italy among my Catholic students, I often envied them their Roman rituals. Conducted as they were in a dead language, such ceremonies could invite a mood of awe while concealing the logical fault lines and scriptural inconsistencies that blared out at me when worshipping in English. Perhaps if Latin chants had crowded out my questions, I'd have found it easier to move away from the mundane and toward the glory of God's presence. Yet Lillian sat at my side during the services we attended, and she was never troubled by the sermons that made me want to argue. Even as a child, she could always quote a bit of Scripture to settle any question I had. As a grown woman, intelligent and knowledgeable, she devoted her life to the Gospel. Lillian had no need of Latin obfuscation to shelter her from doubt.

As the sun rose, I stood at the gate beneath the kaiser's eagle, wearing my navy sport suit and my sturdiest shoes. Bethany was close by, a village on the southeastern slope of Olivet. There, Jesus visited his friends Mary and Martha, and raised their brother Lazarus from the dead, and cured Simon the Leper, but I would explore the town on another day. My destination that first morning was the Church of the Holy Sepulchre, which everyone agreed should be seen in eastern light.

There was, however, an additional consideration dictating an early start. You see, the shrine itself was held in joint tenancy by Greek Orthodox, Roman Catholic, Armenian, and Coptic Christians, but the influence of the Prince of Peace had proved insufficient to facilitate development of an orderly schedule. Between ten a.m. and three p.m. each day, clergy of each sect vied to make their processions to all the holy places within its confines. These events sometimes overlapped acrimoniously. Over the centuries, civil authorities had found it necessary to post guards there to referee the fistfights. I'd already experienced as many riots as I cared to attend, thanks all the same, and meant to get to the church by eight.

There are three ways down the Mount of Olives. I chose the most direct — a natural continuation of the Jericho Road and an easy two-mile walk downhill to the city. This was said to be the very path upon which our Lord traveled during his triumphal entry into Jerusalem on Palm Sunday, and it was easy to picture the two vast crowds of people on that morning nearly nineteen hundred years earlier. One had streamed out of the city to meet Him, moving upward with shouts of "Hosannah!" The other had assembled in Bethany the previous night and now poured down the hill, ready to testify to the great miracle at Lazarus's grave. Halfway down, the two streams of jubilant followers met and became one, shouting, "Blessed is He who comes in the name of the Lord!"

When Jesus traveled this path, the people carpeted His way with rush mats and palm branches; the road I strode was broad, well paved, and suitable for automobiles. For a short stretch, it descended into a slight declivity and all vistas were lost. I leaned into the hill, climbed to reach a smooth ledge, attained it, and then — Jerusalem! The whole city burst into view, its yellow limestone gleaming in the dawn. Sunday school dioramas and pious paintings made its most prominent features familiar. The Tower of Hippicus, the onion domes of Saint Mary Magdalene, the Mosque of Omar, the crenellated walls, the great city gates . . .

I know I should have wept to see it, or thought of some sublime psalm, but really? "It's so small!" I blurted, then looked around to see if anyone had heard me.

No one was nearby, but no one would have been surprised, for mine was hardly a novel reaction. Even Lillian, I recalled, had felt a bit disappointed upon her first sight of the Holy City. "Its size is much less than the importance our imaginations have bestowed upon it," she wrote. "The entire city would fit comfortably within the municipal limits of a small Ohio town."

Seen from the Mount of Olives, Jerusalem appeared to have no streets at all. Rather, it seemed a compact mass, nearly solid from center to edge. On more careful inspection, thin lines of shadow delineated individual buildings, every one of which was topped with as many as six circular stone knobs, low and broad and painted white. Add the famous and impressive domes, as well as those of less prominent mosques and churches, and the overall effect was that of an enormous mushroom colony.

Of course, there is a difference between a tourist and a pilgrim: one comes to see the sights, the other comes to visit sites. A tourist takes in the Grand Canyon, the Eiffel Tower, Niagara Falls. Nothing particularly important happened in those places; the wonderment is visual. Pilgrims travel to Jerusalem because they wish to stand in the very place where the Deity stayed Father Abraham's hand from his sacrifice of Isaac; where Kings David and Solomon ruled; where the Savior walked and died and rose; whence the Prophet rode his mighty steed to heaven. I had come here as a pilgrim, not a tourist, so I shook off my dismay and walked with renewed fervor toward Saint Stephen's Gate, joining the morning throngs that converged on every passage into the city.

Before we could pass within the walls, we were greeted by the usual beggars crying, *"Baksheesh!"* As Lillie wrote in 1906, "Millennia of history have left one thing at least unchanged, and that is the misery of lepers." Dozens of them sat propped against the stone wall that morning, and a more distressing spectacle cannot be conceived. Before medical science discovered a treatment, lepers quite literally fell to pieces. Limb after limb broke down, becoming shapeless first, then lost altogether. Faces could become so knotted with lumpish lesions as to resemble a bunch of grapes; in some poor wretches, the features were scarcely discernible.

In my day, the disease frequently attacked the throat and caused the woeful creatures to make a peculiar sound of heartrending sadness. *"Baksheesh,"* the lepers wailed, as did all the beggars, but more eerily, more hopelessly. *"Baksheesh . . . Baksheesh . . ."*

I had come to hate the relentless importuning — almost as much as I hated my own revulsion at the sight of ragged children and elderly cripples holding out their hands. *Baksheesh* is the alpha and omega of travel in the Middle East, the first word one hears upon stepping onto any public street and the last heard as one takes shelter inside a hotel or a shop or café. How to deal with beggars was a lively topic of concern among foreigners. Lillian always carried coins with her and handed them out with the words "The Lord Jesus loves you, dear." Karl considered *baksheesh* corrosive to society and deplored the way parents sent their most pitiable offspring out to beg. Even so, he often gave openhandedly. When I asked why, he said, "The sages teach us, 'Rather than turn away the one who is truly deserving, give to ninety-nine who are unworthy.' "

Having done a grown man's work from the time he was nine, Sergeant Thompson had no such compassion, and when we'd chatted the hours away, watching Winston paint, he'd counseled me to harden my heart. "If every traveler made it a rule never to give *baksheesh,* but only to pay for some service rendered, all this beggary would stop overnight."

I could not give to everyone; neither could I could bring myself to refuse them all. When I'd asked his opinion during our long camel ride, Lawrence had first offered me an Arab proverb: "Too soft and you shall be squeezed. Too hard and you shall be broken." He suggested a diplomatic compromise: that I prepare myself for each foray into public with three piastres to be given to the first three beggars I encountered and afterward, in good conscience, give no more.

Standing at the entry to Jerusalem, implored by so many for so little, I followed his advice. Remembering the Lord's words, I gave to "the least of these" — three lepers who sat shrouded in the shadow near the gate. Not even Sergeant Thompson could have argued that they were unworthy; God knows none of them were fit to work.

With that, I felt ready to place my foot on

the Via Dolorosa and begin my pilgrimage. It was a narrow street, roughly paved and in some places picturesque, with arches and quaint stone buildings that appeared convincingly ancient to someone from Ohio. It was lined with shops, but Jerusalem seemed to have only two things on sale: lamb meat and souvenirs. Most of the latter were carved from Holy Land olive wood: rosaries, Nativity scenes, heads of Christ, candlesticks. I walked past without much interest, resolutely ignoring the storekeepers' children who tugged at my sleeves and reminded me that there was "No charge for looking, madams!"

Lawrence's prediction was correct. At every Station of the Cross, a knot of English-speaking tourists listened raptly to their guides, each of whom shouted to be heard above the surrounding hubbub. "Here is the site of the Holy Steps trodden by the feet of Jesus on His way to Pilate's Hall of Judgment," cried the nearest. The staircase itself, it turned out, had long since been removed to Rome, but the place from which it had been taken was indicated with great authority.

A few steps farther along, a modern archway spanned the street. To the right, there was an iron gate and then a wooden door. To one side of that door sat a small altar that incorporated, another pious group was told, the *Ecce Homo* Arch. " 'Then came Jesus forth,' " this guide recited, " 'wearing a crown of thorns and the purple robe, and Pilate saith unto them: *Ecce homo!* Behold the man!' "

"Here is the stone where the Savior sat and rested before taking up His cross," I heard a few yards away. Craning my neck, I peeked between the shoulders of the paying customers. Sure enough, I saw a stone.

Descending next into a street that ran north-south and turning left, I worked my way around pilgrims who gazed in reverent contemplation at an impressively shattered granite column, which may well have belonged to some ancient temple. "This is the very spot where the fainting Savior first fell under the weight of His cross," they were informed. "The heavy cross struck the column such a blow as Christ fell that it broke into pieces, and here they are, to this very day."

A few steps farther, and my progress was blocked by several groups whose guides were engaged in a dispute. They agreed, in several accents, that this was the very house where Saint Veronica once lived. They agreed also that when the Savior passed by,

Veronica had emerged full of womanly compassion, and she had wiped His weary sweating face with a handkerchief. They agreed as well that the handkerchief had miraculously preserved the imprint of the divine visage. The argument concerned the current location of the handkerchief. It was, according to the guides, now preserved in each of four cathedrals: one in Paris, another in Spain, and two in Italy.

That may have been when the tautened rope of my credulity began decisively to fray, but turning south, I tarried to watch pilgrim after pilgrim place a reverent hand on an indented stone that made up the corner of a building. "Here, the Lord stumbled, and this stone bears the mark of His shoulder," their guide called out loudly.

Nearby, however, a similar indentation was presented for equal veneration to a different group. *Of course, the Lord stumbled several times,* I could imagine Lillian explaining. To quibble seemed impolite at best and impious at worst. I kept my peace, but somewhere in the crowd an American raised his tenor voice to protest this duplication. Without a moment's hesitation, his guide amended, "That is the Lord's shoulder, but here is the mark of His *elbow.*" At which the American grumbled to the sour-looking lady at his side, "One damn lie after another! Pay 'em enough, these carnies'll tell the rubes anything they want to hear."

In danger of achieving a similar state of disgruntled skepticism, I made a quick assessment. The sun was climbing. Time was running out on the pale eastern light like that which shone upon the Holy Sepulchre on Easter morning long ago. If I wanted to see the shrine before the clerical prizefights broke out, I'd have to move on, and I can't say as I was reluctant to skip the rest of the Via Dolorosa.

Nothing is very far from anything else inside the walls of Old Jerusalem, but I hurried to the Christian Quarter, hoping to change my mood by changing my surroundings. The Holy Sepulchre was easy to find. A domed and towered edifice, its austere exterior was severe enough to hush the voices of those who approached. "Here was where our Lord was carried after his sufferings," Lillie wrote. "Here His body lay for three days. Here He revealed Himself to the women on that glorious spring morn."

Many of those who'd greeted Jesus on Palm Sunday had expected the Messiah to be a warrior-king who would drive out the Romans and restore the kingdom of David and Solomon to earthly glory. Instead they had seen Jesus fall as helpless prey to the criminal justice system of an empire that had no prisons and few punishments to choose from between the extremes of a cash fine and death on the cross. I tried to imagine the shock — the stunned disillusionment — of Jesus' followers, as I neared the Sepulchre. I yearned to feel my eyes prick with unshed tears and my face stiffen with the effort to hold back emotion. What confusion and dismay must have afflicted His disciples! What sorrow the women must have felt as the Master's broken body was borne through the darkness to the virginal tomb "wherein no man had yet lain."

On the threshold of this sacred site, a group of sopranos sang Mrs. Alexander's lovely hymn with voices as sweet as my sister's.

There is a green hill far away,
  without a city wall,
Where the dear Lord was crucified,
  Who died to save us all.

Humming along, I thought of Scripture, and stumbled. Jesus, we are told in Hebrews, suffered *outside* the gate. He was *taken out* to a hill called Golgotha, and laid in a secret place in a garden near at hand. Well! The church is *inside* the city walls, and you have to walk *down* stairs to get to it. And then I remembered that the city that Jesus knew was utterly destroyed by the Romans in A.D. 70, and that Jerusalem was sacked repeatedly by Crusaders.

These were just the sort of nagging doubts that plagued me when I was a child. Of course the early Christians would have remembered where such sacred events took place, I told myself. When the city walls were erected sometime later, an effort would have been made to incorporate these holy places. And since Jerusalem was repeatedly rebuilt on ruins, the city had slowly risen higher than Golgotha, which was now below the level of the modern city.

You see, Agnes? I could imagine Lillie saying. *There's a logical explanation. That's why you have to walk* down *to visit the true site of the Lord's death and resurrection.*

The crowd funneled down to single file in order to enter through a small wooden door. The interior of the church was quite dark, lit only flickeringly by candles. Before us lay a large, thick slice of polished red marble.

"This is the Stone of Unction," one of the many guides declared, "where the Lord's body was prepared for burial."

Gigantic candelabra flanked the stone. Over it hung many glass and brass lamps. Around it tearful believers bent to kiss its surface.

"That marble is not native to the region," a tall British gentleman pointed out with pedantic disapproval.

An explanation was duly provided. "Pilgrims were too much given to chipping pieces off the real stone, so this one conceals it," his guide replied, and redirected the group's attention toward a circular railing. "Here is the very place the Virgin stood when the Lord's body was anointed. Follow me, please!"

The farther into the shrine we moved, the staler the air became. Around the periphery of the shrine, the morning processions were assembling, and at least two kinds of incense began to waft toward us. The cloying scents mixed with the sort of crowd odor that silently proclaims a variable devotion to the principles of good hygiene. Arab workmen were taking a break from their morning's task, smoking hashish near a side altar. Eating and joking, they contributed woozy laughter to echoing wails, a rumble of muttered commentary, and the occasional shocking guffaw. Chants, chimes, and clanking metal chains added to a growing cacophony. Prayers and conversations grew louder in response.

Pushed and shoved from all sides, footsore and increasingly irritable tourists complained indignantly. Pilgrims beat their breasts and wailed. The most devout of these were elderly Italian women dressed all in black, who reminded me of Mrs. Motta. Unlike the tourists, these ladies seemed undismayed by the lack of decorum, lost in their devotion. With their example to guide me, I required of myself the act of will necessary to grasp at some sense of awe.

And then, I was there: standing a few feet from the most sacred place in Christendom.

The Byzantine rotunda is some sixty feet in diameter, decorated with mosaics. A central oculus, open to the sky, is supported by riotously embellished columns. Beneath it sits a small, intensely ornamented chapel crowned with a variety of candle-topped towers, wax dripping down their sides. Above, upwards of forty hanging lamps blaze away. Around, dozens of enormous candlesticks bear bedizened tapers as tall as a man. Sentimental paintings of the Lord and the Virgin compete for attention with the statues of angels and disciples that climb the chapel's outer walls, no inch of which has escaped its burden of decoration. Crenellations, crosses, and medallions provide asymmetrical and unrestrained adornment everywhere the eye could stand to tarry. The interior of the chapel — wherein the Lord lay and rose — is completely clad in figured marble.

No naked rock — sacred or profane — is anywhere visible, but there, in that exact spot, my sister had stood. "I felt the eternal Love and Presence," Lillian wrote, "and wept for my sins, redeemed at such cost."

"It was an absolute nightmare," I told Lawrence over mint tea late that afternoon. "You'd find more decorum at the Cuyahoga County Fair! And if there was a genuine sepulchre somewhere under all that claptrap? Well, you certainly couldn't prove it by me. And the lying! The sheer shameless fakery!" I cried, outraged in recollection. "There was an altar with a stick on it — 'the Rod of Moses.' It was a *stick*. You're told to poke it up through a hole in the marble so it will touch some hidden thing that's supposedly the Column of Scourging. Then the guides point to another slab of marble and tell you, 'Here is where the Roman soldiers sat to plait the crown of thorns.' But both places should be back near

Saint Stephen's Gate — that's where Pilate condemned Jesus as king of the Jews — so what are those things doing in the Church of the Holy Sepulchre?"

"Perhaps they were moved," Lawrence suggested mildly, "when the church was built?"

"And that's another thing! The church didn't exist until two hundred and fifty years after the Romans destroyed the city. I skipped the Chapel of Saint Helena," I told him heatedly. "Now, there's a woman who could have done with a bit less faith. The patron saint of chumps, I'd call her! What did she expect? When the mother of a Roman emperor comes looking for the True Cross, *somebody* is going to make some money by finding it for her! She wants another cross? Why, here's the one that belonged to the good thief! How about a few thorns from the crown? Step right this way, madams!"

"Did you see Godfrey de Bouillon's sword?" Lawrence asked. "I think it's genuine, although I'm not certain he 'cleaved in twain' a *giant* Saracen with it. Might have been an ordinary-sized Saracen . . ."

"My favorite, though, was the chapel of the Division of the Vestments —"

" 'And when they had crucified Him,' "

Lawrence recited, " 'they parted His garments, casting lots upon them.' "

"What a disappointment that was! What? No dice? Every other little detail in the Passion has some sham relic!"

"Not quite," Lawrence pointed out judiciously. "There could have been a chapel for the Holy Hammer That Drove the Nails into the True Cross."

"Helena probably bought it," I said sarcastically. "It's under an altar in some Barcelona basilica."

I went on fulminating and Lawrence listened, nodding sometimes or commenting briefly. Now and then, he sipped water from his glass. It's not true that he never drank anything else, by the way. His time in the desert had taught him to appreciate water, but he was not above a glass of wine at dinner.

"You're right, of course," he said when I finally slowed down. "When they started excavations at the northeast wall of the Temple, archaeologists had to dig through something like a hundred and twenty-five feet of debris before they got to the level of Herod's city. My field was Hittite, but I think this Jerusalem is probably the eighth." He sat back in his chair, looking rather weary but comfortable in the role of scholar.

"The city of David sat on an even earlier settlement. Then there's Solomon's Jerusalem, which lasted about four hundred years. Nehemiah's — three hundred for that one, I believe. Herod's Jerusalem was magnificent, by all accounts. That's what everyone expects to see when they come here, but Titus destroyed it. Later on, a small Roman city was built on the ruins. Since then, Muslims and Crusaders traded the place repeatedly, and burned it down occasionally. And yet . . . the pilgrims come."

"But it's all a fraud!" I cried, feeling triumphant. "It's a house of cards. For centuries, the stories have been sold to pilgrims who pay handsomely to be deceived. That's what makes me angry! How can sensible people be such fools?"

"Was your sister a fool?" Lawrence asked, his blond brows lifted.

It stopped me cold, that question, because that's exactly what I feared: that Lillie had dedicated her precious, short life to a nineteen-hundred-year-old scam. Now, without warning, my eyes began to sting with tears I had hoped to shed for Jesus.

"If it's any comfort," Lawrence said, "I don't believe that she was."

He glanced at his watch and stood. Lawrence rarely gave a reason or said good-bye when he left. I had gotten used to the way he'd simply disappear. He was dressed in his brown suit; the evening's appointment must have involved Jews or Christians, not Arabs. Thinking I was alone again in the courtyard, I allowed myself a single sob, then wiped my eyes.

"Look at it this way," Lawrence said, startling me. He was slouched at the edge of the courtyard, head down, thinking as he spoke. "Jerusalem has always been important strategically. It's been one war after another for millennia. But if you can convince enough people that this place is sacred . . . ?"

He let me consider this until I could admit I'd understood his point: "Then maybe the next army won't destroy it."

The corners of his long mouth turned up, but the real smile was in those tired eyes, already lined at thirty-two. "The present city has survived six hundred years," he said. "That's the longest stretch on record."

The morning after that conversation in the courtyard, I rose from the wreckage of my illusions and returned to Jerusalem. I was determined to experience the city with the tolerance Lawrence demonstrated to me, and even now, I am glad I accepted his challenge.

On second sight, the Via Dolorosa did indeed seem sanctified — if not by the footsteps of the Savior then by those of generations of pilgrims who, according to their many faiths, strove to follow in the way of their Lord.

I returned as well to the Church of the Holy Sepulchre. That Jesus rose, I dared not doubt; that He did so *there,* I could not believe. Even so, decoration that had seemed tawdry and preposterous the day before now charmed me as exuberantly imaginative. Instead of pointless geegaws, I saw the devotion of long-dead craftsmen. I did not even begrudge the modern laborers the hashish that made their employment merry.

No longer driven from the city by my own outrage, I slowed down enough to visit the Garden Tomb, a quiet and unadorned sepulchre hewn from the living rock some 250 yards north of the Damascus Gate. This was the true site of Calvary and the Tomb, according to some. I withheld judgment, but found the place conducive to and worthy of contemplation. Like Saint Thomas's, my doubts withstood more evidence than my sister's happy faith had required. Still, standing there where someone — if not Jesus — had met eternity, I was able to admire those who had not seen and yet believed.

If my mood improved after that second day, poor Sergeant Thompson's patience was stretched thinner by the hour. We often ate meals together at a little square table off to one side of the courtyard, while the "toffs" dined at a large round one in the middle. Neither of us took offense; we knew our place in this august assembly, and it was peripheral.

Our isolation allowed the sergeant a chance to vent his frustration to a sympathetic ear, for my ambling explorations were in stark contrast to those of Mr. Churchill's breathless ministerial tour. Sometimes accompanied by his wife, usually interpreted by Lawrence, always guarded by Thompson, Winston was being quick-marched through a series of receptions and ceremonies. His agreed-upon schedule was punctuated by sudden demands for additional appearances and speeches, which Sir Herbert urged him to make and which Thompson argued against without success.

"I'm never given any notice of a change in plans," the sergeant complained. "There's no opportunity to inspect the site. Even when I have matters in hand, he'll hare off on his own."

Churchill might begin his duties with a public event: laying a wreath at a military cemetery or visiting some dignitary or other. Next he would attend a series of private talks with Arab or Jewish factions, during which he hoped to allay the fears of the former while encouraging settlements by the latter. You can imagine the tension, walking that sort of diplomatic tightrope. Often, while walking between venues, Winston would veer away to get a better look at something that had caught his painter's fancy. Thompson tried valiantly to keep him in sight, but within seconds his charge might suddenly turn and disappear down an alley, leaving his bodyguard nothing to do but dash after him and fume.

You might think it easy to keep an eye on a person as resplendently British as Churchill in Jerusalem, but that small city teemed with humanity of all kinds. Shrouded Arab women, white-turbaned Muslim mullahs, Greek priests, Italian monks, and robed Bedouin in *kuffiehs* joined fashionable French tourists, ragged water carriers, shouting street vendors, store owners, British soldiers, American businessmen, and earnest pilgrims — all these milling amid the beggars, the lepers, and the blind crying, *"Baksheesh!"*

And the streets through which all these people shuffled and pushed and shopped were so narrow! Once I saw a small boy hop across a lane from one second-story window to another; without much effort, he could have doubled the leap and not risked a fall to the pavement. In Thompson's eyes, every building concealed a sniper and every alley an ambush that would take Churchill's life. "I will never get that man back to England alive!" he said despairingly.

Though Winston's wanderlust was a constant worry, my own caused no one such distress. After exploring the nooks and crannies of little Jerusalem, I decided to spend my last day hiking around Suleiman the Magnificent's sixteenth-century walls. Lawrence's insight made me glad that this long-dead Muslim had found the city holy and deserving of protection. I was happy as well that Napoleon had decided against an attack centuries later, and pleased that the pasha of Egypt, the sultan of Turkey, and the British Crown had let the last two centuries pass without finding a compelling tactical reason to level the town.

I turned off on the Jericho Road — the way by which David (may have) fled from Absalom — and walked through fields scrubby with thistle but fragrant with wild garlic, thyme, and mint. When I reached the base of the Mount of Olives, I looked back from the place where Titus (assuredly) massed the Tenth Roman Legion for his assault on Jerusalem, and where Flavius Josephus found the words of Lamentations tragically apt:

> How solitary doth the city sit,
>   that was so full of people!
> How she is become as a widow!
> She who was great among the nations,
>   and a princess among the provinces,
> How she has become a tributary,
>   and weepeth sore in the night.

Sobered, I was in the right frame of mind to visit the Garden of Gethsemane, on the western slope of Olivet. This hillside orchard had escaped the repetitious razing and rebuilding that buried old Jerusalem beneath so much rubble. Of all the places mentioned in the New Testament, it is thought to be the most likely to have been visited by Jesus. It was certainly visited by my sister, Lillian.

Within the garden walls, behind an iron fence, grew eight olive trees of undoubted antiquity. The circumference of their trunks approached thirty-five feet, and after thousands of seasons their branches were fantastically twisted. While I visited, smiling brown-robed Franciscan monks escorted visitors to the (genuine) bedrock where the disciples (might have) slept and to the spot where Judas (reportedly) gave the kiss of betrayal.

In the middle of the garden, however, I was astonished to come across a modern tomb with a wholly unexpected inscription: "Adeline Whelan from Washington was buried here in 1875." Seeing my surprise, a young monk explained. "That good lady paid to have a well dug and a fountain built. The well supplies water to moisten this holy ground so that we may cultivate flowers." And as I was leaving, an elderly Franciscan handed me a bouquet, along with some leaves from the ancient olive trees. The leaves I later carried home to Ohio as a remembrance of his faith, if not my own.

From Gethsemane, I walked onward to Bethany. In my time, the town was an unexceptional huddle of dust-ridden houses surrounded by the blue-flowered borage that carpets Mount Olivet. Was this truly where Martha did housework while Mary sat at the feet of Jesus? I have no idea, but I was glad that the Gospels recorded that homely scene. After walking through sand and pebbles, over cobbles, and up stone stairs, I could appreciate how soothing and refreshing it would have been when a woman bathed the Lord's feet and anointed them with balm. It put me in mind of the way Mrs. Motta ministered to me when I was ill, and I blessed the memory of her kindness.

As I made my way back to the summit and to my room in Government House, Clementine Churchill's habit of afternoon "siestas" began to seem eminently sensible. I washed away the dust of the road with a quick bath and stretched out on the bed, drowsily wondering what Karl was doing, and how Rosie was. And then it happened: lying in the quiet borderlands between dozing and dream, I heard Lillian speak again, her lovely voice as serene as I remembered it.

I always had faith in you, Agnes, she said, as clearly as if she sat at my bedside. *I knew you would find your way.*

It was such a comfort then, but looking back now, in my present circumstances? I may have lost my way forever in Jerusalem. I certainly haven't found it yet.

Supper that evening was an informal but

semiofficial one, with the London delegation and the top officials of Government House gathered. There were ten men at Churchill's table. When Clementine joined them, looking rested and cool, the men rose. Well brought up, and the youngest among them, Lawrence pulled out a chair for her. The talk and laughter resumed.

I was ending my stay feeling pleasantly tired but, like everyone who worked with the relentlessly energetic Churchill, Thompson was exhausted. "It's almost over, isn't it?" I asked him. "Clementine told me you're leaving for Aleppo day after tomorrow."

"And from there, on to Malta and Naples," Thompson said, rubbing his eyes. "Who knows what fresh hell they'll present?"

There was a shout of laughter at the big table, where Winston was holding court with Falstaffian humor.

"He's self-centered. He makes the world revolve around him, and he can be an awful bore, but I'm starting to like the man." Thompson paused to light one of the Turkish cigarettes Winston had insisted he smoke instead of his pipe. "Maybe he just takes some getting used to. Like these things!" he said, blowing out exotic smoke. "There's something about him."

"Yes," I admitted, "I know what you mean."

Eventually, of course, the whole world would know what Thompson meant, but that was years in the future. In 1921, Churchill was still a youngish bureaucrat with a shadowed record. Indeed, the conversation that night soon turned to the defeat that almost destroyed his political career, and Thompson sighed. "Here we go again — Gallipoli and the Dardanelles. He just can't let it go."

Like most disasters, the decisions leading to it had seemed like good ideas at the time. The jolly little war that was supposed to have ended by Christmas of '14 had become a ghastly stalemate. With both sides dug into their trenches, there was nothing but horror to show for the mounting casualties of that first winter, Thompson told me, so England's War Council argued about the way to break the deadlock on land. "Churchill made a case for an attack on Turkey through the Dardanelles Straits," Thompson whispered, "but Kitchener wouldn't release any troops from the western front. And the czar's armies had all they could handle in the Caucasus."

"When Carden said he thought the straits

could be forced by sea power alone," Winston was telling the others, "the whole atmosphere changed! Fatigue was forgotten! The War Council could see its way clear of the western front."

"Carden's mistake was bringing Fisher out of retirement," someone said. "Brilliant admiral, Fisher. Single-minded devotion to the navy, but if you crossed him — ruthless!"

"And widely detested," Winston admitted, "but Fisher and I worked well together."

"You were so young," Clementine said, reaching out to put a fond hand on her husband's. "I think that may have tempered Fisher a bit: the youthful First Lord of the Admiralty and the old salt." She looked around at the others. "I never trusted the man, but Winston was endlessly patient with him."

"Fisher saw the logic of the Dardanelles. He threw his support behind me, and I was grateful," Winston said stoically.

"We'd just taken four hundred thousand casualties on the Somme," Thompson told me. "An eastern front made sense."

"Stop the Turks! Divert the Germans!" Winston cried. "That's why we set Lawrence here in motion: to draw off their troops! Change the balance in the west!"

At Lawrence's name, my ears pricked up. I had never understood quite how the desert campaign fit into the strategy of the war until then, but I did remember the news accounts of the Dardanelles. The British naval bombardment of the Turkish forts holding the straits was fitful, delayed intermittently by bad weather.

"But we were winning," Winston cried. "The Turks were out of ammunition with no chance of resupply. Then de Robeck and Hamilton called off the attack," he said disgustedly.

For Clementine, her husband's colossal military failure remained an intensely personal event. Men who had eaten at her table had turned on her beloved husband, and she was unsparing in her condemnations. Winston was more sanguine, perhaps because he had his wife to express his own dismay at being held responsible for what he still saw as good strategy badly executed.

Have you ever noticed that those who feel guiltiest about a decision will bring it up themselves and keep on talking about it, long after everyone else has grown tired of the issue? One by one, everybody but Winston fell silent, wishing he would, too. "If we'd taken Gallipoli," he insisted for perhaps the fourth time in half an hour, "it could have ended the war years earlier."

Lawrence stood as though to stretch or perhaps to signal that they'd plumbed the depths of this topic, thanks all the same. I thought that he was simply bored until he approached the table where Thompson and I sat. Then, for the second time since I'd met him, I became aware of the slight tremor that could shake his whole body and of a change in the color of his eyes. Ordinarily the rich blue of a clear winter sky, when he was angry they could take on the flat, unreflective gray of carbon steel. To us, or perhaps to himself, he whispered, "I knew the name of *every man* who died under my command." His voice trailed off, and his eyes changed again. In later wars, soldiers would call it the thousand-yard stare, when the memory of a single horrifying minute would abruptly eclipse all the intervening years.

Winston went on talking, and suddenly I understood what had driven Lawrence from the table. Gallipoli was all high-level politics to the toffs. Admirals, generals, First Lords, prime ministers, but not a single mention of the boys! Battleships were sunk, supply and troopships were torpedoed, all hands lost. A quarter million Australians and New Zealanders were killed as pointlessly as their brother soldiers on the western front, and with no breakthrough to justify their deaths. Churchill spoke no word of regret.

Perhaps realizing that he was losing his audience, Winston finally dropped the subject. "Listen here, Lawrence! You really must come back to London with us!"

Eyelids fluttering, the colonel came to himself, saw the reality around him, and shook off the memories. He returned to the other table but remained standing. As usual, his voice was low and rather soft, but I could make out the gist of his reply. He had forgotten how to get on with other Englishmen, he told the others wryly. He'd been happy to serve as Winston's adviser in Cairo and his interpreter here in Jerusalem, but it was time for him to move on. There would be strategy to work out with Feisal and his brother Abdullah. They needed to make plans for the new nations of Iraq and "Trans-Jordan" — a place I had not heard of previously, but one that had apparently been magicked into existence in the past few days.

All at once, I realized how foolish I was to imagine that a man of Lawrence's importance would have time to take me to Jebail. He'd made a spontaneous offer to buck me up when I was saddened by memories of my sister; I should have recognized it as a polite fiction, not meant to be taken seriously. Then, to my surprise, I heard Lawrence say, "— but Miss Shanklin and I will stop first in Jebail." He turned around and told me, "I've organized a car for the journey. Can you be ready by six?"

"Of course," I replied, getting to my feet and coming to his side.

"Too early for me, Shanklin!" Winston cried. "We must make our farewells now."

Everyone rose to shake my hand cordially, and Clementine even urged me to visit her and Winston in England.

"Be sure to give Thompson a few days' warning," Winston rumbled cheerily. "He likes to prepare for the uprisings your presence seems to provoke."

The detective sergeant himself surprised me almost speechless. He took my hand as Winston had, but bent very low to plant a kiss on my cheek. "Take care of yourself, miss."

I was amazed at how fond of him I'd grown, despite his complaints and gruffness. "You do the same," I told him, rising on tiptoes to return his gesture, and we bid each other both good night and good-bye.

I imagine you've had quite enough of my

travelogues. Believe me, I felt the same way myself by the time we left Jerusalem. I was saturated with sites and sights, and felt quite unable to absorb a single additional fact, no matter how edifying.

Lawrence, too, was ready to blow off steam, and his means of doing so involved a borrowed army staff car with a Rolls-Royce engine and no springs. With our luggage secured, I climbed into the front seat and accepted a scarf he thoughtfully provided to tie over my hat. With that, he cranked the engine and, a moment later, yelled, "Hang on!"

During the hours that followed, I made my peace with death while Lawrence made a temporary peace with life. Grinning into the sun, eyes narrowed against the wind, he hurled us along rutted, potholed, crowded roads. The first time he veered off to jounce overland, a small scream escaped me and I braced myself against the dashboard. Lawrence glanced at me, his brows raised in genuine surprise. "Oh," he said, and from then on, he warned me when he intended to drive off the road.

That was his only concession to a nervous passenger, but soon I was caught up in his frank and heedless joy. Flinging the car around rockfalls, lurching onto the sandy shoulders to avoid flocks of sheep and the occasional stray goat, flying past camels and donkeys laden with trade goods, swerving to provide wide berth to anyone wearing robes and sandals, he worked clutch and gearbox, wheel and brakes, all four limbs constantly engaged. if a sudden change in direction startled me, or a thumping bounce threatened to catapult me out of the seat, I got a grip on myself by watching him and admiring the sheer physical mastery required to dominate such speed and power.

Conversation was all but impossible over the roar of the unmuffled Rolls and the noise of the wind in our ears. Only once did I try to ask a question, when we passed the first of several startlingly green enclaves amid the scrub and thornbushes. "What's that?" I yelled, pointing.

"Jewish settlement," he yelled back.

Halfway up the coast, he pulled the car over and fishtailed to a pebble-scattering stop near the shade of an olive grove. For a while, there was no sound except the clicking of hot metal. His face alight, Lawrence turned to me expectantly, and to please him, I said, "That was fun!" To my surprise, I found that I meant it, and when he saw that, he gave a full-throated shout of laughter. That was when I realized that he had lost the giggle in my presence. It was the nicest moment of our time together.

Cross-legged on the ground and comfortable in khaki trousers and a white knit shirt, Lawrence shared out a picnic lunch. We ate flat bread, salty goat cheese, and succulent oranges while gazing at the waves of the Mediterranean as they raced one another up the beach below. If the low mountains and gaunt hills of Palestine were naked and stony, the soft green of the Lebanon reminded me of home. Much of the land around us was cultivated, and I could see why Lillian loved this place. Lemon and almond and fig trees scented the more prosaic stands of ash and cypress nearby, and there were flowers everywhere! Early spring anemones were just past, but lupines were in full bloom: blue and white and yellow. I picked out pink stock and mauve vetches. Blue borage and iris. Lavender clover, and alliums of many varieties. Blood-red poppies, with their sad associations. Pink bindweed, cheerful white daisies.

When he was finished, Lawrence wiped his mouth with the back of his hand and waved toward the countryside. "Your sister brought me here once," he told me. " 'So many blossoms,' she said, 'seen in a single glance on a single hillside, with God alone the Gardener.' She had a way with words."

"And do you share her belief in the Gardener?" I asked.

"I did once." After a while, he said, "Saint George slew his dragon here. Exactly when and where remains unknown, but no dragon has been seen since."

"So George must have bagged him!" I agreed.

He smiled, his eyes on the sea. "This coast was Phoenician once. Then Greek, then Roman. That tower?" he asked, nodding toward a tall ruin across a broad ravine. "Crusader. Eleventh century."

Larks were singing hard overhead, and we watched a cloud of martins gathering to nest in the shelter of the ancient walls.

"Fifty-second Lowland Division took that beach in '17," Lawrence told me. "It's French now, I suppose."

I could hear the resignation in his voice. "And who knows what comes next?" I remarked. "One thing about the Middle East seems certain: another army is always waiting, just around the bend."

For a time I listened to the birdsong and enjoyed the scenery, but Lawrence was somewhere else. When he spoke again, his tone was strangely dispassionate. "When the war was over, a shepherd boy — eight years old — was brought before the military governor in Ramallah. He was charged with bomb throwing."

"Good gracious! An eight-year-old?"

"His defense was that he found lots of those smooth round things out in the fields along the Nablus road — the place was littered with unexploded ordnance. One day when his sheep were loitering, the boy picked up one of the bombs and tossed it at them. The results were splendid. It made a big noise, he said, and the sheep hurried after that."

Caught between amusement and horror, I asked, "Was he convicted?"

"Sent home with a warning."

War after war, I thought. Generations of boys growing up with weapons as toys and no one but warriors to admire . . . "Where is Trans-Jordan?" I asked. "I heard the name mentioned last night, but I've never seen it on a map."

"The maps haven't been drawn yet," he said. "We're still sorting it out. Most likely, we'll split the Palestine Protectorate. West of the Jordan River will be called Palestine, and it will include a national home for the Jews under Arab rule with British administration." How will that work? I wondered, feeling like an old hand, but Lawrence continued, "Across the Jordan — *Trans-Jordan*, you see? — Feisal's brother Abdullah will rule."

"So much of what you hoped for has come to pass."

"It might. Some of it." He lay back, his long Nordic head cushioned on his hands. Watching the sky, he said, "Nothing here is easy. Blood feuds are never settled or forgotten. Compromise is all but impossible. If a tribe is weak, they say, How can we yield anything to our enemies? if a tribe is strong, they ask, Why should we yield anything to our enemies?"

"And where will the tribe of Israel fit, among so many foes?"

He sat up again, and when he spoke there was more energy in his voice. "I have great hopes for the Zionist influence in the region," he said. "The Jews can be a bridge, I think, between East and West. They are an Oriental people with Occidental knowledge. And you saw their *kibbutzim* — their farm cooperatives, those green patches we passed? Remarkable progress in a very short time. We visited a settlement a couple of days ago."

Thompson had mentioned that to me. "Fine, clear-eyed men," he'd reported. "Women of strength and calmness. Beautiful children."

"They have financial support from outside the region," Lawrence said, "and they're experimenting with scientific farming methods. If they can make the desert bear crops, they'll bring prosperity to the whole area. Feisal agrees."

I was surprised by his optimism, given Karl's doubts, but before I could ask anything more, Lawrence uncoiled from the ground in a single fluid motion. He was wearing a wristwatch, but he studied the sun's position on the horizon instead. It was getting late.

"Shall we spend a night in Beirut," he asked, "or push on to Jebail?"

"Push on," I said, and received a toothy grin as my reward.

Traffic in Beirut was terrible, and we reached the American Mission long past the time that visitors would ordinarily appear. The school's porter was amazed to see us, and I gathered our unexpected visit was one of Lawrence's unannounced guerrilla raids.

Word spread. Soon the parlor was filled with staff members, including my sister's beloved friend Miss Fareedah el-Akle. Once everyone got over the shock of our arrival, we were welcomed with much rejoicing and even more food. There were half a dozen bowls of hot and cold salads; a walnut paste spiced with chilies; a mixture of mint leaves and tomatoes with cracked wheat berries and onion called *tabbouleh;* minced lamb with pine nuts and onion. Piles of chicken kebabs and lamb kebabs and two big platters of rice. Finally, when we swore we could eat no more, there were bowls of grapes and apples and oranges, and honey-drenched pastries filled with pistachios.

Naturally Lawrence was made much of, and after heartfelt condolences on the loss of my sister and her family, I was regaled with many stories about Lillie and Douglas, and the pranks of my two nephews. The children did not live long, but I was gratified to know that they must have had a grand boyhood. That night, in fact, we were surrounded by children; they piled in around the adults, listening to the stories while nibbling on fried *falafel* or dipping flat bread into a grainy paste that looked and tasted something like peanut butter. No bedtime was enforced, but neither were there tantrums or demands for attention. Sometime after eleven, a sweet little boy, not quite two, climbed onto my lap with a perfect confidence that he would be cuddled, and I was happy to fulfill his expectation.

For the delighted Miss el-Akle and her Muslim assistant Omar, Lawrence demonstrated the rough-and-ready Bedouin dialect he had added to the literate Arabic they'd taught him ten years earlier. There were many reminiscences of his stay back in 1911. "Do you remember?" he asked. "There was snow on the beach."

"The worst winter in years!" Miss el-Akle exclaimed. "We begged him to stay longer, Miss Shanklin, but he insisted he had to leave."

"I was due at Carchemish," he said simply.

"No matter how we argued, he would only say, 'I must go, even if I have to cross the snow on a sledge!' "

He leaned over and confessed, *sotto voce,* "I got a ride from two English ladies going north in a carriage."

"Whose little boy is this?" I asked, looking down at the small, warm bundle now blissfully asleep in my arms. And I astonished myself by asking, as well, "Is he an orphan?"

The question was translated. A short, plump woman of great dignity smiled proudly. Wearing a transparent white veil draped loosely over her graying hair, she introduced herself as Um Omar — Mother of Omar — and informed me with shining eyes that in addition to the young man who worked for Miss el-Akle, she had five other sons, and two daughters as well. The boy in my lap was her youngest.

I felt an unexpected pang but shook it off, rising to the occasion. Lillian had told me about meetings such as these, and I tried to remember the correct response to a woman's declaration of prodigious progeny. *"Ma shallah!"* I said. The phrase meant "What Allah wills, happens!" Everyone clapped with surprise and pleasure. There was more to the formula, but I couldn't remember the Arabic and said it in English instead: "May Allah keep them in good health."

"Allah ichallik yahum!" Lawrence supplied, and once more there was a round of applause for my small gesture of courtesy. "Omar," Lawrence said then to this lady's eldest son, "how much for Miss Shanklin, who is so learned and polite?"

Omar looked at me and shook his head. "No good," he decided. "Too old."

All the women participated in the howl of expected indignation, so Lawrence continued teasing. "And how much for Miss el-Akle?"

Miss el-Akle was rather younger than I, and quite beautiful. "One cow," Omar declared judiciously. "Too old for two cows."

"Neddy, you are incorrigible," she said.

His eyes dancing, Lawrence continued: "Omar, I think you are mistaken, for a schoolteacher is the mother of minds, and each has many children. These ladies are worth ten camels apiece!"

"Ah, Neddy," said Miss el-Akle affectionately. "Now you are forgiven."

The evening went on like that until well after midnight. Reluctantly, I ceded the small, sleeping boy to Um Omar; I was surprised to notice how cold and empty my arms felt when I let him go. When I was alone in the guest room, Omar's judgment echoed in my mind. No good. Too old. But was that true? His own mother must have given birth to the little boy when she was my age, or even older. Back in Little Italy, many of the students were the eighth or even ninth in their families, born to mothers no longer young . . .

That first night in Jebail, a plan began to take form, one that I hoped would change my life permanently and for the better. I grant you, it was not well thought out. In my defense, I can say only that I had lived too much in my mind, too little in my body until then. I was finished with being sensible and too old to wait much longer, but the moment I so much as thought about it, I heard that awful, inward chorus of objection:

What if he doesn't — ?

— raised you to be a lady —

What will people think?

Conscience makes cowards of us all, the Bard wrote, but these were not the voices of my own conscience. They were the voices of my mother, and her mother before her. It was time to stop listening to the inner doubts that so undermined my confidence. The world had changed. I had changed. When objections rose within me, I ignored them or dismissed them.

Oh, Agnes, you don't want that! Mumma said, pleading with me.

Yes, I realized. Yes, I do. I want. I want!

There was no one left alive to tell me no. Karl was waiting for me in Cairo. And he had promised me the Nile.

At breakfast the next morning, Lawrence told us all he would be driving on that day, to his meeting with Emir Abdullah. This was going to be good-bye. The thought made me very sad indeed, but before he left, Lawrence suggested a walk; naturally, I agreed.

He ushered me out the back door, walking past the school buildings and up a hill near the rear of the compound. "The American missionaries here understood that it was death for a Muslim to convert, so they didn't proselytize," he told me as we climbed. "They opened schools like this instead and welcomed any student who wished to attend. Simply by giving classwork in English and French, they brought important Western ideas to the region. Prosperous families began to visit Paris on holiday. For poorer ones, contact with Americans promoted emigration. There's hardly a family in Syria without at least one son who's been to America for a few years. Those men came home eager to reform the government here."

All this seemed merely informative, something that an academic like Lawrence might suppose a teacher like me would find interesting. Then I saw that he had led me to the gate of the mission's small cemetery. "It wasn't only Syria that was affected," he continued, leading the way along a path that wove through crowded headstones. "One of the Young Turks — secretary for the Lebanon, before the war — he told me that the progressive changes in the Turkish constitution were entirely due to the influence of the American Mission School."

On the far side of the cemetery, we came to rest in front of a small grave surrounded by roses, near the fence on the far side. "Your sister paid a price," Lawrence said quietly, looking down at the stone, "but I think it was good that she and Douglas came here."

Frowning and uncertain, I looked more closely and read the inscription aloud. "Agnes Louise Cutler, beloved daughter of . . ."

I had forgotten: not merely that my tiny niece had been named for me, but that she had lived at all, if only for a few hours. Isn't it terrible, how time goes by and something so important fades from memory?

Lillian had told me, of course, in a tearstained letter, when a pregnancy had ended weeks before her time. "For days I was terribly ill," she wrote, "and did not want to go on living. Then one morning, Neddy Lawrence came up to see me. He sat at my bedside. 'You must be feeling very miserable,' he began, 'as if you'd failed in the most important job in the world. You must be afraid you'll never get over this loss, that you never should have come to Jebail.' On and on he went, describing me to myself, clarifying all my nightmare fears by speaking them aloud, and from my point of view, not a man's. He seemed to know everything that miscarriage could mean, even down to the shame of it. As he talked, warmth and life began to come back into me, instead of flooding out of me, as it had."

He didn't pretend to Lillian that nothing of importance had happened. He didn't try to jolly her out of her grief, as others had, by telling her, "Don't worry. You'll have another." She marked the beginning of her recovery from the day of his visit, and wrote, "Of course, after that, I simply loved him."

With tears in my eyes, I turned to thank him for all he'd done for Lillian and all he'd done for me, but he had already left, noiselessly, while I stood mute, remembering these things. Down the hill, in the mission driveway, the Rolls-Royce engine roared to life. With a spurt of gravel, he was gone.

I never saw him again.

The American Mission School was a comfortable and comforting place that combined Western amenities (the London *Times*) with Eastern luxuries (oranges ripened in the mission's own grove). Even so, with Lawrence gone, I had thoughts only for Egypt. Just under a week had passed since I'd left Karl and Rosie, but it seemed far longer. I left Jebail only a day after

Lawrence's departure.

Staring out at the turquoise sea, standing on the deck of the steamer that chugged from Beirut to Alexandria, I felt myself a seasoned traveler, a new woman ready for the new era, with no one to answer to and no one but myself to please. At the same time, I remembered what Karl had said: To be enjoyed, life must be shared. I missed our daily walks and evening conversations. I missed *him,* and yearned to share all that I had seen and heard and thought.

After the verdant beauty of the Lebanon and the bracing sea air of the voyage, Alexandria's flies and dirt and noise were disgusting, but not shocking or frightening as they'd been a few weeks earlier. Familiar now with how to engage a taxi, how much to pay, what and when to tip, I took a cab to the train station. There I wired ahead to the Continental, apprising them of my arrival and asking that my room be prepared. On the trip south, mirages no longer delighted me, but neither was I depressed by the arid countryside along the railroad. The heat was growing more oppressive, but I ignored it. I knew where I was going, and who was waiting for me, and what I would do when I arrived.

It is a great pleasure to return to a hotel

where your name is known and your reservation secure. My welcome at the Continental felt genuine, not merely businesslike, and seemed almost a homecoming. The bellman chatted with me as he carried my bags up the stairs to the same room I had occupied before. He went to put the key in the door, but it was already unlatched and opened at a touch.

When I stepped into the room, Rosie was circling on the bed, about to assume the doughnut position, nose to tail. Karl was there as well, standing near the double doors that led to the balcony. He had a bouquet in one hand, the faience vase in the other. "You're back!" he cried. "I just found out! Why didn't you — ?"

"Those must be imported from the Lebanon," I said, recognizing blossoms Lawrence and I had seen on the hillside.

"Yes," Karl said. "There is a flower shop that caters to Europeans —"

Anything else we wanted to say was lost in the overwhelming onslaught of a rapturous dachshund reunion. I dropped my handbag and knelt by the bed to receive more wiggling, jubilant, delirious kisses than could possibly be counted. "Yes, I came back!" I told Rosie over and over. "I'm here, Rosie. I came back."

"Look at her! She will make you think I locked her in a box all week," Karl complained.

She was, in fact, sleek and well groomed, and sported a pretty new collar. Her greeting went on and on, until she and I were both worn out with it. That was when I noticed: Karl had not only had her bathed, he'd trimmed the base of her poor tail closely, like a poodle's, leaving the long hair on its crooked end to wave like a cheery little flag.

It was a small and whimsical thing, but the impulse behind it leveled me. Karl had not merely camouflaged her deformity, he'd made it seem attractive and desirable.

If there was any hesitation left, it disappeared at that moment. I went to him, reaching up to take his face in my hands, and rose on tiptoes to kiss him on the mouth.

"It's foolish, isn't it?" I whispered. "Such love we squander on our little dogs."

He took one step back and looked at me, those deep brown eyes questioning. I saw the reluctance, even then, but read it as gentlemanly and caring.

"Agnes," he said, "are you sure?"

"Yes," I said to him. "Oh, yes." And to you I shall say no more.

■ ■ ■ ■

Afterward, Rosie and a thousand questions lay between us.

I did not ask, Are you married?

I did not ask, Do you love her?

Is this the first time you've cheated on her?

Will you leave your wife for me?

I did not ask, Was this a mistake? Have I spoiled everything?

Only one question really mattered: Do you love me as I love you?

I did not ask.

Before dawn, Karl rose and went back to his own room. In the morning, the boy came to walk Rosie as usual. I dressed while they were gone and went down to breakfast when Rosie returned. Karl was already in the dining room and greeted me with an affable public courtesy, as though he had not left my bed two hours earlier.

Waiters and hotel staff are professionally disinterested, of course, but it seemed to me that everyone must know, that everyone was thinking, *They are lovers now.* We had arrived in the hotel dining room separately, so perhaps our secret was still safe. And if it wasn't? To my surprise, I didn't care.

Finished with our meal, we left with Rosie for a stroll in the garden across the street. "So," Karl said. "Tell me about Palestine."

I did and took pride in recognizing how much I had noticed and retained: the overheard conversations, the attitudes, the negotiations, the plans for the Palestine Protectorate and the newly proposed nation of Trans-Jordan.

At first, Karl's questions had a certain distracted abruptness. I recognized the distance in his manner; I had seen it before, that day in the Old City. Once again, I worried that I had ruined things between us. Soon, however, he became engrossed in the information I conveyed, and to my relief, we fell back into the easy rhythm we'd enjoyed during our first days together.

He was especially interested in comments that revealed the British wariness of a French Syria, which Karl seemed to share. "But the French may do better than the British in Arab lands," he admitted, musing. "The cultures are fundamentally similar. Frenchmen and Arabs sit around talking politics all day while their women do the work. French and Arab women are the most industrious in the world because they cannot count on men to do anything but get children on them."

And, "The difference between the French and the English can be seen in their cooking. The English throw a head of cabbage into boiling water and then eat it. The French have a thousand sauces — each a work of art. Thus: the English have no disguises; the French disguise everything."

But, "The French are right about one thing, Agnes. Oil is the blood of victory. There are pools of oil near Mosul — on the surface of the land, like rain puddles. They burst into flame, all on their own. The British know this, of course, and will find a way to keep the Kurdish territory for themselves. From now on, oil will be at the heart of everything that happens in the Middle East."

After a time, we went on to more personal things. When I told Karl of my reaction to the fakery in Jerusalem, I expected him to approve of my new cynicism. *Well, of course,* I thought he'd say, *that's why Jews don't believe the stories. We know they're all nonsense.*

To my surprise, he laughed and told me, "You make a poor atheist. You were angry, not indifferent."

"It wasn't faith that angered me," I lied. "It was the way the people there preyed on the simple and the credulous."

For the first time that morning, he stopped to look at me directly. "You have seen Palestine, Agnes. What do they have? Stones, sand, and weapons! They have to earn a living somehow. Tourism is not the worst choice they could make," he said reasonably, and we continued with our stroll. "Tell me, what did you do immediately after you left the Church of the Holy Sepulchre?"

Not sure why he asked this but certain he had some good reason, I did my best to remember. I could easily call up the Reformation outrage, the fury of Jesus overturning tables in the Temple, but what happened next? I had pushed through the crowds until I reached the exit doors, stumbled blindly in the sudden brilliant glare. When I could open my eyes again, I left by way of the Damascus Gate, where I was accosted by yet another group of beggars — The light dawned, as the saying goes. "I opened my purse," I told Karl, "and gave all the money I carried to the lepers."

"Then you learned what Jesus had to teach you," he said simply.

Just then Rosie came to a sudden halt and began to growl. A few yards ahead, a man sat on the pavement next to a writhing canvas bag. "A snake charmer," Karl said, picking Rosie up before she could pounce.

Loving as she was, Rosie was still a dachshund, and dachshunds are not lap dogs. The standards were bred to follow badgers down holes and destroy them in their lairs. Even the miniatures are quite athletic; despite their size, the drive to capture and kill prey remains strong. For a few minutes we stood and watched a cobra bob and sway, but Rosie continued to produce a low tense whine that sometimes became a snarl. If Karl had lost his grip on her, she'd have attacked without a moment's hesitation.

We left the snake charmer two piastres and walked on to the shoe bazaar, close by and picturesque. Long, neat lines of leather slippers lit up tiny shops with vivid reds and yellows. "Come in! Come in!" each craftsman called. "No charge to look, madams!" I bought a pair in red, and Karl carried the package for me.

Toward noon, the strengthening heat demanded shade. We sat and ordered lemonade and a dish of water for Rosie. While we waited, I told Karl about British admiration for progress in the Jewish enclaves. I believed their approval would please him, but Karl dismissed it all as politics mixed with fantasy.

"There are Christians in the British Cabinet who believe that they can hasten the

Second Coming by encouraging Jews to return to their biblical lands. If we're all in one place, the theory goes, we can be converted wholesale. And if the Messiah tarries?" He cocked a canny brow. "Well, in the meantime, a non-Arab buffer state on the eastern bank of the Suez Canal will protect their sea-lane to India."

As for the *kibbutzim,* they were mainly populated by Jews eager to leave Russia, where they had lived in abject poverty, subject to endless harassment and periodic violence. Karl didn't expect the Bolsheviks to change those conditions anytime soon. For Russian Jews, Zionism was an immediate solution to age-old problems.

"Anywhere is better than Russia," Karl agreed, "but for Western Jews, Zionism is a trap, I think. Once Jews are permitted a territorial center, it will be too easy to drive the rest of us from every other nation on Earth. 'Go back where you belong!' " he cried dismissively, jerking his thumb toward Palestine. " 'Oh, by the way, leave all your possessions behind.' "

There were others who truly needed a nation of their own. "Look what the Turks did to the Armenians," he said. When I admitted I had no idea what he was talking about, he explained, "They were massacred, and the remnants driven from place to place, like cattle, until they died on their feet. And the Kurds — they are Muslim, but never safe from their Turkish or Arab cousins. But I have no need of some artificial homeland invented by the British. I am not a German Jew, Agnes, but a Jewish German."

Things had been difficult in the past, but since the war had ended, everything in Germany was different, he told me. The Roaring Twenties were not just an American phenomenon. In Germany, too, everything was changing. There was a new government, a new way of thinking, new art, new theater, new music.

"Germany is shaking off the dead past," Karl said, "and I am part of that, Agnes. Why would I leave Germany now, when I can help to build the future in my own nation?"

He finished his lemonade and lit a pipe. For a while we watched the crowded street life around us, but where I still saw the exhilarating kaleidoscope of cultures Karl had introduced me to, he saw as well millennia of feuds, rivalries, jealousies, and jockeying for power.

"The Middle East is a paranoid's paradise," he said quietly. "If the Zionists settle here with Christian backing, Arabs will believe it is all a plot against Islam. Jews will be blamed for every act of violence that follows. Black seeds have been sown these past few weeks, Agnes. I fear we shall harvest a tainted crop for generations." For a time, he stared into the middle distance. Then he glanced at me. "When you get home, buy stock in munitions," he suggested with a grin that left his eyes sad. "I promise, you shall become very rich!"

With that, he leaned over to lift Rosie onto his lap, as he had so many times before. Propping her upright against his chest, he ran his palms along her back, from head to haunches, slowly, rhythmically, absentmindedly.

Her eyes closed and she relaxed under the waterfall of sensation, blissful as a Buddha. I watched his hands, and stood. Without a word, we went back to the hotel.

Later on, when Karl was out on the balcony smoking an evening pipe, I could not help noticing his travel documents lying next to his wallet on the little desk. Curious, I opened the passport, and out fell a photograph of his family, which he'd tucked inside it for safekeeping. Had he left it there so I would notice it? Certainly he'd taken no steps to conceal it.

When he came back inside, I said, "Your wife is very beautiful." And neither dead nor discarded. "Your daughter takes after you, I think."

"Yes," he said, and nothing more.

I knew without asking that he had no intention of leaving them for me. There had been no declaration of love, no talk of a future together. I didn't care. Nor was I ashamed of my behavior. I was surprised only by the strength of my desires. At last, I had shared my bed with a man I loved, and in so doing, I had discovered a physical ruthlessness I had never suspected. It was like a heartbeat, that selfishness: *I want. I want. I want . . .*

Beneath the surface I sensed an element of commerce between us that had not been there before: some *quid pro quo* that I could not yet articulate, and willfully ignored. Karl even warned me, in one of those offhand political remarks he made often. "British colonialists establish their superiority and then save you from your ignorance and ineptitude," he said. "The French are quite indifferent to those they colonize, as long as the colony pays."

"And the Germans?" I asked, smiling.

"Ah. Germans will use you like a tool," he said lightly, "and lay you aside when their job is done."

Two days later, he left for Alexandria on the morning train. I recognized the pattern, though I'm not sure I could have told you that, at the time. He was going to report to his superiors, I understood, and to visit his family, I supposed.

"When will you be back?" I asked, wondering if he would lie.

"On Wednesday," he said.

"I could take a Cook's tour up the Nile," I offered.

"I keep my promises," he said.

Imagine a coffee-brown river, lazy between high black banks. Listen to the palm fronds rustle and crackle. Hear the strange crooning of the falcons that soar above you, sharp-winged silhouettes against the luminous sky. Close your eyes against the bright Egyptian light. Feel the thrumming of the engine, the constant subtle vibration of a stern-wheeler.

Imagine that it is April. The Nile is low and shifts in its banks constantly. Crewmen stand in the bow of your steamer's lower deck, testing the depth of the water with long poles. Even so, the boat often runs aground in the muddy shallows. A turbaned Nubian pilot, white-bearded and black-skinned, shouts to his men. Watch them strip off their robes and leap into the mud. Gaze at sinewy muscle and slender bone as they strain to haul the boat into deeper water. Hear the songs as the men work, chanting in unison.

A narrow highway runs along the length of the river. Lie on a teakwood chaise on the top deck, under a red canvas awning. Drowse, then awaken to watch strings of heavily loaded camels swaying along. Donkeys carry men. Women carry water jars and small children. Dust rises at every step, fine as flour. It is dried river silt, that dust. Add water, and the soil is so fertile that you could plant a pencil and harvest a book.

The river is locked, its flooding controlled with immense dams built by the English to regulate the flow of water but, even now, Egypt's farms depend on the river and its silt, as they have since long before Joseph interpreted Pharaoh's dreams.

Whenever the steam engine quiets, its thrum is instantly replaced by the creak and bind of wooden cogs. Water must be raised to reach the fields along the Nile. Oxen circle hour after hour, turning the *sakieh*'s great wooden sprocket, driving wheels that operate belts that carry buckets into the river. Watch buckets lift water up and over the bank, dumping it into irrigation trenches. The friction load of this mechanism is enormous. It makes a rhythmic music you can hear all night long, while the steamer is tied up along the bank.

Dance to that music in your little cabin.

Because you want to.

Even older than the *sakieh:* the rhythm of the *shaduf.* Imagine a deep trench cut at right angles to the river, with two stout poles astride it, driven into the earth. Between the poles, a rigid bar rests on a fulcrum. The bar rises and falls, rises and falls . . . A heavy ball of Nile mud is formed around its short arm, a pottery jar lashed to the other end. A single man — thin, nearly naked, too poor to own an ox — can lower the bucket into the river. It quickly fills and he raises it, using the mud ball as a counterweight, then tips the water into an irrigation ditch six or seven feet above the river. This he does over and over, for hours on end. Farther inland, the operation is repeated, and then once more at a greater distance from the river. By working these *shadufs* relentlessly, three brothers can water a large field.

Their work never ends, night or day, and it has been done by *fellahin* in just this way for five thousand years. You can see their ancestors' portraits on the painted walls of pharaohs' tombs: the same deep bronze skin, the straight black brows, the lushly fringed dark eyes. The *fellahin* live in a circling world where time revolves but never rolls. They know the future by remembering the past. No event is unique. Every event is a reenactment.

I was glad to live in that timeless world, forgetting the past, ignoring the future. I was afloat in sensations that were no less sweet for being commonplace, laughing and weeping when my own high cry joined that of the curlews amid sounds of the river, and the thrumming of the engine, and the relentless beat of the *shaduf.*

My happiness was pure, and remorseless.

Each morning at seven, we were awakened by a boy who delivered cups of tea to our bed, with two sweet crackers on each side of the saucers. A brass bell rang at eight A.M., summoning passengers to the dining room, where breakfast awaited. At one P.M. and again at eight in the evening, the bell rang for luncheon and dinner. Each meal was served in courses, with half a dozen changes of plates and glassware and cutlery.

The crew bought all our supplies along the river: fresh bread and fresh fish, poultry and lamb, vegetables and rush baskets full of the tiny eggs that tiny Egyptian chickens laid. In the evenings, the steamer was tied up, its engine quiet. Passengers were free to walk along the bank or to sit and watch the river turn purple as the sun set fire to the western sky. First singly and then in battalions, stars revealed themselves in the clear desert air. They burned with a brilliance I had never seen before and never would again.

We stopped to explore Amarna, where the strange pot-bellied Akhenaten's worship of the sun flared up and died out with the pharaoh himself. We marveled at the Valley of the Kings, surrounded by steep cliffs and honeycombed with tombs chiseled from the limestone with nothing more than a carpenter's square, a plumb bob, and a piece of string to guide the workmen.

The graves, of course, had long since been emptied of their treasure — gold amulets stripped from the mummies' linen windings, the papery corpses sold for firewood or as curiosities. The walls, however, were still marvelous, painted in dazzling detail with scenes that were familiar to me now: waterfowl amid papyrus reeds and lotus blossoms; flop-eared donkeys laden with baskets of ducks and chickens; peasants grinding flour for flat bread, or carrying jars of beer, or honey, or bright red tamarind juice.

"These scenes are maps, really," Karl told me. "The walls of a tomb are meant to help the dead find their way in the afterlife. The embalmers had no more than seventy days to make the body ready for its journey. If the pharaoh didn't find his way by then, he would wander as a ghost forever."

Across the river, we visited Luxor, of course, where the great temple of Karnak took two millennia to build and two millennia to go to ruin. There one sees the history of Egypt graven in stone, from its glory days as a great empire until it sank in status to a mere province of all-powerful Rome, itself long gone. Avenues of broken sphinxes still line the ancient road. Once upon a time, they witnessed stately processions that bore the mighty dead to their temples. Today, children climb on the sphinxes, playing hide-and-seek among them, while the pharaohs rest in glass cases to be stared at by impious barbarians from the West.

One morning, our first stroll around the deck with Rosie was interrupted by a *BANG!*, a jolt, and a shriek of metal. An Arab waiter was passing just then, carrying two large breakfast trays. Thrown off balance by the shock, he lost his grip. Teacups, bottles of Evian, plates, eggs, toast: everything tumbled onto the engine room, its roof open to the deck above it. With a seemingly endless crash and smash, bits of glass and china were ground into the works. Nobody moved or said a word until the cascade had run its course.

The waiter, nearly paralyzed, slowly looked up and met my eyes. It was a moment of human connection. Try as we might to look horrified, our dismay was quickly subverted by stifled laughter. With guilty looks over his shoulder, the young man put a finger over his lips. We nodded our conspiracy, and he scuttled away, hoping no one else had seen him feed a disastrous meal to the machinery below.

Karl went off to see how much damage had been done. I leaned over the deck railing, watching fishermen in *feluccas* put out from a nearby village. One by one, they reached their favored spot and flung out circular webs, beating the water to drive fish toward the nets.

Oils, I was thinking. Keep your oils! This is a watercolor world, all haze and mist.

"A piston rod snapped," Karl reported on his return. "The crockery made it worse. They'll need most of the day to fix the engine."

He stood behind me. I moved against him, shameless in the sunlight. "What are they singing?" I asked, raising my chin toward the *feluccas.*

"A song for the fish. 'Be careful! We are poor! We are coming to get you!' " He moved to my side, at the railing. "Would you like to join one of them? The river is entirely different when you are close to the surface."

"If we leave Rosie in the cabin, she'll drive everyone crazy, barking. Can she come with us?"

"I'll make it part of the package."

He raised his arm and waved until he caught a fisherman's attention. The negotiations, as usual, took place in shouts. A deal was reached. Ten minutes later, the sailboat had drawn up beside the steamer.

It was smaller than I'd anticipated. The fisherman grinned gummily and beckoned, the music of his Arabic recognizable to me as some variant on: *Yes, yes! Allah-hu akbar! Watch your step!*

"Allah is great," I agreed. "It's the sailboat that worries me. Will it hold all of us?"

"*Feluccas* are built to handle a load of-fish," said Karl.

The *fellah* was transparently delighted by the idea of cash passengers, and I could not bring myself to second-guess the plan. Karl boarded amid much toothless Egyptian merriment. I held Rosie under her armpits and lowered her, amused when she lengthened like a Christmas stocking with an orange in the toe. I followed, glad for the feel of Karl's hands, steadying what felt like an endless drop. The little boat bellied down alarmingly.

With the fisherman in the stern, we nestled in: Karl's back against a net wedged into the prow, me between his legs with my back against his chest, and Rosie in my lap. The *felucca*'s noiseless skimming glide soon quelled my fears of sinking. Karl and the fisherman talked quietly, and we headed off toward a low sandy depression, full of mimosas covered with pale yellow blossoms.

"Hear that?" Karl asked.

I became aware of the birdsong ordinarily drowned out by the steamer's slapping paddle wheel and engine noise. It sounded like human laughter but it was the call of the Egyptian dove, a pretty bird that seems to find everything irresistibly funny. In the city, they nest in mosques and the galleries of *souks,* but here the mimosa was thick with them.

"Listen! That's the blacksmith bird," Karl said.

The sound of hammering was soon joined by a lovely liquid melody that floated toward us. "And a skylark! Where is it?" I asked.

Karl pointed toward a tiny speck soaring above the plain that bordered the river. “Amazing how far the song carries! Ah, and those are bee-eaters.”

Of all the birds of the Nile, bee-eaters are the most gorgeous, I think. They come and go in magnificent flocks, radiant with an impossible color: bronze, purple, green, steel blue, bright yellow, all mingled in an indescribable iridescence. I was just admiring their wheeling, flashing flight when Karl hugged my shoulders in quiet excitement.

“Look, just there,” he whispered urgently. “A hoopoe! There is a legend about these birds. Solomon, the king of the Jews, once lost his way while hunting. He was dying of thirst in the desert when a flock of hoopoes came and led him straight to water. The king desired to reward the birds with tiny crowns of gold, but the hoopoes said, ‘O King, give us not crowns of gold, for men will hunt us then. Rather give us crowns of feathers. We shall remain in safety, but all shall know that we once served you.’ ”

The fisherman said something and directed our attention farther down the shore. Out of the corner of my eye, I saw something large and long ease down a sandy bank, and disappear into the water. “Good gracious! Was that a crocodile?”

We had seen them before, but always from the steamer's deck. Now we were on the river, only inches from the surface. Everywhere I looked, I seemed to see pairs of reptilian eyes, staring at me from just above the low, rippling water.

The fisherman shifted the sail to bring us about, talking all the time. "He says the crocodiles are not so dangerous this time of year," Karl told me. "When it's dry, they have plenty to eat. All the animals are forced closer to the river — easy pickings."

Karl asked several questions, and the man replied at length and pointed. Karl suddenly sat up straighter. "Over there! A float of hippopotamus!"

So much in Egypt must be seen for its sheer size to be appreciated: the pyramids, and the Great Sphinx, and these enormous purplish beasts. Not fifty yards away, eight of them wallowed in the mud. Our approach was making them as nervous as I was. One by one, they began to yawn, opening their stupendous mouths to display great stumps of ivory tusk.

Rosie began to growl, and I shushed her nervously. "Those things could swallow a calf whole," I warned her. "You'd hardly make a snack."

"They're vegetarians," Karl said, "but they

can be bad-tempered."

The fisherman was chattering like a parakeet now, and startled me by pulling up his robe to reveal thin brown thighs. My stomach lurched: one of his legs was horribly scarred where a chunk of muscle had been torn away.

I looked at Karl, and he nodded, confirming my guess: a hippo had attacked the man years earlier. God knows how he survived!

"Shouldn't we go back to the steamer?" I asked. "Really. This is foolish. Why are we taking a chance like this?"

All the *feluccas* nearby were headed toward deeper water in the middle of the current, and the fisherman gestured toward them, explaining. "He says we'll be safer there, but I'm not sure," Karl admitted, disturbingly uneasy himself. "Hippos can close their nostrils completely. They walk underwater as quickly as a horse can trot on land."

Half a dozen sailboats had converged. Our own fisherman was being paid to skip the day's catch, but the other *fellahin* continued to ply their trade, flinging out their nets, beating the water, singing to their quarry. Sometimes we came close enough to bump against another boat, but no one seemed concerned about the collisions or the hippos any longer. I won't say I relaxed, but you can't stay scared forever. I settled against Karl's chest and tried to enjoy the sunshine, though I kept a grip on Rosie, who remained alert and tense.

A yard or two away, a man began to haul up on his net, hand over hand. Suddenly the water boiled with small fish, trapped and thrashing.

Rosie growled and began to bark furiously.

In its frantic effort to escape the net, a fish flopped into our boat, convulsed, and bounced back into the water.

I shouted, *"NO!"* but it was too late. Snarling, Rosie pulled free of her collar and vaulted after the fish.

She sank like a stone. No one moved — it had happened so quickly!

"She'll drown!" I cried, and without thinking, I scrambled out of the boat and plunged in after her.

The river is always muddy, but the flailing fish had roiled it into an opaque soup. Slimy thrashing little bodies beat against my skin. Like a blind man, I threw my hands out around me, fingers stretched, trying to find Rosie.

"Karl!" I screamed. "Help me!"

I meant: *Help me find Rosie,* but my skirt began to tangle around my legs. Suddenly I was sinking. The river splashed into my open mouth. I gagged and gasped, pulling water deep into my lungs. Rosie was forgotten as I fought my way to the surface.

"Karl!" I screamed, frantic now.

I sank again. This was my fever dream come to life, and terror swamped me.

An eternity later, I felt strong hands grip my hips, pushing me up and out of the water. I was heaved, sputtering and choking, into the boat. For a moment I lay in the bottom and coughed up silt.

Rosie's body thumped onto the hull beside me. Certain she was dead, I started to sob and cried out with relief when I felt her struggle to twist off her back and onto her feet. Bedraggled but exhilarated, she shook herself vigorously, flinging sparkling spirals of the Nile into the air. Then the little monster looked around happily, as if to say, *That was even better than chasing chipmunks!*

Weeping, I wiped muddy water and tears from my eyes and sought out our rescuer, ready to throw myself into his dear strong arms.

Hands gripped the side of the boat, and the little vessel rocked as the fisherman levered himself back into it. That was when I realized that it was he who'd saved us while Karl sat and watched the comedy unfold. "*Ach,* Agnes, I'm sorry," he wailed, trying and failing to stop his helpless, ruinous, hateful laughter. "But truly, it was so — *Mein Gott,*" he gasped. "If you could have seen — ! The fish! The dog! The lady! The *fellah!*"

I must have looked a fright: filthy wet clothes, tangled hair, makeup smeared and melting. To all that, I added cold fury as Karl gave in to another gust of incapacitating glee. One of the other *fellahin* retrieved my floating sunglasses and leaned across the water to hand them over to Karl. The Egyptians' sober concern for me made Karl's hilarity more hurtful.

"I called for *you,* Karl. I *called,* and you didn't come."

"This is a new suit!" he objected. "Besides, I don't swim."

Only slightly abashed, he dried my lenses with a white linen handkerchief and straightened their frame. Looking about as contrite as a ten-year-old boy who's just made the whole class laugh by belching, Karl held them out to me, and laughed again when I snatched them back ungraciously.

"Don't be angry," he pleaded, and offered by way of apology, "Perhaps this is good luck! They say that if you drink from the Nile, you shall surely return to it someday."

■ ■ ■ ■

Ever since that morning, alive and dead, I have gone over and over those few weeks in Egypt. Maybe that's why I can tell you about them now in such detail.

One thing was clear, even while I sat there fuming and dripping: Karl could not possibly have planned what happened that day on the river, but like any good tactician, he was alert to changing circumstances. When he saw the opportunity to make clear the facts of our relationship, he did so decisively. And really? He must have been astonished they were not obvious to me from the start, for he had concealed very little. If I was blind to reality, it wasn't his fault.

You see, Karl wasn't the sort of spy you read about in novels — the ones who skulk around in alleys and know a hundred ways to kill an enemy with a fountain pen. He understood that people love gossip, whether it's trivia about the neighbors or scandals involving film stars or politicians. He all but told me straight out, on our first morning together, that he was a German intelligence officer with a long-standing professional interest in Colonel Lawrence. He simply let me enjoy sharing what I knew. Imagine that *you'd* met someone like Colonel Lawrence! You'd have been dying to tell somebody about him, too, wouldn't you?

Karl gathered intelligence by being interested in other people — especially people who felt insignificant and invisible. Waiters like Ash-our could tell him about the men who came to cafés. Chauffeurs and laundresses and bellhops probably enjoyed Karl's attention as much as I had. It's thrilling to share things you know about powerful or well-known people. It lifts you up a notch and makes you their equal, if only in your own mind.

Karl understood as well that sharing secrets is a path to intimacy, both real and artificial. Lonely wives and unappreciated secretaries of officials would have found him a sympathetic listener, just as I had. Perhaps as a young man, even Lawrence had responded to Karl's friendliness and warmth.

At some level, I suppose I knew all along that I was the source of my own romantic illusions, but for an opportunity to live out those fantasies? I was willing to cast aside morality and dignity, and to pay for my pleasure with anecdotes and information about important people I had met.

What passed between Karl and me was not much more than a banal sexual affair of the sort that is often indulged in while traveling far from home. It was also more one-sided than I had cared to recognize. So he let me splash, and sink, and flop gracelessly back into the *felucca,* knowing that it was time — knowing that his booming, good-natured laughter would break the spell.

Even before I took my spectacles from him and replaced them on my nose, I saw everything more clearly. The real Karl Weilbacher was a pleasant man who had shared his knowledge and enjoyment of a foreign country with a tourist who — not incidentally — was able to provide him with useful information. For this, Karl had paid me in the coin I valued most: attention and affection. He was a perfect gentleman until I demanded more of him. Then, against his better judgment, he became more deeply involved with me than he'd intended — perhaps out of gratitude for more extensive intelligence than he'd anticipated.

Or, perhaps, out of pity.

I am grateful to him, honestly. A cruel man would have laughed at my desire the day I first kissed him on the mouth. Instead, Karl gave me what I wanted and was kind enough to wait for the right moment to let me down.

With his assignment in Cairo finished, he would soon return to his wife and daughter. I imagined them rejoicing in the promotion he'd earn through his success in collecting information about the Cairo Conference with the fortuitous help of an American lady he met by accident at his own hotel. He might tell his daughter about his childhood dog, Tesssa, who looked so much like Rosie. And if his wife suspected anything, by his very openness Karl would make our time together sound completely innocent.

I knew all that suddenly, and with absolute certainty, and with a curious lack of distress. The mirror of infatuation had shattered, and when it did, I felt many things, but not regret. I had enjoyed something that did not belong to me, you see. When it was taken away, I was disappointed but not harmed. I may not have made history like Gertrude Bell, but I'd had a grand romantic adventure, and I cherish the memories. Even here. Even now.

The rest of our trip up the river was pleasant in a bland and surprisingly comfortable way. For Karl, the tension was gone; for me, the realities had been recognized.

The river was quite beautiful farther south, especially at sunset, with lavender mountains rising beyond reed-fringed banks against a salmon-colored evening sky. And, of course, the pathetic splendor of Thebes, with its hundred gates, could fill a book, but you may read of it elsewhere if you wish.

What else? Let me see . . . There is lovely pottery made at Kenneh, which is said to be the healthiest place in Egypt. And the Coptic girls in Assiout embroider exquisite net scarves with gold and silver threads. The scarves are sold in Cairo, but don't buy them in the city. You can choose the best in Assiout and pay much less.

The heat grew more oppressive by the day. We decided to hire a car and drive back to the city. It was the end of the season in Cairo when we arrived, and everyone was leaving, not just the tourists. Sudanese boys — waiters, porters, bellhops — were packing up their velvet trousers and Zouave jackets before heading back to the equator for the summer. Bedouin dragomen would soon return to the desert, to their wives and children, to their camels and tents. Hotel hairdressers, barbers, and chefs were already on their way back to Europe. Jewelers and antiques dealers would shutter their shops and go north as well. On the Cook's boats, wicker deck chairs were being folded, their cushions cleaned and stored. It was like an army decamping after a successful campaign. Before long, the heat would become unbearable, everyone said. The flies would make life a misery and sandstorms would become more frequent. Already the pyramids were lost in a yellow haze of particles so fine they never seemed to settle to the ground.

There was one final night's stay at the Continental, but I pleaded headache and slept with only Rosie at my side. To my delight, the little boy appeared first thing in the morning, waking us one last time with his piping offer to "Walk you dog, madams?" Rosie was happy to see him, and when he returned her, I tipped him a princely fifty piastres for his long and faithful service.

Karl and I had one last breakfast, out on a patio, where magpies boldly competed with Rosie for bits of toast. Karl offered to see me off at the Cairo station, but I assured him that courtesy was unnecessary. He arranged for my luggage to be taken down to the taxi.

I lifted Rosie into the backseat. Karl and I faced each other. I offered my hand. Karl held it for a moment or two. Then he said the most extraordinary thing: "Fear not, dear friend, but freely live your days."

There were no hard feelings, but neither

was there an embrace. I thanked him for his companionship and his kindness, and climbed into the cab. As the driver pulled out onto the road, I didn't turn to see if Karl was still waiting in front of the Continental to wave farewell.

As the saying goes, we were even, Stephen. Karl had advanced his career, and he'd kept his promise to reward me with a trip up the Nile. And I? I would get what I wanted as well: a child of my own.

I would stay in New York until the baby was born. That was as far as I had thought the idea through. Maybe I would stay in the city permanently; I could say I was a widow. Or maybe in a year or two, I would go back to Ohio. If the baby looked like me, I might just brazen it out; if it looked like Karl, I could tell everyone it was an orphan I had adopted.

Son or daughter, I would raise my child with the attention and affection I had always craved, and that Karl had given me — if only for a time and with mixed motives. I would know when to tease and when to soothe and when to be silently sympathetic. I would be interested. I would encourage and cheer on, never belittle or subtly undermine.

Childhood should be a sort of apprenticeship, I decided, a progress from small skills to more daunting ones, and from minor decisions to serious ones. I would rejoice in my child's growing strength; I would not try to bend it to my will or snap it like a brittle twig.

Every morning, I would ask, "What would you like for breakfast, sweetheart?" And I would pay attention to the answer.

Even if it was "Oatmeal, please."

The westward crossing was far smoother than the outbound sail. I felt perfectly fine — wondrously healthy, really — with not a hint of morning nausea or seasickness the entire voyage. I played deck tennis in the lee of the steamer stacks and shuffleboard on the forward deck. There was a dance band on board, and I learned to Charleston! I drank and dined with witty travelers and held my own in conversation. When a gentleman offered me a cigarette, I laughed and said, "Why not?"

Mumma, of course, was appalled. *I do wish you would stop acting like you're so special. It's just silly vanity, all this sophistication you pretend to have.*

I'm not pretending, and it's not vanity. It's just who I am, Mumma. You were always afraid of me, weren't you.

Afraid! Why on earth should I be afraid of my own daughter?

I don't know, but it's the truth. Or maybe you were afraid of who you really were. You had ideas of who each of us should be, and none of us was what you wanted. Everything real frightened you.

Well, just look at the real you! Smoking, drinking, whoring with that Jew! Do you suppose it is my pleasure to find fault in my daughter? It is my duty, for all the good it's done either of us. And now, when I think of you living without Jesus — Well, I can't bear to think of what will happen to you when you die. You'll be sorry, I expect. Don't say I didn't warn you!

"Oh, Mumma," I said aloud, blowing smoke at her memory, "do shut up."

That's telling her, my brother Ernest said. *Good for you, Aggie.*

Mumma did the best she could, Lillie whispered. *That's all any of us can do.*

Cold comfort, I thought, and stood to leave my cabin.

"Come on, Rosie!" I said, snapping on her leash. "Life is for the living! Pooh, pooh, skiddoo! Drink up — the night is young!"

■ ■ ■ ■

Part Three: Ohio and Beyond

■ ■ ■ ■

Of course, it is not always easy for a woman of forty to conceive. What might seem a significant delay can be a mere irregularity. Before the steamer reached New York, I learned that I was no longer pregnant, if indeed I ever had been.

It rained that night, and on into the next day. You won't believe it, but I'd almost forgotten rain. Remarkable, how quickly one gets used to good weather.

Rosie and I went out on deck as usual the next morning, and took our walk around the ship in the glassy, gray light of the North Atlantic. "Just you and me again, Rosie!" I whispered to her, my tears lost in the general soaking we got. "We'll be all right, won't we. We'll be fine."

And we were, truly. For a long while, anyway.

It was fully spring when we got home to Cedar Glen. Rosie had a fine time reacquainting herself with the yard, chasing a generation of chipmunks that hadn't learned to fear her. We had missed the March mud entirely and the chilly April rain — that alone was almost worth the price of a trip to Egypt. Late-season tulips and daffodils were still in bloom. Lilacs and peonies were showing bud.

Everything in the house looked powdered, but the weather was so balmy that I opened all the windows and let the breeze help me with the dusting. Seeing me outside flapping the cleaning cloths, the pastor from Mumma's congregation stopped to say hello and welcome me home. "We'd be very pleased to have you come and give a lecture on the Holy Land, Miss Shanklin." I promised I would think about it.

Neighbors caught me up on all the news. There was a big snowstorm in late March. Old Mr. Ellison passed away, which everyone agreed was a mercy. A land speculator had been sniffing around the neighborhood. Name of Hartigan. He was looking to buy up properties for a development like the one those Van Swerington brothers built over in Shaker Heights.

"Oh, and the Beasley girl got married," I was told several times and always with a wink that implied: *kind of a hurry-up deal, there.* Then they'd shrug and say, "It's a different world." Naturally, I'd agree.

"Well," they'd say, "got to get to town. Did you have a nice time on your trip?"

"Oh, yes," I'd tell them. "It was very educational."

It's funny, isn't it, how you can be so different when you're away from home? Then, surrounded by familiar people and things, you slip right back into all your habits, as though you were pulling on an old woolen cardigan: stretched out and unflattering, but comfortable and soft.

Sure enough, Mr. Robert Hartigan contacted me through my lawyer, Mr. Reichardt. He wished to inquire about my selling him the house or, more accurately, the property it sat on, for he meant to tear it down and build something grander in its place. I declined his offer. He must have thought that I was holding out for a better price, but I simply hadn't decided what I wanted to do next.

One fine June morning, Pastor Eastman paid me another call — the third since my return. The last thing in the world I wanted to do was talk about my trip to Mumma's friends, but I was running out of polite ways to decline his invitation to give a lecture to the congregation.

That afternoon I made up my mind to look for an apartment in downtown Cleveland. It was exhilarating to survey all the possibilities, thinking of how my new surroundings would make me feel. The most exciting prospect was down on Euclid Avenue in a brand-new building with its own little fenced-in park, where Rosie could chase squirrels.

The next time I got a call from Mr. Hartigan, he named a truly startling sum, and I agreed to sell. A few weeks later, we met at the bank in Mr. Reichardt's watchful, lawyerly presence. "You're a fine businesswoman," Mr. Hartigan told me as I put pen to paper. "Reichardt here tells me you come by it honestly. I hear your mother was quite an entrepreneur."

"Thank you," I said, and pardon my French, but I made damn sure Hartigan's check was good before the contract was signed! Mumma would have been pleased by that much, at least.

Laying the papers in his briefcase and snapping it shut, Mr. Hartigan asked, "Have you decided what you want to do with the things that are still in the house, Miss Shanklin?"

"Sell them, junk them, give them away," I

said breezily. "Out with the old, in with the new! None of it will look right in my new place."

Mr. Hartigan left the bank happily planning to bulldoze my childhood home. Mr. Reichardt and I went to lunch afterward and talked about investments. "You ought to think about putting some of that money into stocks," he said, handing me a broker's card. "This is my man. He's got the golden touch."

You might be surprised to know how many women played the market in the twenties. In fact, there were so many of us that stockbrokers often reserved special ladies' salons in their offices. These were filled from the opening bell to the close with society women who had money to burn, with the wives of university professors and prosperous businessmen, and with heiresses like me. Perhaps that's what made it easy to speculate in large sums: none of us had earned our wealth with the sweat of our own brows. The other thing was, in the twenties, money just didn't seem as serious as it had before and would again later.

The stock market was like Old Faithful, regularly spouting fortunes. Playing it was fun — like being paid to shop! And it was a social event, as well: someplace convivial to go, like a bridge club but infinitely more exciting. There were the ticker tapes with their exotic alphabetical symbols, clattering along like racehorses. You had to read them in a rush, and the ladies who could decipher them the quickest were held in high esteem. Awed by the panache with which more experienced women snapped out orders to the brokers, neophytes stood by diffidently until they raised the nerve to ask for a translation.

Once you'd cracked the secret code, though, all you needed to know was, "Buy low and sell high." Purchase shares in the morning and by that very afternoon, sometimes, you could sell them for enough to pay for a daughter's lavish wedding, or your own mink coat, or a brand-new automobile.

By then, it seemed we all had gasoline-engine cars. Plutocrats had once travelled at ten miles an hour behind a pair or two of horses, but now women like us could go thirty in a Ford. The fuel-tank wagon was becoming as familiar as the coal truck, delivering cheap and convenient heating oil to factories and dwellings. I didn't own a house anymore, but I could just imagine how lovely it must have been to awaken in a nice, warm home without having to go down into the cellar to shovel coal into the boiler. Why, Americans would no more give up our autos and oil furnaces than go back to candlelight and cooking over an open fire! So I did well with Standard Oil of Ohio, as you can imagine.

I bought into several airlines, as well, having heard Winston rhapsodize about the potential of the air. Man had achieved a three-dimensional existence, and before the decade was over, Trans-Continental could fly you from one coast to the other in under forty-eight hours. I missed out on R.C.A., though. I thought the stock was already too high when I discovered how much I enjoyed radio, but its ascent was only starting. Theaters, newspapers, and pulpits had a new competitor. Before long everyone listened to the radio and every program, night and day, was sponsored by an advertiser, and each advertisement fed the hunger for more and more.

"Nature abhors a vacuum," Mr. Arthur D. Little observed in 1924, "but only because she doesn't have carpets to clean." Appliances, fashions, furniture! The whole world seemed one glorious bazaar, filled with splendid things to buy. So we bought: wildly, extravagantly, recklessly, on credit and on margin.

Many ladies in the brokerage salons were

well connected and hinted at tips from high sources. These women were watched and their bets followed by the lesser players. It was like someone ordering dessert in a restaurant: *Mmmm, that looks good . . . Waiter, I believe I'll have one of those as well.* More often than not, in those days, the speculation paid off; but if you looked carefully, you might have noticed that most people were buying because other people had bought.

I, at least, had some logic behind my choices. I considered, for example, the arms manufacturers that Karl had endorsed, but war was the last thing on anyone's mind in the twenties. With the Great War behind us, we truly believed that the problems of the turbulent past were solved. Yes, there had been terrible sacrifices, tragic losses, appalling destruction, but never again would men of such uncompromising, irresponsible stupidity rise to power. And look how good things were! Why would nations fight when they could do business instead?

So I went into iron and steel companies instead of armaments, on the theory that they would make money in wartime or in peace. I was really quite successful and, after a while, not even Mumma tried to second-guess me. Weeks and weeks would go by without my thinking of her at all, busy as I was.

Looking back, I must say that the twenties and my forties were the best years of my life. I made lots of friends — and yes, I took a lover occasionally. Even Rosie set a style! Several of the stock market ladies thought she was so cute that they sought out the breeder who'd taken Mumma's last dachshunds in 1919. Before long several of Rosie's grandnieces were curled on laps around the salon. If the little ones' housebreaking remained somewhat unreliable, well, the steady flow of our commission money made it worthwhile for the broker to replace his carpeting now and then.

When the morning's killing was especially gratifying, our gang would go out for brunch in one of the fun new places that had sprung up just off East Ninth. Women who'd never been to a restaurant in their lives before the war now considered cooking too dreary to bother with. We'd order waffles and sausages to share with the dogs, and finish up with coffee and ice cream. We spread tips around like rose petals.

After dessert I'd cry, "Let's go share the wealth with Mildred!" and we'd all troop off to Halle's. Every week there was something fabulous to try on: the latest Chanel suit in rose-beige jersey, or patterned stockings to wear under those new skirts with the asymmetrical hems, or "Mary Janes" with the diamanté trim on the straps. We kept up with all the changes.

It never occurred to anyone to think, *I have enough. It's time to walk away from the table.* Tomorrow was another day. We'd all be back for more.

And then, it was over.

To this moment, I can remember every detail of Black Thursday. All around me, disheveled panicky women stared at the ticker tape in stunned despair, or wept, or even fainted as their stocks dropped and dropped again. Balances that had done nothing but grow long strings of zeros suddenly *became* zeros. Late in that afternoon, there were frantic telephone calls, sobbing confessions, pleas for understanding. Husbands who hadn't even known their wives were playing the market found out that they'd been bankrupted.

And it wasn't just the investment money that was lost. Many ladies had borrowed from brokers to speculate on sure things that were going bust before our eyes. "How can my balance be less than zero?" one saucer-eyed lady asked when the broker told her she owed him over $10,000. "That's more than my house cost! I don't understand — it's simply not possible for something to be less than zero!"

It was possible, as anyone who'd taught fifth-grade mathematics could have told her. You may be relieved to know that I was not as foolish as that poor woman. I never borrowed from the broker. For one thing, I'd had a horror of debt since my parents' bankruptcy. And I knew the difference between playing the market and investing, thank you very much. An investment is a transfer of capital to an enterprise that uses it to create future wealth by generating goods and services that secure income or profit. Playing the market is just gambling: betting that some fool will pay more this afternoon for what you bought this morning.

But when prices are dropping like stones, there are bargains to be had. It's time to buy low, I thought with cool confidence, and poured good money after bad. In the next few weeks, my net worth melted like a block of ice in August. Before it was over, even the puddle evaporated. I was forced to sell the last of my stocks at the bottom of the market, in the summer of '32.

By then the full dimension of the Crash

was apparent. A quarter of the workforce was unemployed. All of us were faced with unpalatable choices. I, for example, could starve in genteel comfort surrounded by elegant possessions that nobody had cash to buy, or eat Rosie. "You're lucky you're a stringy old dog," I told her. "It would take too long to stew you. I can't afford the gas bill."

Like so many others, I started each day circling want ads in the newspapers. Then I'd buff up my least run-down shoes, put on my best dress, and hop a streetcar to look for work. Finally one September morning, it looked like my luck had turned. Remember Mrs. Motta, my landlady? Well, she had used the money she made renting rooms to send her eldest son to college, and I read in the *Plain Dealer* that he'd just been promoted to principal at Murray Hill School!

At first, Mr. Motta thought I was there to congratulate him, and indeed I was delighted for his success. We spoke about his late mother and swapped stories for a while, but the moment came to swallow my pride and inform him of my situation. I was over fifty and nearly penniless.

Seeing the look on his face, I stopped before I asked about a job, but he knew why

I was there. There were no openings for teachers, he said, and I understood, of course. There were men in breadlines, fathers with whole families to support, he added. He didn't have to say the rest: single women were the last to be considered for any job. As I rose to go, he promised he would keep me in mind, but I supposed he was only being nice.

Two weeks later, I was wondering if I could hire out as a tutor or a nanny to some family too rich to go broke when a letter arrived in the morning mail. There was a possibility of a part-time position at Murray Hill as the school librarian. The salary was pitiable, but it was the best Mr. Motta could do. Was I interested? Yes. Oh, yes. I was very interested indeed.

And it was *wonderful* to be among young people again. Officially, I got off at lunchtime, but I enjoyed the work so much that I returned with Rosie most afternoons. Even in old age, she was a charmer and liked to snuggle with the children who began to hang around the library after school.

"You know what?" I'd say. "Rosie just loves stories, but I'm awfully busy." I'd hold out a simple book and look very serious. "I hate to ask, because I know you're busy, too, but I'd take it as a personal favor if you would read her a story while I catch up on some paperwork."

This was patently absurd, but doing favors for adults makes children feel very grown-up and magnanimous. The good readers liked showing off, but even the more backward ones were willing to mutter and look at the pictures with Rosie at their side.

One day it occurred to me to bring in "treats for Rosie." I would spend the afternoon in a breadline and bring a loaf in after school. Then I'd watch to see which child gave the bread to Rosie willingly and which looked horrified. To the latter, I would confide, "I think Rosie's getting fat. She really shouldn't have all that bread. Why don't you eat most of it and just give her a little bit?"

Well! Food, books, and a dog to pet — that's a winning combination for any library. I would sit at my desk, shuffling paper but listening as the children read, slyly giving help when they needed to sound out a hard word.

In my experience, most children — even backward ones — can do well in school. They just need one person who will cheer them on, one person who can say with serene confidence, "I *know* that you can do this." When a child struggles, you can say,

"That's the best you've done so far!" Phrasing it that way makes each effort sound like a necessary step along the path to success, you see. "That's better" can sound more grudging, as though everything that came before was failure and it's about time they got it right.

The opportunity to encourage those children was worth more than any salary, no matter how desperately I needed the money. When at last a squiggly jumble of letters began to form words, and sentences, and paragraphs of meaning — Well, it was like witnessing a miracle, and I was amply rewarded with a gap-toothed, face-splitting, ear-to-ear grin.

As the Depression deepened, parents needed every nickel. Once again, sons and daughters were pulled out of school and sent out to sell newspapers or shine shoes, or even — in America! — to beg. Sometimes children would come to say good-bye to me and Rosie. I would dry their tears, open a desk drawer, and help them fill out a card request for the Cleveland Public Library.

"The public library is like a giant bookstore where everything is free," I would say. "Nobody will ever tell you to stop learning at the library. Rosie and I go there every Saturday morning. When it's nice weather, we read stories out under the big tree. Come and visit us."

So you see, in the end, the sorrow borne in my middle years spared me much grief in my old age, for with my own family now long dead, my whole world was little children. To them, I had always been the nice old lady at the library. To me, they would be young forever, full of hope and possibility.

Rosie died in the fullness of her years, and so eventually did I. Mumma was right about one thing: I did regret smoking. That's what killed me in the end. And Karl was right about that legend. Remember? He told me that to drink from the Nile was to ensure a return to Egypt.

Of course, you've had some time to get used to the idea that I've been speaking to you from beyond the grave, but it took me completely by surprise when Rosie and I were reunited in a place of water and lotuses and palms. This is certainly not the afterlife I anticipated. I thought there'd be . . . well, nothing. Even now I don't know if I am closer to heaven or to hell, but Rosie likes it here. There are beautiful ghostly salukis for her to romp with and an extraordinary number of lovely phantom cats to chase, so she is quite content.

I wandered quite a bit at first, probably

because I wasn't buried with the Book of the Dead, which would have guided me away from the world of men. Then I began to encounter others like me — people who found themselves in this place without the vaguest idea how or why. Drinking from the Nile seems to be the only thing we have in common, so Karl's explanation is as good as any.

Most souls are here for a short time and gradually disappear, which is often a pity. Once, a gentleman wearing hardly anything in the way of clothing made friends with me. We didn't talk much but enjoyed our quiet companionship. Then he stood, knit his brows, and looked out into the fog that surrounds us. "When Pagans strive to rule the world, Yahweh defeats them," he declared in a firm voice. "When Jews strive to repair the world, Jesus breaks them. When Christians strive to save the world, Allah humiliates them. When Muslims strive to purify the world, Mammon corrupts them. Therefore, the Buddha advises, Cease to strive. Endure the world."

I thought about that and said, "I'm not sure I agree with your analysis —" but before I could continue, the gentleman faded away just like the Cheshire Cat.

There are lots of Egyptians here, but the

Nile divides the *frangi* from the *beledi* even in the afterlife, and we foreigners still tend to congregate on the west bank. In life, we usually paid attention only to people who could speak our own languages when we visited Egypt. You might say it was as though we were starring in our own private movies. Egyptians became "extras." They served coffee at the edge of the frame or filled the screen with untranslated rage, while we imagined ourselves the "main characters." We didn't even notice we were thinking that way, and now I guess we're stuck with it, though we don't seem to have a language problem anymore.

Some of us here are famous. Did you know Saint Francis visited the Holy Land? I'd never heard that, but it seems he traveled from Assisi to Jerusalem, hoping to make peace with the Muslims of his day. On his way back to catch a boat from Alexandria to Italy, he waded through the Nile and fell in.

I was less surprised to meet Napoleon Bonaparte because I knew he'd been to Egypt. He introduced me to Ptolemy XIII, who drowned in the Nile during a naval battle with his sister Cleopatra. "We were Greeks, you know," Ptolemy told me. "I never believed in the Egyptian gods until I arrived here. My body was never found, so I was not properly prepared for the afterworld."

General Bonaparte was convinced that the Sphinx held him responsible for letting French artillerymen fire on its nose. Francis refuses to believe in the power of a false god like the Sphinx, but despite his own unwavering faith in Jesus, here he is.

It is a matter of some debate why some of us fade away so quickly while others linger for centuries. There may be validity to General Bonaparte's theory. "As long as your name is remembered, you are not truly dead" is what he thinks. Francis and Ptolemy certainly fit that notion, but who'd remember Agnes Shanklin all these years? It's possible that one of my fifth graders still thinks of me, I suppose, or that someone recalls the Library Lady who used to read to children on Saturday mornings, but maybe it's Karl Weilbacher's daughter who remembers me.

I had a letter from her in 1938. When I first saw her name on the envelope, my stomach lurched at the thought that my sins had been discovered and I was at last to be held to account. Such little fears in such a dangerous time . . .

Instead, Fräulein Weilbacher reported that

her father had recently been arrested in the middle of the night — roused from bed in his pajamas, dragged into the street, hurled into a car. Despite the open and increasingly shrill denunciations of Jewish influence in Germany, the Weilbachers hadn't seen this catastrophe coming. Karl had retired from his government position in 1931, his daughter told me, but he had many contacts inside the new regime, old friends who helped him and his family during the Depression. Life was hard, but it was hard for everyone.

"Papa couldn't believe that the Germany he had loved so well would fail to value his long service, but you must know how bad things are for people like us these days," Fräulein Weilbacher wrote. "He sent word to my mother and me that he was lost, but that we must look for help. I am writing to you because your name and address were in his papers. Please, for the love of God and in my father's memory, is there anything you can do to make it possible for us to emigrate to America? I would not trouble you if there were anyone else to whom we could appeal."

That was the moment when I truly regretted the loss of my wealth. If only I had the cash I'd spent on hairdressers during the twenties, or on fashionable shoes, or theater tickets! I might have been able to buy passage out of Germany for Karl's small family.

As it was, I could only contact ladies from my stock market days, hoping one of them had made it through the Crash in better shape than I. Could they lend me money for a good cause, one that might actually save lives? Failing that, did they know someone who might have influence at the State Department, or in the visa offices? No, and no, and no . . .

So I wrote to our representative in Congress and to Ohio's senators. I even wrote to Mrs. Roosevelt, who seemed much more alive to the plight of people overseas than her husband was. Nothing came of my pleas. Eventually, one evening, I set myself the awful task. In the morning, I would write to Fräulein Weilbacher to tell her that all my efforts on her behalf had failed.

I went to bed that night and almost wept to think of how Karl's nation had repaid him. Then it came to me, and I sat bolt upright in bed. Rosie awoke, annoyed by the disturbance. "Palestine!" I told her. "Maybe they could get to Palestine!"

Of course, by then the British had closed the protectorate's borders to the desperate

German Jewish refugees whose influx had triggered the sort of riots I'd seen in Cairo and Gaza. At the same time, I remembered the hospitality I'd experienced in Jebail. Surely, I thought, such generous people would not turn away a poor widow and her daughter.

I rose from my bed, pulled on a dressing gown, and picked up my pen to write. The question was, Whom did I know? Who was still in a position to help?

Gertrude Bell was long gone. She had indeed become a valued adviser to Lawrence's friend Feisal, who was acclaimed king of Iraq shortly after the British saw to it that there were no other pretenders to the new Iraqi throne. If Feisal was grateful to the British, he was subtle in showing it, and not the puppet they expected him to be. He reigned with some success until his death in 1933, which I suppose was a sort of vindication of the Cairo machinations; on the other hand, he was the only ruler of Iraq to die of natural causes for generations, so there you are.

Miss Bell herself died in 1926, so she didn't live to see what happened to the nation enclosed by the boundaries she drew, but she had her triumphs in her last few years. Terms were concluded for a treaty with post-Ottoman Turkey, granting Mosul to Iraq. This denied the Kurds a nation of their own, as Karl had feared, but established Iraq as a reliable source of oil for the British Empire, for a few decades at least.

The last official function Gertrude Bell attended in Baghdad was the opening of a new archaeological museum — the very one that was looted in your time. When her passing was reported, the newspaper included a photo of her on that gala evening. Her slimness had become fragility and her dress remained resolutely old-fashioned, but it was bedecked with ribbons of honor from two nations. She was found dead a few weeks later — a suicide by sleeping pills, it was rumored, but I don't believe that. Like so many Britons of her generation, Gertrude Bell was a great letter writer. There are thick volumes of her collected correspondence, still studied in your day, but she left no farewell note. It seems unlikely that she'd have allowed anyone else to write her obituary if she'd known she was going to die that night.

Given his hopes for Jewish settlement in Palestine and his connection to Karl — whatever it may have been — I think Colonel Lawrence might well have helped the Weilbachers, but he, too, was gone by 1938.

When I met him in '21, Lawrence was still running on nerves, but the strain of the war was catching up with him. He worked himself like a sharecropper's mule, writing that war book of his. Then the original manuscript was lost — lost! just imagine! — but he bore down and wrote it all again. When *Seven Pillars of Wisdom* was finished, he was out of money and desperately tired — physically, mentally, and emotionally.

Many were puzzled by his decision in 1924 to leave both academe and diplomacy behind and to live instead as an enlisted man in the ranks of the Royal Air Force, but I was not very much surprised. Like Miss Bell, he was a great letter writer, you see, and to my delight he had found it worth his while to correspond with me. There were hints of his plans in his letters.

To his misfortune, the predatory *paparazzi* of your time are really nothing new. The press discovered Lawrence in the R.A.F. and hounded him relentlessly, shouting questions, photographing every move. The situation became impossible, and the R.A.F. asked him to leave. Close to despair, he changed his name and prepared to go more deeply underground in the Royal Tank Corps. Fearing rediscovery, he sent printed postcards to warn his correspondents that he would no longer be writing many letters.

On the back of mine, I found a handwritten note: "My past is like a tin can tied to my tail." My reply was itself a few words on a postcard, honoring his own brevity. I quoted Ovid: "*Facta fugis; facienda petis.* Achievement you flee, pursuing new accomplishment." I don't know if he received it, but I like to think he did and that he smiled.

There were those who insisted that Lawrence must have been working as a secret agent in his later years, fomenting trouble in India or the Middle East, or even spying in Germany. They couldn't accept at face value his decision to walk away from public life, couldn't understand that when he finished with something, he simply never looked back.

He was freakishly competent, you see, a sort of serial genius who thrived on change and challenge. Study crusader castles; run an archaeological dig; make maps. Establish liaisons with Arab tribal leaders; develop tactics for asymmetrical warfare. Represent Sherifian interests with the Big Four at Versailles; find a compromise that would allow for Arab aspirations while serving his empire's strategic needs. Write a war book; translate *The Odyssey* from the Greek with a literate warrior's insight. Master airplane mechanics; test and modify powerboat engines . . . No matter what he took up, he worked until he achieved a result that he himself could respect. Then he went on to something else.

Anyway, the publicity eventually died down, and Lawrence was able to transfer back to the R.A.F., an organization he truly loved. He resumed some of his correspondence when it seemed safe to do so, and I was delighted to hear from him again. We rarely wrote of anything historic or political. For the most part, we discussed writers and books, or music and record players. Lawrence had an impressive collection of modern music and firm opinions about the best machinery for playing it. He particularly loved Mahler's Ninth Symphony, which, he wrote, "holds me in thrall. Its spell does not break until the recording has ended, and I hear the rhythm of the needle." On his recommendation, I bought a recording he admired and learned to love it as well.

Apart from the letters, he did me the extraordinary honor of sending a copy of *Seven Pillars of Wisdom* from the initial hand-printed edition. He inscribed it, "In memory of our camel ride — this is the book I told you about." Of its contents, he said nothing, noting only that he wished me to see the craftsmanship he'd marshaled in its production. The book was beautifully bound, with a wealth of illustrations, just as he'd envisioned. There were pastel portraits and amusing cartoons by Eric Kennington; oils by Augustus John; Rothenstein's chalks; a photograph of Meštrović's bronze of the beautiful, sad-eyed Feisal; pencil and pen-and-wash portraits by Douglass, and Dobson, and Spencer.

Later Lawrence sent me a proof of his popular abridgment *Revolt in the Desert,* asking my opinion. Reflexively, I sent a schoolteacher's quibbling list of typos and misspellings, alerting him to occasions when the ship of metaphor had run aground. I also suggested that he reconsider his enthusiasm for commas, colons, and ellipses, a weakness I admittedly shared. I regretted mailing it the moment the envelope left my hand, but he seemed pleased to receive my advice and thanked me for saving him from public embarrassment.

That reply was an opening for me to express the one real reservation I had about the shortened story. He'd left out the emotional climax of *Seven Pillars:* the incident in Deraa. Some people say it never happened as he described it, but something awful did; whatever it was, it scarred him deeply. "I can understand why you would prefer to leave 'the difficult section' out of the abridgment," I wrote, "but that seems to me like skipping the third movement of Mahler's Ninth. Until you've struggled to understand the third movement — with its pileup of polyphony, the crazy complexity that nearly tips into madness — well, I don't think you can truly appreciate the beauty and consolation of the fourth movement." I believe he took my point, though nothing came of my suggestion. The abridgment was published with improved punctuation but without reference to Deraa.

And then one morning in 1935, I read the headline: LAWRENCE OF ARABIA, DEAD AT 46. He had been out on his motorcycle, speeding along a country lane, when he swerved to avoid two boys on bicycles. It was reported that Colonel Lawrence had suffered a compound fracture of the skull, a hemorrhage of the brain, a broken leg, and many internal injuries.

From the first, his doctors were pessimistic, but even in middle age Lawrence was a man of great physical stamina — like a bull, as Karl once described him. He survived the crash for nearly a week, raising hopes for his recovery, but it was not to be.

You can imagine the shock. You, too, have experienced the sudden and unexpected passing of someone vital and attractive and world famous. Whatever distress their private lives hold, the public lives of such charismatic figures seem charmed, almost magical. Their deaths are all but impossible to comprehend. Many people refuse to believe that something as ordinary as a motoring accident could claim such a luminary.

For years afterward, sightings of Lawrence were reported and conspiracies were rumored. His death was a hoax, some said, providing cover so that he could sneak into northern India and foment rebellion among the Muslims there. I permitted myself to believe these notions for a while, but they were all nonsense.

After his death, his brother Arnold published a book of remembrances by those who'd known Lawrence best. I think I told you that earlier, didn't I? Anyway, Mr. David Garnett was not alone among Lawrence's friends in finding "something clerical and celibate" about him. Despite, or perhaps because of, the fervent evangelism of his mother, Lawrence was not religious, but the monastic life in the Royal Air Force had suited him, and he was genuinely happy there. As an elderly Miss el-Akle recalled years later, Lawrence "used all his gifts, great or small, in service to others." Her observation might seem at odds with what some took to be a shameless seeking after fame, but Winston Churchill agreed with her assessment. "Home, money, comfort, fame, and power meant little or nothing to Lawrence," he wrote.

In my opinion, Lawrence's celebrity was as much a tool as his clothing. He used whatever he had to advance causes he believed in, and made himself insignificant otherwise. He was actually quite consistent about that. To work among comrades, doing something useful with his mind and his hands — that was God's work to him.

When I read about the accident that killed him, I thought, It was a good life, well lived. I wept, on and off, for days.

You might be surprised that Winston Churchill was the last person who came to mind as I cast about for someone who could assist Karl's family. When you know that Churchill led Britain through the dark days of the Second World War, it's hard to keep in mind that he spent the years between the two global conflicts without much influence. His party was out of power, and he was relatively unimportant within it. Even among Tories, it must be said, Winston was widely disliked.

In France and Britain and America, we were simply sick of war. Our dead soldiers needed no freshly slaughtered company. Governments around the world were strapped for cash and beset by troubles, left and right. The Depression had impoverished so many; most people were struggling day by day to keep body and soul together. As odious as Herr Hitler was, the very thought of another war with Germany was unbearable. And frankly, so was Winston's tedious insistence that such a war was inevitable and that it would be better undertaken sooner than later.

Unlike some war lovers I could name, Winston had actually served under fire; unlike most combat veterans, he had relished the experience and never washed his war paint off. You will say that he was right about Hitler, that appeasement was wrong; in the end, the Second World War was a necessary struggle. Too true, but you should also know that going to war was always Winston Churchill's first resort. Even a stopped clock gives the time correctly twice a day, as the saying goes. You're still better off with a clock that actually works, in my opinion.

Anyway, I did write to him about helping "my friend Miss Sarah Weilbacher and her mother." Several weeks later, he replied with a promise that he would see what he could do. "Clemmie sends her regards," he wrote in closing, "and Thompson says it's been too long between riots. Do visit, if you can."

I never heard from him again — not surprising, considering what he had on his plate as war came closer. Nor did I hear from Fräulein Weilbacher after the spring of 1940. I continued to write to her, apprising her of my continuing efforts on her behalf, trying to keep her spirits up. When I wrote in April, the letter was returned marked with the German equivalent of "Addressee unknown."

Perhaps Karl's widow and daughter did make their way to safety in Palestine. Perhaps Sarah married and had children. Maybe now, when she tells her *sabra* grandchildren stories about her escape from Nazi Germany, she mentions the American lady who convinced Winston Churchill to help her get to Israel, and that's why my name is remembered. I know the odds are horrifyingly against it, but I would like to think that's how things turned out.

If she survived, Sarah must be quite elderly now. Even the youngest of my little library friends are getting on in years. I don't have much time left, I expect, and to tell the truth? That's fine with me. Even General Bonaparte has stopped being smug about the longevity of his fame.

You see, we seem to have a sort of aerial view of the world from here. There's nothing much to do, so we spend a great deal of time watching human history as though it were a sort of film projected on the shifting misty air around us. It was fascinating — at first.

I was sadly amused, for example, to observe how things turned out for the "Lost Generation" of the 1920s. Relentlessly unlucky with the history they were born into, they fought two world wars and bore the brunt of the Depression. With their savings wiped out, many were forced in old age to move in with their grown children. Ancient flappers and decaying swells would shake their heads as their serious sons and respectable daughters raged at teenagers for dabbling in illicit drugs, thoughtless sex, "jungle" music, and lewd dancing.

"Why, we used to drink until everyone was falling down, peeing-on-the-carpet, puking-in-the-streets drunk!" the Lost would mutter, recalling the bootlegging, the jazz, and the parties that went on all night. "How could we have raised such stiffs?"

I myself lived long enough to see the defeat of the tyrants of World War II. Before I died, I thought that people had learned some enduring lessons from the stupendous carnage of that war. The United Nations was formed, and it appeared that the world's wisest men and women would gather together and find ways to bring reason to bear on their differences. After all that suffering and destruction, I honestly believed people had finally learned to value peace and progress and prosperity.

When I expressed such sentiments in the afterlife, General McClellan laughed at me. (Oh! I forgot to mention it, but he's here, too. Did you know George McClellan had a great interest in the Middle East? He visited the region shortly after the American Civil War and drank from the Nile during a barge excursion to Luxor.) "You just watch," he said cynically. "It'll turn out to be a swindle."

Francis agreed, with a weary sigh. "Usually the next war is being planned before the ink on the treaty is dry."

"Peace is the womanish pursuit of cowards," Ptolemy declared. "My sister put an asp to her breast and died for love. She should have murdered Marc Antony and fought to reclaim Egypt's glory."

"At least you died fighting," General Bonaparte said. "Real men," he informed me, "will always choose peril and power."

Not always, but consistently enough. Observing human history has turned out to be a terrible exercise in monotony.

As Mr. Mark Twain observed long ago, there's hardly a square yard of land anywhere on earth that's in the possession of its original owners, and I suppose that's true. The dead don't blush, but I would if I could when I think how I lectured Winston about colonialism, for my own country rests on the whitening bones of countless Indians. Nobody's hands are clean. We might not rape and kill and pillage personally, but an awful lot of us were happy to inherit the stolen goods.

Poor Francis has witnessed the cycle for centuries. Armies arrive and lay claim to somebody else's land. Generations suffer humiliation, theft, and murder. The dispossessed call upon their gods to witness this injustice; theirs is a righteous anger and so retaliation is sacred, for it is meant to redress an affront to all that's holy. "Savages!" the conquerors cry then. "These rebels are devoid of human morality. We have no choice but to hunt them down and kill them like the wild beasts they are." They always claim that they have no choice, but what are they doing there in the first place?

"You can see why God weeps," Francis often says. "How sad, to grant free will and see it used so poorly."

I haven't told Francis, because he might be upset by the idea, but I've come to pity God, who has observed our kind for millennia, not merely decades, as I have, or centuries, like Francis. The good Lord must find our world a brutally disappointing place.

If He exists at all . . .

I'm sorry to have to tell you this, but apart from the steadfast faith I see in Francis, there is no sign here of the deity my sister, Lillian, worshipped. Far more in evidence are the gods of war, whom I once assumed were merely mythical: Mars, Ares, Thor. Indra, Guan Yu, Wotan. Ogun. Ashur, the Morrigan. Huitzilopochtli, Bishamon, Sekhmut . . . All of them are real, and in their numberless hordes, they watch human history with gleeful satisfaction.

Here, along the Nile, Mentu the Falcon-Headed seems to be in charge. "The children of men may prate of peace and mewl of love, but anyone can see the truth," he roars, lifting his great feathered arm toward his legions. "They worship us!"

I wish I could argue, but the twentieth century certainly didn't provide much evidence to deploy. I've come to believe that Mr. William James was right. (He's not here, by the way. I just remember what he wrote.) Most people welcome war. Rare and precious as it is, peace seems boring and banal by comparison. People believe easily that battle is a sacrament with young men the necessary sacrifice. They believe darkly that without war's mystical blood payment, society goes soft and rots from within. And most of them can be swayed by lofty rhetoric and crafty slogans. As war approaches, Mr. James wrote, nations experience a vague, religious exultation. That's when the blood-red gods begin to dance. "I am Empire," Mentu howls as the others whirl in ecstasy. "I am the King of Thieves!"

The irony is that each new war begins in hope: hope of restoring lost honor, hope of redressing injustices and reclaiming tarnished glory, hope of a grand new world. Each war ends with the black seeds of the next war sown: honor newly lost, injustice freshly inflicted, a world more broken than before. Always, someone steps forward, ready to water and weed and harvest those black seeds, dreaming of the day when they will bring forth their bounty of vindictive vindication. Into that dreamer's ear, a blood-red god whispers, "Offer flattery in one hand, fear in the other. Rule or be ruled! Dominate or disappear!"

The rationales warp and twist and shift. The closer war comes, the simpler and stupider the choices. Are you a warrior or a coward? Are you with us or against us?

"All men dream," Colonel Lawrence wrote, "but not equally. Those who dream by night wake in the day to find that it was vanity; but the dreamers of the day are dangerous men, for they may act their dream with open eyes, to make it possible."

"It's the dreamers who do all the damage," I decided as we watched yet another reckless rush toward calamity. "I swear, the world would be better off without them! You know what I'm starting to think? If you meet a dreamer of the day, you should wait until he sleeps again, and then just — just shoot him in the head!"

Francis stared, not so much aghast as disappointed.

"Well, that's what the Bible tells us," I said, defending myself. "It's in Deuteronomy. 'If there arise among you a dreamer of dreams, a false prophet who arises among you, thou shalt not harken unto him and neither shall thine eye pity him, but thou shalt kill him!' "

With half-closed eyes, Francis began to recite, "I have a dream . . . I have a dream that one day on the red hills of Georgia the sons of former slaves and the sons of former slave owners will sit down together at the table of brotherhood. I have a dream that one day all of God's children — black men and white men, Jews and Gentiles, Protestants and Catholics —"

"— will join hands and sing in the words of the old Negro spiritual, 'Free at last! Free at last! Thank God Almighty, we are free at last!' " General McClellan finished with him.

"Oh, my," I said.

"There were those who believed the Reverend King was a dangerous man," Francis reminded me, "and someone killed him for his dream."

"All right then, what about Hitler?" I said.

"Gandhi," Francis countered.

"Pol Pot!"

"Mandela."

"So how can we tell the false prophets from the true?" I asked.

"By their deeds shall you know them," George McClellan said. "Wait and see."

"Wait and see," Napoleon mimicked in a

prissy voice. "That's why Lincoln fired you."

"And in the meantime, the damage is done!" I cried.

No one answered.

There was some excitement a little while ago. The ghost Nile has currents and eddies, just as the real river does. Every now and then someone new washes up. George spotted a man wearing antique armor climb onto the foggy bank, across the water. Ptolemy says the armor is Greek. He thinks the man might be Alexander the Great, so he and George have been trying to attract the newcomer's attention. General Bonaparte is sulking. Just between you and me? I don't think he wants the competition.

The idea of another soldier among us is making Francis restless, but I've begun to hope we can lure someone new to our group, if for no other reason than to distract our two generals from what's happening among the living.

General Bonaparte has been particularly agitated lately. *"Non, non, non!"* he'll cry. "Imbeciles! You cannot win against an insurgency that way! *Mon Dieu!* Doesn't anyone study the Peninsular War anymore?"

"This is going to be a military blunder as catastrophic as your invasion of Russia,"

George predicted.

You can imagine how well that went over with Napoleon. Things have been pretty tense since then.

I'm sure you've realized that Karl Weilbacher was tragically wrong about his own nation but largely right about the Cairo Conference. Black seeds were sown, and I'm afraid you're still bringing in the harvest. Rarely has so much been decided by so few to the detriment of so many as in that fancy hotel back in 1921. I thought at the time that Winston and his Forty Thieves were a high-handed, arrogant bunch, and I knew the Cairo Conference was significant when I stood on its edges. I never imagined that decisions made then would dictate history for a hundred years or more, or that America would get tangled up in it all.

I guess it's easy for some people to convince themselves, as Mumma always did, that they're doing something nice for others, something they suppose others must truly yearn for, something anyone ought to be thrilled and grateful to receive. And perhaps others do want it, or maybe they don't, but people on the receiving end can't help feeling that they should have been asked before somebody charged in and bestowed it. Naturally, people are resentful of ham-handed efforts to run their affairs for them, especially when they can plainly see a benefactor's ulterior motives. And even when you mean well? Sometimes things are just none of your business.

"Americans have always looked at the Middle East and seen themselves in a mirror," George McClellan told me recently. In his opinion, "Anyone could have predicted how all this would turn out."

Well, I didn't, but I certainly know something about gazing into the mirror of infatuation. Eventually it shatters, and you're left with nothing but broken glass.

Francis says he's fed up with the generals and wants to know if Rosie and I would like to try moving upstream. I'm thinking about it, but I may wait a while longer. This bend of the river seems to collect military people, and I am still hoping to run into Colonel Lawrence. Surely his name is remembered, and I can't imagine that he never drank from the Nile.

Which sort of dreamer was he? I wonder. He seems to have concluded that he was a dreamer of the day, and hated himself for it, but I don't think it was Lawrence's fault that things are such a mess in the Middle East. There were many forces at work. He did his best, not that good intentions count for much.

The Arabs he lived among had every opportunity to shoot him while he slept and bring his head to the Turks for that enormous reward. They understood that Lawrence was for them, not merely using them for his own purposes. His dream was that they could be more fully and truly themselves, not just darker reflections of himself in the mirror of infatuation.

Maybe that's the way to tell the dangerous men from the good ones. A dreamer of the day is dangerous when he believes that others are less: less than their own best selves and certainly less than he is. They exist to follow and flatter him, and to serve his purposes.

A true prophet, I suppose, is like a good parent. A true prophet sees others, not himself. He helps them define their own half-formed dreams, and puts himself at their service. He is not diminished as they become more. He offers courage in one hand and generosity in the other.

Well! I was hoping I could end my little story by saying something wise and uplifting, and I'm afraid that might be about the best I can do. Perhaps if I'd read more philosophy when I had the chance, I'd have something more impressive to leave you with but, you see, I just taught fifth grade and lived my own little life. When it comes down to it, I don't have much in the way of advice to offer you, but here it is:

Read to children.

Vote.

And never buy *anything* from a man who's selling fear.

Oh, dear. It might be too late now, but one last thing? Try not to remember my name.

ACKNOWLEDGMENTS

Dreamers of the Day is fiction. I have changed a few dates and historical details to make the narrative work, but it was my intent that readers looking for fact not be led far astray. As often as possible, I let historical figures write their own dialogue.

I would like to mention sources I found especially useful while writing the novel. *Assignment: Churchill* by Walter H. Thompson (New York: Farrar, Straus and Young, 1955) is a funny and informative behind-the-scenes book about Winston Churchill. The Cairo Conference section is short, but since Thompson had just begun work as Churchill's bodyguard, his impressions of great men and affairs of state were fresh and bracingly irreverent. I also drew upon Thompson's eyewitness accounts of the Gaza riot and events in Jerusalem. Winston Churchill's enthusiasm for oil painting can be found in his 1921 essay "Painting as a

Pastime," which was republished in his book *Thoughts and Adventures* (London: Butterworth, 1932). I found *Desert Queen* by Janet Wallach (New York: Doubleday, 1996) an insightful biography of Gertrude Bell. I recommend *Images of Lawrence* by Stephen Tabachnick and Christopher Matheson (London: Jonathan Cape, 1988) as an excellent and concise analysis of the many biographies and opinions of T. E. Lawrence.

Celandine Kennington's remembrance of Lawrence's kindness to her after she suffered a miscarriage, which I made use of in Lillian Cutler's letter to her sister, Agnes, can be found in *T. E. Lawrence by His Friends,* edited by A. W. Lawrence (New York: Doubleday, 1937). That book provides essays by dozens of people who knew Lawrence. In aggregate, the essays portray a versatile and complex man, and I relied on them more than on any formal biography, since Agnes's reactions to the man would have been similarly personal.

A. Edward Newton's *A Tourist in Spite of Himself* (Boston: Little, Brown, 1930) was a gold mine of incident and attitude, and the source of Karl's observations regarding national character in the 1920s. I also made use of a variety of Middle East travel memoirs from the early twentieth century.

These sources included *Nomad's Land* by Mary Roberts Rinehart (New York: George H. Doran, 1926); *The Innocents Abroad* by Mark Twain (New York: Signet Classics–New American Library, 1966); *Things Seen in Egypt* by E. L. Butcher (London: Seeley, Service, n.d.); *Crusader's Coast* by Edward Thompson (London: Ernest Benn, 1929); and *On Mediterranean Shores* by Emil Ludwig (Boston: Little, Brown, 1929).

Ladies Now and Then by Marie Manning, writing as the advice columnist Beatrix Fairfax (New York: E. P. Dutton, 1944), was a lot of fun generally and provided details about ladies' salons at stockbrokers' offices during the Roaring Twenties. The novels of Edna Ferber and Mary Amelia St. Clair, writing as May Sinclair, are enjoyable sources about women's emotional and social lives in the period of this novel. I particularly liked *The Girls* by Ferber (New York: P. F. Collier and Son, 1921) and *Mary Olivier* by Sinclair (New York: Macmillan, 1919).

Among the more modern resources for *Dreamers of the Day* were *The Great Influenza: The Epic Story of the Deadliest Plague in History* by John M. Barry (East Rutherford, N.J.: Penguin, 2005); *Sultry Climates* by Ian Littlewood (Cambridge: Da Capo,

2002); and *Flapper* by Joshua Zietz (New York: Crown, 2006). And anyone attempting to write about American history would do well to consult *Generations: The History of America's Future, 1584–2069* by William Strauss and Neil Howe (New York: William Morrow, 1992).

The details of Lowell Thomas's multimedia lecture about Allenby and Lawrence are from *Lawrence of Arabia and American Culture* by Joel C. Hodson (Westport, Conn.: Greenwood Press, 1995). Thomas's tours began in late 1919, not earlier, as indicated in this novel.

The 1921 Cairo Conference rarely rates more than a few lines in texts referring to it, but *A Peace to End All Peace* by David Fromkin (New York: Henry Holt, 1989) is magisterial, and the title says it all. For my purposes, *Churchill's Folly* by Christopher Catherwood (New York: Carroll and Graf, 2004) was more useful.

For Colonel Arnold Wilson, the best source is *Late Victorian: The Life of Sir Arnold Wilson* by John Marlowe (London: Cresset Press, 1967). Miss Fareed el-Akle is mentioned in many biographies of Lawrence and wrote an essay for Arnold Lawrence's collection *T. E. Lawrence by His Friends* (op. cit.).

Mildred Rosenquist really did work at Halle's Department Store and dated Bob Hope when he lived in Cleveland, though before the period during which this novel takes place. Other characters were merely suggested by history. For example, T. E. Lawrence is thought to have known the German Jewish intelligence officer Max von Oppenheim when both men worked near Jerablus in northern Syria, under the cover of archaeological research. Karl Weilbacher, however, is fictional. His name and some details of his childhood were borrowed from those of Massimo Weilbacher's grandfather. The real Karl Weilbacher was indeed in Cairo in 1921, but he wasn't a spy — as far as we know! He later settled in Italy, where his grandson grew up to become the Milanese lawyer who helped me so much with *A Thread of Grace.*

Early in the twentieth century, Mrs. Emily Rieder taught at the American Mission School in Jebail. Letters to her from the young T. E. Lawrence have been preserved; the one in which Lawrence asked Mrs. Rieder to obtain Colt .45 pistols for him was the impetus for this story.

The Shanklin family is entirely fictional. The narrator's name honors the memory of a woman who taught freshman English students to diagram sentences at Glenbard East High School in Lombard, Illinois, in the 1960s. I know almost nothing about the real Agnes Shanklin, who died many years ago, but she laid the foundation for everything I have written since 1965. This book is, in part, a long overdue thank-you note. May her name be remembered.

As always, I have greatly benefited from the comments and suggestions of a number of prepublication readers. The following have influenced this novel, and I am grateful: Susanna Bach, Richard Cima, Mary Dewing, Louise Doria, Linda Eastwood, Miriam Goderich, Martin McHugh, Nancy Miller, Daniel Russell, Donald Russell, Martha Smith, Kate Sweeney, Ann Thoma, Bonnie Thompson, Jennifer Tucker, and Polly Weissman.

My gratitude goes as well to my superb agents, Jane Dystel and Miriam Goderich, to Robin Locke Monda for the jacket design, and to the team at Random House: Nancy Miller, Lea Beresford, Simon Sullivan, Jennifer Hershey, Dennis Ambrose, Barbara Fillon, and Jennifer Huwer. It's a real pleasure working with you all.

ABOUT THE AUTHOR

Mary Doria Russell is the author of *The Sparrow, Children of God,* and *A Thread of Grace.* Her novels have won nine national and international literary awards, including the Arthur C. Clarke Award, the James Tiptree Award, and the American Library Association Readers' Choice Award. *The Sparrow* was selected as one of *Entertainment Weekly*'s ten best books of the year, and *A Thread of Grace* was nominated for a Pulitzer Prize. Russell lives in Cleveland, Ohio. Contact her at www.MaryDoriaRussell.info.

The employees of Thorndike Press hope you have enjoyed this Large Print book. All our Thorndike and Wheeler Large Print titles are designed for easy reading, and all our books are made to last. Other Thorndike Press Large Print books are available at your library, through selected bookstores, or directly from us.

For information about titles, please call:

(800) 223-1244

or visit our Web site at:

http://gale.cengage.com/thorndike

To share your comments, please write:

Publisher
Thorndike Press
295 Kennedy Memorial Drive
Waterville, ME 04901